Penguin Books

BETWEEN MEN

Katherine Govier is a native of Edmonton who has lived in Calgary, Washington, D.C., and London, England, and now lives in Toronto with her husband and two children. She has taught at Ryerson and York University in Toronto and at Leeds University in England. Her first novel, *Random Descent*, was published in 1979 to immediate critical success. Her second novel, *Going Through the Motions*, was published in 1982 and has been adapted for the stage. Govier's short stories have appeared in many magazines and her first collection, *Fables of Brunswick Avenue*, was published in Penguin Short Fiction in 1985.

D1253401

KATHERINE GOVIER

Between
=Men=

Penguin Books

PENGUIN BOOKS

Published by the Penguin Group
Penguin Books Canada Ltd., 2801 John Street, Markham,
Ontario, Canada L3R 1B4
Penguin Books, 27 Wrights Lane, London W8 5TZ, England
Viking Penguin Inc., 40 West 23rd Street, New York,
New York 10010, U.S.A.
Penguin Books Australia Ltd., Ringwood, Victoria, Australia
Penguin Books (NZ) Ltd., 182-190 Wairau Road, Auckland 10,
New Zealand

Penguin Books Ltd., Registered Offices:
Harmondsworth, Middlesex, England

First published in Viking by Penguin Books Canada Limited, 1987
Published in Penguin Books, 1988

Permission has been received to reprint excerpts from the following
songs: "A Whiter Shade of Pale," words and music by Keith Reid
and Gary Brooker, © 1967 Westminster Music Ltd., London,
England. TRO-Essex Music, Inc., New York, controls all
publication rights for the U.S.A. and Canada. Used by permission;
"Goody Goody," by Johnny Mercer and Matt Malneck, © 1935
Chappell & Co. Inc. Copyright renewed. International copyright
secured. All rights reserved. Used by permission of Chappell Music
Canada Limited.

Manufactured in Canada by Gagne Printing Ltd.

Canadian Cataloguing in Publication Data

Govier, Katherine, 1948-
Between men

ISBN 0-14-009774-0

I. Title.

PS8563.O85B48 1988   C813'.54   C87-093523-2
PR9199.3.G69B48 1988

This book is dedicated to my sisters,
Trudy and Sue

Acknowledgements

First, the author wishes to thank Professor Donald Smith, Department of History, the University of Calgary, for his enthusiastic help in directing her to research and source material.

Other individuals and institutions who provided guidance and documentation for the historical aspects of this novel include:

Professor Louis Knalfa, Department of History, the
    University of Calgary
Calgary Public Library
The Provincial Archives of Alberta and Brian Speirs, the
    Alberta Legal History Project
Ms Donna Martinson QC, Calgary
and The Glenbow Museum and Archives, without whose resources such histories could not be written.

A variety of published material on Calgary history has been consulted. The author acknowledges Max Foran, John H. Robertson, among others. The author further wishes to acknowledge the financial assistance of The Canada Council and The Ontario Arts Council.

Between Men is a work of fiction built around events which took place in Calgary, in 1889. Rosalie New Grass lived and died in the manner described. Some of the major characters named existed; others were created by the author to tell Rosalie's story.

Any resemblances between the characters in this book and persons living today are entirely coincidental.

Prologue

February 28, 1889. Calgary, Alberta

At four o'clock in the afternoon, having just got off the train from Banff, William "Jumbo" Fisk turned the corner onto Scarth Street and walked north towards the Turf Club Saloon. Ahead of him was a choker of snow clouds. The temperature was heading for zero. His hands, bare from the cuffs of his coat down, were blue-black, but not with cold. They were always like that, charred like the instruments in his smithy. The smudge didn't wear away, even though he'd been up in the mountains drinking and playing cards for the last three days. There would be another game that night too but he had a few hours to put in first.

He passed a livery stable, a scrawny stray cow. He passed the rail where he'd hitch his team if he hadn't sold it. The stairs were wide in front of the saloon: he made for the door; he'd owned a piece of this club too but he sold that a month ago — gambling debts. This trip, he'd done very well, though; he had a thousand dollars in his pocket, and he was feeling good, or he ought to be feeling good. Something nagged and twitched inside him, trying to get out. He was almost up the steps when it made him stop. He looked across the street. Three Indian girls stood watching him.

"You waiting?" He jerked his head towards the door.

One of the girls stepped forward. She wore a red blanket for a shawl. That red twigged a memory: back home in Ontario in the last haggard, ice-bound month before spring you might see a redwing blackbird, and feel that relief was coming. She looked at him flat, her face not moving. Small. Young. He beckoned. She hesitated but didn't look back at her companions. She crossed the street to him. He went ahead through the outer doors and then held the batwings. His breath lasted outside, a white puff, and she walked through it.

At the bar the men sat on their stools like a row of cardboard cutouts, hats pushed to the tops of their crowns, elbows and knees apart touching the next man's. Kelsey stood behind the bar, his hands mirrored on the marble surface, looking over the hats at the door. Jumbo signalled upstairs, and Kelsey nodded. Jumbo and the girl moved across the room, behind the drinkers' backs, to the stairs. No heads turned. Kelsey pointed overhead, to the left, his own bedroom.

Fisk had already climbed three ahead of her when the girl halted at the foot of the steps. Not hearing her tread, he turned back.

"You want a drink?"

She shook her head. Nevertheless, he came back down and went around to the end of the bar, and ordered a round for everyone.

"Winnings, Fisk?" It was Murphy talking, the newspaper man. Murphy wanted to know too much about other people's doings. He stared hard at the Indian girl, who dropped her eyes.

Fisk grinned, and tossed the whisky against the roof of his mouth. It flared, burning off the clouds that lingered in his head. Instead of answering Murphy, he looked at the girl, who stood where she had stopped at the foot of the stairs. She was new. "What's your name?" he said.

There was a moment. She wouldn't speak. Her eyes fell

like stones at Murphy's feet. Murphy's eyes seemed to water but he didn't blink.

Fisk set his glass back on the bar, hard.

"What's your name?"

"Rosalie," she whispered.

Upstairs in the room the girl picked up a candle in two hands and brought it to her face, gazing into it. She was muttering something; it sounded like a Hail Mary. He took the candle from her, and put it down on the washstand. Then he put out his thick hand and cupped her chin. As he looked into her scared eyes a question idled through his brain: why was she doing this? A dumb question if there ever was one. They all did it for the same reason. He pressed hard, and then jerked. Her chin flew upward. She was nobody, not his sister, not his mother, not his wife — not that he'd ever had one. By the looks of things not even a real prostitute. She was nobody.

"Wash your hands," she said.

He laughed comfortably at the impertinence. His breath was coming deeper now, his tension easing. He looked around. The room was the colour of coal. There was only an iron bedstead with a mattress and rough linen, a grey woollen blanket. A washstand and pitcher. He took off his coat, his laced boots. He could have turned on the gaslight but he preferred the gloom. She spoke again.

"Wash your hands."

She was looking away from him, at the wall. He put his hand on her upper arm and pushed her back onto the bed. She lay still, looking at him, her chin pulled into her neck, her face three flat triangles — forehead, cheek, other cheek.

"Wash your hands," she said. "I don't want to get sick."

Something about that made him laugh. "Whatever you say," he said, and turned his back to her, rolling up his sleeves. He did not undress further. She did not seem surprised.

He must become aroused. The fear was of not being aroused. He leaned over her. The red blanket fell back on the bed. He pulled at her flannel dress, and it parted beneath his hands like ribbons.

Kelsey heard a thump over his head. He cocked an ear with faint curiosity. What would Fisk be doing? Neither he nor the girl looked drunk enough to fall. When another muffled thump came, and then a groan, he moved down the bar and tried to get in on a conversation.

"You heard about the Eau Claire Mill? They say they can give us electric lighting on the streets by summer."

"They're talking like we can't live without it," Kelsey remarked, coughing to cover another noise. The man he spoke with, a hack called Lee, gestured to the ceiling.

"What kinda business you running here?"

Kelsey was new to his job, and didn't know how to respond. He gave Lee a cold stare and moved down to serve another man. The moans continued.

"Hey, George, what's the noise?" That was Murphy talking, Murphy with the long nose. Kelsey cursed Fisk; it was the last time he was going to let him use his room.

"It's my dog. I've got her tied up out back. She's in heat —" he explained further, but Murphy had already turned his head away. In another minute Kelsey slipped from behind the bar and, calling the floorman to watch the cash, went upstairs.

The hallway was nearly pitch dark; the early February night had come before the afternoon was gone. "Time to light up," he said to himself, talking to keep back a certain feeling of nerves that was coming over him. The noises were awful, wretched and deep, regular, about a minute apart. Two shapes emerged from the far end of the hall. He jumped.

"Lowry!" He'd forgotten; one of the owners and a prospective buyer were inspecting the premises. Kelsey didn't need to lose his job, did he? He prayed they hadn't heard the groans, although he didn't know how they could not. The men passed him in the narrow hall. They said nothing. He went along to his room. They'd better not come looking this way. The last thing he wanted was for someone to walk in on Fisk.

He put his ear against the door. He heard only a faint rustling, as of bedclothes moving. "Fisk!" He knocked against the wood softly. "Fisk, you in there?"

There was no answer, and no more noise.

"Passed out," he said to himself, "and just as well."

Thinking he'd keep Fisk from crashing out into the hall, and give Lowry and the gentleman time to get out before the girl reappeared, he took out his key and put it in the lock, turned it, and tried the door. It was locked: good. He went downstairs and slid back behind the bar. He looked along its length to the outside: the bar and street were like the same slab of marble, white and grey and clouded with cold. He felt his hands. They were sweaty, his forehead too.

"Trouble with this weather," he said to no one in particular, "your body overheats once you get inside." There was no answer. It seemed to him the row of faces was turned to him for an explanation. The groaning began again. But surely not, he was hearing things, it had been quiet upstairs. Anyway the men were laughing now, and couldn't hear. He turned to light the lamps.

"Drink up," he said. "It's time for dinner."

At last the bar began to empty out. Lowry and the would-be buyer came down, nodded and left. Only Murphy, bloody Murphy still sat at the bar. Then Kelsey heard the knock. It came softly. Stopped. Then came again. Kelsey looked at Murphy; his long nose was bent over his newspaper. "Bar's closed." He sidled out hoping not to be noticed and took the stairs silently, two at a time.

"Jumbo?" he said outside the door.

No one came to the other side. "Jumbo?" he whispered, sorting his keys. He found the one, turned it, pushed the door open. Fastidiously, he refrained from looking in, but stepped further back into the dark hall. He should have lit up long ago. No one came out. Kelsey stepped into the doorway. There was no light in the room. He peered through the gloom, unable to make out anything but the bedpost. He feared something, he did not know what. Then, with relief, he saw the huge man standing beside the washstand, drying his hands. The Indian girl lay on her back on the bed. One of her legs was bent up beside her. The other foot stuck out straight towards the iron post at the head of the bed. Kelsey looked away. He didn't have much to do with women himself.

"Fisk? Is she sleeping or what?"

"Dead drunk, I should think."

"I heard a noise."

Colour was coming into Kelsey's vision now. The sheets, part of the wall and the floor seemed to be wet; a deep crimson streamed from Fisk's hands into the basin. Kelsey blinked. Perhaps it was a trick, a dye. She had been wearing a red shawl.

"Aren't you going to get her out of here?" His voice had raised up a little, there was a whine in it. Fisk had come to be in charge, although it was Kelsey's room.

The big man turned from the mirror. It was no trick; the basin was full of blood. Sweat burst out of Kelsey's brow and he instantly averted his eyes. He turned his back on the whole scene and walked out of the door.

In a minute Fisk appeared beside him. "How about some dinner?"

Kelsey looked at him.

"I expect she'll be all right in a few minutes."

"Something female?" said Kelsey in a hopeful voice.

Fisk shook his head. "Must have been. Didn't realize it till I finished."

Closing the door, Kelsey sought for one second the depths of Fisk's black eyes; he wanted the other man to tell him it was all right. He saw nothing there, which frightened him even more. He found he was in this man's thrall.

"She has to go. I've got to sleep in that bed tonight."

"She'll get up soon."

"I don't want to, but I'll leave it unlocked. You know anyone might go in there and see. There's been folks here looking to buy."

Fisk shrugged. "The Windsor suit you?"

Kelsey led the way to the side door and down the alley; he didn't want to pass Murphy whose back he could still see at the bar. The floorman ought to tell him they were closed.

The dining room had white tablecloths and silver on the tables. They were by a window: cold buffeted the glass and the darkness returned their own thick profiles. Kelsey found he kept his eye on the time. By the mahogany clock it was six-twenty when the roast beef came. Soon the half-hour chime would go. He waited for it, and the ten minutes seemed to be an hour. He thought about the girl on the bed and hoped she had got up.

Fisk said a kind of grace with his eyes open, staring into the plate. He had the manners of a gentleman, and kept his elbows off the cloth. The beef was coated in brown gravy and the potatoes were crusty. Kelsey picked, but the big man ate with enthusiasm, cutting through two slices with a flick of his knife.

He was called Jumbo because of his height, and the thickness of his neck and chest, but in fact he had short forearms and small hands. There was a finger missing off his left hand; people said he lost it when he volunteered at Duck Lake to help the police when they got routed by the halfbreeds. He was taken for forty, but he was much younger; his wide beard and sideburns and his face and hands, ill-treated, rude and thick, made it hard to guess. He looked like an easy-going fellow, enjoying his meal, completely absorbed by what he was doing at that moment.

He'd come from somewhere east, and people said his family was important down there. He'd been in Calgary three years at least, long enough to belong. Everyone knew him, but for all his friendliness, he didn't look a man in the eyes when he spoke. He seemed aware there was — when you caught it — something naked about his glance; it had to dart away or let out too much.

Facing his plate, he was going on about the card game that night. "Got to get there 'fore it starts, get the lay of the land," was what he said. "You play poker?" Kelsey knew it was just conversation.

"I don't think I'd like the feel of it, being in a position to lose everything," he said. Kelsey's stomach was queasy. The clock now read twenty minutes to seven. They moved on to civic issues, with which Kelsey was becoming acquainted. He'd come up here from the States only two months ago.

"You in favour of this electric lighting for the streets?"

"What's wrong with the moon?" said Fisk, looking around for a toothpick. "I reckon the Lord's got his reasons for darkness."

For some reason, Kelsey didn't like this mention of the Lord.

"You could say the same about cold weather, and we do what we can to keep warm. I'm right for it," said Kelsey. "Keep the riff-raff and the savages from destroying us."

"They say this alternating current is dangerous," Fisk remarked in an agreeable way. "I heard it said if you fall asleep under one of those electric lamps you can wake up dead." He wiped his mouth. The words clapped over the table like big hands. Wake up dead.

Kelsey could no longer sit. He pushed back his chair. "Guess I ought to get back," he said, "open up again." And, taking up his courage with him, reminded Fisk, "Check on the girl. What's her name?"

"She said it was Rosalie," said Fisk, as if there were reason to doubt her. "She'll be gone by now, likely, 'less she's waiting at the bar for money."

"Didn't you pay her then?"

"She passed out, didn't she?"

Kelsey opened the door to the room. He felt the girl lying there before he saw her. There was no sound. Of course not. Suddenly he knew for a sure thing that she couldn't be alive, not now. He spread his lips and hissed through his teeth a sound that included all the obscenities he had never dared to utter. Fisk stayed close to the door behind him.

"Rosalie," he called sternly over Kelsey's shoulder.

"She's dead," said Kelsey.

Fisk headed towards the bed. He pressed his hand down

on her chest, as if he could push out a sound. He picked up her hand and quickly passed it over to Kelsey. The fingers were cool but the wrist warm. Fisk stepped back to the end of the bed feeling for tobacco in an inside breast pocket. He did not seem alarmed.

"Well, I say she's not too good. Not surprised actually."

Kelsey dropped the hand with a shriek. "She's damn well dead, Jumbo!"

The two men looked across the bed at one another. To cover his shaking, Kelsey felt for matches and went to light the gas. The light jumped up the walls, creating shadows that magnified Kelsey's panicky motion as he doused the match. His voice went high.

"Why did I ever let you use my room? Look at all the blood!"

Together they looked. Blood had soaked into the mattress, and splattered on the walls. There was a pool under the washstand and smears over the china pitcher and bowl. More was around her face. Kelsey felt his stomach reject the little roast beef that he had eaten. He was starting to shake. He made an effort to come to grips with himself, with what was happening. Blood now, blood then, thumps and groans before. He told the men it was his dog tied up. But it wasn't; it was the sound of a killing. Fisk had killed this squaw. Fisk was an animal, an animal. And it was all on Kelsey's hands, in his room, even. Kelsey quaked. God help me, he prayed, I want to get out of this alive. He gripped his fingers inside his cuffs and gave it everything he had.

"I mean, what do you think she's got?" he said affecting his companion's nonchalance.

"She musta had something, bleeding all that much."

"She looked OK when she went up."

Slowly, backing to the door so the madman wouldn't turn on him, Kelsey shook his head in fake wonderment. "Should we get the doctor?"

"Bit late for that, I'd say. Let's get the police chief."

Fisk shrugged, and put his pipe away. "If you like." As

they reached the door he put one of his hands on Kelsey's shoulders, as if to console him. Kelsey bent a little under the weight. This time they locked the door.

It was only eight o'clock but the town was still. Constable Dillabough stood on the street corner. He reached into his pocket and pulled out a sulphur match, and lit it. The yellow flame leapt up, blotting out the night. He sucked it down into his pipe and looked over the bowl down Scarth Street. In front of the Turf Club there was a group of Indians. Maybe six or eight of them. Did his eyes deceive him? The group had doubled since he'd come to this corner half an hour ago.

The moon was up, a skeletal circle half solid and half glimmer in the ice crystals that hung over the town. Tomorrow March would begin: there would be two more long months of winter with the ground frozen like brick underfoot and the air shrinking the skin. As Dillabough watched, a thick-set body separated itself from the darkness at the front steps of the club and, passing the Indians, came towards him.

"Fisk! Abroad in this cold?" The blacksmith had his coat open and he wore no gloves: now he was near enough for Dillabough to see his hands, unnaturally pink and scrubbed. "You'll catch your death."

"Chief, I don't mind telling you I'm not here for my health. I'm in a bad fix and I've come to turn myself in."

Dillabough offered his tobacco; he knew the big man. "Is this a little joke you're playing?" Over Fisk's shoulder he saw another man watching from the door of the club. Murphy. Two, three more Indians had materialized.

"There's a squaw dead in there and I want to tell you all I know. It could look bad for me."

This was news Dillabough didn't know how to take. Although he was chief he was also the sole officer; he'd been on the force less than a year. This would be his first corpse, Indian or otherwise.

"Ah!" he said. Somehow he got his fingertip into the

bowl of his pipe and burnt it. Frowning, he peered through
the grey light into the face of Jumbo Fisk, a pleasant
enough man, but one who kept bad company. If what he
said was true there could be trouble for all of them. Nobody
had forgotten the Indian uprising four years back. The
treaties had been signed since then, but things could easily
get bad. Dillabough spent half his time trying to get the
RCMP to drive off the starving Indians who came to town
from their reserve.

"You sure she's dead? Maybe we could get the doctor."

"There's a lot of blood."

A short silence fell while Dillabough drew on the pipe.

"You taking me into custody then?" said Fisk hopefully.

"Guess I'll go in there first and see what it's all about."

The two of them had to walk back through the group of
Indians. They went together across the frozen ruts of the
road, the police constable's buffalo coat making him almost
Jumbo's size. He was only young. He prayed.

By then the hall outside Kelsey's room was crammed with
bystanders. Dillabough had to push his way through.
When he passed the doorway Kelsey came out with a basin
of water and some lemon. "You're not to touch anything in
here," said the officer.

"It's my room."

"All the more reason you shouldn't, fella."

Kelsey's eyes spun with fear and he backed off.

The gaslight was on high above the washstand and sent a
beam of light from the mirror directly onto the bed.
Dillabough's eye was drawn there unwillingly. The woman's
feet were where the pillows should have been. Her face was
closer to him, an awful sight. The bottom lip was swollen to
a grotesque purple pout, her eyes cast upward. The bed
around her was saturated with blood, in widening circles
from the centre of her body. The sight reminded him of one
of his mother's religious pictures, the colours, the sad
expression of suffering on her face. She had painted the
room with her blood, it ran from the bed to the floor, even

the walls were touched with it. There was a flamboyance to the scene, a look of death not ordinary.

It was hot in the room. Dillabough was wearing his buffalo coat. He felt weak. The two men looked at him, presenting their finding.

"You see, she's kicked it," said Kelsey bitterly. "I never saw her before tonight. I never let men take squaws up here."

Fisk went forward, putting his hand on the woman's breast bone. "Rosalie," he said. "Get up. It's time to go."

"Hands off!" shouted Dillabough. He whirled on the little crowd of curiosity seekers and found there was only one of them left: Murphy. "If you're going to hang around, make yourself useful. Get Dr Lafferty. Get Murdoch." Murphy vanished. Fisk moved to go too. "Not you!" Kelsey moved. "You neither! How did she get into your room?"

"She came in with him."

Unbidden, Dillabough's eyes had found the girl again. She wasn't one of the regulars. He thought of the group of Indians out front. They knew something had happened. They had ways of knowing. God forbid they knew it was this.

"Get the mounted police," he began, and then his stomach revolted and he headed to the door.

"Wait," said Kelsey weakly. "She's getting up —"

The constable turned around. He was about to faint, and had to prop himself up on the door frame. The three of them stood without moving, and saw the Indian girl sit, gather the red shawl around her shoulders, separate herself from the form on the bed and stand. She was extremely pale, almost transparent, but that could be explained perhaps by the loss of blood. The light seemed to pass right through her. Her head down, she took a step or two, but as the way around the bed to the door was blocked by the men, she stopped. Hastily, Fisk and Kelsey stepped back. She passed by Dillabough. There was a second when none of them saw her.

"She's gone."

"She is?"

"How did she get out?"

Relief made them giddy, until they looked back at the bed. She was still there, more sodden than ever. Definitely dead. Dillabough swooned.

Chapter 1

The high electronic warning had been sounding since the beginning of the hour they spent in bed. *Beep, beep, beep,* as Ace opened the front door and walked across the hall of the empty townhouse, Suzanne following. *Beep, beep, beep,* as, eyes hooked to his, she laid her clothes on the single chair in the bare room. He approached her; they adopted the strange/familiar positions. *Beep, beep, beep.* Gradually the sound grew fainter, and then it disappeared altogether.

When they were still it asserted itself again.

"What on earth is that noise?"

She strode to the bathroom as he opened his mouth to answer. She had the habit of walking out of rooms while he spoke; it had infuriated him during the years of their marriage. She came out of the shower minutes later, wrapped in a towel. "What did you say?"

"It's the dump trucks. They do it when they're backing up, as a safety measure." He was still lying there.

"They've been backing up since one?" She went to the chair for her blouse.

"Dump trucks back up for a living," he said, and laughed, showing his perfect teeth. The faint lines that had shown in his forehead when he came in were completely gone. He had

1

a baby face, a smooth pink visage, after making love. Perhaps that was why he did it, because it kept him preserved.

"Oh, I shouldn't have," she said.

He did a nip-up from the mattress, landing heavily on his feet in front of her.

"Still want to talk about the divorce?"

"I thought we agreed," she said grimly. In the huge mirror which hung alone on the wall, reflecting only other walls and her pale form, she looked older than she had that morning: wrinkled, smudged, unrested. And when she opened the door to step out into the day again, the electronic sound pierced the bright air ominously. It reminded her of something. Of the alarm sounded by a life-support system when the patient was in distress, when the patient hung between life and death.

Ace sat behind the wheel of his low car, chafing in the glare of the late spring sun. A crane had wheeled into the eastbound lane of the Crowchild Trail in front of him and the procession of cars was caught in its slow wake. Trucks and heavy equipment surrounded them. A new subdivision was going up; the whole hillside was under construction.

"Everything's always going up in this place, nothing's ever finished. Nothing ever gets old." So said Suzanne disconsolately. "Ace? Don't you think? Am I the only person in Calgary who likes things old?"

He puffed the dust away from his small, straight nose. He had his elbow out the window, his palm propping his chin as they crawled past low stucco houses set on freshly seeded lawns and poplar saplings encircled by guard fences to save them from being knocked over by dogs.

"I like one old thing," he said.

"What's that?" Falling for it.

"My old wife."

"Take me back to my office," she said.

"If you hated us that much," he said, unperturbed, "I figure, you'd have stayed east."

She scoffed. "The east! I couldn't live there. You can't

see the sky. It's like being up to your eyeballs in hills and trees. It's like standing on a bed that's gone soft."

He shook his neat blond head. "That's no reason." He was dogged, sure of himself. "You haven't got what you came back for, yet. Or you'd have stopped complaining about us."

Why had she come back? She told everyone it was the tenure-stream job; you just didn't get offers like that any more. He rather hoped it had something to do with himself, her erstwhile husband. He had her request for a divorce pegged as the re-opening of negotiations.

"Is it so unreasonable to expect the place to age a bit, like the rest of us? Like me, anyway," she corrected, looking over. The tender line under his pointed chin was taut, the sleek hair solid to his forehead. Lines fine as baby hair showed beside his eyes only when he looked into the sun. He was thirty-five but he looked like twenty.

The crane was still ahead, blocking the view. They turned their heads to look sideways, up the hill. New houses stood square, naked, as if they had just come out of a box the night before. Above them was a row of timber frames you could see through; and above that, a planner's idea, a row of surveyed lots marked off by posts with red plastic tickets. These, having the best view, would be the most desirable.

Around the marked plots, the hard pale earth was turned over, showing its moist underside. Where the lawns would be it was rototilled to brown corduroy. There was a mechanical violence in what they did to the earth here: in summer, men and machines dug under it, shaved it, shoved it, all under pressure of time in the short warm season. In winter when they couldn't work it for the cold, people got on snowmobiles and aluminum toboggans, and scored lines over its hard white head.

Both Ace and the city were tuned, engineered, bright with progress. He belonged to the good times, and hadn't been hit by the bad. When it seemed the oil boom would end, the family company had diversified.

Now he got his chance, pulled out and passed the crane. He couldn't stay behind anyone, especially anyone bigger than him. They sped past a bit of prairie dropped like an old shirt between developments, wrinkled and dusty and out of place. Then they curved around towards the downtown.

"What are you doing this weekend?"

"Nothing much," she said shortly. "Marking papers. Gemma's coming for dinner."

He grunted. He wasn't much concerned about what she did, as long as it didn't involve anyone new. Gemma's visit wasn't important.

Suzanne didn't ask what he was doing. He let her off in the parking lot by the college; she gave him a hand signal and didn't look back.

As Suzanne crossed the parking lot to the arts building, a pickup truck pulled alongside her. The driver leaned from his window to look down the neck of her blouse. Then he gunned his motor, and a piece of dirt popped from under his tire into her right eye, making it water.

She entered the building, one eye weeping into a Kleenex. With the other she inspected the yellowing leaves of the giant fig tree under the central skylight. The tree was the third of its kind to be planted and it looked as if it weren't going to make it, either. *Failure to thrive*, they called it with babies. She turned towards the elevators. The ten years of her absence from Calgary had been marked by a conspiracy of local millionaires to endow miniature jungles in public spaces. Every hotel and shopping centre had its solarium, summer and winter a shocking lime green against the yellow-white land. Even Foothills College, a cluster of low grey buildings on the dumpy south-east side of town, kept its modest pseudo-tropic, or tried to keep it. A curled leaf landed in front of her. This ficus wasn't fooled.

Stepping off the elevator at the third floor, Suzanne attempted to pass the history department receptionist unnoticed. But Nola, seated outside the head's office with a telephone hooked under her chin, rolled her eyes.

"Psssst!"

Nola hissed. It was a technique. Nola hissed to give weight to her messages; she whispered to invite confession. She hissed because she sat by herself all day and she wanted people to come up close.

"Roberta Asp was by looking for you," she said.

Suzanne nodded but didn't slow down. She was not up for a chat with Nola. Neither was she up for a visit from Miss Asp, one of those students who missed the lectures but showed up at her office later with an urgent need for nothing in particular.

The right eye was still running and the left one had begun, too. She could barely see the writing on her door: Room 535, Dr S. Vail. She opened it, peering through a mist of tears. It had seemed like a good idea at the time to do battle with the physical plant to have her own pine harvest table installed, instead of the usual steel desk with the secretary's arm. It had also seemed essential to remove the fluorescent ceiling lights, which robbed the body of vitamins, and replace them with a small lamp with a driftwood base. She'd hung rice-paper blinds in the windows and a birchbark painting on the wall to make the room her own.

But she had only succeeded in drawing attention to herself. She was already set apart, the first woman hired to teach full time in the department, the first home-grown Albertan. Her colleagues were from Pakistan, England or the United States; one was from Toronto. The head favoured male scholars with foreign credentials. But change was coming; she had been hired to stave off an order to comply with equal-opportunity regulations. In any case her attempts to make her office her own had been a mistake; anyone who looked in the door could see that whoever felt at home in 535 didn't belong in the rest of the place.

Suzanne swayed in her office doorway, dabbing her eyes with a Kleenex. I'll take work home, she said to herself.

She let go of the doorknob, crossed the floor to pick up a file folder from her table and slid it in her briefcase. Returning to the hall, she closed the door behind her.

"I'm going home," she said, passing Nola. The Kleenex was black; her mascara must be running.

"Must be nice."

"I'm not feeling well."

Nola tipped her chin. "You don't have to make excuses to me, I'm just the secretary."

"You're right," said Suzanne. "Thanks for reminding me."

A year ago, when Suzanne had first come, Nola had presented herself as an ally. It was Suzanne's first real job, after sessional appointments here and there; she didn't know how to be a boss. Meanwhile Nola had a surfeit of bosses and knew only too well what to do. Tacitly, they arranged to switch roles; Nola would take charge while Suzanne would listen to her complaints and be grateful not to have to give orders. The arrangement had served well. Today, however, Suzanne bridled. Why should she feel guilty for leaving the office at three on Friday? No one else in the department even came back after lunch. Only because Nola was still sitting there, and would be, until 4:45 on the dot. Ducking her head, she got into the elevator.

She was in her own car at the first stoplight. She couldn't see out of her right eye, and her foot shook on the clutch, so that the car popped into gear and stalled. Judging that it was early enough to cut through downtown, she took Fourth Street under the railway tracks. It was a mistake.

Rush hour was on. Women in high heels clattered over temporary board sidewalks towards a line of blue-and-white buses. Alongside Seventh Avenue, people were standing on an elevated platform, waiting for the C-train. The C-train had been built to give rail service to the city after it was too late, or too expensive, to go underground. It pelted along on raised rails through the downtown office and shopping streets. As if to encourage the natural suspicion held in these parts for public transportation, it was accident prone. In its first week of operation it had jumped off the track and into a crowd. Most of the populace chose to stay with their cars.

And their cars sat in traffic. Forced to a standstill, Suzanne looked up at a sky pocked with half-built skyscrapers started in the boom and now stunted by recession. Hoardings alternated with glassy walls alongside the sidewalk. Lines of men and women funnelled out of doorways. They looked like miniatures on the base of an architect's model. And this used to be the land where a man could stand tall.

Suzanne wedged her way into the left-hand lane for the bridge, and then pulled into the drive-in croissant stop on the island between the four lanes of traffic. She bought two croissants and got back into her car. She'd had nothing to eat, what with her ill-considered visit to Ace's new town-house and its consequences. She began to chew on one as she crossed the Bow River. Immediately, her mental state improved. When she turned left on the north side of the river the sun, hanging white over the mountains, bit into her eyes. It would take another five hours to sink, growing larger and more orange in the western haze until finally it would drop behind the horizon.

She turned onto 11A Street. She was heading for a little frame bungalow with a saddleback roof and a picket gate set in its honeysuckle hedge. It was her own, a house she had chosen, paid for, and decorated alone. Her thirty-five previous years of life had been spent in other people's homes; twenty in her parents', three in an apartment dominated by Ace, ten more in assorted flats. This was home.

She leaned forward over the wheel now. She was almost there. When she got inside and dropped her briefcase and changed her clothes, she would be safe, safe from other people, safe from her own weakness in the face of other people. She sped up on the straight street. She was almost into the intersection when there it was, a long white van, speeding silently eastward across her path. It took a second for Suzanne to recognize the charging vehicle. Sirens were outlawed except for fire engines, danger to person not warranting a disturbance as did danger to property. But it was an ambulance, blank, sudden, soundless. The van swerved and she saw the word on its side: EMERGENCY. *Emergency*, emerge. In her head she heard the piercing beeps of the dump truck. Now she knew what that sound reminded her of. It was not the malingering, not the death held off by machines. It was a birth. A prolonged, dangerous birth. She slammed on the brakes.

Dropping her head, she burst out crying. Why had she done it, why? Her car stalled. A horn honked behind her, and then another one. Suzanne wiped her eyes with the back of her hand, turned the key again and drove the last block home.

Suzanne and Gemma sat in wicker armchairs on the front porch, drinking white wine. Suzanne had her bare feet up on the porch rail. Gemma wore high heels and crossed her legs at the ankle. Gemma was thin with concave cheeks and neat, catlike features. She had frizzy, rust-coloured hair and great false eyelashes that tickled the plucked pouch of skin under her thin eyebrows. In profile the glue showed. But straight on, she looked ingenuous as a baby. She had come straight from work, wearing a white ruffled dress that exposed her bony chest. Directly across the street, the Ringroses rocked on their swing, glaring. Suzanne put the wine bottle on the floor, out of sight.

Gemma pushed her straps off her shoulder to get more sun.

"Did you go to work like that?"

"'Course I did."

Gemma had trained as a teacher but had given it up after a few years of the restricted social life in an elementary school in Brentwood; now she was a secretary at an exploration company downtown. Hers was a case of voluntary downward career mobility for the purposes of matrimony. Unfortunately even the geologists had already found women.

"Put your wineglass down," said Suzanne.

She was concerned about the Ringroses. They didn't like her, or more accurately, they didn't like the drop in prices that had allowed a single woman to buy a house on the street. Not that they were wealthy, on the contrary. They'd simply lived in their house for forty years. When the price of oil went up, technocrats from Paris and bankers from Toronto had rushed to these river flats with the clapboard houses in the prairie style. Renovators had enlarged the windows and stuck gables out of second storeys; they tore down half a dozen houses and put up a complex of neo-Victorian prairie townhouses in their place. Sitting still, the Ringroses saw their house triple in value. Then the price of oil went down. The house value was reduced by half and the Ringroses figured they'd lost a fortune. They couldn't blame the businessmen, because businessmen meant progress. And the government out east, well, it was too far away. The Ringroses both came from farm families. Then it had been the weather, jerking them around. Now it was politics. They folded their arms, telling Suzanne this, and let it be known that perhaps worst of all was that a woman without a husband, a *career* woman, had moved in across the street. And who knew what sort of life she led.

"Anyway," said Gemma, "I thought we might go downtown after for a drink. Someone I know is going to be at the Greenhorn."

Suzanne wiggled her toes up on the porch rail. She'd experienced Gemma's friends before. They were all over-weight and had wedding rings dropped in their vest pockets. She said nothing.

"D'I tell you Len is leaving?" Gemma said.

Len was one of the big, married men at the office whom Gemma coveted.

"No, where's he going?"

"Vancouver. His wife's making him. I think it's probably

because of me." She examined her false fingernails with critical pride.

"You never told me you had an affair with Len."

"I didn't. But she can tell he's madly in love with me."

Suzanne had heard all this before. She groaned at the persistence of Gemma's illusions. "I guess this means you'll be looking for a new job."

"Don't laugh. That's why I want to see these guys tonight." Now Gemma put down her glass and held her right forefinger in front of her face. She frowned and picked angrily at the nail. She used to bite her fingernails down to the quick, making them bleed; it was one of her more obvious ways of doing violence to herself. Because she couldn't break the habit she had large, rounded acrylic nails glued down over her own once a month. Now she painted the acrylics and then picked off the polish as a substitute for chewing.

Suzanne looked away. They were very old friends. They were such old friends they weren't really friends any more, they were refugees from a common past, they were individuals with ever diverging beliefs locked into a treaty of mutual defence.

"Len's wife!" Gemma went on. "Dumpy little thing too, I met her once." Gemma was of the opinion that women could be divided into two groups — wives and mistresses. Falling by default into the latter category, she ran a constant battle against the wives of the world, who she believed always "won." "Anyway, there's no point in keeping that job any more, there's no one left there I'd even bother to try for."

"When are you going to stop making major life decisions on the same grounds that most people would choose a singles bar?"

"Since when was taking a job a major life decision?"

"Since women began to take themselves seriously," said Suzanne, seriously.

"You don't really believe that stuff, do you?" said Gemma. "You just say it to annoy me."

"I'm going to start the fire," said Suzanne, and stood. The soles of her feet and her calves ached, as if she had walked a long way carrying a heavy sack. If she could throw off her past, she'd run down her porch stairs and through the picket gate, and back to Toronto. But she'd tried already. There she'd had too little weight, no depth; she had passed along the streets like a shadow.

"So tell me," said Gemma, digging, "how's your gorgeous ex?"

Suzanne let the screen door bang behind her, and padded down the hall.

"If you don't want him you can always turn him over to me," Gemma called, to her back. She followed Suzanne through the little kitchen, and out onto the back stoop, where the barbecue stood. She watched as Suzanne poured lighter fuel on a tepee of charcoal. Gemma had a radar like a bat.

"You've made that clear," said Suzanne. The flames leapt up and she dodged sideways. Soon the orange flames would die, and in half an hour the coals would be turning grey with ash; then she could cook on it. The first fire was merely graphic; only when it looked like it was all over did its heat rise. It was like her marriage, a big blaze which she'd hardly felt until it seemed to be over. It lay there for years and now when she came back it was too hot to touch.

They had suited her, while she was away, those silent grey ashes. Nobody knew Ace in the east, in truth nobody had really known her. For Suzanne, as a graduate student, life had been an intellectual affair, something to read about, to see in films, to analyse over coffee, something intense and equally impersonal. Being separated but not severed from a husband 2,500 miles away had helped keep it that way.

But now she was here, where it had all happened, and she intended to end the mordant marriage. It had come to stand for everything she thought was wrong with her. Despite an air of accomplishment and control which most people found convincing, Suzanne felt herself to be *undefined*: neither married nor single, young nor old. Holding a job but not committed to it. If she was going to grow old the way she feared she was going to, as a spinster and an indifferent scholar, she should at least clarify the terms.

Hence, the divorce. She had waited nine months to re-establish residence in Alberta. Today she'd met Ace to get him to agree to start proceedings. And while doing that she'd idiotically —

"Know what Gemma?" she said, turning suddenly, the poker in her hand. It was a moment she was going to regret. But, moved by the sight of those scrawny shoulders in their ruffles, moved by the day, reminded that she, like Gemma, was vulnerable and most of all female, she wanted to confess. "I went and slept with him today."

Gemma was silent. Her mouth was a little open, the curved upper lip lifted; her eyes were wide and assessing.

"I don't know why. It's been nearly a year since the last man —" The poker waved into the air between them. Suzanne giggled, abashedly.

Gemma slowly shook her head from side to side. "I don't know why you're ashamed of it. It's legal after all."

Suzanne swung around and poked the charcoal.

"He's a hunk. I always said. Lots to offer." Gemma rubbed her forefinger and her thumb together and winked. His money, she meant. "If it's not you it'll be someone else."

Suzanne sniffed. Gemma was disgusting. Why had she told her?

"You're just lucky we've still got our deal," Gemma went on, blithely. Years ago, at university, they'd pledged never to go after each other's men, before, during or after the fact. "No, don't worry, I wouldn't. Anyway, it's hopeless. He's hooked on you." She sighed. "What a waste."

"I think he's just fond of me," said Suzanne, carefully.

"Oh, that too, I suppose." Gemma leaned back on the rail and went after a different fingernail. She had no interest in subtleties. She took account only of the more basic human emotions — envy, lust, fear, and — surprisingly —

loyalty. The latter, in her case blind and energetic once in place, explained the lasting friendship, because Suzanne was subject to fits of violent antipathy to her old high-school pal. She was having one now.

The flames were reduced to a low red glow. Grey crept grain by grain over the charcoal.

"You know I always felt sorry for Ace. You really did him in."

Suzanne gritted her teeth.

"You did. You just decided you were through with him and dumped him, flat, the way only you could. Without batting an eye."

Suzanne thought Gemma had a nerve, assuming this tone.

"It's over and done with," she said coolly.

"Apparently it's not."

"I was never what he wanted, Gemma."

"That's not what he says."

Suzanne brought the poker down on the edge of the metal barbecue with a clang. She took a deep breath, in through her nose, out through her mouth, the way she'd learned for self-hypnosis. She had to get herself in hand, to control her emotions. All the retorts she could make clamoured in her throat. But she absolutely would not explain. She would not burden anyone. She was a listener, and as a listener, quickly discovered that other people have their own problems; they don't need yours. Friends ought not to be asked to deal with one's confusions. Perhaps they could not deal with them. It was a point of pride that no one understood her, least of all frantic, shallow Miss Starchuk, who had been trying for years to get rid of her last name. She tightened her lips.

Gemma watched. She let up on her fingernails for the moment; she had a particularly alert gleam in her eyes.

"OK," she said, "OK. You're right. You broke up because Ace didn't want you. You're right about that, and you don't need to talk, and you've got things under control. Unlike poor desperate man-eating me." She grinned her cat grin.

"Don't pick on me, not tonight." Suzanne's voice rose in mock distress.

"I won't, dear."

"We're almost ready to put the meat on." Suzanne put down her poker and went into the kitchen.

"Just promise me one thing," shouted Gemma through the door.

"What?"

"You'll put on some shoes and come down to the bar with me after dinner to meet these guys."

"Oh, Gemma. No."

"One of them is famous."

"How famous?"

"I forget his name. He's in politics."

"Do I have to?" Suzanne was gay; the situation had been rescued.

"Yes."

"Why?"

"Because," said Gemma, sticking her head around the door and pulling her square grin. "Because you've been getting away with this 'I'm on top of everything' number for too long. Don't you think we're all tired of waiting to see if you're human?"

Chapter 2

Nobody knew who the greenhorn was any more; he had bought some bad land by the river which turned out to have oil under it, and then lost his fortune to an operator. The bar in his name had red leather booths with brass studs; the stools had stirrups on their sides. Along the walls were photographs of bronco busters. Suzanne examined the nearest one. His arms were outstretched, his legs poked down below the horse's belly like pegs, the fringe on his chaps flew. He looked like an angel expelled from heaven, braking as he came to earth. She put her hand around a glass of beer.

Gemma's male friends were from Toronto. Or Ottawa. They were certainly eastern; their eyes darted to the door every few seconds. One was Gemma's type, big and amiable and bearded; the other was older, with curly hair shot with grey. He wore thick glasses and a long tweed jacket with a single button and narrow lapels, something out of a fashion magazine. He also wore a smile as he listened to Gemma talk about her great-aunt.

"She was a full-blooded Cree," said Gemma, "honest."

"Amazing," said the bearded man.

Suzanne laughed. It was funny about these Indian relations.

The great-aunt had been the family's shame until the last influx of outsiders to Alberta had granted cachet to having been here a long time. Indian blood was OK as long as you didn't have too much of it and as long as you had got it in the previous century. Now everyone had to have one red antecedent.

"It's a way we have of expiating guilt," Suzanne explained. "There used to be natives here. If you don't see many it's just that they've married into the best families."

"Suzanne here was born right by Hell's Half Acre," said Gemma. "You know about that?"

Now the thick horn-rimmed glasses and the pointed face of the wiry, grey-haired man turned to her. "Sounds exotic," he said. His smile was wider.

"Not really."

He kept looking at her. His eyes were very large behind his lenses. He had a certain ruined glamour.

"It was just where they burned off the natural gas at the well sites. The price was so low, they couldn't afford to send it to markets. And so there were always these great walls of flame shooting up, you could see it from miles around."

"Was it hot?" he said.

She laughed. "You got used to it."

"You seem to have survived it rather well," he said. His voice was low, almost croaky. She could have told about the little row of houses called Poverty Flats and the house owned by the gas company. About how her mother used to go out to the front door with a fishing rod and come back with trout for dinner. But of course now you couldn't buy a place in Poverty Flats for under two hundred thousand dollars, and anyway her family was hardly poor. She guessed she'd lost the right to tell it. She shrugged.

"I've been away for ten years."

"Down east?" As if there were nowhere else to go.

She nodded. Immediately, his face relaxed. There were common assumptions then, she wasn't an untutored westerner after all but someone who had been in the centre, who had learned the proper order of things.

"I'm just here for a day or two, government business," the one with the beard was saying. "But Simon's staying."

The glasses on Simon jogged as he nodded, admitting to it.

"He's consulting."

"Consulting?" said Suzanne. "Whom are you consulting?"

The beard laughed. "Oh, they're consulting him. On energy."

"I used to work for the feds," said Simon quietly.

The beard coughed, dropped his head back and rolled his eyes at Gemma and Suzanne. "He's too modest. He practically wrote the legislation."

Suzanne was taking the measure of this man called Simon. She'd heard of him before. She'd seen his pictures in newspapers. Always in a group of men, over a stack of papers. She didn't associate him with any particular event or idea. In person he seemed wily and intense. Arrogant, she suspected. Nevertheless, she was drawn to him.

"I thought I'd come out where the action is, set up an office," he said.

"Teach the oilmen how to manipulate the laws you wrote?" Suzanne said.

"You know a bit about the business then," he said, a little eagerly.

"You can't live here and not."

He tipped his head towards her. The chin was narrow. The skin was loose around what had been a heart-shaped face, a harlequin face, now badly weathered.

"Let's face it, it's got an image problem. I happen to have a few skills, a little useful know-how. I thought I could deal with internal and external problems, analyse corporate behaviour, let them know how people see them."

"Like a shrink," she said, half smiling.

"Exactly."

Suzanne tried to imagine the businessmen she knew going to a shrink because of an image problem and failed. "Well," she said finally, "Gemma's looking for a job."

"She is? What can she do?" Simon was still looking at

Suzanne. Gemma leaned over and put her face between them. Her fingernails were out on top of the bar.

"I'm rather good at public relations," she said, dimpling and causing her eyelashes to fan her cheeks. Gemma was never able to resist a chance for double entendre with men.

Simon leaned back.

"Take her, you'll need her," Suzanne said, swivelling around on her stool. She had her purse in her hand; she'd had enough for one evening. The beard was ordering another round. "Not for me," she sang out. As she got to her feet she found herself idly looking for the telltale white stripe around the fourth finger of the left hand of the man called Simon. There was none.

He sprang to his feet, and caught hold of her by both elbows.

"Don't leave. You've got to help me," he said quietly. "I don't know anyone in this town. Except you."

She noted the curly hair and narrow collar, the tight facial muscles, the voice with a chuckle backed up in the throat. He was old. Much older than any other man she'd dated. Almost as old as her father but not quite. Fifty, anyway.

"You don't know me, actually," she said mildly.

"Then I must get to," he said. "I'm desperate. It's culture shock." He leaned even closer and his voice fell. "The men in this town are like overfed steers. I can't find my way around. It's so spread out. Haven't they ever heard of downsizing? I could get out of touch with reality. Don't you see I need you?"

"I've had a rather long day," said Suzanne. "Can we make it next week?"

He swayed back, pulling his face down into a comic pout. "Next week? What on earth does that mean?"

"Tuesday or Wednesday."

"No, it doesn't. It means the brush-off. Don't do this to me, Suzanne, really, I'm in need."

He saw that she was weakening.

"Look," he said, "here's what we'll do. You say yes, I come over, I talk, you listen, you talk too if you like, then I go away to my hotel room and you go upstairs to bed. Nothing happens."

She noticed that he had set this scenario in her house.

"I don't seduce you," he continued.

"No, you don't," she said, "but you might annoy me by trying."

"That's the last thing I want," he said.

Did he mean to seduce or to annoy? Suzanne drew up her back. He was still touching her arm. Her body was reacting strangely. She was growing warm, and a heavy pulse had begun in her veins. She was suddenly fiercely hot. She desired this man; she could not move. It was a violent, persuasive desire she had never felt before. She stiffened, resisting it. He misunderstood.

"Look," he said. "I know I talk too much. Don't listen to what I say. Just listen to what I feel."

Suzanne burst out laughing.

"Now that is a really good one!" She pulled her elbows out of his grasp. "I'll tell you what. Give me a call this weekend and I'll give you the Cook's tour."

Alone in the car, Suzanne drove west out of the downtown and crossed the Bow at Fourteenth Street. She was going up Nose Hill to the old look-out point at the Winter Club. The first rise was steep, the second steeper.

It was ten-thirty, and finally dark. The hill as she approached it was magnificent, blue-purple and bristled, like a whale beached at the edge of some faintly glittering ocean. The city ended abruptly just here, at the crest of the hill, and would go no further, because the hill was leased for ranching. Several cows moved across the night sky, their flat, low silhouettes companionable as she nosed her car into the end of the row at the look-out parking lot.

The sky was clear. Each vehicle was separate, distinct. When she had come here before it had been winter; the cars lined up at the edge of the drop had been wrapped in steamy exhaust. Tonight was warm and clear; she was exposed, alone where everyone else was in twos.

She turned off the motor. The quiet was sudden; it was all around. Nobody was building anything or tearing anything down. No cars were honking or gunning their motors. The lights slid down the hill and across the valley to the river and rose up the hill on the other side. In the centre, where she had come from, they blurred into strokes, jagged eruptions skyward. Lesser lights mapped the neat crescents, wedges and boulevards of a city which was planned and happened almost at once.

In her mind Suzanne was telling someone about the city, about something she loved, despite the cranes with their red-lighted tips to warn off low-flying planes, three cranes she could count now, striking off at an angle against the pattern. It was a striving kind of place. Always trying and never, by accident of geography, arriving. Becalmed on a sea of grass. Not becalmed, perhaps, but — temporary. She could look into the future and see the grass replace it all.

You see, she said to herself, bringing her fingertips to her thumb and then blowing on them, opening her hand. It's like a dandelion puff. Complex and formal, damageable. She was speaking to him, to Simon. She hadn't really wanted to come here alone. She had wanted him. But she had pushed him away. She was angry, as angry as she had been attracted to him. She hit the steering wheel with her fist. "...*We're all tired of waiting to see if you're human,*" Gemma said.

She turned her head to peer into the car beside her. Two heads were one, joined down the cheek, looking the same direction down the hill. The night was warm and the windows of other cars were open. She could hear, suddenly, a pop song on a radio. It was time to go home. Friday was over at last.

On Saturday night at ten o'clock Suzanne sat at her desk at home, in the spare room. It occupied the top back gable, behind the front bedroom, above the narrow kitchen and the back porch and the small pantry, all of which fit one person perfectly. It was a house with no more than the essentials. Except for this room, this spare room, almost empty, painted yellow, with a bare polished pine floor, a desk, a rag rug, and a goose-necked lamp, a room such as one discovers in dreams, forgotten and ready to be lived in. She was working on a research paper for the academic journal *Studies in Western Canadian History*.

The telephone rang in the hall. She stood up to answer it. It was Simon, as she expected. After she put down the receiver she returned to the room and carefully put away all her papers into yellow cardboard file boxes. Then she slid her notebook back into its place in the bookshelf. She shut the door of the room behind her. It would be exactly the same, no page turned, no paper shifted, when she returned.

She'd left the front door open to the birds and insects. They were crying; the long sundown had just ended and the dark was falling fast. He arrived almost immediately. She saw the yellow top light of the taxi flash on in the middle of the street. He was paying from the outside, through the window, the way they do in big cities. Then he turned and looked at the house.

She saw him seeing her and for a minute she was in his place; facing the outline of a broad-shouldered solitary woman in her tiny clapboard house, the archway of the hall, the pillars of the porch, the picket gate. Suzanne had the sense something was beginning.

He walked towards her up the path. He was not tall, not small. His face was pointed and lean, his bones sharp, his thighs surprisingly thick. He had grey-blue eyes, the eyes of a fanatic, she remembered from the night before, eyes which grew hard and almost clear with concentration when they lit on her. He did not look as old in the dark. He had a roman nose, and dark skin, a high forehead rising to a dome under the thinning grey curls. His mouth had a touch of humour though not enough, she thought, to laugh at himself. Just watching him she felt the jolt of desire go through her again.

She pushed open the screen and met him on the porch. The air was thick with the scent of lilac. He touched her hand. Now the urgency was gone, the physical panic. She felt only warmth. He was here. There would be time for all that.

"Let's walk," she said.

He turned with her. They went down the sidewalk and towards the river. She was gay.

"I'll show you the neighbourhood. This is, dare I say it, the bohemian part of town."

Along Kensington Road the lights were on in shop windows. A man was standing on a ladder in front of the Plaza Theatre taking down letters which had spelled African Queen. The top of the theatre was a false front, cut in peaks like a crown; it stood forward, a pop-out against the sky. There was Judith's bookshop, where Suzanne often had coffee and loitered. Around the corner, the little clinic where one of her friends practised medicine. And the deli and the exercise club.

"I see you've got a safe kingdom here, populated entirely with women friends," he said.

"I hardly have to go anywhere else, except to the college."

Two couples came out the door of the basement Chinese restaurant. The men were both blond and wore open-necked shirts with sweaters looped around their shoulders. They had bare feet in their loafers. Side by side they stopped to look in the window of the wind-surfing store.

Simon and Suzanne passed them, crossed Memorial Drive and cut over the grass to the bicycle path by the water. They fell into step, with shoulders touching, in the direction the water flowed.

"How come you aren't married?" he said.

She told him she had been. It wasn't exactly a lie.

"Not me," he offered. "My whole life since school has been politics. And boy am I sorry. It wasn't worth the last twenty-odd years. I'm out of that now. *Fini. Terminé.*"

She knew enough about politics to know that after that kind of service you get a reward, unless you leave on bad terms. "Did you get bumped?" she asked.

"Hell no. Going out is going up. After what I did on the legislation they offered me a vice-presidency. But I'm not big on Crown Corps. And I was sick of the game. It's a crock."

"You spent twenty years figuring that out? I'd just assume it."

"Assuming is easy," he said. "All kinds of people assume all kinds of things. But there's nothing you can say about power till you're near enough to feel it."

His conversation did a curious thing to her. It beckoned her into a chamber reserved for very adult, very weighty matters. At the same time it told her these matters were simple, quite within her grasp, that she belonged in that room, she had something to add.

"You see," he continued, "power is one thing, but needing it is another. I was right hand man to — " he said a name, someone she'd heard of, "and I worshipped him. He was a brilliant thinker. I hung around long enough, though, to see what the whole thing did to him. He used to tell the PM what the country needed, how much of it people would accept. For a while the PM listened, but then he started to fall in the polls. He didn't like what my man had to say. So my man changed his tune. Started to go against all his principles, flatter the guy. Then he'd call me up and try to rationalize why he did it. You see he'd been close to it too long. He needed it too much. He needed the prime minister to call him up and ask for his advice. It made me sick."

"Aren't you working for the government now?" said Suzanne.

"No, no, this is all on my own. Sure I know people, I can make things happen, but what I'm doing isn't politics. It's just resting. I got tired of working for other people. No, if I went back it'd be for the big thing. Run for office, that'd be it."

They stopped under the arch of a bridge, at the place where Suzanne and her friends used to land the rubber dinghy after drifting in from outside town. She was supposed to be showing him, but he was doing all the talking. The world had walked up to her doorstep and had begun to make explanations. Odd that she could understand so easily all he said, and even believe she understood things he hadn't said. She thought his "rest" was forced and that it wouldn't last for long; she thought his zest for politics was still there. Listening to him was like picking up a new book by a familiar author. Odd revelations and news were followed by patches of the known.

He was wearing cologne, a brand advertised in connection with one-night stands between glamorous executives. The suddenness of their confrontation and the intensity of his bristling self-absorption put her on guard. But you are always on guard, Suzanne, she told herself. And where has it got you? They turned back towards her place.

"You know why I'm like this, of course," he remarked, as if in direct answer to her suspicions. "I'm an outsider. Have been always. You probably don't know what that means. It means you've got to make it totally on your own, no one has marked the path. I never knew the right people, I never went to the right schools."

"Lots of people didn't."

"Not lots of people who are where I am. But I had this thing going for me. I had an idea. I figured it out in second grade. I figured out that I was nearly the smartest in the room. The second smartest. All the time. But see, the smartest always had something wrong with him. That's what I could see. You know what I mean? He was too weird, or he didn't care. So I pushed in and took his place. It's so easy. It's been the same everywhere I go. Doesn't matter how big the pond. It's universally applicable."

"Even here?" Suzanne relaxed. The wind was blowing the cologne away from her.

"I have no doubt, no doubt at all. I am the second smartest person walking on the bicycle path by the Bow River, and the smartest doesn't count."

She laughed. He turned towards her, stretched his arms over her head and brought them down behind her back. He was about to hug her, and then he didn't. "The smartest isn't playing the game," he said. She laughed again.

"Well it's an idea but it's not going to change the world."

"You'd be surprised."

"I would." They took a few more steps in silence. But she was caught now, she had to know what he thought. "How come I'm not playing the game? Because I'm a woman?"

"Oh no, there are lots of women who play the game. Your friend Gemma does. But you don't seem to recognize the usual stakes. You've counted yourself out."

Beside them the river chugged, thick and green. She could see through the darkness that the sky had lowered; a wind was bringing clouds from the west. The air had picked up the chill of approaching rain. There was an onrush of cars from a distant traffic light; it reached them and drowned everything for a moment and then was gone.

"I don't know why you'd say that," she said.

"Obvious. You're an insider here. You could have anything you want."

"You think so," she said in a neutral tone.

"You're not in it for marriage, you're not in it for money. You've been away and you came back. I don't know what for."

"I came back because of work." It was what she always said. People thought that she meant her job. But the job was just earning a living. *Work* was something else, her secret pursuit, her obsession. That was what gave her whatever he chose to call it, this curious autonomy from events. Work was taking the wrapping off these shapes in her mind. Shapes that had been there before she returned to her hometown, that led her here, that she came back to finally see, and make clear. Because of the work, a part of her was always living in another story. The story that appeared, in layers on the desk in the spare room. The story had to do with an event in this town a hundred years ago.

"I do a bit of research," she said.

"Research — historical? You mean you write?" He stopped in mid-bounce. "What are you writing? A book?"

"Oh, nothing so grand."

His body drew into a little convulsion of excitement. He turned to look into her eyes. "Oh, I think it is. I think it's poetry. Oh, poetry, poetry," he exclaimed, scooping the art up into his bag of enthusiasms. "Poetry was always what I wanted. I got into this game as a speechwriter — did I tell you that? And it was only because I didn't have the nerve for my own words. That's what I mean when I say if I gave up politics it would only be for absolute power. Like to write."

People say they're going to write when they retire or when they're too weak to do anything else. Suzanne never admitted to that eternal fantasy of the amateur.

"I knew a couple of poets," she said, "at university." Her mind went back to some fellows who'd had rumpled pants and a whipped look. "And I wouldn't say they were experiencing real power."

But he wasn't listening. He cupped her face in both of his hands, and tipped it to his own. He breathed on her. "That's what we have in common," he said. "We're poets, together. You inspire me."

She couldn't deny poetry, and him, at the same time.

They were back at the place where they had to cross the road. There was a small crater in the asphalt at the edge. He stood on the curb and stared down intently at it. Then he gathered his legs and sprang over it, into the street. He reached back for her hand. She stepped out after him, surprised at his agility, his quickness. On the other side he spoke.

"Phrase," he said. "That's it. Phrase is where poetry and politics meet." He paused. The pause was for her exclamation. "How do you like it?"

"What?"

"My slogan. That's what I used to do for politicians. Invent slogans. To sell some idea to the public. Borrowing from Peter to pay Bill, that was mine. You'd be amazed how much a good slogan can do for a concept. 'Phrase is where poetry and politics meet.' That's for us."

"I like it. Is it true?"

"It makes no difference, if it sounds good. It's a winner, in fact. I can come up with all kinds of them."

They were nearly at her door when the spats of rain hit, exploding into gleam beneath the porch light. He still had her hand. He could have used the accident of the weather and demanded to come in, but he didn't. Instead, by way of saying good-night, he put his hands again lightly on her shoulder and leaned towards her, close enough for a kiss. Then he peered around behind her head into the dark hall.

"What have you got in there that you're so secretive about, a wild animal?"

She said nothing. Her eyes were closed. He drew his head back, reluctantly.

"Suzanne Vail," he said. "I'm going to see a lot more of this woman," he said, as if pledging into a mirror. "I'm going to have a tremendous love affair with this woman."

Chapter 3

Suzanne stalked past Nola with her chin out, trying to look as if her mind was on other things. It was no good. Nola hissed from her desk in the alcove. Suzanne slowed, making it clear she intended to carry on in the direction of her office.

"That's a pretty colour on you," Nola said, eyeing the yellow cotton lace dress with the red trim. "So bright."

Suzanne drew the skirt in towards her legs. "Oh, summer's coming, you know I can't resist the temptation — "

"If you've got it, flaunt it, right?"

"I didn't think I was exactly *flaunting* — " And lifted her wrist ostentatiously to her eyes. "Got a two o'clock class." She kept moving down the hall. The louder hiss came over her shoulder.

"Asp was looking for you again. I told her you'd be in before that class."

Suzanne made a face but did not turn.

"Suzanne!" Grimly, Suzanne turned round. She'd gone too far past; now she would have to walk back to Nola's lair.

"Suzanne, tell me, what does an orchid look like?"

"Like an open mouth and throat. Why?"

Nola's lips twisted sideways; suspicion confirmed. "I figured you'd know."

Suzanne stepped closer. She'd been feeling good when she came in. Now she began to fold inward. "Why?"

"Because he's gone and bought some, of course." Nola jerked her head towards the Head's office. She never called him by his name. "Turned in the biggest expense form ever claimed for a conference, and there's orchids on it, from the hotel florist, can you beat it? I'm supposed to sneak this by the finance people for him."

"Well, he didn't buy them for me."

"Oh I know that! He's gone and taken his girlfriend to another conference, that's all. I just thought, God, the ironies of life. It's my job to make sure he gets away with it when I've never seen an orchid in my life. I knew you would have, though."

"Why don't you tell him you know?"

Nola darted a glance over her shoulder towards the half-open door. She claimed he lurked in his office, eavesdropping on her, and that he got this idea out of a book on power politics. Certainly if he eavesdropped, Suzanne agreed, it was not his own idea. God knew the man had never had an idea.

As they stared at the door the Head materialized.

"Girls," he said pleasantly, and stepped in front of Nola's desk.

"Dr Vail if you don't mind," Suzanne snapped.

He swung his astonished face towards her.

"Or Suzanne, if you'd rather." She giggled, her face flaming. He smiled carefully and went on his way.

"Damn!" said Suzanne, watching his back. "I blew it." She'd waited for a whole year to tell him she wasn't a girl.

"Plucky today. What's caused this new mood, may I ask?" But Nola did not want an answer. "Orchids, can you believe it? This is the last time. Better still, I won't do it at all. I'll resign this afternoon."

"What was the conference?" Out of habit, Suzanne

sought the details of the Head's fiscal irresponsibility. She had decided earlier that such knowledge could be useful in the future should the Head oppose her on some academic issue. She saw his back grow smaller down the hallway. The Head was not fond of Suzanne; he didn't like her approach. History was grand, and elsewhere, to him; he was offended by the suggestion that any of it had happened close by. "Local history," his term for her field of interest — Western Canada in the nineteenth century — was first of all a contradiction in terms. If she insisted there was such a thing he might concede that it could be a useful hobby for members of Women's Institutes.

Nola said something, but Suzanne wasn't listening. She was thinking that the possible reason for the Head's disregard for Suzanne was her friendship with Nola. His back had swung around a corner. The girls, he called them.

"What was that?"

Nola respected the name, but the second the words were uttered, Suzanne forgot them. She was losing her zeal to gain the information which could bring her up higher on the totem pole. She looked around the beige hallway, at all the closed, grey doors, at the wide elevator lobby with its glass case of soapstone seals and silkscreens in an exhibit called, "Inuit at their Play." If she was not mistaken the whole place was fading. Or perhaps it was just that it was summer, and a drama had begun. She might be in love.

"Well, well," she said, nodding assent to whatever Nola had said.

"And red shoes, too," said Nola.

She headed off down the hall to her office, her face grave with concentration. Was it really happening, was she becoming detached, losing interest in her familiar and, she had to admit, soothing situation? Perhaps. Take the yellow dress, for instance. For years now she had gone to the universities where she studied and taught dressed as a spinster. She tied back her hair, wore long pleated skirts, dark stockings, no makeup. For a while she even affected round glasses with transparent frames. As an undergraduate she had been what was considered attractive, in her pale way. But after Ace there had been this deliberate conversion; she had taken up scholarship the way women used to go to convents.

And the men. Of course there had been men. But they were hand-picked not to last. They had been racially exotic, and mostly non-verbal; one a sound man for television, another a carpenter. It was remarked upon. "She's doing a tour of the United Nations," said Gemma. Suzanne's mother flew up from the south to give counsel.

"Do they wear their skirts that length in Toronto?" Mrs Vail had asked mildly at the airport. Then, "Would a little lipstick hurt?" The showdown came as they climbed to Suzanne's third-floor apartment. Her mother said a woman needed a profession but Suzanne was taking it too far. You got a training in the event of disaster but ought not to put the cart before the horse. You needed a man to look after you. You couldn't go on living this way. Had she left Ace and the good life for good? Even if she had, there was no harm in looking decent, was there?

"In other words you want me to pretend to try to attract a man when I am preparing for a life without one," said Suzanne.

Suzanne's mother never believed Suzanne made decisions. She thought her daughter was the victim of other people's actions.

"I didn't know he'd hurt you that much, dear."

And Suzanne said the trouble with her mother was that she hadn't stayed the same as she was when she had the power to mark Suzanne for life. "You told me never to live for a man. Now what are you saying?"

"I suppose I was unhappy dear, when you were young." Her mother basked in older middle-aged contentment.

Even her father, an ally in accomplishment, backed off after the Master's degree. Two degrees had been tolerable, but the upcoming third would eliminate the last possible mates from the field, he implied. So be it, said Suzanne, and grew paler and left the tangles in her hair.

Suzanne tried, in the first few years after the Ph.D., to
strike the right tone with students, to put off *badinage*
without being rude, to charm, as a teacher must, without
being seductive. To turn them on to the message without
turning them on to the medium. She wasn't clear how to be
with them, too young to be a schoolmarm, too old for a pal.
Needing authority, she became brisk and sharpened her
tongue. The resulting persona had been — well, perhaps
forbidding.

But today she unlocked the office door of Dr S. Vail,
plump and satisfied in her yellow and red, her hair fluffed
around her ears and swinging long in a ponytail behind. No
wonder Nola was rattled. Suzanne was rattled herself. Was
it written on her that her stale romantic life had taken a
turn? And more than that, she liked it? On her chest or
forehead, the scarlet letter? And what if it was? She was not
about to question what had broken the vow of celibacy or, if
celibacy had not been strictly accurate, then at least
emotional stasis.

Suzanne leaned into her file-cabinet drawer searching for
the file marked History 301, Reinventing the West. A
person came into her doorway; she looked up.

"Miss Vail?"

"Who are you?"

"I'm in your class."

Suzanne stood up. "What's your name?"

"Asp."

She had thought she remembered Roberta Asp but she
didn't recognize her now. It was an androgynous-looking
person with white makeup all over her face, a headlight
hanging around her neck, and hair that stuck up all over in
little greenish white spikes. "Are you in disguise, Asp?" she
said.

"I'm in fashion."

"Thank you," said Suzanne. "I ought to have known."
She eyed the chrome and glass neckpiece which hung out
from her waist, swinging dangerously.

"I designed it. You can get them in the craft gallery," Asp said. She was grinning; her head bobbed and all the hair trembled in place. Suzanne looked across the harvest table to her Boston fern which bore an uncanny resemblance to her visitor.

"Have you two already met?" said Suzanne.

But Asp didn't smile. She pushed herself out of the door frame with a graceful arm, crossed the office in two steps, touched a couple of books on the shelf and then turned to the window. She lifted the paper blind in her fingers, and looked out across the air-conditioning equipment on the roof towards the foothills to the south-west. "You're a different sort of teacher, aren't you?"

Suzanne looked her dead in the eye. The girl had attended one lecture at the most, at the beginning of the second term, back in January. Then, she had long dark hair and dark skin. Here it was almost May, and Asp had the nerve to show up in a different incarnation. Suzanne interpreted her altered appearance as a trick aimed at her personally.

"What have you come to see me about? To tell me how much you like history?" she said.

"Why do you have to call it that?" Asp said crossly. "It's like you're putting it away, in a box."

That was exactly what Suzanne felt about the Head. She lifted her hands from the top of her file cabinet, and tucked a hair behind her ear. "What exactly do you mean by that? If you mean that it wasn't so long ago, I agree. It's fresh."

Asp laughed out loud.

Suzanne flushed. "I'm waiting, Asp. For you to say what you're doing here. You've missed every class since possibly the first, and the course is almost over."

Asp sank into the chair. Her legs stretched half-way across the office. "You're a lot more approachable. You give me the feeling you're almost human, know what I mean?"

"What do you want, Asp?"

The girl grinned. "You mean aside from an A?"

"I might be prepared to give you an extension on that paper, if I was convinced you have some interest in the subject." Suzanne pulled her lips in tightly.

"Nice dress," said Asp.

"Nice try," snapped Suzanne, "but let's stay on the topic. You ought to be concerned about your work. What are you going to do? Withdraw from the course? Stay in until you get a failing grade on your record?"

"Hey! Take it easy," said Asp, standing up. "I'll do it. I'll do the paper, all right?"

"I'm not asking you to," said Suzanne. "It's your funeral, not mine, if you don't."

Asp grinned. "That bad is it?"

Suzanne grimaced.

But Asp didn't want to leave. She had something to say.

"Hey you know, what you were saying, at beginning of term, about whether the west was wild, or tame? Well, I think it depended on who you were."

"How did it depend?" said Suzanne, wearily letting herself be drawn in.

"For the right kind of people it was lawful and safe. For the rest of us — "

"Who were the rest?" said Suzanne. But Asp only looked at her, sardonically. Suzanne's interest was caught. "Who were your people then," she said. "Where did they come from?"

Asp smiled. "Round about Edmonton, a little farther south. My grandparents, and my great grandparents. And before that."

"No, I mean where did they come from before?"

"They didn't come from anywhere. They were just there."

"Of course they came from somewhere..."

Suzanne began to flush. She felt she was being teased. She tried to place the name Asp etymologically. It couldn't be European. Perhaps it was Egyptian? or changed, assumed? There were many like that. But Asp?

"It's Cree," said Asp, and sank further back in her chair, arms folded, smug.

Not you, too, Suzanne was about to say. And Gemma's great-aunt. But she stopped herself. Something told her it was true. The dye-job and pale-face paint were a disguise. Asp was native Indian. But why was she putting her on?

Some students had to fight their teachers before they could start to learn. And afterwards they had to love them. When she was first teaching, these emotions smote Suzanne; to the extent that she was a guardian, she was rebelled against; to the extent she was a guide, she was adored. By now she had learned that these extremes were impersonal and was not bothered. Today however, her calm seemed to have abandoned her.

Suzanne closed her eyes and drew a deep breath. She put her hand down on the pile of papers, shaking her head. Was it possible she was cornered in her office by a green-haired Indian mannequin? Was she losing her grip altogether? There was a story about a guy who'd gone mad in the History department and had driven to the Badlands and pitched himself off a ledge into a pile of dinosaur bones. When she opened her eyes, Asp was gone.

Suzanne's footsteps rang out separately from the students', shuffling in their loafers and boots. She strode down the colour-coded hall to her lecture in L213, in the yellow section. The halls were colour-coded for those who achieved them without achieving literacy. Yellow was for humanities, blue for science, red for the professions, green for physical education and fine arts.

"Hey Miss Vail, you want some tickets to the Talking Heads?"

"I don't think so, thank you."

"You could come to the frat house after. We're having a wet T-shirt party."

Oh, but Suzanne had been there, at the wet T-shirt

parties, the beer bashes, the toga parties. She had been
picked up by bus to be presented as a pet at the pledge
parties; her name and a head-and-shoulders photo had been
on the wheel they turned to come up with their favourite
dates. Suzanne had been there but she wouldn't be back.

"I'm looked after this weekend, thank you."

"Who's looking after you?" A wide grin. "The guy with
the Porsche?"

She smiled enigmatically; she registered that they'd seen
Ace in the parking lot. "You're a bit old to be spying on
your teachers, aren't you?"

She rounded the doorway into the classroom and set her
books on the lectern. A sadist in the physical plant had
filled the room with child-sized desks; all thirty-two students
sat with elbows and buttocks protruding over the seats into
the aisles. They were waiting for her to bring them to life,
earnest young men with thick brows and affected women
with too much makeup. A piquant boy with an earring in
his left ear, a sallow, intense girl with circles dark as bruises
around her eyes. It was like peering into a muddy stream
and hoping to see the bottom. There were a few glimmers,
possibly a stone, but nothing strong enough to raise hope.

Fifty minutes, and then the students in the front row
would slide their books into tidy piles and plant their feet
flat on the floor, ready to bolt when the buzzer sounded. If
they stood up too suddenly, they'd take the desks with
them. Fifty minutes, and then they would be released, and
so would Suzanne.

Chapter 4

Murder Most Foul
A Shocking Tragedy Last Night
An Unfortunate Squaw Murdered and Mutilated...
A Mysterious Affair

"Probably due to the fact that Calgary is an exceptionally orderly town and has been singularly free of crime, a profound sensation was created last night when the report circulated that the mutilated body of a murdered squaw had been found in a room over the Turf Club Restaurant on McTavish Street. The first reports were as usual considerably exaggerated. The case was represented as rivalling the worst of the Whitechapel tragedies in terrible detail. Although these reports were overdrawn the case is a truly [*illegible-folded*] one. Chief Dillabough of the Town Police Force was patrolling Stephen Avenue at eight o'clock last evening when accosted by a well-known character about town named William Fisk, commonly known as Jumbo Fisk, an appellation he [*smudged-illegible*] for greatness in size. Fisk who appeared considerably excited, told the chief that he had come

TO DELIVER HIMSELF UP

He explained that he had been spending some time with a dissolute squaw and that she had 'died on his hands.' The chief at once took charge..."

Suzanne raised her head from the greyed papers, frustrated. Newspaper accounts were notoriously bad sources, even if she could make out the words. *Facts*, she needed facts, the hard centres in this fatty flesh of description, but there were few. Few facts and many accounts, here and elsewhere, the story of the story, impossible to verify, leading her this way and that. Fact, the supposedly irreducible thing, was not so easily preserved.

What she wanted was to be transported to the physical world of Calgary, one hundred years ago. But it had been a transitory world and for the most part was gone to dust; there was precious little to be found — a few clay pots, stone edifices and burial grounds. On the prairie the longest surviving relic was the printed word; it had replaced the artefacts of history; it was the object of her search.

And there were many. To man's and woman's amiable, half-mad desire to leave behind their version of what they'd seen she owed the memoirs, the census, the police records, the settlers' account books, the letters home. These written words were her mediator when she sought to confront that bygone world. They were her medium in an occult journey backward, her tour guide, translator, her means of transport too.

She loved the words, and despaired of them. They were flimsy, unreliable and odd. Some survived the years only to be lost in the creases of the old paper as she copied it, so that what was "flowers" one minute was "curses" the next. Some dissolved before her eyes, reduced to scratch marks on the magnifying glass. Some had been employed in the first place to disguise the real event.

In the bright artificial light of the reading room, Suzanne put her hand on the small of her back, where it hurt, and pushed aside the magnifying glass she'd been looking through. When she was a graduate student, she used to say that truth was her goal, its glittering transparent shores luring her like a mirage on a highway in the hot sun. Now she little believed in such an uncomplicated thing, but she journeyed on regardless. Her work might even be amusing if it weren't concerned with so desperate a deed. Prodded by curiosity and directed by guesswork and hunch, she hardly knew what she was looking for. But the story drew her, it had a shape which, laid bare, might explain more than itself. This murdered Indian woman, that dark club and the men who frequented it, the town's panic: it was one of those occasions where the layers of paper and politeness broke open, revealing the core. But to see that core, Suzanne needed a way in. Something was missing. She needed a guide, a torch, a pick-axe. Something, or someone.

She looked at her notes. What she had so far was a story of men. Of Jumbo Fisk, twenty-three, a giant, with bad habits and good connections; of George Kelsey, a newcomer in town with a job as barkeep in a cheap hotel. Fisk's barfly friends, a faint-hearted cop, some men of importance with feet of clay, and even a couple of heroes, a feisty frontier judge and an unimpeachable doctor. And then there was Rosalie. Rosalie New Grass, who did not cry out in the hours of her death.

That was what she had. So far nothing to lift the story out of its gloom and perversity, nothing to illuminate its dark byways. An Indian girl and a lot of men, perfectly ordinary in their time and place — almost.

Except for one. She had almost forgotten him. He was a spectator to the entire sequence of events, a man of whom she had by now some passing acquaintance. He was always there but never mentioned, the invisible man. She had read enough of what he wrote to see him witty and at times pompous, to see him dig and then refuse to dig. He was a strange character, tied to his chosen town, but certain of his superiority. He was the man who wrote up the Rosalie case for the newspaper. Who was he?

The accounts were unsigned. But, Suzanne thought,

suddenly, I bet I know who it was. There was a character in town at that time, a big Calgary booster, a former easterner, a compulsive letter-writer. She stood up and went to the index. His letters were in the archives, as she thought. The clerk was pasting photographs on grey mounting. She passed the white card over the counter to him. In four minutes his leather-bound copybook was on her desk. She scanned the list of entries, with brief descriptions of contents. Perhaps he made reference to his journalistic efforts, perhaps even to the case? Yes, there was a letter addressed to the Reverend Williams in Montreal, Fisk's uncle. She turned to it, and skimmed. "...and as I have chanced to be sitting in on his trial in my role of correspondent for our paper..."

Suzanne sat back and let out a long-held breath. These were the rewards of her work. This moment of discovery, *her* discovery. She enjoyed it, for a moment, and then took up her pencil and began to work.

This man had a name of course. But Suzanne did not, for the moment, write it down. Instead she pondered on what she knew of his characteristics. He could describe the weeping parents of the murdered Rosalie as creating "a most affecting scene." A dry-stick kind of man, patronizing, Victorian. A parent himself, more than likely, she deduced, from the emotion he so primly alluded to. A man whose opinions could go from the extremes of calling Rosalie a "dissolute squaw" to, later, "the flower of her race." A man who tried to keep his lead on public opinion while in fact following it.

He fancied himself a thinker, didn't he, for look at his digression on Jack the Ripper: he postulated that by a "morbid contagion" the murders had become photographed on the minds of folks with an "unnatural disposition." "In times of excitement such people would be liable to act upon what was so forcibly stamped in their minds..." And how he meddled! Imagine writing letters to the relative of the accused, professing sorrow while turning in accounts of the trial which were inflammatory, even accusatory, if she read

them correctly. This man was more involved than he ought
to be in this case. And ambitious, as well, and energetic,
and having an axe to grind. He was perfect. She could use
him.

She could use him, but only by breaking the rules of her
kind of scholarship. She did not know and could not
discover why he took such an interest in the Rosalie case.
She would have to make assumptions, to invent. But she
was sure that if she did, this man would be her vehicle to
carry her past the great century behind her. He could cut
through the intervening rings of darkness and light, the
banal seasons of freeze and thaw, as if it were not time but
mere geography. But if he were to be the means for this
ungeographical journey, and she to follow him, she would
have to make him her own.

Aware that she was offending the standards of the likes of
Studies in Western Canadian History editors, and somehow
not, for the moment, caring, she stroked out his real name
on her copies of the papers. She would call her man — what
would she call him? She put the end of her pencil in her
mouth, and thought. She would call him Murphy.

All during the next day Indians accumulated silently in
front of the Turf Club. By nightfall there were several dozen
standing, their standing itself speaking the news. A squaw
had died by a white man's hand. They said her spirit had
been seen, that she walked the streets.

The town was held in awe and fear. Two men were in jail,
taken out of the club in handcuffs. The squaw's body
remained locked in the room over the bar. The mayor
warned of Indian violence; her people could not be allowed
to see what had been done to her. The coroner's jury was
meeting downstairs in the Turf Club around the bar tables,
but after a day the stench of her rotting caused them to
remove to council chambers.

The Turf Club regulars had moved to the long bar at the
Alberta Hotel. I stood at the other end and called for a
whisky. I could hear them talking.

"What do you make of that moaning we heard?" said Lee.

Driving hack, Lee got around the town well, and he'd got the impression Fisk had got off the train somewhat the worse for his journey. "Kelsey said it was his dog." Lee breathed noisily through blocked nasal passages; he always did.

"How were we to know?"

"Damn strange."

"She ought to have screamed."

"Kelsey must've been in on it," said Whitbeck, a cook by trade. The idea that it was a conspiracy somehow made him feel easier.

"They say the Indians are bent on revenge." Air hissed in the gap between Lee's front teeth.

"That's a crock of baloney, Lee," said Lowry. "You're looking to stir up trouble." He was mad mostly because he thought, now a squaw had been killed in his club, he'd never sell it.

"Plenty of settlers'd be willing to take up arms," said Whitbeck. It had not been many years since the Riel affair.

I hated to be one of them and yet I had no one else. They were ignorant, and a poor class of man; besides I am older than the others, but not as old as I look, with my white beard and my white, horned eyebrows. Finally I slid uninvited down to their end. No one looked up to greet me. I drew out my tobacco case, and carefully began to roll a cigarette. I tapped both ends. They were watching my hands.

"Saw your friend Fisk this morning," I said.

None of the men moved. Whatever they might say to each other they wouldn't say in front of me. They knew I had a finger in everything in town, and reported for the newspaper as well. "Not surprised, Murphy," said Lee.

"I told him, 'Jumbo, it's a bad mess you got yourself in. I hope you can get yourself out of it.' 'Oh,' he said, 'there's no trouble.'" I opened my mouth and let my teeth show, giving emphasis. "I hear he's got big connections in

Ontario. Widowed mother with lots of money. His uncles are big too; one in the church, one works for the *Globe* newspaper."

"They'll get him off?" said Lee. Lee was the kind of man who regularly came up too close to you when he talked.

"He may not need the help," I said. "Who's to say he did anything? Looks as if it coulda been anyone. There's only the one curious circumstance going against him. That's the fact that there was no weapon. It's a hard thing to understand. It was done with bare hands." I stared at Lee. "You ever killed anyone with your bare hands? It's not easy. Fisk is strong, he might be the only one who could have done it."

"I 'spect she did it to herself." Lee backed off a bit.

"And flung a piece of her flesh clear under the bed while biting through her lower lip from the pain? Come, come," I said. They knew I was laughing at them.

"He turned himself in; 's a sign, isn't it?"

"It's a sign, I'll give you that. But is it a sign of innocence? Or just a sign that he thought he was in trouble and counted on his friends and the police chief and the justice of the peace to help him out?" I cackled; I was enjoying this. They stuck together like a gang, like they wouldn't want to be alone, listening to me. "Mind you, I liked Fisk just as much as the next man."

Whitbeck picked up on this. He chose to trust me, a little.

"Quite a thing, I say. It must've scared him good. They say Dillabough's still gibbering, you can't calm him down."

"Quite the thing." Heads were shaking all around.

"I guess we're going to be on the map with this one."

The men nodded, shifting their glasses. This matter of getting on the map: first it was the railway that was going to do it, then the boom, then the fire of 1886. And still it hadn't happened. There was a sense of something owing. This was the biggest murder they'd ever had, in fact it was the only one since, a few miles south, a black man from the States had put an axe through a shopkeeper's skull and robbed the cash.

"Anybody know the girl?" I said casually. I pressed my palms on the table, and leaned back on the hind legs of my stool.

"Couldn't say for sure, but they don't think she'd ever been at the saloon before."

"That so?" I said.

"If *you* didn't she's got to be the only girl in town you aren't acquainted with," said Lee.

I didn't like that. I don't like people commenting on my habits. I'd never have fallen into this life if it hadn't been for my wife leaving me, just vacating like that, the way no woman had a right to do. And for the biggest whoremaster in the west.

The room grew smaller as the light escaped, and the dinner hour approached. A rancher who had come in to town for his bridles and found the blacksmith closed came looking for Fisk, and had to be told.

"I deal with him regular," he said. "You can't tell me he'd do a thing like that. Strong, but gentle as a cat."

The picture of Fisk came up before us then: at his smithy, with the white sparks, the solemn ring of his hammer. I don't know the man well but I know his arms are thick and his face leathery, a thickness of texture, not contour.

"You'll find him in the lockup now," I said.

"I'll be damned." The rancher pursed his lips and frowned his readiness to keep Fisk's secrets, even if he might only guess at what they were. Then he went out, into the afternoon which had almost become night.

"Fisk never said much about himself," said Whitbeck. "Must say I liked him for it."

I called for another drink, but I pushed back my stool. I really didn't like to imbibe in the present company. His breath hissing in his passages, Lee reached beside his chair and picked up his hat. He stood and pushed it down on his head with the flat of one hand. He backed away from the bar but didn't quite leave it yet. I put my legs around the stool backward like a buckle. Lee was waiting for something.

He wanted a fight, I guessed. I knew how to give it to him.

"Tell you one strange thing. I recall as Fisk's been greatly interested in this Jack the Ripper story that's been going on in London. He'd been reading all the accounts of it in the newspaper, asking me what I knew. Always wanted more details than you could get. I've got it in my mind that this is some kind of copy-cat thing," I said.

But it was Whitbeck who got mad. "You ask me that's where this kind of trouble starts. Fools trying to sell papers is all. I don't like the way you newspaper people..." he spit, and seemed at a loss for strong enough language, "...write things up."

"I'm not accusing anybody," I said. I let my stool tip forward; it banged on the floor. "I just noted it's the same sort of thing. They're saying in London there's more than one Ripper, see, the other just got the idea from the first. Down in the slums there's thousands of these low women, shrieking outside the gin shops, fighting with the drunken sailors. Now there's been a couple of attempts on these women with knives. Some of the crowd tried to lynch the men doing it, but it turned out to be just a regulation squabble. See what kind of thing could start to happen here?"

"Couldn't ever."

"You'd be amazed the sort of thing human beings can get used to, provided it happens often enough."

"We don't need your fancy theories," said Lee. "Your *Times* of London." He shifted his feet, ready to go.

I laughed. I'd never waste my time with these men but for the fact that I had time to waste. I raised my hand. "I got nothing against Fisk. Absolutely nothing. I got nothing against whoever did it. I take a philosophical point of view." I lowered my voice. This was the kind of thing no one would say, no one but me.

"It's the sex, and the killing going with it, interest me." Smoke from my cigarette puffed up in front of my face, and I couldn't see their expressions. They said nothing. I could feel their determination to say nothing.

"I say Fisk'll be back drinking with us in another week," said Lee finally. "We've got to stick together in this, specially if certain people want to make a big case out of it. I say we bury her nice and not have a trial at all, it's just going to stir up the Indians." He jammed his hat down harder on his head.

Rosalie's coffin sat on the board platform in front of the Fire Hall for all to see. It was of polished cherry and the mountings were silver, as good as could be got in the territories. The Indian agent had thought that the federal government should pay, but the town decided that would take too long. Town Council was in a hurry. It voted the money for a showy one. I was there for the paper, taking notes.

Dillabough, looking pale, and Murdoch, the Justice of the Peace, sat on chairs on the platform, a scattering of whites before them on the street. The Indians stood close together, their shapes concealed in blankets. In his heavy, final voice, Father André spoke to the Indians. A halfbreed translated his words for the whites who listened.

"He say the white man mean no harm by this. It is not an act against your race, but an act by a single man."

An Indian moved forward, his blanket falling back across his shoulders, and called to the priest. He put his hand out flat in front of his face, as if to stop something coming towards him. The halfbreed spoke again.

"They ask where is the white man who killed her? They say he has taken Rosalie and in turn they must have the murderer."

Father André spoke again.

"He says vengeance is the Lord's."

The Indian voice came again, and then the halfbreed's. "He says will white man's law take care of punishing the murderer, for them to see?"

The priest made a short answer.

"Assuredly, this will be so." Dillabough and Murdoch nodded vigorously.

"The Indians say they are pleased," concluded the halfbreed, although the Indians had said nothing at all.

Father André raised his eyes to the sky. New Grass, the father, and Rosalie's mother, whose name I did not know, walked up to the platform. Behind them came a young man who fell on his face before the coffin, a lover or a brother.

"They say they want to look upon her face."

"It is not done," said Father André hurriedly. He had been instructed to tell them God wouldn't want them to see. The repair work had been beyond what the amateur undertaker could manage.

Father André raised his arms, and began to pray. First he spoke in Cree, foreign sounds to his white listeners; his prayer was stranger still to the Indians. His voice, a thing apart, tumbled down the platform over the heads of the crowd.

"Sometimes my heart is very weak and falls down, but He lifts it up again and draws me on to a good road. His name is Wonderful..."

The old woman began to cry.

"Sometime — it could be very soon, it could be very long, it could be a long, long time — He will draw me into a place between the mountains. It is dark there but I will not draw back; I will not be afraid; for it is there between the mountains that the shepherd will meet me...."

Standing in the back, I shifted my feet on the frozen ground. I don't know how these people could stand still for so long on packed snow without proper boots. The cold grew right through the foot and up the leg, that's what it did, and the sky pressing down like a swollen udder over your head. But I admired these people. I'd rather be a savage than a white man, that was for sure, at least today.

"Sometimes He makes the love rope into a whip but afterwards, He gives me a staff that I may lean on... All tired is gone and my cup He fills up till it runs over..."

The prayer was all very fine, but what I wondered was how they were going to get Rosalie into the ground, weather like this. Back in Ontario, we'd have kept her in the ice house until spring. Indian custom would have been to wrap the body in skins and put it in the fork of a tree. Such bundles were still seen around Calgary. But that was out of the question for Rosalie. They couldn't have her hanging about, in full view, reminding people. She would have to be hidden somewhere until thaw. The whole idea of this ceremony and the coffin was a joke anyway. It was a lie to say that even dead she was as good as a white woman.

"What I tell you is true, I lie not . . . these roads that are many and away ahead will be with me all through my life and ever afterwards . . ."

At last André was done. Four white men showed New Grass and the young man whom I now took to be his son how to pick up the coffin. They had to let go of their blankets to do it. One of them tripped, and the coffin overbalanced, and nearly fell.

At the foot of the platform stairs the Indians wanted to go west, the whites east. Dillabough tried to direct, waving an arm overhead like a lariat, but no one paid any attention. The coffin lurched sharply to one side; again it looked as if it might fall. But the men hoisted it once more, and Father André, who in his black robe caused others to move aside, went to lead the procession. He and the bearers moved down the snow-packed road eastward. They passed me. I stamped on the ground to get the circulation back in my feet, and then took out my notebook.

"A most affecting scene," I wrote.

When they couldn't look back and see me, I followed the pall bearers.

Behind the chapel New Grass and his son stood awkwardly beside the coffin. The priest had bade them goodbye, but they made no move to leave. I stood in the trees, in earshot, not exactly hiding, but not visible either. Father André asked what he could do. It was a brutal winter; would New Grass take a little meat away with him? New Grass said nothing. He appeared to have a great capacity for saying nothing.

Father André at last concluded the man wished to be alone with his daughter's coffin.

"We do not lift the nails, you understand?" he said. "It is not done to look at her now." He went further. "You will endanger her, in the afterlife."

New Grass and the young man seemed to assent.

"I will leave you then," said Father André. "When the ground thaws we will have a burial, as God wishes." André walked a little way and then turned back. New Grass signalled that he was going but he sent his son ahead and only withdrew a little into the trees. Unable to play the waiting game any longer, the priest went inside. The young man returned. He had two friends with him. I stayed where I was. New Grass and the others lifted the coffin easily. Silently they bore it away through the trees. It was very difficult to follow. I lost them. I assumed, however, that they were going to the flat land on the western edge of town, before the first hills to the south, where the few Indians had their shelters.

In about half an hour's time I made my way there. It was easy to locate the log cabin New Grass had built when he came to town to work for the white man. They had set the open coffin down in front of it. There was a fire lit inside, and voices. I waited outside for half an hour or so. It was now completely dark and I was able to stand near enough to see in through the chinks. They had unwrapped the body and examined the wounds. She was two days dead now, but the cold and half-hearted embalming had kept Rosalie to be seen once more by these women, no doubt her sisters and sisters-in-law, her mother and grandmother.

The women tore off the garments which had been put on by the white man. The patch-up job was awful, and so was the smell. The Indian women touched her wounds and cried out and tore their hair. They spoke one to another in hushed voices; they argued, pointing at her broken lip, and the gash that had discoloured her lower body. I could only imagine what they were saying. To them it must have been a great mystery. Not even the Blackfoot did such things to women. New Grass stood back from all this, his face dark and flickering in the fire shadows. He knew something of the ways of white men.

It was frigid out there and yet I did not want to leave. This was the true funeral; this was the best part. I didn't know if I could write it, mind you, but all my instincts told me I should be there. I took a calculated risk; I stepped out of the shadows and into the doorway of the hut and gestured that I wanted to come in.

I suppose they could have turned on me then, as the representative of whoever the white man was who had done it to her; I suppose I could have fallen victim to their rage, as their feelings were much aroused at the moment. No one calls me brave, they call me slimey, but I know where I have been and what danger I have put myself in to get my story.

There was a moment of pure suspense. The Indian women hid their faces and cried at their men in confusion. The men without moving let their eyes meet. I stood. They stood. Then New Grass beckoned me to enter. From that moment they did not look my way again. Whether they thought I came as a mourner, a representative of the town, or as a reporter for the newspaper I did not know.

Now an argument sprang up between the old woman and the old man. From what I understood she defended the girl; he disowned her. Some suggested Rosalie had been chosen by the white man's god for some special punishment, that they might even look upon this death as an honour. I interpreted his short rejection as saying, no, she has brought us great disgrace.

Crying and wailing, the women washed Rosalie and dressed her in a red beaded dress. They painted the frozen face, the bruises pallid lavender now. They lifted up the long, heavy fall of hair which came down to her knees and combed it, and rubbed it on their cheeks. Even I could see that this hair, alone of her physical being, was not cold nor hard. It looked warm, like a thing alive. It sprang back when it was bent. I watched curious and moved, hiding my feelings.

Smelling the hair, the women wept. Rosalie was gone from the rest of her body, but in her hair she remained. They braided it, and bound the braid with sinew. When she was ready, they laid her on skins on the floor of the cabin. The braid, stretched northward, caught the firelight, its twining a languid dance.

Rosalie's brother began to conduct the mourning. First he cut gashes in his forearms and thighs. Rosalie's mother let her own hair loose; it tumbled down her back. The brother lit a pipe, drew on it, and passed it. At first the men told tales, singing and laughing. I imagined these tales were of Indian bravery, of how plentiful the buffalo had been before the white man came, how fierce the warriors, how protective the great spirits.

The night was long. I took a corner and folded my legs under me on a rug through which I felt the frozen earth. Now and then someone rose and put another smudge of sweet-grass on the fire. They seemed to be arguing about what should be done with the body. Speeches were made. I thought I understood them questioning how young Rosalie, who had taken up the white man's god and studied in his school and worked in his home, who had been obedient to her parents, came to be in that place where white men drank and did terrible things with women. They called the spirits to come to them and make them understand.

It was common knowledge among whites that Rosalie's ghost had been seen in town. I didn't know if the Indians saw her or not, if they imagined that her disgrace prevented her being given entry into the spirit world, if they thought she waited to be avenged. But I saw Rosalie's misfortune in life — to be caught between a red and white world — continued in death. Her people did not know if they could take her back. Those who wished Rosalie buried as a good woman rather than as a bad were more numerous, but the father's voice was stronger. At last they concluded. She would be buried in the old way but apart, neither dishonoured nor claimed.

Dawn was breaking as the men dragged Rosalie out in her robes into the cold white air. She was coloured like distant rocks, silvered with the light snow which had begun to fall. Lifting the robe she lay on by its four corners, they set out over frozen ground pricked out yellow with the stubble of last year's grasses. The women followed, wailing, and their low voices caught the sides of the shallow bowl of land and returned to them. Although they were only a dozen, they sounded like many. I fell in step behind, and even let my own voice be heard.

When the procession reached the edge of the river they stopped. Rosalie's brother chose the spot. It was a place where the hill to the south crested slightly over the bank, leaving a drop of ten feet facing a small, low island on which grew several willows. They lowered the body to the ground. Then the brother strode to Rosalie's head and drew out his knife. Raising his voice high in a fearsome chant, he lifted the braid and slashed it off. He held it up, a trophy.

A natural cave was there, in the side of the hill. The women wrapped the robe over Rosalie and bound her tight with sinew. The bundle that was now her was placed in the mouth of the cave and then that mouth was blocked with sticks and rocks. I watched as New Grass drove a stake into the ground before the mouth of the cave. He took Rosalie's braid from his son's hand and hung it there on the stake. The old woman kissed the braid before they left the place. When we all left it still hung there: perhaps later the mother would come back for it. It is said they carry the relics with them, in the little pack of magical things they keep on their backs.

Chapter 5

"So what do you want to talk about?" said Suzanne. She had the safety chain on her door, and peered through the three-inch space that opened. Ace was trying to slip his toe in the bottom.

"You know we need to."

Talk was a bitter word with them. Besides, Simon had only left an hour ago. It was unseemly, if not unsafe, to entertain her husband. But Suzanne let him in anyway.

He had never been in her house before. He sat with his back pressed to the corner of her loveseat, with one loafered foot bouncing on his knee, looking all around and nodding, as if it all confirmed some suspicion. Ace didn't enter a room, he took it on. He took it over. When they lived together Suzanne had no refuge from this competition he carried on with space. She might stay home potting houseplants and listening to Bach and be content. Then he came in and the rooms rearranged themselves in his favour; her earth and plants were a mess, her music a nasty background tinkle. It all came back to her, and the anger too.

"So talk," she said, "I didn't know you knew how."

"Don't be clever, Suzanne," he said, "it doesn't become you."

It didn't, and neither did the marriage, the whole relationship. People said it went wrong because they were too young. But their childishness had been the best part of them. They wrestled and played water-guns and drank champagne in bed. It was on adult terms they failed.

Ace and Suzanne met at the ages of six and seven at the gas company Christmas party. Ace's Dad, Block, was Santa Claus, an in-joke for the staff because there had been extra big bonuses that year. Ace was small for his age, and had to push to the front, and Block/Santa pretended to have forgotten him. Suzanne remembered him that way, as the boy who cried because Santa snubbed him. She hardly noticed him again until he began to play badminton. It was an obscure sport but Ace, by then handsome and jolly, gave it glamour.

Suzanne's natural companions had been the intellectuals, the skinny guys who worked on the school paper, the under-developed girls with glasses. He moved with the jocks and their female equivalents, "the blondes." She wanted to go to France on her own: she had a poetic notion of sitting in Paris cafés. She ended up with Ace's crowd on a charter flight to Europe only because her parents thought she would be safe with young people whose parents they knew. In the end Suzanne didn't care whether she went or not, but she knew this gang would get up to trouble. At Orly, Derek Prowse rode around and around on the baggage carousel, too drunk to pick himself up.

Most of the guys went after French girls because they thought they would learn exotic tricks. Ace went after Suzanne. They chased her roommate out and made her share with the hard-nosed guide, a lace-draped divorcée with Continental tastes and a need to support herself. She congratulated Suzanne at breakfast. Ace was a catch.

The song playing in Greece, in Rome and Seville that summer was "A Whiter Shade of Pale." They chanted the senseless lyrics everywhere. The blondes and the jocks. It was *their* time, and their world. Two of them stayed on to live in

Greece. Two went to South America, which was becoming fashionable. Ace and Suzanne went back to Calgary.

It was the summer of the black-light parties. You could see your date's teeth fluorescent behind dark lips; bra straps glowed through filmy, coloured shirts. The blondes bleached their hair lighter still and ironed it flat like sheets. Still the song played everywhere. "We skipped the light fandango. Turned cartwheels 'cross the floor. I was feeling kind of seasick. The crowd called out for more —"© It was a languorous dirge, a song of mourning. Perhaps they were passing through a portal. Perhaps now everything would be serious.

But no, no; they insisted on being sillier than ever. Ace took Suzanne to a fraternity party in a rented community hall. In the cloakroom he took her jacket and told her to stand on the table. Then he left the room, returning with some of the brothers, pointing at her, laughing while she asked him why she couldn't get down. She didn't understand the joke. The joke was the fact that she did it at all. When she climbed down he gave her his pin.

Ace's best pal in the frat was called the Weep. He got his name from the initiation ceremony when he had broken down and cried. He was tall and thin with a little boy's face and a sunken chest; he was an electrical engineer, a genius with wires. That night the brothers had a Weep Hunt.

The cry went up — *Weep, weep, weep, weep*! The Weep started running, the whole pack of boys after him. Out the doors to the playing field, and through the ghostly birch trees. The women stood by the jukebox and looked out the window to the men's silhouettes streaming across the turf. The Weep, long-legged and in stark terror, was out in front, the rest lumbering, gaining on him, eventually catching him where they threw him to the ground and pummelled him, bumping and shoving one another ecstatically.

"That's my intended out there, chasing his best friend," Suzanne said to herself. And the music played on.

Later that summer he shut down the motor suddenly

when she was on waterskis behind the boat at Bragg Creek. He circled her in the freezing water saying she had to promise to marry him before he'd pick her up. First she cried. Then she promised. He was a sport, you see, and she was too sensitive. All the tricks were a necessary training. She had been banded like a migrating bird in one season. The only other boy she ever dated was Jason, the twin of her oldest friend, Jennifer Beecham.

It wasn't until the day of the wedding she rebelled. Their families and fifty friends had gone up to the Banff Springs Hotel. The wedding would be in the chapel in the town. Suzanne sat in the bathtub in her parents' hotel suite staring at her toes and announced that she was calling it off. She hadn't really chosen Ace, not for herself.

Her mother came to perch on the edge of the tub. "My dear, by all means, if you're not sure, don't do it."

"Don't be ridiculous," said her father through the door. "She's got to do it. They're all waiting."

"Thanks, Mum." It was brave of her to be willing to flout the flower arrangements, the minister. "I'm confused. I can't remember if I love him."

"I can't remember if I ever loved your father. I think it's more important to be able to handle them, actually."

"Don't encourage her," said her father through the bathroom door. "You're half the problem, yourself."

"And you're the other half!" shouted Suzanne in an unprecedented outburst. The bathwater began to turn cold and the suds were congealing on her skin. Her mother went out; above the noise of the television football game she could hear her hissing at her husband.

"If the gir...ssss...her life...you and I *never*....I will *not* stand by and..."

It came to Suzanne that there was no happiness in marriage but that none the less it was the only way of getting away from home.

"What do you think you'll find to fight about when I'm gone?" she called back through the door, reaching for the towel. An hour later, she came down to the piano bar in her ivory satin wedding dress with her grandmother's crocheted train. The brothers bore Ace towards her on their shoulders. In the receiving line his mother turned to her and said, "Dear, my advice is to keep separate bank accounts."

Ace decided not to go into the gas company. He decided to keep up his badminton and to make shuttlecocks. He and the Weep made a robot to test the birds. It was called the Ace-R and it duplicated his serve. Suzanne watched all the tournaments; she loved him best when he played. He looked like the ballet dancer who had air instead of marrow in his bones. But they were all getting old. And so many were dead. Or perhaps Suzanne just collected the dead. One of the brothers was killed driving on black ice; another burned up in his absent parents' home after an all-night booze party. A third did himself in with tubes in the four-car garage, leaving a letter saying he'd brought his family shame. The women began to have babies, Suzanne too. Her baby weighed a pound and a half, took one breath, and then died. Ace was there. The doctor laid the child on her breast, looked at Ace and said, "She was just like you, Ashley."

But Ace wasn't looking at the baby, he was looking at Suzanne. "Maybe it's just as well, Suze," he said later. "You can go back to university. You're not cut out for a mother." She had not forgiven him that remark. From then on she knew that marriage was not only sad, it was a temporary thing. Marlyss (they called her Marlyss, you have to call them something, even if they're alive only for a second), though gone, was hers always. Marlyss and she would always be related, but she and Ace were only married. Marriages could end. Theirs had taken another year or two.

"I want to know why you won't meet me for lunch," said Ace. She had refused him the last three Fridays.

"I need to eat to keep up my strength," she snapped.

A red mark like a slap appeared on his cheek. "I don't know what I've done to deserve that," he said. His knee bounced up and down, his foot jogged loosely where it lay crossed over his other leg. His energy could turn her furniture to dust, her faded loveseat with the carved feet could collapse under him, her wicker tea trolley might fall to pieces. She wanted him out of her house.

"I don't think I owe you any explanations," she said.

"You don't. I already know."

But she hadn't known, had she?

Ace told her about his girlfriend on a Sunday. They had gone for the weekend to his family place in Canmore, and were woken up in the morning by the sound of a tractor lawn mower which seemed to be coming through the window and up the bedspread. They might have made love but the roaring scotched any rites; Ace jumped out of bed cursing Block. They decided to roll the motorcycle down the side drive and sneak away to the Hoodoos.

She swung her leg over the black lozenge which held the motor behind his seat and buckled her helmet under her chin. They took the TransCanada west through the park gates and turned off into a cloud of dust. He parked the bike where it couldn't be seen. On the way up the path he said that he didn't like to cause people pain.

"But I've done it," he added. "And I'd do it again. To save myself."

She missed the warning.

He continued. "The only way the world will work," *tramp*, *tramp*, over the dead pine needles and the rotted branches, "is when people put their own needs first; if everyone did it we'd all be less screwed up. If you save yourself, you save others."

She was hiking in front; her face flushed, hidden from him. "I wish," she said.

"But you believe it too," he protested. "You're the same as I am. That's what I always liked about you."

The back of her neck began to stiffen.

"You save yourself and I save myself and my father saves himself. My mother doesn't; that's what's the matter with her. That's why she's such a mess at fifty-eight. Her legs are good and she has a year-round tan, but inside she's a wreck.

Her problem is she never learned to tell the rest of us to fuck off."

Suzanne loved Ace's mother. Miss Amy was her friend.

"In this life," he said, puffing slightly as the path grew steeper, "sacrificers are never rewarded. But you, you're tough. You'll look after number one when the crunch comes."

She'd been slow, but she wasn't stupid; by this time she knew. She turned around and looked at him.

"Let's stop here, Suze," he said, gesturing to a rocky ledge.

She looked up. The Hoodoos were above them, sandy druids at the top of the hill looking over the valley southward. Their hooded figures conferred with one another, and the wind. The soft stone drifted off their backs as they stood, ancient and fragile, disappearing and leaving grit in the eye. "No," she said, "that would be too easy."

They tramped in silence until they stepped over an upturned knot of pine roots and came to a place where the rock was gone and there was only sand. The orange pine-needle carpet made uncertain footing; sometimes it was only a web over a hole between tree roots. Suzanne stumbled and went on, looking at her feet. "We are the hollow men, we are the stuffed men," she chanted, to annoy him.

He found the spot he knew, climbed to it and beckoned. The Hoodoos loomed in a row before them.

"Suzanne," he said, in a formal way, "I am having a relationship with another woman."

Perhaps she would have looked the same if some very old friend told her he had a wooden leg; sad, but also titillated by the novelty, the successful way he'd kept his secret. She wanted to know how it felt. Then she cried; she was expected to. She said she loved him. He said the same. They began to kiss. They made love, but it was different than it had ever been. They both kept their eyes open. The Hoodoos were there, hour-glasses of sand without the glass, hour-glasses from which the sand did not run down to be caught and turned the other way up to start again. From these ones the sand blew off slowly, little by little, and was gone forever.

"So who is it?" she said, finally.

It was a girl called Titian, the one blonde who'd been a redhead. She had dropped out to work for a travel company. Suzanne recalled that Titian was dumb and skinny and suggested that Ace could have done better. Ace was hurt.

"You should appreciate," he said, stuffily, gathering up his blue jeans from the ground, "how difficult it is for me to bring these things up."

"Why do it then?"

He said they hadn't been communicating and that this was a peace gesture. He hoped that it would spur her on to improve the marriage.

But the lights were going on in Suzanne's memory, the bells ringing.

"All those trips east to test the shuttlecocks?" she said. (At the time he was still in sports.) "Did she set up your itinerary? Did she go too? Work on the marriage? Is that what I'm supposed to do while you have an affair?"

"I didn't say affair. I said relationship. Anyway there are certain things you could do for our marriage on your own," he said. The sun was rising over the hill behind them now; the late mountain morning had arrived. "Like learn French cooking."

"I know what I can do," said Suzanne, now ready to stun the mountain tops with a full-blown scream. "I can call your goose-necked redhead and have lunch with her."

He was so startled that he stopped dressing. "What ever for?" he said.

"Because I'm curious. I want to know how it is possible for anyone to have a relationship with you."

"Well, don't ask for Friday," he said, "because that's the day I see her."

"If you know, then why do you ask?" said Suzanne. "It's true. I am seeing someone." As this was her revenge she waited for satisfaction. His pain, shock, fury; her justified pleasure in same. Nothing. Perhaps she had taken too long about it. Perhaps she was made up wrong.

"But," he said, "I thought we were going to give it another try."

She could see she'd made a big mistake going to bed with him that day. A muscle in his thigh was jumping. She wanted to put her finger on it, press it down. She wanted to put her head against his chest. She was shocked at herself. She had just been with Simon.

"You thought. But no."

"What was all that about then? In the townhouse that day?"

"An aberration," she said.

He bowed his head. She watched him anxiously. She was cruel. She was torturing him. In five seconds his head came up. He winked, an eye like a god's and as imperative.

"Would I like this guy?" he said, grinning. "You know you deserve the very best."

"I don't believe you ever really suffer about anything!"

He only grinned more broadly. "You wanna have lunch next week anyway?" he reached over and took the lobe of her ear between two fingers and squeezed.

The pool sweep, a white plastic snake which propelled itself on the surface of the water, backed out of the corner and swung hard across the shallow end in front of Jennifer and Gemma. It slurped up a few dead needles off the potted pine trees, and then settled to a quiet sucking. Summer was sudden and would be short. Two days ago they were walking around in hacking jackets and jeans; then came a hole in the clouds over the mountains and the new season swept in. Right away it was hot. Gemma and Jennifer were out in their bathing suits, their limbs pasty and obscene. One week from now they'd be brown, casual in their white shorts and halter tops. There would be tables on the sidewalk in front of the café at the base of Jennifer's apartment building

Now the rooftop pool was deserted except for the two

women. Gemma wore the smaller bikini but then she would
have been the first to admit she could afford to. She had a
concave stomach, long legs, and toenails painted to match
her blood-red fingernails. She was stretched out confidently
on her cot, angled so that her shadow fell exactly under it
and no ray of sun was wasted.

"Guess what I hear? Suzanne is going back to Ace."

"She'd better not be," said Jennifer. "I've just referred
her to a woman I know to do the divorce." Short, buxom
Jennifer was a lawyer. She worked for the Crown, in the
Prosecutor's office. She spent her time trying to convict
people, criminals, mostly. Those who weren't criminals she
had to try to convict too, which was where it got sticky.

"They're getting back together. He's spreading it all over
town. Besides, she told me..."

Jennifer closed her eyes to the sun, and to the indiscre-
tion. "Well, she ought to tell her lawyer first."

"Suzanne and her big talk about the single life. Suzanne
and her 'I just want to be alone.' I remember when she used
to be a party girl. I think she's only pretending to be a
hermit."

Jennifer spoke. "I suppose if she is, it's not your
business. But legally speaking —"

"It *is* my business. It's a waste of a perfectly good man.
Furthermore, I suspect — haven't I always said this? —
that she spends as much time and energy telling herself and
everyone else that she doesn't need a man as I do trying to
get one."

Jennifer laughed.

This was not a disloyal conversation. It would have been
much the same if Suzanne were there. Suzanne allowed
herself to be discussed. She even, somehow, invited it.
Suzanne liked to be between people, in the middle. It had
been that way when she was a child, her mother and father
always arguing; they had argued about many mysterious
things. It had been a relief when the subject turned to
Suzanne; at least then she knew what the issue was. If she
provided enough issues she could keep them together.

Of course it was an illusion; the fights were about problems more serious than her. Her parents had shown that they could manage without her as habeas corpus. They had made a kind of peace, and retired to Arizona. Her brother went adventuring in Australia. Suzanne had once found a place in Ace's family, but that was gone now. Jennifer and Gemma had taken up the roles of warring parents.

Greedy Gemma, and judicial Jennifer; sensitive Suzanne. They made a bizarre trio, they always had. They were paper, scissors and rock, like the game they played. Make a fist and pound three times. One, two, three. Gemma would put out two fingers to cut. Jennifer would keep the fist for a rock; Suzanne laid her hand out flat for paper. "Paper covers rock," she would say. "Scissors cut paper," said Gemma. "Rock crushes scissors," said Jennifer.

Suzanne and Jennifer met saddling horses at Pioneer Ranch Camp. In high school they wore matching camel-hair sweaters and grey flannel skirts. They found Gemma in the lunchroom at Western Canada High. She lived on the wrong side of the district, near the zoo. She was a fan; she admired their clothes, she admired their boyfriends, she admired their cars. She admired Jennifer's touring Volvo so much she took it for a spin and drove it into a creek. It had to be taken apart and dried piece by piece.

Gemma (formerly Gerta) Starchuk was so terrible she was wonderful. She told lies to guidance counsellors to cover up the fact that her parents worked as caretakers at the municipal building, and was found out. She borrowed money and couldn't pay it back. Once she was caught in the mat room with the gym teacher and was suspended. They couldn't decide if she was going astray or if she was ahead of her time. Jennifer and Suzanne took her on regardless. They dragged her through senior matriculation and on to university.

But on campus the trio began to move apart. Suzanne got pinned to Ace, and simultaneously began to preach about being one's own person. Jennifer marched on to her long-standing goal of law school, serious and rational.

Gemma ran around in racoon coats waving pennants, and
cast herself at the feet of a hockey star who had a wife back
in Lacombe. They tried to educate her. At first she was
merely amused. She'd come here to find a husband, she
announced out loud in the Students' Union cafeteria. And if
you must have women lawyers there ought to be a limit of
one to a firm. It was just fun, just Gemma singing for her
supper.

Suzanne went on talking about her inner resources, and
Jennifer did her articles. Gemma finished a lacklustre
degree in education and did some supply teaching, expecting
to be relieved of the necessity to work, and of her last name.
She traipsed out to dances alone. As she fell behind her
friends, her dissenting voice gathered conviction. Jennifer
married one of her law professors and within six months
began to find love letters from other students in his pockets.

"It's too humiliating, I'm leaving him," announced
Jennifer on the telephone to both her friends. Gemma, then
a disgruntled grade-seven teacher living with her parents
and spending her month's salary on shoes and purses, came
running. Suzanne, separated from Ace and in Toronto
working on her Master's degree, flew home for a summit
meeting. She was on Jennifer's side: infidelity, and the loss
of face it meant for the wife, could not be supported. But
Gemma strode up and down the room in front of the sofa
Jennifer's parents had given her for a wedding present and
argued urgently against splitting up.

"Don't give up now! Just when you've got it made!
Think about it! He doesn't want to lose you. He doesn't
want a scandal. He just has this little bad habit — he had
affairs with students — and he wants to keep it up. For you
it's an enviable opportunity. Think of the *deals* you can
make. All you've got to do is decide what you want, and ask
for it."

Jennifer sat dignified and speechless.

"You've got him over a barrel! You're the lawyer. Don't
you see? You can get anything you want out of him now."

"All I want is to trust him." Jennifer's eyes filled with tears.

Gemma guffawed. "I thought you were in favour of progress for women. Nobody trusts their husband any more, do they? Like you're always saying, we've got to have marriage contracts, we've got to have family-law reform."

"That's different," said Suzanne loyally, although she wasn't sure how.

It seemed then that Gemma had finally and irrevocably taken her own road, and that her road and theirs had divided around a very large rock. Jennifer became a driven woman, getting up at four in the morning and working until eight at night to make things better in the world. Gemma, despite her practical skills, failed to find a way to change her name from Miss Starchuk to Mrs Anything. Suzanne's search for true love and freedom too led her down the rabbit hole of history. When she moved back to Calgary, she called Gemma.

"I'm back," she said. "Can we have lunch?"

"I see Jennifer occasionally," said Gemma carefully. "In fact we're meeting at Bibi's at noon." Suzanne found them just as before, bickering.

"Isn't it time you got out of this grimy criminal work and into some clean-hands law?" Gemma was saying. "You're never going to make money unless you deal with wills and titles. People are a dead end."

"Make a fist, bang three times. One two three," said Suzanne.

"I'm paper."

"I'm scissors."

"I'm glue," said Suzanne.

"I've got a new approach, do you wanna hear?" said Gemma. She lay absorbing sun, without moving anything but her mouth.

Jennifer wanted to hear.

"You know I'm between men."

Jennifer raised an eyebrow, but Gemma couldn't see,

behind her sun-glasses. Between men was an old expression. It meant finished with one and not on to the next yet. Gemma had been between men as long as Jennifer had known her.

"And I've decided to do something positive about it. I've founded a group. I've already got ten members."

Gemma was looking very pleased with herself, her lips for once relaxed to an upward curve. "I'd ask you to join but I know you'd think it was beneath you. It's called SWARM. Single Women After Rich Men."

"Good grief."

"Now hear me out. You're going to put it down. I know. You're going to tell me I'm giving women a bad name. But this time you're wrong." Her voice gained authority. Her thin neck strained accommodating it.

"I know what you and Suzanne think of me. I know I'm a joke to you two. But I take it, you know why? It's because I owe you so much. I've learned such a lot from your mistakes."

Jennifer snorted, and then caught herself. She kept her mouth shut.

"From you I learned that you can't legislate equality. And from Suzanne I learned that you can't count on the perfect man to give you what you want. I figure the only thing that will get women up there enjoying life the way they deserve to is money. And how are you going to get it? You can't earn it, can you? The safest way, the way to use your natural talents, is to marry it. It can't be that hard to do. Rich guys are out there, and they've got to marry someone."

"SWARM," said Jennifer, thoughtfully. "I'm surprised it's taken you this long to come to it."

"It's an idea whose time has come. We've got seminars lined up on behaviour that appeals to the high-income male. We're going to have lectures on dress and makeup for the upper strata. We're commissioning studies on where they live, how to meet them..."

"Maybe you've found your calling, Gemma. Maybe you

could run it as a full-time job. Better yet, do it as a nightclub act."

"Just because you never needed lessons," snapped Gemma. "This is the ultimate in democracy. Rich men for those who weren't born to them. A redistribution of resources. What's wrong?"

"Nothing," said Jennifer. "Absolutely nothing. I'm reserving judgement."

Gemma was tapping her fingernails on the plastic armrest of the deck chair and looking very intently at her friend.

"I know what you need," she said. "You need a session with us, with SWARM. There's a meeting right across the street at seven-thirty."

"That's the very, *very* last thing I need," said Jennifer firmly.

"You're absolutely wrong. What you need is a group of women to talk to. What you need is to let down your defences and open yourself to getting some help. Listen," said Gemma, leaning over and taking Jennifer's wrist between her thumb and forefinger, "I never said this to you before but you are living in the dark ages of womankind. I know what you think about SWARM but you don't see it clearly. This is not just a bunch of man-hunters. It is women helping women. It is members of an oppressed group sharing their individually acquired wisdom. You stopped believing in sisterhood when you gave up on the placards and the demonstrations. But it still exists, and this is where it is. This is what happens to movements, doesn't your legal history tell you that? They become a lot of people trying to get more of what they've figured out that other people have."

SWARM. Jennifer thought of bees, things that bite you. "So do I have to tell them my problems."

"I thought you didn't have problems."

There was a silence. Then Jennifer gave a long sigh.

"I think I shall finally give up trying to teach you self-respect," said Jennifer to Gemma.

"So who wants self-respect? I have enough trouble getting a man."

Jennifer laughed and sat up, splitting her legs and putting one foot flat on the tiles on either side of her lounge-chair. Gemma shouted at her back.

"While you're at it why don't you give up trying to save people?"

"Oh Gemma," said Jennifer, as she placed her feet side by side on the edge of the pool. "I *have* quit. At my stage I'd be perfectly content trying not to make things worse for them." She pulled off a neat little dive and disappeared without a splash.

Gemma pushed herself up and walked to the deep end; gingerly, she slid herself down into the water, keeping her head above the surface. She screamed with pain at the cold. Then she sculled over to Jennifer. Together they rotated to face the sun. They sat in the water as in dentist's chairs, knees bent, bodies angled back, hands scooping identical figure eights beside their hips.

"Oh, poor dear little advocate," she said. "Your prostitutes giving you trouble?" Jennifer was always given the worst cases in her office; this one involved a bawdy house called Pharaoh's down by Electric Avenue. The police had tapped the owner's phone for months and were about to get him for living off the avails. Jennifer worried that the hookers had nowhere to go. Meanwhile, the men in the office had fun watching her tortured conscience as she twirled around trying to find the perfect moral position on the issue.

Jennifer's eyebrows drew together. She said nothing.

"You can't take them home with you."

"That's enough, Gemma. Stop."

"You mean I'm getting to you?" Gemma's cat-smile appeared, then disappeared. "Tell me how."

"You have this way of making me feel that everything I do is irrelevant," said Jennifer.

"Irrelevant to what?" Gemma's eyes were rounded.

"I don't know. Real life. The biting and clawing of it. If it's legal or not doesn't seem to have much to do with anything. Except maybe keeping out of jail."

Gemma thought about that for a moment. "You're just saying that because you're disappointed. You used to think law had everything to do with everything, and now you've found out it's only a small part."

Jennifer rotated to face Gemma. "What if I told you the Crown only wants Pharaoh's closed because certain property developers want to buy the land it stands on? And these developers are people you and I — and especially Suzanne — know? What would you say about that?"

"What would I say? What would Suzanne say, you mean."

"No, I mean you. I'm not going to tell Suzanne."

"Is it Ace?"

Jennifer put her face in the water and blew bubbles. Then she lifted it. "What would she do?"

Gemma grinned. "Oh, she'd want to run out and investigate and write it up for the newspaper. Cry scandal, all that." Then she thought a little. "Or maybe she'd brood on it and try to understand how and why it got that way." She dropped her hands under the water to support her body, which was sinking. "On the other hand probably she just wouldn't want to know." She stroked to the edge, her hair out of the water.

"I can't help her get this divorce if she goes behind our backs and sees Ace," said Jennifer shortly.

"She *is* seeing him," insisted Gemma from the deck. She arranged herself on the edge of the pool, paddling her crimson-tipped toes in the water. "What did I tell you? She pretends that nothing's going on in that little house of hers but it's all a front. The thing I really hate is this discretion. What are friends for if you don't let them in on your secrets?"

Jennifer walked along Kensington in her seersucker suit, the glare of the low sun on her back. She rarely went out in the evening; most nights she worked. But she had agreed to meet Gemma for a drink under the Pepsi umbrellas on the corner. Before she saw her, she heard the high, forced giggle and the rapid-fire of her voice. She was talking to the

waiter, a young blond man in khaki shorts with a shrunken
T-shirt. Jennifer sank into a chair. The waiter went to get
her a kir.

"Got your eye on someone new?" she said, without
enthusiasm.

Gemma gave her square smile, her top lip rising to each
eye tooth like a curtain on invisible ropes.

"He's not in my bracket."

"No, of course not." Jennifer couldn't face the sun; she
was too tired. No one else in the office was doing much
work, but as Jennifer always said, crime did not take
vacations. She was going to let Gemma do the talking all
evening.

"How did I let you talk me into this?" she groaned.

"You don't have to say anything," Gemma said brightly.
"If anyone asks, you're with me."

The woman at the door wore a white sticker that said *Hi,
I'm Hilda and I'm SWARMing*. There were already a dozen
women in the room, talking in twos and eating pieces of
broccoli and squares of cheese. Jennifer kept her back to
the wall. She told a woman with a face like a Pekinese that
she was a lawyer for the Crown; and the Pekinese was
ecstatic: "People always need lawyers," she said. "Lawyers
are terribly useful." Jennifer fell to inspecting the floral
arrangements, tulips, freesia and iris, until order was called.

"You are fortunate enough to attend one of the first
meetings of the new women's network, SWARM. The rules
here," said Hilda, a diminutive woman with pearls, "are
that you must stand and say who you are and what you want
from the group. I know that might be hard for the new ones"
— she smiled at Jennifer, "so we'll let Gemma start."

Heads went up and down around the table. About half
the women had their fingers lightly laid out on the top of
the library table, as if it were a typewriter or a piano.
Gemma spoke.

"I think we'll just start right in since most of you already
know our intentions. Our name," she smirked, "is self-

explanatory. I'm handing out a list now of the speakers we expect to offer in the next few months." She opened her briefcase and drew out a sheaf of paper. Jennifer had never seen her look so efficient. Gemma continued.

"I'm still working on those contacts for getting us into business parties. We've got to have lists of upcoming corporate functions. And I need someone to give a lecture on upscale ethics."

"Are there any ethics up the scale?" threw out a woman with *Hi! I'm Darlene* on her white sticker. Gemma cast her a short glance, and stood silently drumming her fingers as the others scanned their mimeographed handouts.

The list contained the following items:
1. Haunts and habits of the local R.M.
2. What to say, what not to say when you meet one
3. Understatement in Hair and Clothing
4. You deserve the Best — A Lecture on Self-Enrichment
5. Psychology of the Corporate Male

A heavy-set woman directly across from Jennifer struck the table with her fist.

"This is retrograde! If you're so interested in enriching yourself, why spend your time looking for a man?"

"We've been all through this," said Gemma quietly.

"We've been all through it, and we agreed to keep the discussion open. We all come to SWARM with different points of view. *I'm* here to raise objections," the heavy woman glared.

"Remember," said Hilda mildly, "it's all about choice. If Gemma has seen that a rich man is what she wants and has also seen that her need can spur action to meet the needs of other women, who are we to criticize?"

"Hear, hear," said the Pekinese. The heads began to nod. The large woman struck the table again and shook her head.

The voices were coming all round the table. It wasn't what they said that impressed Jennifer, it was the way they said it. The sureness of their manner. She imagined the relief for each woman, knowing that her problem was on the table, the efficient fingers were tapping over it, it was no longer just hers, it was outside, a phenomenon.

Exactly ten minutes had passed since they sat down. Jennifer liked it better than she imagined she would. The morality, or lack of it, intrigued her. It was like a contemporary tribunal, an airing of otherwise unstated principles. It seemed rather an innocent form of relief for a lot of timid women who didn't have a husband and wanted one.

"I hoped to meet men on my own," one of them was saying, "because I felt it was wrong to — I don't know — *try* too hard. They tell you, if you try it won't happen. But men try, don't they?"

"Absolutely. Men go after what they want. They spend their lives learning ways to get it. Now we're going to do the same."

"But isn't — *love* — a little different?"

Gemma was very good at this. Her chin was high, her voice full of assurance. "Why should it be?"

"Well because it's not — a thing — you can just get like that. Or is it?"

"It's a thing you earn," said someone.

"Bullshit," said someone else.

It's a thing you give, Jennifer thought.

"We at SWARM see love as an exchange, a give and take," Gemma said, triumphantly looking at Jennifer. "We're just making sure we're in the right market."

Jennifer was sure all this had nothing to do with her. She stayed to the end, for Gemma's sake, and then went back to the office.

Chapter 6

It was Sunday. Suzanne sat in her rocker in a silk kimono with her feet on the coffee table, listening to Mozart. She had been working on her paper all morning. Outside the sun blazed but the curtains were closed; she needed a little more time before she let in the light and its clarity.

There was a knock on the screen door. She folded her newspaper carefully and moved on bare feet; the varnished floor made no sound. Simon was on the porch in his jogging suit.

"Hey," she said, "am I on your route?"

"Designed with you in mind."

She tried to look stern. She had always disliked being taken by surprise, especially when she was alone at home. No one ever dropped in unannounced when she lived in the east. Here the practice persisted, part of the myth that Calgary was a small town. Apparently even a lover, who ought to give more warning than anyone, felt free. But in truth she was glad he'd come. It saved her wondering if he would.

He was red in the face, and sweat which had escaped the band around his head fell just in front of his ears in a crooked rivulet. He wore a jagged smile. She still felt, when she saw him, that inner jolt. He was an old man, a stranger. There were only small points of recognition in his face — eyes, lips — the rest of him she did not know. The heat began to spread down her limbs. They were uneasily involved. They met either by last-minute arrangement or by no arrangement at all, as if by doing so they could pretend the planets were in charge.

"Am I to invite you in?"

"I need a shower." He pulled a backpack around for her to see. "But I wouldn't want to put you out. I brought my own towel."

She opened the screen. The sweaty heat of his body was palpable as he passed. He had a dark growth on his face. She hadn't seen a man like that for a year. Her lurch of desire was not simply for sex, but for something more threatening, for intimacy.

He went into the bathroom and shut the door. She retreated to her rocker and the newspaper, but this time she was really posing. She could hear the full rush of the shower. Like the sound of teeth cutting through the flesh of a fruit, it made her mouth water. She poured herself some cold tea. The water rushed on. She could go and knock on the door and ask if he needed shampoo. Too obvious. He could poke out his head and invite her in. He wouldn't. He probably thought he'd gone far enough in coming by to dress. He had made himself available; she was to make the move. It was the kind of trick women were reputed to use, not men.

She took her feet off the footstool, hating to break the standoff but knowing something he didn't — the size of the hot-water tank. Soon it would begin to run cold. It was now or never. She was shy although she knew he wanted her. She forced herself to stand. She untied the kimono and let it slide down her arms, down her back and thighs to the floor. Her nipples were already erect. She walked down the hall to the bathroom door, conscious of her breasts and pelvis swaying. The shower was so noisy he didn't know anything until she put her arms around his chest.

Simon picked the Northern Italian place on Centre Street

South for brunch. He said he'd surveyed and that it was the only place in town that served things other than red meat. It was in the area south of the railroad tracks which was being reclaimed. An Indian lay across the doorstep, unconscious.

"That's what I like about the west. You can still see your native peoples," he said cheerily, offering his hand so Suzanne could step over him. Suzanne bridled.

It was the first time they'd gone out together in public, in daylight. At one o'clock in the afternoon the street was dusty, bright and still; a line of two-storey sandstone crowns stood up against a transparent robin's-egg-blue sky. When they stepped over the sill it was as if a slide was pulled from the projector; the darkness became a sudden absence of image. Then the red-brick foyer materialized, and in its bronze-trimmed mirror, the pair of them.

Suzanne had imagined they would look illicit: the younger woman on the arm of the grey-haired, distinguished man. But they did not. It was not such an uncommon sight, a couple with a decade or two age difference. She was slightly disappointed. Simon was smaller beside her than she expected and less substantial.

The hostess nodded at Simon's name and took them through the dark hallway into a glassed-over court. Their table was in the centre. Suzanne saw heads turn as they walked by. People knew Simon's face but not his name. No one spoke to them. Only old friends acknowledged each other in public in Calgary. It was hard to say if this was out of respect for privacy, or merely to avoid giving others a sense of their own importance. Suzanne glimpsed old man Gildoff, who had a drilling company. She'd gone to school with his sons. One was a kleptomaniac; the other ran off to work on a schooner in the Indian Ocean. She didn't want to introduce Simon. She wanted to be mysterious, to float over this world with her lover.

Who seemed to have a touch of the exhibitionist in him. "You're gorgeous today, Suzanne Vail," he whispered, not very softly. He liked public expressions of love; he had already kissed her passionately on the front porch in full view of the Ringroses. In her new reckless mood, she'd given up worrying. She was doing them a favour, letting them know that their worst suspicions of what went on in her house were true.

"My cardboard cowgirl. All fierce and stubborn, with those broad shoulders. But then you get damp and curl up. Look at your feet." He pointed under the table where her feet were wrapped around the chair leg. "Like the tendrils of a vine. Your fingers too, so delicate." He reached for her hand.

Maybe she was cardboard. She did not put up much resistance. He had become beautiful to her too. His body, its bones and veins so obvious, the marked, toughened skin, had been shocking at first. Now she revered them, signs of his longer life, his wisdom. The thick hairs on his chest could even raise a nostalgic tear to her eye, although she didn't like to think for what. A month ago all this had been unknown territory; now it was property. She pressed his knee under the table.

"Where would you be today if we hadn't met?" he said.

"Where would I be indeed?" she said. It was impossible to think.

"You'd have gone back to that husband. Women do that. The moment there's no man on the scene they panic."

"Hardly! Men are the ones who don't know how to be alone."

He smiled indulgently. "How can you say that, Suzanne? Look at me. I'm fifty-three. I've lasted all this time."

"I bet you haven't really. You're never unattached for very long. There's always someplace where you leave your dirty shirts." He had tried the shirt trick at her place, as a matter of fact. There was a pile in the bedroom. She hadn't touched it; she had the feeling if she washed them some delicate balance of power would be destroyed. "Talk about panic, anyway. Didn't you tell me you dumped your last love as soon as she wanted a kid?"

"That wasn't panic, that was ennui." He winked through the crystal of his wine glass. The comment would have put her in a rage if it came from Ace. But Simon could get away with it. He was a member of a different generation. It was fun to fling her modern notions against his implacable calm.

"You don't make yourself sound like a very good risk," she said.

"You know what people say about me."

"I don't actually. No one knows you." There was the bearded man in the bar that first night, but after his encounter with Gemma, he had flown, like all the others. Suzanne had taken up with men of unknown history when she was away, but it was different at home. Here, she had never dated anyone whose parents didn't know her parents or who didn't golf or ride or have a cottage in the same places as the rest of them. She had not realized how closed her world had become, until Simon showed her.

"They will," he said.

"They will, but..." said Suzanne.

Calgary was a club. Membership meant holding dear a few tenets: the mountains were beautiful, and business was good. These two tenets periodically came into conflict, over such matters as putting hotels on fragile alpine meadows. When this happened, business won. Further tenets were a handshake meant a deal, and art without a horse in it was pretentious.

This Calgary club included the descendants of the ranchers and the meat packers who'd made their fortunes, and the town's, a hundred years ago. It also included the lawyers who came with them and turned into politicians, and the earliest wildcatters and drillers. The rest of the élite was made up of local oil people and Americans on rotation from their parent companies in the States. Sure there were new people around; doors were open. It was said that a presentable man could get into any dining room in town. But this did not mean he could get into the club.

It only meant that in the old days, even twenty years ago, there were no good restaurants. Private dining rooms were places to do business. Anyone could do business in Calgary. But although making money was Calgary's credo, and a continuous influx of fortune-seeking strangers necessary to its functioning, mere seekers after gold were disdained. They came, they found their stake, and they left. Club members had come the same way a hundred, or seventy-five, or only forty years ago. But they had stayed. Staying, after the majority had made its bundle and run, or had lingered only to be worn down by the natural and cultural discouragements, endemic to the place, was the key to membership. Certain families had lasted through three or four boom-and-bust cycles and now they owned the place. Club members were more than willing to do business with you but until you'd lived through a bust and lost your money and started again, you wouldn't belong.

This exclusivity was, like all such systems, a defence. It was the Calgarians' answer to the national assumption that they were lesser because although they had made it big they had only done it in this out-of-the-way place. Nevertheless it was there. Simon was never going to be part of the club. He had come for the wrong reasons, and too late. He would not last it out. Suzanne rather liked his nonmembership, but Simon did not. He didn't understand why he couldn't sell his skills.

"I don't get these guys, I just don't see their thinking. They give me shit about the legislation. But now I'm here, why don't they use me? I tell them, I wrote it. I can make it work for you. They don't want to play ball."

He talked through narrowed lips and looked past her shoulder. "That legislation is a work of art. There's knobs and buttons in there that only they can push. That's what I put them in for. So then these guys say to me well, if you made it like that, full of loopholes, why did you bother to make it at all? They don't understand the process. Haven't they ever heard of politics out here?" His elegant fingers flew up repeatedly, from table to air, to punctuate his speech.

"They're not used to people like you," Suzanne said. "They're used to people who build or dig or at least make money. Not people who make phrases." She smiled.

His eyes focused on hers. The knot between them loosened. "You'll explain all this to me, I know."

Suzanne took a proud breath; her eyes fell modestly. Imagine that she could teach him anything. She thought that she was the pupil. For all these years she had been circumscribed, on the surface. Simon opened up the country to her, and made the range of it; the depth of human feelings seemed to be in reach just by his words, his ferocity.

"I wish I'd met you when I was eighteen and married you on the spot," he said. "I wish we had three children and a summer cottage. I know I've wasted my time, but how could the other men have missed you? I can't believe my luck. How come you're not already taken?"

In his drive to reinvent himself, he wanted to invent her too. There was one thing she couldn't leave out. "I *was* taken, you know."

There was a palpable strain, and darts from his eyes.

"So tell me about this husband. Why have you been keeping him from me?"

"I told you, it's over. I have — um — seen him now and then," she said. "We have things to discuss. Loose ends. If it wasn't over, why would I have left him? I *did* leave him, you know."

"That's right, you did," he said, reverting to reasonableness. "It must have been difficult for you, being so young and all. Tell me about it."

"Not now." She didn't want Simon to analyse her marriage. He was so categorical, so quick and sure.

"How come it didn't work? How come no kids, no cottage?"

She lifted her shoulders. As if she hadn't spent years trying to figure that out.

"Was he a bastard?"

"No, he was a very nice man. The nicest I knew."

"Aha," said Simon, smiling in his knowing way, seizing on this as an explanation. "And you've been hating yourself because it didn't work out with the nicest man you knew."

She spun her wineglass. "Maybe I've had it with nice men."

"I'm not a nice man," said Simon.

"I know." She turned her gaze down to her lap, lifted her napkin and spread it there in a gesture of finality.

Suzanne met Simon at the college tennis courts for a game. He said he didn't play well, but he sprang around the court like a goat; he could jump around from his forehand to get a backhand overhead. His shots were long and hard and he made no concessions to her lesser strength. Suzanne played a good game but she couldn't get the ball past him. As she dashed and leaned, gasped and grunted at the back of the court a lump rose in her throat. He ought not to hit it so hard. He ought to make allowances. When she served an ace, she cheered immoderately. Simon came to the net and chuckled gently.

"You want to beat me don't you?"

Did she really want to, or did she just think that he ought to have *let* her beat him. As if she was a child. His being older made her younger.

They walked around the campus; she showed him all three buildings and the parking lot. The place was deserted. It was a hot weekend in June; the spring term was finished and summer school hadn't begun. It was a little like wandering on the surface of the moon. There was dust everywhere from the hole that was being dug for the new library. She was still out of breath. He had his arm over her shoulder. She felt as if this man, who she'd met a month ago, was part of her body. She touched his fingers with hers.

"You never did tell me what they say about you," she said, thinking of their conversation in the restaurant. "Those mythical people who knew you in the past."

He looked into the distance; there were pouches under his eyes. He played with the fingers of the hand he'd been holding.

"There are some," she said. She was desperately curious about his past.

"Some what?" He often had an absent look; if he turned to her question it was to humour her.

"Some women in your past."

"An endless stream, I'm afraid," he said happily.

"Why an endless stream?"

He looked surprised that she'd asked.

"Because there is an endless supply, I suppose. I'll explain something to you later."

"So what," she persisted, "would one of this endless stream of women say about you?"

He looked at her with a great air of confession. "That I'm great for an affair when I'm passing through town but a bad risk for falling in love."

"That's my office," she said, pointing straight up to a window. "Fifth floor, fifth from the left." She did not like his answer.

Simon hastened on. "Now that I've said that," he said, turning her to face him, "I'm not so sure it's true anyway. I mean you are a superior woman and therefore not likely to mess up the way the others did." He looked a baleful challenge in her face.

She squeezed his arm. "You're so silly." She found this flattering.

"And anyway," he said, taking her fully into his arms, "this is different."

They were in the open air. Suzanne wondered if there were a gardener or someone watching. There was always someone watching, wasn't there?

"Why is it different?" she said. She gave up her struggle to get free.

"It's the grand love. You are going to reverse the pattern."

That weekend it seemed the city had been vacated for their pleasure. In utter quiet they lay on her bed, watching the late afternoon sun dance on the far wall of her room. The sunlight was like liquid, like water; it moved, carrying the shadows of branches with it. It was as if the fourth wall of the room had disappeared and they were open to the air on a platform exposed to a long reach of transparent and open space. Desire had been satisfied for the moment. But it would return, the steady heat that invaded with his presence, the craving she felt for him to take her up and to take him up, into the centre of her being. The power of that temptation was astonishing to Suzanne. The wanting was so great it almost overshadowed the act itself.

"Why are you so delicious to me?" she said.

"Perhaps it's my age."

She laughed.

"I'm not kidding. Perhaps it's because I'm so much older."

She was reminded of his endless stream. "Is it like that with all the girls?"

He hugged her loosely and went on looking at the ceiling. "A jealous little thing, are you?"

She was cut; her eyes watered. There had so recently been no distance between them.

"I'm going to explain something. You ask why there's been so many. They used to complain that I picked them up and dropped them. I guess it became a habit. But it wasn't only me. The older I got, the more they were offering themselves. If I had to give reasons I'd say they'd all missed out on having a father."

"So it has to do with my father?" Simon was not the least bit like her father. For one thing Simon teased and played games. For another he adored her. "I don't believe it," she said.

"What was your father like then?"

Suzanne got out of bed. The back wall of the room was in place, yet she couldn't escape the feeling she was on a platform, being examined. She looked away from Simon.

"He wasn't there, that's all. He wasn't particularly cruel. He was just — absent. My mother was unhappy. I knew that. I blamed him at the time."

Simon nodded his head; he was not surprised.

They had a glass of wine together in the living room before he went back to his hotel. He sat in the chair where Ace had sat. Briefly that other entanglement came to Suzanne's mind. But it was easy to dismiss. Simon was talking again about the grand love, how she was the perfect woman for him. He'd a bad record with women but his life would be different now. Suzanne was not really with him. She was in her bedroom in the little house in Poverty Flats, awake in the night crying for her father. The day before she'd gone to Sunday school and learned about hell, the other hell, not Hell's Half Acre, but the real one, where people went for punishment. She was sure her father was going to go there. She actually prayed for him. And she never prayed. Not before, not since.

He worked double shifts at the plant. He'd be gone for days it seemed, and then he'd come home. He'd lie on the couch to take a nap. He picked her up and hugged her then. He wrestled her and she cried out to get free of the lock of his arms. Before, at school, she'd had to memorize "Invictus." She didn't like "my unconquerable soul" at all; her favourite phrase was "in the fell clutch of circumstance." She liked to be got hold of, to struggle out.

"To you." Simon was raising his glass. "May you rewrite my character. How's that for a new motto?"

"Don't you think I'd have a better chance of rewriting my own?"

"You're doing something like that already, aren't you?" He jerked his head upwards and back. "In that spare room of yours?"

"Not at all."

"Well, what *are* you doing?"

"None of your business." She was uneasy at the thought of him knowing about her other domain, of his judgements being brought down on it. She did not trust him.

"Of course it's my business. We're in love. What's the point of holding back?"

"You hold back. You go off and make telephone calls and don't tell me who they're to."

He did not deign to answer but reached over and took her head between his two hands. "Oh my little bird," he said, "we've come so close together. We become one person and we don't know how to go back to being two. But we'll learn."

He got ahead of her that way, with his overview, his great experience. He took over. He got into first place, as he said he would. She almost caught sight of the mechanism working, and then it evaded her. She stood.

"You're very determined, aren't you?" she said.

"Aren't you?"

"I'll admit I am determined. But not like you are, not to take hold of other lives. My machinations are all inside me. I soak up life and then carry on an internal sorting and ordering, trying to make sense of it. Trying to impose my own order. I don't particularly care if other people take my view of things," she said. "I'm only interested in laying out a pattern."

"I suppose that's why you're a historian."

"I'm not a typical historian." In graduate school, when her lecturers spoke of the fourteenth century's three crusades she said yes, but that's the easy part; what was really going on? That's the record, that's the observable fact, but haven't you left most everything out? What did the men discuss in the markets? What did mothers teach their children, what games did they play?

"I actually don't care about the coronations, the campaigns. I only care about real life."

He laughed. "What on earth is that?"

"I think politics and military matters are peripheral. More than that, I suspect them to be screens, flags thrown on the field to disguise the true events." She dared him, hoping he'd bite.

"Sounds like mushy revolutionary polemics to me," said Simon.

"No," she said, although she had to admit she wasn't explaining it well. "Maybe I want to be a time traveller. It's probably just a very advanced tourist bug."

He shook his head. "Just when you've got a good point to

make, you undermine yourself. No wonder you're not making waves in your department."

She flushed. "It's not just my manner," she said. "I'm different. The men — emphasis on *men* — who wrote history didn't like to guess. I don't mind it. That leaves the field nicely open: certain left-alone areas can become my special pasture."

"Pasture as in 'being put out to pasture.'"

"It's not at all an easy way to work," she retorted hotly. "Disregarding most of what has been done before, or at least taking it for false evidence. I have to start from tiny clues, events that stand out for their bizarreness, because they've never been explained. I have to weave my way through the sources, visiting the living, the dead, sifting the detritus. I have to interpret a lot from a very little."

"You work by instinct," said Simon. "How very female of you."

It seemed they had to argue to say goodbye. She was getting flushed and her hands were in fists. "Men do it, too. They just have fancy names for it. Think of geological drawings. You know how they look at the structure of the layers of the earth, where one stratum buckles up, to see if oil's underneath it. They predict as well as they can but finally they have to just make a guess and try it. See if they strike it."

Simon retreated. "I gather you have your detractors."

"Oh yes. My kind of history is sometimes called 'modest,' sometimes 'blinkered.' I am considered by most of the men in the department to be sinfully unambitious. In fact the Head took me aside a few months ago and advised me that I couldn't make a reputation and certainly couldn't be promoted as long as I worked in these 'fringe areas.'"

"I think he's wrong," said Simon. He stood up, touching the top of her head. The touch went down to her heart. His unpredictable kindness had the force of blows. He made her valuable. He had that power. "I think you've got a great deal of drive."

She bowed her head. Drive, he called it. Drive was a

gross motor activity, something you did in a truck. What she did was not driving but exploration, a progress with tentacles. Perhaps she had no will to impose, but she had the strength of the vine which, growing on rock, gently, relentlessly probes and may, after many long years, crack open a boulder.

Chapter 7

I made my way along Scarth Street at nightfall. I'm always identifiable, even in the dark; my weedy legs swing outward from the hips so that my trunk rocks from side to side with each step. My sea walk, as my wife used to call it, moves me along deceptively quickly. Which is fine if you have a destination, but since the bitch left me I had no need to go home and nowhere else to go, except hell-holes like the Turf Club.

Now as the dark dropped its nightly sentence over my chosen town, I was lonely. I cursed Evangeline. She humiliated me. I am a man of my word. I took her as a wife and whatever she did, even if it was to live with the worst whoremaster in the country, she did as my wife.

It was the day after Rosalie's funeral. The Turf Club saloon was open again. I went in out of curiosity. The men were talking about the coroner's discoveries. The most talked-about thing I knew already. There was no weapon, the coroner's opinion being that the injury had been done with bare hands.

"Let's say he didn't mean to kill her but he did anyway, what does that make Fisk?" said one man.

"A better man than me," said another, spraying the foam

off his beer. But the laughter was short, uncomfortable. Behind the bar, Kelsey's hand shook on the shot glass he held. He put it down, got out his rag and began polishing, pressing hard to be steady. When the men looked the other way he checked the clock.

"It'd be different, if she was a white girl. That's why Kelsey here didn't say nothing about the groaning isn't it? An Indian girl upstairs with the blacksmith, you look the other way."

Kelsey did not acknowledge his defender. But he must have been grateful for him. There was a feeling against Kelsey in town, since the inquiry, a finger pointing. Fisk had been here longer, and he mixed better. If one of the men had to be named a killer, they'd pick the newcomer.

"Still, she was a Christian," said Whitbeck.

"Some Christian."

"Heard we've been written up in the *Globe* newspaper."

"You know who made sure of that," said Whitbeck. "I wish they'd never of put in those overnight wires." With a clenched jaw, he looked at his own watch and then slowly replaced it in his pocket.

I know when I'm not welcome; I drained my glass and with a nod to my unsavoury companions and a tip of my hat to Kelsey I pushed through the doors into the night. Sure I was the one who sent the notice in to the *Globe* on the wires. I know a timely story when I see one, don't I? And unlike some others, my pride in my home town won't stop me from letting it out.

Part of the interest in the Rosalie case came from the fact that the Ripper's latest victim had been announced. Her name was Alice. Alice Mackenzie. "Professionally bad," the *Times* of London, my favourite paper, said. By that they meant "whored for a living" I suppose. I got a laugh out of this bit of editorial circumlocution. Reading on, I'd discovered that Alice Mackenzie had in fact been a char-woman. She charred for Jews, said the *Times*, themselves a very hardworking and poor class. She had no bonnet or hat, but only a shawl. She had no home either and when she did not have five pence for her lodging she stayed on the street all night. She only whored for a little extra. Still, once in a while was as good as all the time, at least, for the *Times*. Enough to merit her classification as a professional; even enough, it seemed, to merit her reward.

I smiled into my beard, remembering the writer's implication that Alice Mackenzie had been lucky, rather than unlucky, to have met relief in the form of her killer. I wondered what the writer thought was Alice Mackenzie's greatest misfortune, that she had no bonnet? That she was an occasional prostitute? Or that she had to work for Jews? I wished there was someone in town who shared my brand of humour. Then reverie gave way to a curse on account of the cold. I thought I'd better be getting home.

As I went down the stairs, I noticed someone coming out of the alley beside, leading a horse. His movement was furtive, the profile of his hat a dead give-away for Whitbeck. My nose bent a little to the right, my lips to the left. I've been a lot of things, minister, teacher, coroner, salesman. But I know I have the soul of a newsman; things happen to me, things happen where I am. I ran, crablike, softly, and reached the alley's shadows. Behind me I heard a sound, and turned to look just as Kelsey came out the door.

The horse was darker than the night. Ears back, tail slightly raised, it stood without moving while Whitbeck handed Kelsey the reins. There were bags on either side of the saddle. Whitbeck handed over a sack of what looked like cash.

"That'll give you a certain immunity," he whispered. "When you've reached the border."

"I'll be frozen solid by the time I get to MacLeod," whined Kelsey. "Why'd I come up here in the first place, why?"

"You'll thank your friends for this," hissed Whitbeck, "You stay and I swear they'll pin it on you."

"Hey!" I said, stepping out fast enough to catch the horse's reins. "You wouldn't be thinking of leaving town?"

Whitbeck slapped the horse's flank. It reared up, its tail

an unseen swat across my back. The horse's shoes clapped on the packed snow, it neighed, an eerie echoing cry, and bucked again, but I am stronger than I look. I still had the reins. The other man began to run. "Ride out, fool! You've got time. Ride!" he cried over his shoulder to Kelsey. In seconds he had disappeared.

Kelsey did not move, not even to kick the horse.

"You wouldn't be thinking of leaving town, would you?" I repeated. I shortened the reins in my hand. Kelsey sat unanchored on the horse. His hands were occupied trying to put the sack of money into his jacket. I spoke soothingly. "It would look very bad for you if you did. I suppose you thought if you crossed the border you'd be safe."

Kelsey said nothing.

"I'm surprised at you, willing to let your friend Fisk face the music alone. Not that I'm of the group that's so sure you have a crime to answer for." Kelsey's hands went slack in his lap. Safety had been only a day's ride away. Now he was caught.

"She got up and walked out of the room," said Kelsey. "They say she's not even in the coffin any more."

"I fancy the best solution for your nerves — you can never tell what a man's going to do once his nerve is gone — is to go and see Murdoch and have you locked up with your friend. Just for a witness, you understand."

"No," said Kelsey, "no."

"But you might bolt."

"No. It was Whitbeck's idea."

"Everything is the fault of someone else, is it now? Come on, let's take you in." I smiled at Kelsey as I got hold of his horse and led him. "It's for your own good. What if the Indians rise up, and you standing in the bar open to any kind of attack? You'll be better off there."

Kelsey tried to get off the horse. "Held for a witness? And what am I going to say? She never even screamed."

And that's how it was Kelsey came to be in jail along with Fisk. His bail was set at four thousand dollars, but he couldn't post it. I figured the two of them could keep each other company. Meanwhile, the juices running in me all over again about this story, I went down to the little building where the *Herald* had its offices, east on Stephen Avenue past the Bodega restaurant. It was quiet in there. The editor was out, and the printers elsewhere. I thought an editorial would be the right idea at that point, as opinions were forming and reforming everywhere. But what would I write?

The town was divided on Rosalie's case. Most of the top men wanted the whole thing hushed up, and quickly. I understood their concerns, which were mostly for the safety of the town against the Indians who were always resentful (and a great deal they had to resent, the way I saw it) and now very restless. George Murdoch, Justice of the Peace, led this group of thinkers. He said the murder had been blown out of proportion. Well, Murdoch cut a real figure in town; he'd been the one to choose our city's site along the Bow River, even though some questioned his taste. When he'd spotted what was to be Calgary it was a little bend in the river filled with the stinking carcasses of rotting cattle. A harness-maker, Murdoch had been the first man to hang out a shingle here, and he'd been mayor too, the first year of incorporation. Personally, though, I couldn't agree with him.

A murder's a murder, just like a corpse is a corpse, the way I see things. I toyed with the title "Dead is dead, white or red," on my sheet of paper, but decided against it. This was no time for word play. The fact that our little murder came on the heels of London's Jack and his last strike in Whitechapel had fanned the flames of panic; I suppose I didn't want to encourage them any more. Mine is an academic interest; though some think me ill-willed, I'm just as happy to see right as wrong.

Indeed there were reasons for caution. Indications to which I was sensitive led me to think this was no ordinary story of a whore and a squaw man in a drunken fight. First of these indications was the fact that Dillabough still swore that Rosalie stood up and walked out of the room, that she was all in white and wore a red shawl. This could only be explained by the idea of a ghost, although some said there had been two Indian girls and that it was some kind of hoax. That was nonsense of course. But, perhaps because of Dillabough's persistent ravings, rumours of another kind began to circulate. It was now established that Rosalie had been a mission student; she had been at the Dunbow School near town. The priest there was the famous Father Lacombe who, it was said, knew the girl personally, and testified to her devoutness, and even suggested — again, so it was said, and I had not verified these remarks — that she was not a whore but a holy martyr. While no one quite believed it, these ideas had the effect of drawing up the town in a fit of wonder and worry so that it was no good for anything else.

I repeat, I believed little or nothing of what I heard, I merely took the whispers and rumours as evidence that this was no cut and dried case. Things were happening in our town. Certain activities that had previously been tolerated came into question. Why did the Turf Club have to be there? cried the wives. What did the men do? On this point, when approached, as I inevitably was, in my known position as a mediator between the top and the bottom of our society, I equivocated. My personal feelings began to press in on my professional feelings, and I pride myself on not letting that happen. I abhor those hell-holes and the men who go there, I can make that clear in these writings. But since Evangeline left me I know something of the desperation that drives men there. I am not wholly without compassion, particularly, I suppose, for persons with whom I feel something in common.

But compassion I throw back, as I soldier on in my adopted profession. I traffic in information. I have no loyalty to people. I like to make what is not known, known, in so far as it can be. I never miss an opportunity to demonstrate the power of knowledge — not of learning, for which I have only limited use, but of knowledge, such as the sort Eve gave to Adam. I do so even if such opportunity conflicts with my personal interests.

Having said that, however, I can go back a little and add

that I do not know what made me press this case, the journalist in me, or that other, the compassionate man. I just know I did press it. The day after the funeral, I went out to the mission to talk to the nuns about Rosalie. I heard that she loved dramatics, not a surprise, and that she had taken a place in the fan drill, and had been a passable singer as well, but was too slight to fare well with dumbbells. I ascertained that they hadn't been in touch with her since she left them, for which information I was very grateful.

There was another thing I did, as well. People often remark about me that I know everyone, that I am always to be found behind the scenes pulling strings. It is true, and it is partly my nature, but it is also my art. I said that Fisk had relatives in the east, and I knew this to be true. I sat down to think about this and got out my old book of names from when I lived in Ontario, east of Toronto, and then I recalled what it was that nagged at my mind.

I had met these relations of Fisk. In a previous walk of life, I had once been sent to propose an investment to the uncle high up in the church in Montreal. There was his address: the Reverend T.J. Williams, in Montreal. I have a book with many such names and addresses in it, it is part of my trade. I often forget just where I have got them from, and why I thought they would be useful. However, there was the name, and the address. I was having no luck with the editorial, in fact I had been thinking myself round in circles. I put a new sheet in my typewriter and sent off a letter to the uncle, describing the sad predicament Fisk was in (whether he had done this deed or not), certain that the uncle would be most concerned to know. And then I put it in the mail.

I had just completed this task when I saw, hurrying down the street avoiding faces and shop windows, that whore of whores, my wife, Evangeline. She looked terrible. Her blotched reflection I knew would have humiliated her, as much as the cuts she received from the ladies formerly of her acquaintance. I jumped quickly into a space between doorways as she passed. After a moment I walked silently down the street after her, keeping a safe distance between us. She seemed very distressed. She bit her tongue to make her tears stop, and dug her fingernails into her palms. I think I knew what tormented her so. She simply could not fathom that Rosalie, her own sweet Rosalie, had ended like this. She was always soft on her. I blamed her, when the girl wouldn't come to work any more.

"The friendlier you are with them, the worse they'll do you in the end," I said. But she had never been angry with Rosalie even though when the girl disappeared without a trace three months ago, it was like losing her best friend. Not long after that she left me herself. I suppose I was jealous, the way they play-acted as they hung out the wash in the yard. I can still hear their piping voices.

"How now my love; why is your cheek so pale? How chance the roses there do fade so fast?"

"Belike for want of rain, which I could well beteem them from the tempest of my eyes."

Remembering that, and feeling my wife's pain even from my unseen position at the end of the block, I was moved to feel something for the girl I knew as an innocent child. Why did God, or whoever, or whatever made up the design of things, consign that bright dancer, quick-study of the poetry she barely understood, to those dark and final moments, the ill-kept room above the laughter in the bar, the staggering weight of the big man, the towering, obliterating pain? For what purpose?

I am no innocent myself; I understand that something primitive, even mad, is loosed in men by the act of sex. Still I saw no reason why the blood feud of men and women should come to settle its score on Rosalie. That woman before me, hurrying with half-shrouded face past the shop windows, had chosen her punishment, had chosen to flee respectability for the risk of passion, knowing she would be shunned afterward. In some ways it was not so great a sacrifice. Who cared about being an outcast here? The north-west affects some one way, some another. There were people who became more and more proper in the territories, fighting off that wilderness out there, dressing for dinner in their shanty huts, so as not to revert to savages. There were others who tasted a little wildness and wanted more. Evangeline was one of those.

Indeed, I thought, still on the trail of this woman who had tried to ruin my position in town along with her own, that if anyone could be held responsible for this death, it was Evangeline. *She* had picked Rosalie from the other Indian girls at the convent. *She* had gone sledging with her on the North Hill, had been friends with her, had been responsible for her being between two worlds that way. If it weren't for Evangeline, then Rosalie might be walking on this street now. Mind you, Evangeline would say she only needed Rosalie because I was no fun. And I would retort, "Someone should have warned you about marrying such an old man, an old man with one wife dead already and a son almost your own age." Then Evangeline would give her own inimitably scornful laugh. "Oh Murphy," she'd say. "Don't you think I know there is no sage voice to warn us in life?"

I watched Evangeline turn onto Scarth Street and begin to walk towards the Turf Club. She never came this way, no white woman did. But I could only hold my breath. She was clenched up as she walked, as if in hatred. In front of the Turf Club a solitary Indian stood. It was the tall and straight young man who had prostrated himself before the coffin, who later I had seen slice off the braid at the grave: Rosalie's brother. Evangeline stopped, watching him, looking for a sign. He looked right past her. She waited. I waited, out of sight by the side of a dray which was pulled up in front of the greengrocer.

None of us moved. I thought she would go up to speak to him but she didn't. It was impossible to tell from his rigid posture whether he had seen her or not. He was a fine figure of a man and symbolized all that is noble about the savages. At length, slowly, Evangeline retreated, forcing me to retreat as well. But it was no matter. I turned and ran back to my office, because I had an idea for my editorial. I sat down and quickly wrote it off.

"We believe," I said (it was always a pleasure for me to use the editorial we), "that there is, as some folk say, an Indian haunting the town. But it is not Rosalie. It is her brother. The young man has come, several days in a row now" (there was no harm in a little exaggeration) "to stand in front of the Turf Club and say nothing. He stands so still it is as if he wants to be, himself, a monument to her death. He stands as if he contemplates revenge, but not of the expected variety, not the rape and murder of an isolated white woman on a ranch out of town. He seems to want something more exact and purgative, something that will not stain him and his people as Rosalie's murder has stained us."

I read it and was greatly impressed with my work. I went on to advocate a trial in town, and the quick and full punishment of the man or men concerned.

Chapter 8

Stampede was not just another rodeo. It was ten days of scheduled mayhem to which the city was tradition bound. On the first Monday Suzanne took the bus out to the campus, so she wouldn't get stuck in the traffic jam created by the parade. Classes were over, but she had to get her marks in.

It was nine o'clock in the morning. She sat near the front. Do Not Talk to the Driver, said the sign beside the ticket box. A man hung on the handrail and talked to the driver.

"How goes it this time?"

"Worse every year." The driver wore a checked shirt and string tie instead of his uniform. His cowboy hat was pushed up behind him on the seat. Stockbrokers and waitresses and courtroom lawyers would also be wearing their cowboy outfits. It was obligatory; the obligation came with citizenship. "It's not the cars so much either. It's the jay-walkers do the worst. They should have open season on 'em, that's all, one hour a day all this week just to keep 'em, to keep 'em" — he searched for the word — "primed."

Someone was cooking flapjacks on the sidewalk at Broadway and 14th Street. The crowd of people licking maple syrup off their forks blocked the two lanes going west.

Across the bridge Suzanne could see the row of backs —
families lined up to watch the parade pass. The rotary
street-cleaning machines stood ready to follow the horses.

Suzanne wore her old blue jeans and a ruffled shirt with a
fringed vest over it. She had a beaded belt and a white
Stetson hat over her hair which was tied in a ponytail at the
nape of her neck. Everything was fake; none of it had ever
been worn on a ranch, except for her boots. They were
genuine; as a teenager, she had been through a long and
passionate horsey stage which had left her with this single
accessory, leather riding boots with high heels and lots of
stitching.

Stampede was big when she was a kid. Stampede was
bigger than Christmas. Suzanne and her brother saved up
their allowances so they could go to the midway. They
bought pink cotton candy that stuck to their fingers and
dissolved on their tongues, turning into sweet water. They
went on all the rides. Suzanne had been fearless about the
rides, the ferris wheel with the creaky seats which swung
when the wheel stopped to unload, sometimes leaving you
stranded high over the fairground. The dizzy-making ones
she liked just as well, even though her brother would
stagger off behind the wiring to vomit. And the Wild
Mouse which ran on a circular track, throwing you into the
corner, jerking your neck so that your head rolled, too
heavy to control. Faster and faster, the Wild Mouse went,
until it had to stop. Suzanne rode them all but her favourite
was an old-fashioned one called the Caterpillar. You took
your seat, you jolted forward and a cloth tunnel came over
your head, leaving you in the dark. Suzanne knew she
wouldn't like the ride now; when she grew up she learned
too much to enjoy danger.

She used to stand outside the freak shows too, the Reptile
Lady and the Fat Man. Her mother forbade her to go in to
see "those poor things." She was fascinated with the ladies
of the Club Lido, who leaned beside the barker advertising
a sex show every hour. "Sad," said her mother, "so sad."
Sadder yet according to Suzanne's mother was the Indian

village at the end of the midway, where Blackfoot and Cree from nearby reserves came and sat in skins and feathers, under their painted tepees, with sour faces. But Suzanne liked them too.

Suzanne didn't see how it could be that sad, when everyone had fun at Stampede time. Suzanne's father did the ring toss and her brother played bingo. They bought hotdogs and cobs of corn at the Imperial Order of the Daughters of the Empire booth. They went to the chuck-wagon races and cheered while the outriders fried eggs and the wagons crashed.

It was just innocent family fun, then. But over the years Stampede became wilder until, like a midway ride, it had to stop. Suzanne remembered the episode with an antique fire-engine. A trio of boys, the Weepstick among them, had come to pick Suzanne up in an antique fire-truck, where she was working selling popcorn outside the fairground gates. They had stolen it from a backyard in Mount Royal; someone's father had given it to someone's mother for her birthday. They got it running and they rode it down to Elbow Drive. They were on the long hill when they realized they didn't know how to put on the brakes.

Suzanne squeezed her eyes shut at the memory. She was hanging onto the side, the horn blaring. The fire-engine was half way down and gaining speed. Almost at the bottom, flying. And then, what saved them? A sharp turn, an upward slope? That part she didn't remember. The boys had been punished. Suzanne got off easy, an innocent passenger.

It was a good thing her students didn't know that episode, she thought. The bus pulled over at the corner of the campus. Walking across the dusty parking lot to her office Suzanne composed herself for the assessment of her colleagues as much as her students, for the act which would be, like her cowboy outfit, convincing only if you kept your eyes down.

"Miss Vail!"

Groups of summer-school students leaned on the hoods

of cars, and smoked with conspicuous lethargy, projecting a lack of necessity to go anywhere, do anything. Suzanne smiled vaguely in the direction of the voice, and kept walking. It sounded like someone she had known once, but she saw no one she recognized.

"Suzanne!" hissed Nola as she got out of the elevator. Suzanne obediently turned into the alcove next to the Head's office. "Would you believe what he did to me on Friday? Would you believe he gave me these letters at 4:15 P.M. saying he wanted them out that day?"

Suzanne crumpled her brows and shook her head.

"Told me to leave the ordering till later? I always do the ordering on the last Friday of every month!" Nola drew her spine up in her chair, elongating her complaint. "It was the weekend, and my sister was coming in, and I told him that I have to leave at five sharp, I *told* him — "

Nola invented these dialogues with the Head. Suzanne knew for a fact that Nola never told him a thing, certainly not in anger. She told it all to Suzanne, instead.

" — give me credit for some brains at least, I can plan my time myself!" She wanted Suzanne to tell her how brave she was and how badly treated.

"Oh dear," said Suzanne. From the edge of Nola's desk she picked up a white piece of paper with damp purple lettering on it. Normally she did not pay much attention to purple ink; it meant mimeographed sheets asking for nominees to the committee to review applications for sabbaticals, or announcing that faculty must remember to lock the door to the screening room. On this one, the letters were still wet.

"Oh yes, did you see the memo? They're cutting 202."

History 202 was "Reinventing the West."

"My course?"

Suzanne thought this was perhaps Nola's little joke. But Nola hadn't the nerve to go that far with a joke, not so far as wasting supplies of paper and mimeograph fluid.

"Why didn't he call a meeting? They can't do this without asking me."

"I thought you wouldn't like it," said Nola not without

satisfaction. "There was a meeting but it was in June and you didn't come..."

"I didn't get a notice." She gave Nola an accusing stare.

"It was in your mailbox!" Nola's eyes were very round and her lips had pulled down away from her nose, closing over her upper teeth.

"But you send notices home during the summer. Nobody comes into the office!"

"Well, you usually do." Nola chewed on her upper lip, maintaining her eyebrows at the top of her face. *Tch, tch, bad girl*.

"What about the students who have already registered?" Suzanne's voice was going high, helpless.

"They'll be notified." Nola did not meet Suzanne's eyes, but her voice sank. "A lot of people would have been with you on this particular decision but they weren't at the meeting either. We nearly missed getting a quorum, in fact."

"I don't believe this. He can't do it." Suzanne crumpled the memo in her hand. She'd have to go in and see the Head herself. Raise a ruckus. Even if it *was* too late. She should have done something when she first saw that he was against her. She was an institutional moron. She'd forgotten to attend to the business at hand. She'd been too busy working on the course to make sure it stayed on the curriculum. Recreating the past, she'd let the present go. She made more progress in the last century than she did in this one. Something was wrong, with her, or with them. With her was easier.

The heels of her boots clopped slowly down the hall. She unlocked her office and put her books on her table, thinking of another possible interpretation. This was Punishment. Wildly, she considered the idea that Nola and the Head knew about her romance and had set out to teach her a lesson. No, that was ridiculous. That was Suzanne feeling guilty and confused. She walked around her table and began to open and shut the drawers, putting things in place. Envelopes. Elastic bands. Pencils. A stack of scrap paper on which she wrote telephone messages. Someone tapped on the door. It was Nola. She held a long, thin piece of greenish paper with a row of holes down each side.

"See," she said. "It's dropped off the printout."

"What's that supposed to mean?"

"It's dropped off the printout. That means your course isn't on any more."

"Is your famous printout a complete list of all significant events to come?" Suzanne demanded, her voice quavering. She knew she was being irrational, and if anyone told her so she'd have killed them. "Does it come from the Creator? Say yes, Nola."

Nola was transfixed. She kept her hand on the doorknob.

"Does it describe the entirety of what can happen in this institution between next September and January? Say yes, Nola."

"No," said Nola distinctly. "It isn't and it doesn't. It is a list of all those courses that students may register in for next term, as of August 15th."

Suzanne tossed her head back and rolled her eyes. It was too exasperating to get angry at someone as obtuse as Nola, who didn't even understand an insult when she got one. The eager confiding face had gone crafty, the chin was pulled in. Nola's eyes were round and very bright. She took the edge of her bottom lip beneath her teeth and rolled it back and forth. Could Suzanne have missed this simple point? The case was closed; the course wasn't on the printout. Nola's eyes narrowed, became inpenetrable. No, Suzanne had not missed the point. She was disagreeing. She was telling Nola that she was stupid. Suzanne was just as arrogant and high-handed as the other professors. Nola had thought that Suzanne was different, that she knew how to treat a secretary like a human being. But Nola had been wrong.

"Well," she said, backing still further into the hall. "I've got to get back to my phone."

Suzanne stared out of her window. In the west clouds were accumulating, blocking the mountains. It was going to rain on the Stampede parade. All those crepe-paper roses on the floats would wilt and their colours would run. The clouds were building up quickly. She watched until they filled half the sky. She ought to record her grades. She ought to go down and see the Head about the course. She couldn't let it go, not without at least a fuss. No doubt the Head expected a fuss; he probably wanted her to come in and beg. She couldn't stand the idea. She couldn't be sweet and charm him to gain her ends. Play the game, as Simon would say. If you didn't play it, it played you.

On the weekend she and Simon went canoeing in Bowness Park. The banks were green and the sky was blue. The water in the threading channels was absolutely still but channels wound off to hidden pools. The lagoon was full of rented rowboats and canoes. Simon paddled and she sat in front, her back in the direction they were going, a useless fixture, Cleopatra on a miniature Nile. They were drinking wine from a bottle under his seat.

"You're not a very good Indian," said Suzanne. He paddled awkwardly, shifting on his knees. "You're supposed to be able to kneel for days."

"I've got knobby knees."

She dropped her hand over the side into the water. Her skin was green under its surface. Pinprick white bubbles rose from the sides of her wrist, like breath.

"Anyway, I never had any desire to be an Indian," he said, irritably.

"You didn't? I thought everyone did."

"That's typical of you, Suzanne, typical. Identifying with the underdog."

But she hadn't wanted to be that kind of Indian. She'd wanted to be an Indian before the white men came. A wild Indian woman on horseback. It would have been better than growing up to be like the women she knew.

"Indians were untrammelled. They had moveable houses and wore mocassins; they didn't have to wear makeup and entertain the business friends of their husbands," she said.

"That's shameless romanticizing."

"I know. I'm just telling you what I thought. Also they had a religion. I had none."

"They didn't have a real religion."

"Don't you believe in medicine then?" she said.

"Medicine-man medicine?"

"Medicine — like magic. Spirits. In trees and roots and people. If a child is sick and will die, it's because of medicine. Evil spirits that can get inside people and make trouble."

"No, I don't," he said, sitting back on his heels and putting the paddle across his knees. The canoe parted the water smoothly in front of them. "I don't believe in spirits, evil or otherwise. I don't believe in bad medicine. But I do believe people can get in the habit of sabotaging themselves."

"Miss Vail?" said the voice at her office door. Suzanne? It was a croaky, ironic voice. Suzanne swivelled her head around from where she had been staring as the rain began. It was now after lunch. Her marks were in. She ought to be on her way home.

"Who is it?" she said, and when no answer came, swung open the door.

Roberta Asp wore a large purple sweatshirt torn at the shoulders. Instead of her headlight necklace she wore the sign of an apple with a black X on it. Her hair was now burgundy coloured; thin orange braids were scattered throughout its frizzy cloud. She was the first person Suzanne had seen all day who wasn't wearing Stampede clothes.

"Asp," said Suzanne. "If you spent half as much time on your work as you do changing wigs...What's the apple mean?"

"Don't be an apple — red on the outside, white on the inside. I'm the opposite."

Suzanne laughed.

"Wanna have a beer?"

"You mean you don't want to know if you passed?"

"Not really. A beer?"

Suzanne was charmed: all most students wanted at this time of year was marks. But she was reluctant to venture out into Stampede frenzy. "I don't want to go anywhere noisy."

"I know someplace," said Asp.

It was pouring with rain. Against her better judgement, Suzanne agreed. "But you've got to get me back by four," she said.

Asp's car was the colour of rusty primer; it had no doorhandles on the outside. Asp opened the driver's side with a screwdriver and leaned over to push the passenger's door with her foot. Suzanne took careful note of how it was done. Once in, she wanted to be able to get out.

They spun out of the parking lot, shooting gravel. With Suzanne clutching the dashboard, they drove over the bridge and down to Bowness. The flats had been a poor little village of displaced Indians and blacks, with a trailer park and a couple of gas stations, until five years ago when townhouses with cedar-shake roofs had been built into the valley. Gentrification had only gone half-way, however; a mini-boom must have busted while building was half way through. They pulled up in front of a low plaza with several faded signs — Imelda's Beauty Parlor. Mike's Milk.

On the smallest door, wavering black paint announced The Northwest Rebellion; under the letters could still be seen the old sign — Ye Old Pizza House. The place was dark, with a low ceiling. Waist-high metal doors showed they really did make pizza once but now the kitchen was empty. Asp strode cockily down the narrow hall to a windowless back room. Half a dozen dark-skinned men were there, sitting on linoleum covered chairs at bare tables.

"You're gonna love this," Asp was saying. "Check out the walls."

Suzanne checked out the walls. They were papered in brown wrapping paper, and written all over from floor to ceiling. The writing was done in red pencil, black pencil, lipstick, charcoal, mustard, ketchup. Drawing of cars, of wolf heads and females shaped like squeezed balloons dotted the few blank spaces between names and epithets — Indian Rights for Indian Women, The Rhinoceros Party Wants You, Mary Blows Peter and Paul.

Asp pulled Suzanne a chair alongside the wall. "You

wanna see what I call history?" She patted the seat for Suzanne to climb on it.

High up near the ceiling, the writing was spidery and strained. "Nelson Small Legs," it read.

"Remember him?" Asp looked triumphant.

"Sure I do." Nelson Small Legs led an abortive sit-in of Calgary Indians at City Hall. When the Indians failed to get what they wanted, he had committed suicide. Suzanne ran her fingers over the writing.

"Every five years or so they paper this over. But they always cut around that one. Underneath they must have stuff that goes back to the fifties."

Suzanne was beginning to think Asp wasn't so bad. "I call it history too," she said. She'd driven past this place a thousand times, always on her way to the ski hills, or to the Canmore townhouse with Ace, or over the mountains to early spring in Vancouver. She'd never known it was here. "It's wonderful."

Asp shrugged defensively. "I hear they're gonna tear this mall down anyway."

A man pulled up a chair with them. He had fleshy cheeks and a square moustache. He nodded his head. "Hi, I'm Rod." Asp seemed to know him; Suzanne smiled uncertainly.

"You live around here?" he said. Suzanne shook her head.

A glass slid to Suzanne across the table top. It was damp on the outside, standard tavern issue with a wider top and narrow stalk. There was a thin white line around it half an inch down from the lip. Someone started the jukebox. Suzanne drank her beer. It tasted marvellous.

"My grandfather had a job down here," Rod was saying. "He used to run the gravel pit. I used to ride in the back of the truck with the shovels and the bags of gravel. They gave him a little house by the gate. He lived in it till he retired."

"I remember that house!" She remembered an old man too, standing by the road, trying to stop the children who came in to play. But Rod had turned to talk to a couple of women.

"Everybody starts washing hair," one of them said. "It

takes a long time to work up to where you get to stand beside the stylist while he makes decisions like whether to layer it or not."

A couple of overweight men with lanky pigtails came in, followed by two women in black slacks who went immediately to the jukebox, put in a quarter, and began to dance together. The music was loud. Suzanne saw Roberta on the other side of the table, watching her, running her fingers back through the red spikes of her hair. The waiter put a cluster of beer glasses on the table. The elastic in Suzanne's ponytail felt tight; it was giving her a headache. She pulled it off and threw her hair forward, to let the strands fall in the opposite direction to the way they'd been pulled.

"I'm *so* pissed off," she said, inadvertently.

"Are you? How come?" said Asp, without apparent interest.

Somehow this made it easier for Suzanne to talk. "They've cancelled my course. It's off the printout for fall. They don't think it's important." Telling this went against Suzanne's rules of personal deportment. A lecturer did not confide in her students. A woman of substance did not ask for sympathy.

"That's terrible," said Asp. "It's the only course about real stuff."

Suzanne smiled. "Fat lot you know. You barely passed." But the temptation to go on was great. "It's all political," she said. "They don't like 'local' history. Oh I don't know. Maybe it's because of me. I should have pushed it harder. I should have talked it up. I just got buried in this... writing." Her head felt heavy; she propped it on her wrist.

"What writing?" said Asp.

"It's either an essay or a mystery story," said Suzanne, offhand.

"Sounds good." Asp had a way of following a conversation without seeming to care. It made it easy for Suzanne to talk. The younger woman stared with narrowed eyes across the smoke-filled room. And Suzanne told the story of Rosalie and Jumbo Fisk.

"Violent murder of women: a cultural constant," she finished. "Easy to exploit, difficult to understand." She stopped to drink her beer, embarrassed. "Anyway that's what I was thinking about when I ought to have attended to departmental matters."

Asp was still, in her chair across the scratched table top; her cloud of tangled hair and the apple T-shirt with the large X in the middle merged in Suzanne's vision. She looked like a cross between a tree and a highway sign. Perhaps Suzanne had drunk too much.

"No wonder you're hooked on it," Asp was saying. "I would be too."

"No, no," Suzanne waved her hand. It was too difficult to explain. The last thing she wanted was for Asp to catch her obsession; it felt like a dangerous one. "You see it's really something about *me* I'm looking for," she stumbled on. "To do with my own — "

"Poor Rosalie," said Asp. "Everyone's victim. Yours, too."

Suzanne felt that she had disappointed Roberta Asp.

She watched the two women performing for the fat men and drank some more beer. She wondered who slept with whom. A male person wearing earphones came and sat beside her. He smiled and nodded. She wondered about the earphones. Did he prefer his own choice of music to that in the bar? Perhaps he was listening to silence. He signalled. Did she feel like dancing? She nodded.

Gliding in the small space between aluminum table legs, not touching her partner but referring to him, facing him with eyes averted, she reminded herself that she never went for drinks with students. They couldn't handle it, she always said, or else she couldn't handle it. There were divisions, gaps that could not be crossed between teacher and student. Like all divisions, these required vigilance to maintain. And most certainly she never danced with strange men in bars.

The music went on and on, plodding, steady, mindless.

Her partner was moving like a robot, backwards, his heels snapping up one after the other. Every minute or two he did a jerky mime, pretending to unscrew his right forearm, and then his left, then to take them both off, then to unscrew both legs below the knee and take them off, then to unscrew and remove his head. After he'd done the whole set he jumped up and down with a strange growl, and then he began again.

Suzanne understood she was meant to dance out some fantasy of her own, but she didn't trust herself to improvise. Instead she kept to her tried old two-step. It got boring after a while. She didn't know how to get her partner's attention; whenever she tried, his head was turned the other way. He couldn't hear her call him, with his ear-phones on. Finally she walked away. He danced on.

"I'm ready to go," she said to Asp. How easily they'd traded places; the girl had become her caretaker.

"You'd better write your name on the wall first. You've got to have your place in history." Asp gave a crooked smile. "I'll find you a spot."

"It's OK," said Suzanne. Her legs were aching. "What time is it?" She wanted to go to bed.

But Asp got up on the chair and found a place beside a certain Brian who had loved Denise in 1977. The pen didn't write on the vertical; they had to keep shaking it before they scratched out the dry letters S-U-Z-A-N-N-E V-A-I-L among the others.

Suzanne handed Asp the pen.

"I'm on there a few times already," said Asp.

"Be on again."

Asp stood up on the chair and wrote "Rosalie New Grass" on the wall.

Suzanne followed Asp's long, jean-clad legs down the hall to the outside door. The rain had cleared and a pale sun cut into their eyes. In the front seat of the booby-trapped car, Suzanne groaned. "I had too much to drink."

"Two beers? Not possible."

But she shouldn't have said so much, to a student especially. "It's all breaking down, all breaking down," she muttered.

"What's breaking down?" Asp spun the steering wheel with her usual indecipherable smile.

Suzanne didn't answer.

The footsteps on the porch were light, they hit the wood and rebounded like a basketball. Suzanne had only just turned her back on the door, aiming to the stairs and to a collapse in bed.

"Hey, Suze!"

Ace was there in his tight, faded jeans, his low belt with the Mexican silver buckle; his fingers were looped through the belt holes. He grinned. "You wanna hit the midway?"

Her head still spun. "I couldn't possibly make it!"

But he pushed his face onto the screen; it smeared his features making him look like a burglar wearing a nylon stocking. His nose went flat, his lips outward.

"Why not? Like we used to." He squinted at her. "I do believe the lady's drunk!" he said.

"Not at all. I just had a few beers with a student."

"It looks good on you," he said. "Come on out."

She could hear the car radio blaring a good time down the street. He stomped his boot heels on her hollow proch, and she said all right. She had promised herself not to see him again. But she was breaking all kinds of rules. The more she did, the less she wanted to be alone to think about it.

She echoed him: why not?

They walked down the midway, a mass of shoulders. Suzanne's eyes were glittering, her head light. They edged side to side down past the carnies, the sno-cone sellers. The children with their lips stained fluorescent green and blue from syrup, the spit of fat from beefburgers and the burble of glassed-in popcorn popping. Oscar the Mouse found his hole to run down, the red or yellow or blue you could put your money on. You could have your weight, your age

guessed and if you fooled the guesser by more than three
you got a prize. She used to win, being under-developed.
Or you could swing this mallet, hit the base and send a slug
up the post to ring a gong. He used to win, because he tried
so hard.

Now their heads floated in that swirl of hats and the
combat of cries and bells and buzzers announcing take a
chance, Take *Your* Chance, Three chances for a dollar! Past
the wooden balls to throw and keep in the bucket with the
sprung bottom. And the weighted milk bottles you tried to
knock down but which held amazingly upright. It was all
rigged against you but you had to take a chance and try to
win one of those blue stuffed poodles or elephants. You
could walk triumphant back along the midway clasping it,
envious eyes on you.

The midway was smaller now and not so evil, nor
magnetic. Ace played the Arabs on camelback who raced
along a lighted path if you put the ball in the right spot.

"This one's not chance, it's skill," said Ace and she
laughed as he kept winning, but then one white-winged
Arab on a red camel pulled ahead and beat him four times
running. He supposed there was an element of luck after
all.

At the top of the midway were the rides. She couldn't
stomach any now, except the ferris wheel. It glittered silver
in the sun, its swinging seats full of children leaning down
to wave to Mum and Dad. When she moved forward and
stopped, Suzanne put her head against the backrest and
looked straight up at the sky.

She was on the front of the wheel, gently swinging. It
turned a dozen feet and stopped to load. She saw her years
stacked beneath her in stages; she had ridden on that seat,
and then that one. She could see up to the North Hill,
down to the river. There was so much out there, in this
large bowl offered of the city, much more even than she ever
thought. The higher she got the more she could see. There
was no need for limits. The wheel turned and stopped,
turned and stopped. At last it was full. Grandly lifting to

begin the descent, she rose up from the centre and went over the top.

Suzanne woke up in the master bedroom of Ace's empty townhouse. The bare window looked over the roofs of the houses on the next crescent down the hill towards town. She caught herself sleepily thinking, a large Roman blind or some plantation shutters might do there. When they were married such details were the mainstay of conversation — over the sound of the shower, the dinner forks, the cocktails; before, during or after sex. These conversations interrupted nothing. They were grateful for them, they wore a system of paths through the mutual wild space. Now there was no path to cut, no ground staked out, nothing shared but rash moments.

Ace's eyelids remained unmoving, his breathing regular. His head lay half off the pillow, his hand on his breastbone. Amazing: a man could do a simple thing like lose consciousness after climax and she felt protective. She read somewhere that a hormone released in the male at ejaculation caused this loss of conciouness. Mother Nature had done it for him, not Suzanne. Then why this tenderness?

She looked down on him. His cheek was turned into her breast. He was muted, his cheek hollowed under the squared, high bone, his nose not long or short but perfectly straight, if anything a trifle too blunt at the end. He had been dominant before, but now she was the pilot of their enterprise, alone at the controls. She was making connections, taking measures, in silent preparation for landing.

"The house is for us," he said, without raising his eyelids.

Suzanne grew alert. He was talking in his sleep, perhaps. Presuming. He couldn't. Today was just a mistake, a falling back together for old time's sake. But she looked around the townhouse anyway. It might have been for them, once; a compromise between the new ranch-style house he'd have liked out south, and a renovated Victorian place in the Beltway that would have been her style. But any compromise had always put them in limbo. Besides, they were almost divorced.

"We can move in whenever you like."

There was still no sign he was conscious. Poor Ace, imagining these rooms as witness to the rituals of their married life, the elegant brunches with a few friends, the deep leather couch for Friday night television. She didn't think she was expected to say anything, particularly since he had chosen to make this offer lying down. That way he risked no rejection.

"There's a nursery upstairs," he said.

Suzanne banged her head on the headboard as she sat up. The sun had passed out of sight behind the bare back of the house down the hill.

"All right," he said, sighing, rumpling his already rumpled hair. "Let's talk about your boyfriend."

"It's none of your business."

"You can at least tell me how it's going," said Ace. "If you keep me posted, I think I can tolerate it until you make your decision."

"That's an indecent suggestion if I ever heard one. I have no decision in mind," she said, stiffly.

"Oh," he said, grinning, "hardball."

"No. No ball. Just my life going on, which has nothing to do with you."

"I guess you wouldn't bother seeing him if he weren't great in bed." His blue eyes were dark, the lashes stuck together in spikes.

She felt pity, and patted his arm.

"Well is it? Is it good? Is it better than us?"

They call revenge sweet. Perhaps that was indeed the taste in her mouth. She could afford to be gentle. She stroked his stomach, where the muscles buckled in towards each other perfectly, like a charioteer's belt.

"Come on Ace, relax."

"You're screwing around on me." He got up on an elbow, scowling.

"That's ridiculous," she said. "I can't do anything 'on you.' We're no longer involved."

His eyebrows went up. The muscles in his chin tightened. Something kept her going.

"You're the one who said, why not? This, this trip to the midway. It was an accident. It doesn't mean a thing." But the feeling of falling came back to her, of sinking down from the top of the ferris wheel, and her gorge rising up her throat.

"Suzanne, there's no point in fighting it. We're fated."

"Were we fated when you took up with Titian? And what about all your other women? There must be more."

"Oh, bring that up, will you?" he said sulkily. "I didn't know you were vindictive. It doesn't become you."

She could smile. They were on old ground. She could be superior; it was over.

"It's not the same for women," Ace continued. "Your pride isn't on the line."

"That's the most absurd thing you've ever said." She took the opportunity to get up, and put the sheets back onto the bed.

"What are you doing then, Suzanne? Just testing to see which one of us you can give up? At least I never did that. I never considered leaving you. Titian was always on the side."

"Like an order of fries? Easy to say now she's gone off and married someone else and has two kids."

Ace was sitting up now, his arms folded across his chest, the picture of propriety wounded. "I had you first," he said.

"Had me?" Her voice rose. "I'm not a thing to be had." ("It's a wonder you weren't taken already," Simon had said. "I was," was her answer. She had been truly taken, staked, mined.) She pulled the blanket up, straightening it on her side. The bed was five feet wide, and had been freshly made. For the first time she wondered about the townhouse, sitting there empty. It wasn't Ace who did those hospital corners. He got someone to prepare it. He had planned ahead for the "accident" of their coming here from the midway.

"Did your maid change the towels in the shower, too? What do you call this place on your tax return? Under what category are you writing it off?"

Ace's eyes went flat in the corners. She might have hurt him. "I call it the home I hope to move into with my wife."

Suzanne walked away from the bed, and stopped at the bathroom door. She was nauseated, her knees felt weak. She had been so pleased with herself before today, with a new lover and an old flame petitioning. But it was no fun. She had no talent for dissembling. She wanted an explosion, the door to slam in her face. But he didn't do anything. His eyes were there, taking her in, his look catastrophic.

At last Suzanne lay in her own bed, watching the broken rectangles of light from the street lamp on the floor under her window. A car went down the street slowly; its headlights made a curved pass over the ceiling. When she was a little girl she thought the lights on her bedroom ceiling came from the helmets of giant soldiers walking on the street below. She didn't know how she had learned to fear soldiers. She was born five years after the war. Her family hadn't been touched, oil and gas being an essential industry. Perhaps it was the same way she learned to fear everything; by hearsay and imagination, by not having been there. She was afraid of what she did not know.

The room was luminous grey although night was at its deepest. Self-hypnosis had failed to lull the whirl and surge of thoughts. She would not sleep, although she was very tired. She was alert and still, and waiting. She was hanging, suspended. Up there for all to see, even for herself to see, a different woman than she had been six weeks ago, a different woman than she imagined herself to be. Who was she, once so controlled, now to be stricken alternately by desire and remorse?

Only harmless Suzanne Vail, the broad-shouldered, book-ish woman with red-blonde hair and a sardonic smile, who never spoke up loudly enough to be heard. She stopped holding off the world, and now she was in the middle of it. Two men. First came Ace, then Simon. Pursuing her when she didn't want it. That's what she had thought. But now an idea came; she was responsible for this herself. One lover begot another. Two men being less than one man; two men equalling no men. Two men making her safer, because one man was too dangerous.

Gemma had given her a talking to, Gemma with her new SWARM wisdom.

"You realize it's nothing to do with you," she said. "It's between the two of them. Competition, you know. They're probably much more interested in each other than you."

"Motives, motives. Why do you assume everyone has motives?"

"Because they do. Even you, little innocent. What you're doing is attempting to reduce men's power over you. That's why I'm encouraging you. It's an evolutionary stage. The best way to get through it is to indulge in it."

"I liked you better when you were just plain nasty, Gemma. Now it's all systematic, your bitchiness."

"I'm right, you know," Gemma had said, serenely. "There's only one reason for you to have done what you've done. Just when you clear the decks from your old marriage you take up with your husband. And just so *that* won't work you find a foil for him, this old guy, totally unsuitable, for insurance. You're deliberately avoiding involvement."

Maybe Suzanne *was* using one man to neutralize the other. Yet it was that neutrality, that blankness she feared. She could not compare one against the other. She could not retain the impression of one, carry it past the other.

She tried to remember Simon, the feel of his skin. She thought back to the last time she was with him, here, in this bed. The more recent memory of Ace was blotting out her sense of touch. Ace was too perfect. There was no texture with Ace, none of those dry spots, nodules, bristles, islands of moles (now it was coming back) that made Simon's skin like a relief map, topographical. Simon was old, his skin loose. It slipped over what was inside; it was a little thick; it was something to get through. It was skin, in other words, while Ace's seemed merely to be an outer manifestation of his golden interior.

Likewise, Ace's crystal eyes were outlets for the power of the mechanism. He tried to melt her in place with them, to weld her attention exclusively to him. With those eyes on her it was not permissible for her to think of someone else; she would not be allowed to escape. In loving him once more she had been allowed knowledge so potentially damaging that she had to stay or be destroyed, like the witness to some gangland slaying.

She lay open-eyed on her pillow, frightened, and stared into the darkness.

Chapter 9

Suzanne stood in the hotel lobby holding the house phone in her hand. She wore a flounced dress with ricrac around the skirt; they used to be called squaw dresses. Now they were called "prairie-style" dresses and were made by Ralph Lauren.

The hotel had only recently come into existence, a hulk of stone and glass, new Ozymandias in its own little desert of gravel and tractor prints. The front doors were bronzed and opened inward; in the ceiling large light fixtures of pale paper had grown up overnight, like poisonous fungi. Today there was a horse in the lobby. Two men ran around it, shouting. The horse ran the other way, in circles, on a short rein. It was last Saturday of Stampede. Suzanne covered her ear with one hand to hear Simon's voice through the receiver.

"Come on up, let's have a drink first." The gravelly sound of his voice stirred the pit of her stomach.

"I'm illegally parked."

"I need a drink," he said, plaintively. He was going to his first Stampede party.

She went to the bank of elevators and pushed thirteen. Along with the unlucky floor number he'd drawn a room

which was less a room than a ledge, long and narrow with
windows along the side. As soon as she was in the door, she
felt for the wall; she should be edging along it with back and
fingers to be sure not to fall off. It had the worst view in
town and plenty of it. The huge windows looked over the
south-east of the city across railway yards, oil storage drums
and stockyards. He was standing in front of the mirror
pulling a string tie under his collar.

"Tell me how you wear these things."

She stopped moving, about five feet behind him. They
were communicating through the mirror. "There isn't
much you can do with a string tie," she said. When they
were apart she believed that this was it, this was love. But
when they met again, she was shocked. Could this be him?
He was old. This pinched, worried face, unlovely large
hands and feet, small chest and round stomach, could this
be what she loved?

"When in Rome."

"You're not in Rome, you're in the provinces."

He turned towards her. She was not immediately reassured. He took several steps, she one, and they embraced,
held on for a few seconds. His cologne came over her first,
something called Figment; now she understood that he
wore it because he was self-conscious about his personal
odour, but she still didn't like it. She held on another few
seconds. The chemicals gave way to the smell of damp
forest ground in deep shade, a fermenting, rich musk. The
real Simon. She thought he was like earth; he said she was
like water. One day they could be air and fire.

His hands lingered on her shoulder; she pulled them off.
If she didn't, they'd never get to the party.

"I'll just go away and leave you alone then," he said,
pouting.

"I thought you wanted a drink before we went."

He poured something in a glass and threw it back,
looking at her squarely, as if he'd never said what he just
said, as if there had been no threat. "Have it your way," he
said, "you always do. But I still think you're perfect."

"Don't say that!" The affair with Simon had grown so intense that it felt dangerous, as if it were an enormous cargo that might slide down, crushing them. Touch was explosive, even language had become self-conscious. They talked about it too much. What they said began to sound like poetry, like a conversation between two writers about their creations.

"I'm not perfect," she said.

"You're right, you are. You could use a little loosening up."

"You could use a few manners. You haven't offered me anything to drink."

He put down his glass and went over to the wide, empty closet, pulling a hat box off the overhead shelf. He was showing her something. "It was a gift," he said, pulling out a ten-gallon hat.

"Not from a friend," she murmured. She watched him in the mirror again. "Nobody really wears those things," she said, "it's sort of a figure of speech."

He put it on his head. The brims folded up like giant ears on either side of his face. He looked so silly that her arms involuntarily lifted from her side as she stepped forward, putting them around his shoulders. She would have kissed him except that he grabbed her first. His quickness made her pull away.

Not fast enough, however. His fingers went into the flesh of her shoulders. She was shunted stiffly forward again. His lips were muscular and moved all the time, forcing hers to give in, to open. She kept her teeth clamped shut. They kissed in mute argument. She didn't know what the argument was about; it had begun almost as soon as the affair. She said he wanted her too much, too suddenly. He was greedy; he had to be with her always, to take her in through all his senses. She told him not to give in to that greed, because he would consume her, she would be all gone, he would have nothing but himself, he would be there loving himself. He said she enjoyed resisting.

"Let's get out of here," he said suddenly, releasing her as

if she had been detaining him and stooping to pick up his hat where it had fallen on the bed. He drained the end of his drink. As they headed for the door their shoulders bumped.

"Excuse me," they said, simultaneously.

Glenbow Trail wound around the western edge of the city, past Ace's new townhouse. Suzanne carefully looked away from it as she drove by. Simon sat with his hands flat on his knees, making an effort to keep still. They were going to a gas company barbecue with Jennifer and her twin brother Jason. Simon had never met her friends, except for Gemma, who didn't count. Suzanne's friends didn't know much about Simon.

As they came up the driveway the Beechams, Sr, came out the door, dressed for the same party.

"Hi, there, young fella," said Mr B to Suzanne. It used to be the best way to tease Suzanne and Jennifer when they were teenagers, to mistake them for boys. "Who's your friend?" He looked at Simon. "Taking your hat out for a walk?"

"Simon Ross. He's moved here from the east," Suzanne said.

"We've seen you on the news," said Mr B, without extending his hand.

Mrs B was tiny with a sweet voice. "Moved here," she said. "How interesting. And how are you finding us? We have a reputation for being rednecks."

Simon opened his mouth to answer as Mr B slapped him hard on the back, and then pawed the ground slightly in his eagerness to get away.

"I haven't found —" Simon said. But Mr B was dragging Mrs B by the arm towards the door.

"Now that's enough, dear," he was saying. "We can't have you standing here yacking all night." Mrs B allowed herself to be settled in the passenger seat of the long, lean car. On the porch, Jennifer and Jason stood side by side watching the car roll backwards down the curved drive. Jason was short like Jennifer and blond, and turning slightly portly.

He stroked the tight stretch of gingham over his stomach, as he shook Simon's hand.

Inside, Simon asked for a martini.

"Martini?" said Jason. "You drink martinis?"

"There something wrong with a martini?" said Suzanne, quickly.

"No, no. I just thought you might have learned to drink scotch by now," said Jason, grinning wickedly.

Simon flushed. Suzanne looked at him, the elder statesman, the wise and well-known consultant, the worldly one. He looked a fool. He managed a smile; he rose up on his toes and down again as he looked around the room.

The Beechams' house looked small from the street, but the back fell away to two storeys of glass with a view of the foothills to the south-west. Suzanne always felt distracted in that house on Ermine Drive. If you looked straight down from the window you were looking into twelve feet of chlorinated turquoise water. It was all the glass and the view: undulating distances made her want to throw herself into them, as onto a bed or a stack of pillows. At lively parties people dove off the balcony. There had been a serious accident once; an associate of Mr B had broken his shoulder hanging by one hand from the balcony.

"There you go, fella. No stuffed olive, I'm sorry."

Jason winked at Suzanne. Stuffed olives, was it? Long ago he had appointed himself guardian of his sister's virtue and by extension, hers. Suzanne drank her wine.

"Nice view," said Simon.

"Why did you come to Calgary?" said Jennifer, with characteristic forthrightness. Simon mumbled.

"I thought I'd drum up a little ... business for myself, in the oil patch." Suzanne knew the business wasn't going well: he said it now like a challenge.

Jason and Jennifer wore identical fixed smiles. They didn't know why Suzanne liked him. Silence fell. They saw a jaded fifty-year-old politician.

"How are Deborah and the kids?" said Suzanne to Jason.

"Picking berries on the shores of Shushwap. I'm going up the end of the week."

Jason and his wife had the Senior Beechams' cottage Suzanne had visited as a girl; she remembered the black-berries on the far shore, and after, ghost stories in the sleeping cabin. There had even been an incident — it returned to her now, Jason's thickened face recalling to her the soft, inquisitive boy who'd kissed his sister's friend.

"Aren't the mountains beautiful?" Simon was saying.

"They look so close."

"Magnification factor in the dry air," said Jason. "Have another? Terribly sorry about that stuffed olive."

They followed the twins' car down Macleod Trail past the Chicken on the Way sign, muffler shops and pizza huts, past the old roller-skating rink. A new district had Tudor-style homes and a manmade lake. Long ago the suburbs had hugged and eventually enfolded Fish Creek where Jennifer and Suzanne used to go fly-casting, smoking cigars to keep away the mosquitoes. They passed the railway station at Midnapore, its grain elevator now sunk in a suburb. They took a sharp turn to the west; the fields opened up ahead like the pages of a book.

On their left was a small log cabin with a chicken coop in front.

"That's for me," said Simon, "that's where I ought to retire. Write my memoirs. Write my masterpiece."

"You wouldn't like it out here," Suzanne said. "The country is too personal for you. You'd have to see your neighbours, you'd have to rely on them." She discouraged him whenever he talked about writing. She didn't like his having this fantasy; he had taken it from her. Besides if he found out too much about writing, he would find out she wasn't what he imagined her to be.

"You can come and live there with me. Finish that book of yours, whatever it is you're always doing."

"I hardly do it any more."

"Get back into it then. Commute to the college." The

cabin had disappeared now in the back window but the
dream was just appearing in his mind. "We could convert
the chicken coop for your office ... I wonder if we'd need
two cars. ..."

He was always planning. He made plans and remade
them, repeated them, as if by doing so he could print them
on her, tell her her future would be changed, had already
been changed, by his efforts. Her future, that dreary vision
of it she'd had before she met Simon, herself in a tweed suit
and oomphy shoes stalking the yellow section halls like
some new-age nun, was being redrawn.

And her past, too. The fences of the McBean ranch
appeared, white and lime green. Until Suzanne had moved
to the city, she had passed those fences several times a
week, driving in and out of town in the old Austin to the
orthodontist and gymnastics class. They enclosed pastures,
a jumping course, the ranch house where the Queen stayed
when she was in the vicinity. In those days oil was just the
stuff in the ground that people were trying to find. Men
talked about dry holes and scouts and strikes, well fires and
sulphur gas. Oddball Americans came up with wives called
"Little Joe" and children who went to prep schools in the
south. They were part of companies that operated like large
patriarchal families. The members stayed a while, looking
for oil, and then the parent sent them somewhere else.
Every now and then somebody's company found some oil.
Then the men talked about price on the barrel and at the
wellhead, and pipelines. The little axe-headed pumps
began to go up and down in the fields. The oil flowed
invisibly out and was sent away and nobody was much
changed for it. It seemed a dull, uncertain business, not far
removed from farming, another way of being dependent on
the ground under your feet.

But then Simon came, and told her about supply and
demand, OPEC and shortages. Men who had seemed like
perfectly normal people to her were "barons." Those
Americans who called her "sugar" were villains: they made
deals with sheiks who cut people's hands off for petty
infractions. But a decade ago in the east Suzanne had been

called a hick. It seemed that this folding, grain-coloured bit of land where she was born was a fortune cookie; baked in was a new message.

A cowboy at the gate waved the car around to park in a pasture down the hill. Getting out they could see the three peaks of a circus tent, bright turquoise and orange stripes against a still brighter sky. Music came, on the wind, from two directions. A four-piece dance band played on a wooden stage. Another platform was bouncing with square dancers, the corner, the allemande, skirts tipping up on each twirl. The caller, in a checked shirt, cradled a microphone with his elbow and clapped.

Suzanne and Simon held hands. To their right, men and women in chef's hats and stained white aprons worked over fire pits where the headless black carcasses of large four-legged animals turned on spits. A waitress passed, wearing a hard hat covered with sparkles and cowboy boots which slapped against her thin legs, exposed to the edge of a pair of fringed panties.

"Nurse! Nurse!" called Jason, getting out of his car. "I need a drink. And bring this man a stuffed olive."

The waitress took off her hat. The leather straps inside it made lines of sweat across her brow and through her hair, from ear to ear. Every year the McBeans made them dress more uncomfortably than the year before. Once they'd been saloon dancers in net tights with stiletto heels which sank into the dirt.

"I'm not your nurse," she said.

"She's not my nurse," said Jason, who was getting in a party mood. "Is she a little bit touchy?"

"Jason," said Jennifer.

"I need a beer, nurse. And my friend here needs a stuffed olive."

"Keep that up and you'll need a crutch," said the waitress. She wiped back the drips of sweat on her temples.

Jennifer started to laugh.

"Pretty please," said Jason, making a grab for her tray. The girl walked off.

"Can you beat that?" said Jason. "I'm an invited guest!"

He was doing this for Simon's benefit. He was determined to live up to an image. Suzanne grabbed his arm. "Jason!"

"Whose side are you on?" said Jason, looking hard at Suzanne. Then he shook off her hand. "I'll go and find us another." He lunged forward into the crowd. Someone hailed Jennifer from the other direction and suddenly Simon and Suzanne were alone facing the crowd.

She could recognize people: a certain Fran from her high school who had married a man who owned a drilling company and had taken on three or four delinquent step-children. A guy who'd once tried to tear off her dress in the car after a fraternity formal. She couldn't remember his name, but she'd heard he was now a judge. Her boss from the summer she worked as a receptionist at an oil company, later purged when the parent corporation was investigated for using bribes in Arab countries. Gemma was there, too, she saw as she continued looking. Gemma in a fringed bra and tight white jeans, laughing her high raucous laugh and shaking her bangs out of her eyes. SWARM must have been staking the place out.

"Is that who I think it is?" said Simon, pointing at a barrel-chested man with a black moustache. Suzanne said the name. "Just the guy I need to meet," he said and darted off too. Suzanne stood alone. The hard-hat waitress passed by with a tray of wine. She took one. Sipping and walking carefully on the uneven packed earth she moved towards the food tent.

Inside the open flaps was a table bearing a life-sized ice sculpture of a polar bear scooping fish. His paws were laden with caviar and around his feet lay smoked salmon and strange little green fruits that looked like shrunken heads. The bear's back was shiny and wet, his features a little dissolute. It was hot, even in the shade. Suzanne moved around him, looking for some non-violent form of food, a soft cheese, perhaps. A light claw lit on her shoulder in the dark. She turned.

"Miss Amy!"

Ace's mother stood before her, white-haired and pale, her

large blossom-like head drooping, one hand rigid on her cane. Behind her was Block, Ace's father, with oiled grey hair the colour of a ball bearing. Suzanne embraced her mother-in-law, not wanting to crush her, or dislodge the Brie from her paper plate. Then she shook Block's hand. They stood, nodding wordlessly. The women embraced again.

"You look better than ever," Block announced. "My son's an idiot."

It was a pleasantry; he referred to the divorce. But Block had thought Ace was an idiot to marry her in the first place.

"Dear," murmured Miss Amy, "where have you been? Are you divorcing me too?"

"Never."

An errant cowboy pounded Block on the back and he turned away. Suzanne moved closer to Miss Amy. Her thinness had always given her a spiritual look. It was her argument against a life that was resolutely, grossly material. But even her considerable wit and cunning had proven insufficient in the resistance. There was more than thinness now. The red stars under her cheeks and the expanded pores on her nose, only partly hidden by powder, were evidence. Her hands were drawn up, arching and pinching.

"I thought you were moving south," said Suzanne. It was to have benefited Miss Amy's arthritis.

"I'm having an operation," Amy said. "My hands will be like new. I'll be back at the piano."

Suzanne smiled. Amy had never played piano.

"Yeah sure, and I'm a ballerina."

"If you can't laugh," said Miss Amy, "why carry on?"

"No reason I guess," said Suzanne softly, though she could think of some. Amy pressed her grand, frightening face closer.

"Oh don't get all polite! You used to tell me what you thought."

It was an uncomfortable reference to a past that was gone, but not very far. "Why don't you come by for tea? Surely we can do that now, and you won't think I'm trying to entangle you in our wacky doings again?"

Suzanne heard the slow trickle of water behind her back.
It was the ice bear melting. They were jostled apart. Amy
poked ahead on her cane, seeking her husband. With her
cracker and wine glass Suzanne set off in the opposite
direction. On either side she heard men talking about deals.
Not mud and gushers and diamond bits, the way they used
to, but deals with the banks, deals with the feds, who was in
on the deal. She found Simon, telling a woman about his
legislation, the work of art, about the buttons and knobs
you could turn.

"This is Darlene, from Mecca Oil," he said. The tanned,
blonde woman looked over with calculating eyes.

Darlene from Mecca was famous on the local scene. She
had been personal secretary to a company president. Her
boss took her into meetings, where she watched fiercely and
said nothing; apparently her speciality was the psyche-out.
Then she was promoted to vice-president, the first woman
to be one. Subsequently Darlene was feared and hated, as if
witchcraft were the issue.

"Weren't you Darlene Jamieson?" Darlene Jamieson had
been captain of the Western Composite High School cheer-
leading team. Western's team had been intimidating in its
precision, and Darlene's hawk-like profile at the right had
kept the other girls stamping in time.

"Darlene Anndaughter," she said, "I went back to my
mother's name." Her eyes defied Suzanne to comment further. In any case, Simon was looking impatient.

"I was just saying there are buttons in there," he
continued, "that no one knows how to push." Suzanne
fancied Darlene's shoulder turned slightly to exclude her.

Suzanne sipped her wine. Perhaps Darlene did not wish
to be reminded of her cheerleader connection. A shame. It
had been, after all, a sign of adventurousness, athleticism,
arguably more useful in the long run than, for instance, the
United Nations Club. There on the sidelines of the football
field, intimidating the opposing teams, Darlene had learned
the psyche-out. She had early exposure to rhetoric, mass

hysteria, the losing complex. Didn't businessmen always talk about being team players? And that women didn't know the rules? Cheerleaders knew the rules, even if they weren't on the team.

Turning away from Darlene and Simon, Suzanne watched a pickup truck pull onto the far corner of the pasture. Two men in coveralls unloaded a large package. It was a wicker basket about the size of a café table. They set up the basket. Then they pulled out a great wrapped parcel and some kind of motor.

"The entertainment arrives," Darlene said.

"What do you call this?" Simon waved behind at the two competing bands, the whirling dancers.

"Foreplay," said Darlene.

The men began to untie the package. It was not actually a package, not in the sense of having contents; it *was* its contents. It was orange and blue and stretched out on the ground like a great collapsed skin. The men in coveralls walked around it, pulling and hooking up ropes. Then they started the motor. Air blasted into it and slowly the thing began to resurrect itself, whale or cloud, from its repose. The noise was terrific. The fabric seemed to rip in the high wind; the pistons banged. The partygoers began to shout and gather around. In minutes the skin had swelled and rounded to reveal the writing on its side: Mecca: West, it said. It quivered sideways on the ground, full but earthbound.

"Who's going up?"

"They'll pick someone," shouted Darlene.

"The way they do at benefit symphony concerts?" said Simon. "Some guy who always dreamed of it gets to raise the baton?"

Her smile drew her lips back over her teeth. "Perhaps you'd like to?" Her eyes were narrow. Suzanne would not have trusted her.

"Do you think I could?" For someone who was so smart, Simon could be stupid. He grinned confidently at Suzanne. She did not blink.

"Stuffed olive," she said. It was meant as a warning: watch out for the local sense of humour. But he didn't get her meaning.

"That's a great idea," said Darlene. "Send you back where you came from."

"No, seriously," said Simon. "I'd like to."

"But what an opportunity for you to meet people! We'll introduce you."

Darlene took Simon by the arm. Leading him by the elbow, she began to push through the clumps of people towards the balloon. The banging engine was now so loud it obscured all other sound. Suzanne watched the dumbshow as Darlene introduced Simon to the Mecca executives. There was a lot of nodding. They pointed at the balloon, at the sky. Simon smiled delightedly. Behind him the balloon quivered, a giant udder. He doffed his ridiculous hat and waved it around the circle. Dozens of hats waved back. Women whistled. The band began to play "Up Up and Away."

A man in a green jumpsuit led Simon into the mouth of the balloon. Their feet made little bumps visible from the outside. Someone started a propane burner. Simon and his guide neatly stepped from the mouth of the balloon as the yard-long flames sprung from the burner, directed into the flabby orb. As the air inside became hot, the balloon bounced slightly on the ground. Then it began to rise in an arc until it hung directly over the basket, upright and ready to go. Applause broke out.

Instantly the banging motors stopped. In the silence the crowd was still: the President of Mecca picked up a microphone. Suzanne didn't listen to the introduction; she could hear the voice but not the words. The crowd was cheering. When she turned back the man in the jumpsuit helped Simon over the edge of the wicker basket.

"Hands off!"

The thing began to rise. Simon leaned over the edge and waved in a theatrical way.

"Hot air for hot air," shouted the man beside her. She started.

"Tell 'em we don't need any."

"Don't come back!" yelled someone. "We won't miss you."

Poor Simon, he probably thought that once they'd had their fun with him, he'd be in, that the balloon was the Trojan Horse. But the Trojan Horse was brought into the city, not blown out. Even as the excited spectators ran about the field, Suzanne felt smaller, knowing how he was seeing them from above.

"Can they steer that thing without a wheel?" she said. The woman beside her wore a white dress with rows of gold ricrac down the front. She held up her lorgnette on its chain. "If they just go with the wind, where will they end up?"

"Wherever," said the woman. She had a deep voice, dry in tone. "But politicians know all about that."

"If they want the thing back, they can get out a gun and shoot it down." The laughter was giddy.

The balloon travelled at an angle, sideways and upwards. The orange looked lovely against the blue sky; the basket hung underneath like the dot under an exclamation mark.

"Lose your date?" said Darlene Anndaughter pleasantly, returning.

"It wouldn't be the first time I got left at a party," said Suzanne careful to be unconcerned. "But I suppose it's the most original."

But when Darlene moved off and she stood sipping alone, Suzanne began to feel sorry for herself. She strained her eyes into the endless blue. She imagined she saw Simon, apelike, arms over the side, running around the rim, unable to control his flight, like Curious George in the children's books. She headed for the square-dance platform. Perhaps she could find a partner. Or that waitress with the wine. They all had hard hats, though, you couldn't tell one from the next.

She was stepping over a slight hill when she felt a nudge at the small of her back, stronger than a nudge, really, a distinctly unfriendly shove. She heard his voice. (Of course Ace would be here, how could she have forgotten that he would be there?) As she turned to Ace, there was a thud on the back of her neck. And that was all she thought, for the moment.

She woke up on the ground, smelling grass. Above her was a lazy Susan of pantlegs and skirts, the blue sky like a plate holding it all. She was very confused; only her hatred of cliché stopped her from saying "Where am I?" Someone had his hands under her armpits and was trying to pull her up. She was very heavy.

"I can do that myself," she said, prying off the hands. She rolled over and tried to get a foothold in the grass which ran beneath her feet like liquid. "I must have tripped."

Everyone was looking. It seemed that she was not going to be able to get herself up. She lay down on her stomach and resigned herself to the pasture. She was growing comfortable on the little hill, looking at the food tent, listening to a nasal caller going on about bringing your little darlin' back home. Then Ace stood her on her feet and dusted her ruffles. In his hand was a Prince tennis racquet.

"When did you switch to mid-size?" she said, querulously. And then, looking around, "What happened?"

"I believe this man came up and tapped you with his tennis racquet," explained a woman bystander with some satisfaction.

There was a knob at the back of her neck. She had been slow to catch on but now she was getting it.

"Thank you," she murmured, "I see." She turned to look at Ace. He was industriously brushing twigs of grass off the back of her skirt. She tried to walk away with dignity. Ace followed.

"Leave me alone," she said.

"Don't be silly," he said, "a friendly tap. Harder than I expected. I am sorry. You know the famous stroke." He smiled in his most engaging way and took her by the arm, leading her away from the little group that formed. Suzanne's eye went to the orange and gold exclamation point in the sky. The balloon was far off and still travelling; no hope for help from there.

"Here, let me get you a seat. A glass of water will help." Ace scanned the heads, presumably for a hard-hat waitress.

"You idiot. You hit me with that thing!"

He hung his head. "You exaggerate."

"It's amazing the trouble you can get into at a family picnic," she said. "I ought to tell your mother on you." In fact she didn't feel at all like joking, joking was just what she did when she was scared. "If you can't laugh... why carry on?" Miss Amy would say. It certainly wasn't that she thought this was funny. It was because she thought she couldn't do anything else.

The waitress came with the water. The moment she turned away, Ace squeezed Suzanne's elbow.

"Good god, Suzanne, I can't leave you alone for a moment and you're off with some other guy. What do you have to say for yourself?"

"You struck me." He was hurting her elbow too.

"That's not the point."

"It's the only point. Wife-beating ..." she began.

"Oh don't give me your political dogma! It's not *wife*-beating."

They were getting rather loud. Suzanne looked out of the corner of her eye for help. There was none.

"You mean it's not wife-beating because we're divorced?" she said.

"We are not!" he said.

"I had a date!" Suzanne protested to the party at large. Simon was over east Calgary now. Why didn't somebody else come? There was no shortage of people but no one was paying attention. Ace had hit her. And knocked her down. She felt humiliated, although it was Ace who ought to be embarrassed. "I should go home," she said finally.

"And miss the party? Let me get you something to eat."

"Now I'm going to be sick." At last her eyes lit on

Gemma across the field. There was Jennifer, too. Walking towards them she staggered; the two of them held her up.

"Take me home." Going limp she could hear them talking excitedly about which car they should use.

All four of them were in Suzanne's car. Gemma drove, with Jennifer beside her. Somehow Ace had got into the back seat. Suzanne was trying to evade his arm. Gemma was humming, pretending not to overhear his entreaties, but Suzanne could tell by the set of her neck that she was gobbling up every word.

"Just let me explain. You don't understand."

"What's to explain? You came up and clubbed me to the ground. The only thing I don't understand is how I ever came to know a monster like you." She meant to have done with Ace for once and for all.

"You aren't thinking clearly, Suzanne!"

"If you want her to think clearly you shouldn't hit her on the back of the head with a tennis racquet," said Jennifer.

"I think she's got a headache," said Gemma, inexpertly guiding the car into the four lanes of traffic curving around the city. Jennifer was trying to watch what went on in the back seat and navigate at the same time.

He appealed to Jennifer. "You've got to see how it makes me feel, when she shows up with another guy."

"After all, it's only been — how long? Ten years? Since you split up?"

"Seven," he snapped.

"I rest my case," said Jennifer. "You have no right. You never did."

"It's got nothing to do with right. You may not be aware of it but we are getting back together."

"We are not." The car went over a bump. Pain shot up through Suzanne's head, and down her shoulder blades. Perhaps she was going to be paralyzed.

"Don't try to be logical. Hitting you wasn't anything reasoned. It was just — an outburst."

"First you want me to think clearly, then you don't want me to be logical. Make up your mind."

It was still the middle of the afternoon. The sun was so bright it fired the inside of Suzanne's eyelids. She didn't want him there. She didn't want him anywhere. "I'm hurt," she said.

"I hurt too, Suzanne," said Ace. He hung his head. "I'm sorry. But I couldn't stand to see you with him."

"These things don't happen to me," said Suzanne quietly, "I am a private person, as the saying goes. A month ago I lived undisturbed, unnoticed, a dim little researcher dallying a little with a not quite divorced husband. And now look, I am public property. I couldn't even get beaten up without a panel discussion."

"If you cared for me you wouldn't be so intolerant."

"I would so! It has nothing to do with who I care for. Nobody gets to hit me."

"Not even your ambitious little consultant?"

She opened her eyes and looked out the window. They were at 34th Street South. Ten more minutes and she'd be home.

"This is obscene," she remarked to the car ceiling. She shut her eyes.

"Leave her alone, Ace," said Jennifer. "She's tired." The car swerved to the right. "Take 14th," she said to Gemma. It swerved back left.

"You're so strict," Ace was going on. "You don't forgive." He took up her hand. "Can't you see it wasn't me who did it but the old bad actor inside of me?"

"Where shall I drop you, Ace?" said Gemma.

"I'm going to her place to look after her, of course," he said.

Suzanne started to cry. Gemma stepped on the gas. Jennifer leaned back and put her hand on Suzanne's knee.

"Left here," she said to Gemma. The car went on two wheels. "Where's your Kleenex?"

"Is she crying?" A hush came over the car. "She never cries."

"She's crying," said Suzanne.

She tried to give them a nice noisy show, since none of them had heard it before. Crying wasn't so bad. What happened was she ran out of jokes to fight it off. Doing it, she felt just as silly as she had before. Jennifer found a box of Kleenex. Ace gave her one, and then put the box up under the back window. Both front windows were open; Jennifer and Gemma had their elbows out. A wind came through Gemma's side, circled over the back seat, and went out Jennifer's side. This wind ripped a Kleenex out of the box, just one. The Kleenex flew straight over Suzanne's shoulder. Steadily, the wind continued to pull on the tissues. One by one they came out of the box, one by one they flew around inside the car, like pale yellow hats. Three, four, five of them. They began to go out the window, behind Jennifer.

"Will you look at that?" Suzanne said.

"Amazing."

The car had a little cycle going, the Kleenex mobilization. It was funny. Someone started to laugh. Things were almost normal.

"Suzanne," said Ace.

"Ace, listen to what she just said. She just said she doesn't want to talk to you."

"But she's got to talk to me. We've got to work through this problem."

"What problem? We have no problems. You came up and clobbered me. Now I don't know you any more."

Beneath her feet, Suzanne could feel the buzzing of the metal strips of the bridge. Almost home. She felt like the polar bear in the ice sculpture, dissolving into a puddle of caviar beads and mushy crackers, while the others made their bargains. Finally they drew up outside her house. Ace jumped out to help her out of the back seat. Muscles all over her back had began to ache and seize; she longed for the bathtub.

"Suzanne, you aren't making this any easier. You're upset. I'm going to get you inside and get you a nice cup of tea ..."

"No, I'm going to bed."

"All right, well I'll call round later tonight and we'll talk it over."

"No, Ace," said Jennifer in her best threatening voice. "Don't go over there. She doesn't want to talk it over."

"Let me at least take her inside."

He took her hands. She went stiff. He was begging. His eyes forced her to see him. He whispered, "Remember it wasn't me doing it. It was the bad actor."

"The bad actor," she said. It was what the brothers used to call the guys who went out of control, drunk. Only those guys were bad actors for life.

"Don't you think I've got a little bad actor inside? You hardly ever know he's there. Today he just — got out." He stood there chagrined, pleading.

"Just don't come near me again," she said. Her eyes went up to the sky. She wondered where the orange and turquoise balloon had gone. She thought if she stood on her toes she might be able to see it, over the roof of the house next door.

Chapter 10

The telephone rang. Suzanne woke with the impression that she was paralyzed. Papers were all around her on the sheets; she'd been working in bed and had fallen asleep on her research. Her back muscles were in spasm as a result of being struck with the tennis racquet at the Mecca barbecue. The ringing continued. She reached slowly for the receiver.

"Suzanne, dear, you've got to come and help me. This minute — "

"Miss Amy?"

"I'll unlock the front door."

The line clicked at the other end. Suzanne dropped the receiver and hoisted herself up stiffly, faster than she thought possible. She found her purse in the bathroom, and the car keys on the stereo where she had dropped them when she came in. That was Saturday. This was Tuesday. She couldn't imagine what had gone wrong. Block left his wife alone for ages, sometimes, she knew. He was supposed to come home for lunch and take her out for a walk, but this good deed was like all his others, subject to arbitrary cancellation.

Suzanne could get to the house on the other side of the river in ten minutes if she was lucky. She ran flat-footedly to the car, trying not to jar her back, and took the Louise

Bridge down through town and up the hill to Mount Royal.

The ornate knob turned easily in the centre of the two carved wooden doors that had been brought across the Atlantic from some Spanish monastery.

"Miss Amy!" Suzanne stepped into the echoing hall. She expected prostration, heart attack, or cat burglars with sawed-off shotguns. Instead she saw Miss Amy dance into sight in the middle of the foyer, bone thin in her blue jeans, her eyes popping. Her right hand was in a cast halfway up her elbow.

"Oh, you're here, thank God —" She had her left hand on the waist of her pants, the bandaged right waving impotently in front. "Help me undo this snap. I have to go to the biffy and I can't get it with just the one."

Suzanne popped the bright metal snap open.

"Oh thank heaven, you're marvellous." Amy scampered into the guests' powder room, leaving Suzanne feeling like an idiot, standing on the black-and-white marble tiles. They were cool. She looked down. She'd driven over in bare feet. She let out a sputtering sigh.

"So you're all right?"

"Oh, oh, at last," Amy moaned through the bathroom door. "Just a jiff!" Amy had all kinds of merry little phrases like that. "Toodle-oo" for goodbye, "tickety-boo" for tidy. She sounded faint, far away through the door. "Block dressed me this morning and the maid comes in after two but I just never thought about what would happen in between. You know what it's like when you just have to go and you can't even look towards the ladies or it's all over…" Now Miss Amy reappeared, smiling, offering her waist to be re-buttoned. "Will you have some coffee, now that you're here?"

Suzanne padded after her, grumbling. "You scared me half to death. You shouldn't have done that to me."

"Well I had to get you here somehow, didn't I?"

Amy had been ill forever, but now she was worse, much worse than before. Her hair was dull and matted against a porous scalp, her back in a sickle curve. She was thinner than anyone should be, and still be alive. Suzanne knew she should have visited; her mother-in-law had been her friend. But she hated going to the Cummingses' house.

Amy poured the coffee in the old yellow china mug with the handle with leaves crawling up it. Suzanne held it, and looked through the greenhouse wall into the backyard. The magpies Amy detested were perched in an arc around the birdbath which was meant for the little songbirds. They made Suzanne nervous. In livelier days, Amy, an expert trap shooter, had gone out with her gun and shot them. Fat, with their slick black-and-white uniforms, the birds hung around like the security guards of a new, yet unseen regime.

"You had your operation, did you?"

From Amy's plastered wrist the tips of her fingers protruded, senseless little pink gumdrops. "They say it'll be like new when the cast's off. If I like this one I'll have the other one done. But you see I can't even —" she waggled her fingertips.

But arthritis was the least of her ailments. Amy looked as if she were being sucked into some vacuum inside herself. She was without makeup this morning, the tiny blasted veins showing everywhere under her eyes and around her nose; her cheeks were livid and her eyes raw around the lids. Only a woman once truly beautiful would have the courage to look so ugly. She sat at the flecked white and gold table: her good hand drifted over its surface feeling for the dust which never had a chance to collect. The kitchen was white, gleaming; it was like the cockpit of a high-speed jet. The dishwasher, the double oven, the range top all had chrome buttons and tiny dials. It was a work of art, thought Suzanne, like Simon's legislation, with buttons and knobs, buttons and knobs.

Beyond the kitchen, the room opened into a family area with games tables; athletic trophies crammed the book-cases, the triumphs of little Ace and Big Brault framed on the panelling, beside Block's mounted deer heads and shellacked trout. Amy's trophies were the empty liquor bottles stuffed under the sink, in the oven, behind the record player. They included the pills, here on the lazy Susan in the centre of the kitchen table, pills — liver-red ones, tiny pastel yellow ones, multicoloured lozenges. When Suzanne and Ace were first dating, Amy was an impressive matron with a "nervous condition." The treatment got out of hand along with the condition.

"You were walking funny when you came in here," said Amy. "Is it true that Ace knocked you down?"

Everyone knew everything. Suzanne smiled at his mother, who did not need any more grief.

"I think it was an accident."

"Huh!" said Amy roughly. She turned this way and that in her chair. "Did he do it because you're divorcing him?"

"I was already divorcing him."

"Huh!" said Miss Amy again.

Suzanne could not tell her about Simon.

The house was absolutely quiet, and clean. What would the maid do when she arrived at two? What would Amy do when the arrival of the maid forced her out of the kitchen?

"Would you like me to take you down to Verily, Verily?" said Suzanne. "The new fall things should be in." It was Amy's own rule. When in pain, purchase. Some of Miss Amy's friends ran a dress shop. It used to be when Amy and Suzanne went down, the owners set out chairs in the middle of the broadloom between the racks, and served old-fashioneds in pink glasses.

"I don't go there now. They're frightened of me."

"How about to the club, for a whirlpool? It might be good for us both."

"I don't like going places," said Amy petulantly. "People don't want to see me. You know what they're like. They don't like sickness. It ruins the ambiance. They think of it as defeat."

Suzanne couldn't argue.

"You know where I'd like to go?" said Amy suddenly. "Home."

"To Virginia?"

"There's no one there, of course."

"But it's a grand idea. See the summer house. Take a trip!" Suzanne was a little too enthusiastic. She should offer to take Amy home. But it had been impossible to interfere when she was in the family; now it was unthinkable.

"Block says he'll take me but I don't want him to. If we go together, they'll see me walk down the hill to the bay and they'll say, 'there he is, he's brought her home to die.' 'Here comes the old thing,' they'll say, 'for one last look at the place before the end.' I hate being felt sorry for."

"Amy! Don't talk that way!"

Suzanne couldn't stand the enclosed air of the kitchen. She slid open the glass door and stepped out onto the patio. The magpies were not disturbed by her presence. By now they had all the water out of the bath. They were chattering and hopping from hedge to post. She ran at them, flailing her arms. Amy followed her to the door.

"Don't be like that, Suzanne. You've got to accept this, for my sake. You're as good as my daughter, you know. It's coming to us all, it's only coming to me a little sooner."

Suzanne turned around slowly to see her mother-in-law's face. She was standing inside the door Suzanne had left open. Slowly she drew the screen across in front of her. It cast a skin over her face, taking away the light. There she stood, an emaciated, yellow and grey stick figure with a piquant child's gaze, round, wide-apart eyes, full mouth, all pressed flat. She moved her lips against the screen. Suzanne started. It was just what Ace had done at her front door, when he came to take her to the midway. They both had a habit of pressing themselves against things. And Suzanne thought, do I love the part of her that is him, or the part of him that is her, or does it even matter?

"He's won, you see. My husband has beaten me."

"Nonsense, Amy."

"He had to fight off half the boys in town to get me. He came in off his ship, they all did, there were thousands of them. They used to see us, my sister and I, going in and out of the butcher, the pharmacy. He got to know Daddy somehow, the devil. He got into the house and then he got out of the Navy and he was going places."

Suzanne nodded. Block had gone places all right.

"They all thought I'd be looked after. I suppose I was a bit of a problem, even then. Can't think what it was made me that way." She grimaced, a little joke on her. "He

wanted to move off to Texas. Texas! I thought. I thought
that was the most dreadful, uncivilized place there could
be. Then it was Canada."

Suzanne smiled. Miss Amy had never been a patriot.

"I always thought, he'll divorce me, and I'll go back. But
he never obliged."

"You could have done it yourself. Perhaps you didn't
want to."

"I just could never make up my mind. You see — "

Amy leaned onto the screen; it bowed out. She was
suspended over the patio, as in a net.

"No, I don't see," said Suzanne.

"You don't see because you still have it. I've lost it. I
might have wanted this or that, once, but I had to hide it.
As soon as he found out he squelched it. He knew about
wanting, knew it was the most important thing. He'd stop
it somehow. 'Not now, Amy,' or, 'Why don't you just learn
to play bridge with me instead?' He'd give me things before
I thought of them. I can't explain. He paralyzed me." As if
the telling of it gave her energy, Miss Amy pushed with her
good hand against the door frame and bounced back
upright.

"You let him."

"So you see I'm sure you're doing the right thing," Amy
went on, not listening. "Even though I wish my son could
have kept you."

Suzanne thought that for her whole life she had been
listening to women tell her they were helpless, they were
victims, men had done them in. She was forewarned. It
would not happen to her. She was sympathetic, but she
could not stand to hear any more. Her tolerance was
running out, and her life was going on, regardless. Going on
to include a man.

She ran two fingers along the ridges of her coffee cup
which represented vines, stems of ivy whose leaves
intertwined. One thing she was sorry about. She was sorry
that she had avoided Amy. There were relationships which
were neither blood, nor love, nor law. There were connections of gut and sinew, entanglements of dependence,

sympathy, proximity. These you could not divorce, or
disown.

"On another subject," said Miss Amy briskly. "When I
die Block will remarry. I just want you to know it's part of
our understanding. Don't think I would be offended."

"Amy!" wailed Suzanne. "Must you?"

"Don't write me off yet. I may be able to do something
for you. I still have a card or two left to play!" Amy slid
open the screen and reached out her hand to Suzanne.

Slowly, Suzanne drove back down the hill. She held the
wheel firmly, determined to get away. She had promised to
go back again; she hoped she would have the courage. The
wide curve of pavement was deserted; the leaves hung still
on the trees. It was mid-morning and the children, if there
were children, were not at home. Only the postman trod the
path from door to door up front walks lined with juniper.
The dogs didn't even chase the cats, they sat like ringed
posts on the doorsteps. This was what prosperity had
brought, this flatness, silence, this ordered vacancy. This
was Amy's world, and Amy was what happened to people in
it.

When she crossed the bridge into Kensington, there were
the tables out in front of the Stromboli. A metal rack of
T-shirts hung in front of the dress store, and in the
bookshop window Judith was arranging a display. She wore
her T-shirt that read "I survived the recession." Suzanne
slowed the car and honked. Judith waved.

The sun was hitting the side of the flat-iron building, and
all the reds and greens stood out in relief in the village. On
11A Street, four children had their bikes in a huddle. The
Ringroses were weeding their flower beds. Suzanne waved
at them too; they looked up, quizzical. A curious elation
filled her as she contemplated what she had escaped. Here
was her little house, her funny old furniture, her oddball
lover who'd never fit in, never make her play bridge, and
her obscure researches which she did whenever she wanted
to. Free, free, free. She *had* chosen right. She had chosen life.

Simon and Suzanne were going camping in the Kananaskis.
They had her car packed with a pup tent, a Coleman stove,

some tin pots and a picnic basket. The picnic basket had in it smoked salmon and caviar — Simon's contribution.

"For hors-d'oeuvres," he said. Neither of them camped much.

"Mosquito repellent!" she said, standing beside the driver's door. "I knew we forgot something. We can't go without it. Cutter's is the best."

Simon was putting candles for their dinner in the glove compartment. He'd brought *The Rubáiyát of Omar Khayyám*; they were going to read this together at a waterfall. He wore short khaki shorts, a pair of heavy hiking boots with woollen socks, and a Panama hat.

"Fine, we'll stop at the drugstore," he said.

Suzanne trained the sun-visor over her eyes and set off westward. It was a little late in the afternoon to be leaving. They stopped at the drugstore, and then went on to the liquor vendor's, because Simon decided they needed a bottle of champagne. It was four-thirty when they sped past Bowness. Suzanne looked at the Northwest Rebellion out of the corner of her eyes. Then she set her sights on the mountains.

"We may not be able to get into the campground," Suzanne said. "I think people make reservations now."

"Oh well, never mind. Can't we just pull off somewhere and climb up a rock beside a little mountain stream? Who needs a campground?"

By the time they reached it, the campground was full. There was another ten miles down the road, the ranger said. It was not full, but it was not very picturesque, either, flat, too close to the road, and full of screaming kids. It was now six-thirty. In the mountains the dark came much sooner; already the sky was deepening to marine blue. Simon was in excellent humour. He was poring over a trail map, trying to find them a perfect spot for the night.

"If we take this trail by the creek here for just two and a half miles it says there's a rest spot by the lake. It's not serviced. But it'll be cleared. Let's go there," he said.

Suzanne looked. The trail was marked intermediate to advanced. The lake was called Pole Cat's Plunge. It looked dangerous to her and it looked like a lot of work. But he said he'd carry the tent and sleeping bags. By the time she had them tied to the frame on his back, it was seven o'clock. They set off up the trail, passing the first wooden picket with a sign: Lake, 8 km. What was eight kilometres? Over a mile and a half. The mosquitoes were out. They stopped to smear Cutter's all over their faces and hands and ankles. Simon insisted on leaving his legs bare.

"We are insane," said Suzanne tramping upward. "We'll never make it before dark."

"Dark isn't really dark, you know," Simon said. "We'll be able to see just fine."

"You don't know the mountains."

Suzanne began to stumble on roots and stones in the path. She stopped looking at where they were going — up, alongside an increasingly steep rock drop — and started looking at her feet. Simon was in front: she could hear the squeak, squeak, squeak of the leather straps across his back frame as he walked. *He* wasn't falling. The sky was a deep navy now, the ragged silhouettes of pine trees emerging velvety against the sky. She missed the next sign.

"Lake, five kilometres," he said.

"If there's no campground there why do we have to make it all the way to the lake? Couldn't we just stop here?"

"We don't have any water."

"But there's a creek somewhere. We're supposed to be climbing up a creek." Suzanne could hear it, rustling in the darkness.

"Down there," said Simon, pointing to their right, down the pebbly slope. "But we can't go down. We'll never get back up."

She resigned herself to it. She thought about mountain lions and bears, about falling down and breaking a leg, about running into maniacs with homicidal tendencies. She listened to the drone of the frustrated mosquitoes who wanted to land on her neck and couldn't, because of the smell of her ointment. She wouldn't have had anything to do with her neck either if she had a choice. Her back began to hurt, where Ace hit her a month ago. It was eight o'clock and almost pitch dark now. But it was a clear night, and a vast scattering of stars was emerging over their heads.

"We must have missed the last sign," muttered Simon. The path had got very narrow, and wasn't well worn. "We should be there by now."

"Is this the path?"

"I don't know. Maybe it went that way."

The undergrowth was thin. Simon scrambled under a few scratchy lower limbs of spruce and investigated the other side of a boulder. "I think this is it, over here."

"Isn't the rest spot supposed to be on top? I suppose if we just keep going up ..." said Suzanne.

"Hard to imagine there being a lake up there," said Simon, gazing up the side of the dark, tree-covered mountain. They began to walk again, simultaneously. They had to come out to something, eventually. It couldn't go on being steep and narrow forever.

"A sign! What does it say?"

Simon approached the board plaque shaped like an arrow. It was so dark he had to feel it to read it. It was pointing back the way they came. "Lake, one kilometre," he said.

"That's it!" said Suzanne, putting down the picnic basket. "We stop here."

"But there's no water. What about our dinner?"

"We'll have to have just the champagne and hors-d'oeuvres."

Simon dropped the frame off his back. The cooking pots jangled on a rock. He took out the champagne. The cork came out like a gunshot in the dark.

"Here come the rangers," said Suzanne. But no one came.

They ate smoked salmon and caviar with rye bread, and crawled into their sleeping bags to drink the champagne. It was difficult to put the tent up, because there was no light. It was night in the mountains. Suzanne kept lighting the candles, which fluttered in the low breeze and went out.

"Didn't we bring a flashlight?"

"We must have."

There was no flashlight in the pack, none in the picnic basket.

"I think it's in the glove compartment," said Suzanne. She began to giggle. "Anyway I don't think I want to know what's out there." She stayed seated as much as she could, only crawling a little way to the packs, and back to her sleeping bag. They had begun to think they were high up over the lake. She didn't want to plunge over some ledge.

"There might be animals around," said Simon. "I think we should light a fire, but I don't want to do it unless I know there's water so we can put it out."

The mosquitoes were a symphony in the background.

"Let's go for a walk and find it," said Simon.

"I think I'd rather lie here and get mauled by a bear," she said.

She was a little drunk. She was also very frightened.

"Don't you know how to walk in the dark? I'll teach you," he said.

He stood up, and pulled her up behind him. He put her hands around his waist, and began to shuffle forward; she shuffled behind him, holding a candle. "You've got to put that out," he said. "They just make your pupils contract." He blew on the candle. "Now. Stare directly into the dark. Let it enter you. Let your eyes adjust. In a minute you'll be able to make out shapes."

All she could see was the back of his head. Then she realized that the back of his head was more solid than what was around it. The sky was growing lighter; she could make out outlines of the trees, see a gap, and through the gap, a great expanse of sky with stars. Light began to stream from the stars, dividing out the mountainside from the forest, the ground from their feet. She could see her feet, and where she was stepping.

Simon shuffled on. The path had been thick in texture, almost rubbery; now it was pebbled and shifted under foot. And it had begun to slope down. More light was ahead. Suzanne let go of his waist; she could walk by herself now. The whole night had become transparent. They had penetrated the darkness.

"There's the lake, down there," said Simon.

His voice was louder. The opening in the trees allowed it to travel; it returned to them from across the lake. All Suzanne could make out was a wide space, and on the other side, the dark mass of a rock. Her fingers touched a branch;

the dry sharpness of a needle, the glue of sap, the small pointed scales along the branch told her what it was, but the touch was more telling than ever before. She reached out, but Simon had moved ahead quickly, and there was nothing in front of her.

Now the moon had risen over the rocks behind them and illuminated the surface of the still, circular lake. It was grey-blue, a reservoir of light. Cold air rose up from it and clung to Suzanne's face.

"Shall we swim?" she said. It seemed the extension of their exploring, breaking into another element.

"It'll be freezing," he said.

She climbed down the side of a rock. She could only see his outline. "Come on," she said. She could be the leader now. Would he follow? She looked back up the rock. There was a dark pile: he'd sat down.

Briefly they had deceived the mosquitoes. But now they descended, and hastened Suzanne's plunge. From the quiet rose the hollow plonk and rustle of water as she gently disturbed it.

"Cold!" she said, her voice echoing. She didn't mind it. The water took up her body. She gave in to it. The water was there, had been there, all this time, mysterious. It would swallow her. She paddled away from the edge. The surface of the water, visible only a few feet around her, seemed to roughen. She could hear Simon somewhere, splashing at the water's edge.

"Come on," she said.

"I won't jump. That's how people become paraplegics." He slid off his shoes, peeled down his jeans. "What will it be like?"

"First will be the shock," she said. "Your heart might stop. Everything will disappear for a second. Then slowly feeling will return. You'll remember yourself."

He pulled his sweatshirt over his head and stood for a moment on the rock. Then he squatted, slid his legs down in and struck out through the water toward her.

Suzanne raised her eyelids a fraction. She was inside a luminous orange prism. The tent. She could make out the outline of a pine branch beyond. She looked to her right. Simon was half out of the sleeping bag, one leg crossed over the other, his eyes shut, his arm flung open as if to receive an embrace. His glasses were beside him on the ground-sheet. His eyes began to open.

And what could he see? Without his glasses, Simon was nearly blind. Pumpkin-coloured clouds, an impression of walls? The beige stretch that was her? Unless she was within six inches of him he couldn't make out the freckles on her shoulders. He was sightless in bed, exploring with his hands, his mouth. He put his face close to her skin so that his breath coated her. He gazed at her with round, soft eyes, a gaze without peril because it did not focus, it did not judge. It simply took her in.

Last night she had been blind too. Simon had been in front of her and she could only see him, nothing else. She had heard their voices in that intense way one heard, in darkness. It was romantic; she loved it. She let her eyelids drop, and slept again.

When she woke up, Simon was sitting up with his glasses on. His eyes were quick to meet hers. She struggled to focus.

"How late is it?" she said. She thought it must be very late. The tent was stifling. She was still in the dream of last night, but he had emerged. He had moved on. He had been sitting there, plotting. She pulled the sleeping bag up over her breasts.

"There are two ways to do it," he said, as if she had been following his thoughts. "You can make history or you can make a career. I was interested in the former. That's why I'm not there any more. I've got ideas, vision. You don't last long with that."

"But I should think those were desirable qualities," she said, burrowing closer. It was difficult to keep up with Simon's mood changes.

"That's one of the most idiotic things you've ever come out with, Suzanne, if you don't mind my saying." Animated by this thrust, he leaned forward in a straight line and reached for his shirt. "You westerners are so naïve."

Thus was union finished, and division begun. Suzanne

struggled up on her elbows. He bent, grizzled and gnome-like, against the tent wall. He was unshaven, and she could see now that his beard grew in white. His eyes drooped at the corner. With his bottom half furred by the sleeping bag, he looked like an ageing satyr. She tried to fit this image of him with the man she'd met in the Greenhorn that night, the well-dressed sophisticate, the *éminence grise*. He had the *grise*, but she was no longer so sure about the eminence. He didn't actually have a job. It is hard to be eminent when unemployed. But that nebulous "fame" he'd come to her with still clung; it gave his observations a certain resonance. Suzanne did not mind that he wasn't working. The fact that he had descended from the most private government chambers, and the most public photo wires into her life, her bed, seemed marvellous. But he minded.

"Naïveté goes, I suppose, when people realize their power," she said.

"But that's just the point. The west will never *get* power. Power doesn't travel from east to west. Only the sun and eager young men do that." He leaned back, looking for comments.

"Nice," she muttered.

"You like it."

"Yeah. And balloons?" She couldn't resist. "Don't they go from west to east?" He was pleased with his party stunt. It had made him a name around town. So far, however, it had not brought more oilmen to the little office on Tenth Avenue for instruction in how to use the buttons and knobs.

"Balloons travel like wind and water, according to gravity," he said. He was not going to admit there had been a way to steer the thing. Certainly he hadn't found it: the crew brought him down at the end of the day near some gas fields on the border with Saskatchewan. When the Mecca people came out to claim their balloon they were astonished to find him gone; he'd walked to a gas station and called a cab. A cab! From Brooks! That made a better story than his going up in the thing in the first place.

"Power went from England to America," she said.

"That's not growth, that's revolution. And even that

moves west to east. Revolutions are reactionary things anyway; they're aimed against the main power base. Growth is
only useful in the direction that is of greatest benefit to all."

"If there were such a direction," said Suzanne. She
pulled her legs up out of the sleeping bag and began looking
around for her clothes. She must have left them down at the
lake.

"Ah, you're a cynic," he said. He had his clothes. He
had greater instincts of self-preservation; he had remembered
where he put them in the dark, and brought them back up.
As he stood up and dressed she watched him. He had had
the left side of his face to her; now he turned the other
direction and opened the tent flap. Light poured onto his
right profile.

It came to Suzanne that Simon had two faces. One of his
faces was civilized; the other was wild. It was the left, the
civilized one, he'd turned to her this morning. On that side
his nose was long and pointed, his eye wise and well-
shaped, his teeth even. But the other side, the wild side
which she saw briefly now, was utterly different. On the
right, his nose was thin and bent under, his eye narrow, the
pupil a bead rolling sightly outward, and his lip was not
straight. Also one tooth was longer and more pointed than
the other. He had two faces, and he was two people.

His civilized face was considered and thoughtful, controlled and rational. With his civilized face he was a tutor,
and kindly. But his wild side was unpredictable. His wild
side walked in the dark. It was passionate, and could be
cruel. Both sides were possible. But Suzanne didn't ever
know which face she was going to see at any time.

"I may be a cynic," she said. "But I don't cheat." She
wound a towel around herself and scrambled down the
slope to the lake, where she found the pile of clothes,
ridiculous testament to last night's abandon.

The debate continued at they marched back to the car.
She walked on his left, listening as he declaimed.

"Of course we *cheat*," Simon said. One of his rhetorical
tricks was to switch from "I" to "we," thus outnumbering

her. "We cheat the natural order. This is what government is for. To 'cheat' as it were, redistributing wealth, fostering the needy. Is it cheating to shape the future? Is it cheating to take from the haves and to give to the have-nots? Cheating to try to achieve the kind of balance that can keep this country together?"

Suzanne pushed the spruce branches away from her face. The path was not meant for walking side by side. And besides, he took the middle.

"It is *not*, Suzanne, it is creation. People like McBean, like Block Cummings — " by now he had learned the names, "the grand old men around here, they were nothing but labourers. They dug the clay. Think of us as sculptors." He stopped and peered down. "Vision!" he said, clapping his chest.

"But it's your vision, not theirs."

"Does Michelangelo ask the stone what it wants to be?"

"Well yes," she said. They had reached a point on which she had an actual opinion. "I believe he did. He would have to, if he wanted to do a good job. He couldn't make the sculpture on his own. He had to find out what was in the stone, didn't he?" She stepped ahead of him on the path, a little primly, victorious as her point went home. He stopped dead.

"My God, I think you're right," he said. "I lost the thread of that one."

He followed her slowly, pondering. His index finger went up in the air, pointing at her. "When you said it was our vision, not theirs, then I should have said, no, it is not, it is the country's vision, and then —"

"You're just like my in-laws were at the bridge table. Talking over each hand before they finish playing it. Eventually all they had to do was deal. And he said, you play this and that and she'd say, you play so and so. They figured the whole game out in their heads. No need to bother playing."

"But of course," said Simon. "Strategy is the only interesting part of the game. All the rest's a waste of time."

They found the car where they left it, and loaded up the

camping equipment. All the uncooked dinner food in the picnic basket went in the trunk. They'd stop at a restaurant for hamburgers; it was too late for breakfast. Simon took the wheel.

"Government. Bridge. Conversation. You don't imagine there is actually a right or wrong in these things? Success is merely a matter of organizing your material."

She thought of that first evening when they walked by the river and he said he wanted to be a poet. "I don't agree. Everything in life is not a contest." The slopes of the mountains began to turn green beside them as they descended towards the main highway. "A poem is not a contest."

"A poem *is* a contest. A poem is a perfect example. A contest between the poet and life, with words as the chess pieces, if you like. The poet wins by arranging the pieces so as to hold life at bay. Give it a more perfect order. Isn't that what you're doing in that little spare room of yours?"

Suzanne took a sudden breath. "What do you know about what I do in that little spare room?"

"I know a lot," he said absently, taking the car around a steep curve, "because last week you left your papers all over the bed. I took them back to your study, and while I did, I had a look."

Suzanne pressed herself against the seat of her car. She pressed herself hard, so that he wouldn't catch the enormous thumping in her chest. He drove on, not noticing, or pretending not to notice.

"And now I understand you a little better. I understand what this obsession with history is all about. You are trying to find an order inherent in a chaotic past which you find distressing. You are arguing with history."

"What papers?" she said, dangerously.

Now came the romance she had wanted when she woke up. He pulled the car over on the gravel shoulder, and turned to look at her. His face was flat, neither wild, nor civilized. She did not know which one was talking to her.

"I want to know you," he said, "even the parts of you you don't want known. You see, I am ruthless. When it comes to *this*." *This* was her. He put his hand under her chin. It put into her mind the moment when he came to her door that first weekend, how he had pledged to love her, referring to her in the third person. Her words muffled by her trapped chin, she spoke.

"Where did you put them?"

"On the desk. Beside the pile of Xeroxed microfilm. It looked like old newspapers."

Her desk. Her papers. Her spare room, her perfect, pristine uninhabited room, the room no one went in to.

"And you read them while you did this?"

"Most of the manuscript. The clippings I just glanced through." He shook his head. "Pretty sordid story, isn't it? A hooker done in by a john?"

"You read it all?"

"No, not all." He leaned back from her and turned to start the car again. Now she saw his hooked nose and crooked lip. The wild, unprincipled side of his face. Outside the car window the rich velvety green of the pine forests swayed. She gathered up her courage.

"What right did you have to do that, Simon?"

His tone was innocent. "Come on, Suzanne, you *left* them there. You must have wanted me to see them." He smiled, then turning a kindly look on her, pulled out onto the highway.

Chapter 11

Alone, Suzanne walked east on Seventh Avenue to the library. It was Saturday morning. The secretaries were not trotting out for lunch, nor were the blue-suited young geologists. The little yellow jeeps from messenger services did not dodge down the sidewalks. Overhead the glass hallways strung between buildings, called "plus fifteens" because they were fifteen feet above street level, were empty and blank in the sun.

She had the city to herself. With its steep shadows, its oversized sky, it felt like a movie set. The inhabitants were actors now off duty. They had abandoned their places on the streets for private lives, as if this mounting of sidewalks and buildings deserved no more, as if it were just something they used. They had the land to love, didn't they? Their city they could afford to treat with contempt.

Dust was older here in the east end, litter around the storefronts deeper. Optimistic city fathers had placed the main library in the bad section, hoping to improve the area. Suzanne's colleagues complained they were accosted by drunks and prostitutes when they came to consult the collection, but she had no such problems. She liked coming here.

This was the faded cowtown she'd visited as a child when, once a month, she drove in from the Valley with her mother. She knew that painted cup of coffee behind the grimy restaurant window, yellowed steam rising in a friendly S from its brim, with its red circle reading "25¢." She knew that fat man, or his predecessor, who leaned beside a doorway, his shirt parted in a downward V over his navel, which flickered in his belly like a lazy eye. There was a country-western bar advertising a group called "Hearts of Flame," and a woman in a hippy leather store, sitting on a stool, threading beads. There had been an old bookstore here too; Suzanne and her mother usually stayed an hour or more to paw through secondhand paperbacks selling for ten cents. Sometimes her mother wanted absurdist drama, sometimes female psychology, for a while the occult. She and the owner, a skinny, sallow young man, drank coffee and exclaimed together over their reading. What had his name been? It was gone.

But a memory rose, clear, unbidden, from that childhood which had seemed unremarkable, free from shock. On a day like today, hot, still, dusty, the city nearly deserted, Suzanne and her mother were driving southward, home, after their trip. The sun hit the windshield straight on, throwing white over their eyes; her mother wore sunglasses, Suzanne squinted. The radio was playing: Nat King Cole sang. "Love is and love was and always will be, all over the world." Suzanne's mother hummed along.

"Why are all the songs about *love*, Mum?"

Her mother stopped humming. She did not turn her sunglasses from the road.

"Because most people think it's the most important thing in the world."

Suzanne knew what her mother meant when she said "most people." She meant "other people." It was the same as when her father talked about religion: "most people need something like that." He left the clear impression that he and his family were above this general weakness.

Echoing her husband, her mother did not include herself

then in those who thought love the most important thing in the world. And yet she sang the song. Sang about love and thought about the bookstore man.

Suzanne knew then. Her mother was a fake. When she worked, facing the wall in the kitchen, turning her face with a smile to the child who asked for some little thing, she was not happy. Not happy when she took the children skating to the rink and they held hands to the Blue Danube waltz. Not happy when her father was working and they went out to have hot turkey sandwiches at the truck stop on the highway. Her mother was happy now, humming in the car, and she had been especially happy when she saw the bookstore man. Suzanne knew and because it was too much to know she put the knowledge away from her.

Today it returned. Suzanne stood where the bookstore used to be. So her mother had a lover. For twenty-five years this knowledge had rested in Suzanne. Today it was brought forward, only today. By now the knowledge had no power to hurt her: it was merely interesting. Or more than interesting, a message. Her first feeling was pity. Her mother had loved that man, perhaps as passionately as she, Suzanne, loved Simon. But they had seen each other so seldom, and for such a short time! And then he had gone away. Suzanne and her mother had returned to the store, and it was locked; boxes half full of books were strewn on the floor. They'd gone to ask in the restaurant.

"That one! He was a fly-by-night," said the fat man. "Something caught up with him, I expect. He ran out on his rent too." The fat man had said this in a peculiar, savage burst of words. He must have known why they asked. Suzanne's mother must have come other times to see him, left the store with him.

Her mother turned away from the door of the restaurant, white-faced. But Suzanne had been pleased. He had been a threat, this bookstore man, an unsuitable friend. Any man who was not Suzanne's father would have been a threat, but this man was also a low life, a lost cause. He had come from another world which Suzanne found drab and vaguely dangerous, and which she now sought.

It had been a hopeless romance, even a child could see that. Suzanne's mother was not about to abandon her home, up the hill from Poverty Flats by then, with its new furniture and modernized kitchen, their new car, and most of all, her own children, for this scrawny loser. She was only flirting with the possibility. Her mother had then, and continued to have, a tendency to commit herself to lost causes. She agonized over the black-sheep relative on whom everyone else had given up. She tried to help the welfare mother who kept losing her child to a foster home, and getting him back only to lose him again because she took an unscheduled trip with a boyfriend. Her mother, like a lot of women she knew, like a good part of the female population, tried to save people. Occasionally she even succeeded. People laughed at these women even then. And the rescued ones never failed to reward their benefactors with a cruel deed, a careless slight.

Suzanne turned the corner towards the library. There was no bookstore now. She didn't think her mother even read books much any more. They had been an interest, an outlet which she gave up. Like the bookstore man. Suzanne wondered why *she* had been taken on the errands to meet him, if it had been necessary, or if there was a message in it. Perhaps her mother had intended Suzanne to know about the lover. Suzanne had no way of finding out. The days for that kind of communication were over, had been over before Suzanne could afford to hear it. Everything had been out of time in her and her mother's duet, discordant. Their reciprocal dependencies made sympathy impossible. Then Suzanne needed to believe her mother was perfect, and her mother needed Suzanne not as a child, but as a confidante. Now her mother was too old. She would not remember, or she would claim she didn't remember. So much was forgotten, and the places changed and lost, and with them the explanations of things. Time pushed everything apart.

Suzanne wanted to conflate the events of the centuries. Only the enormous, sustained effort of a fanatic could do that.

The library door spun around; she left the sun yellow and dove grey shadows for the uniform fluorescence of a public building. A group of Chinese students at the counter stuffed their knapsacks full of books. To the right was the local-history collection. Suzanne claimed a table and got out her notebook, stretching her sandalled feet across the space under the table. She had come to look for information on Rosalie, whose death was the only recorded part of her life.

Mostly out of curiosity, and not expecting to find anything, she got up and looked under *Indians — urban* in the card catalogue. There was nothing she hadn't already seen. Several small encampments of Indians had existed in Calgary in 1889. The inhabitants sold firewood, picked berries, and hired themselves out to whites for chores. The Mounties tried to chase them out of town for vagrancy, but there was nothing for them back on the reserve, only the old, the sick and the hungry. The ones who wanted to survive drifted back to town.

She pulled an article from a file. The Toronto *Globe*, 1887. "3,000 Indians at Fort Macleod Starving"; the story occupied two inches in one column. The buffalo were gone, and the land had been given to settlers. Smallpox and tuberculosis were raging amongst the natives unaccustomed to European viruses. She pulled out a photograph of a log hut; the logs were sticks really, only as big as a man's forearm, the cracks filled in with mud. There was a small fire and a few blankets. That would be how Rosalie's family lived. They had none of the homesteaders' skills, no knowledge of how to grow a garden or line the walls with newspaper to keep out the cold. But this was nothing new.

Suzanne sighed and looked up. On top of a cabinet, a new hardback book was displayed. *Women and Indians*, it was called. There was a chapter called "The Pochantas Perplex." Suzanne began to read. It was all about the two myths of Indian womanhood — the pure princess myth, and the corrupted "squaw" myth. Theories from the academy, definitive, removed, yet it held a certain truth. Hadn't the town been divided, after Rosalie's death, on whether to call her a whore or a saint? She was never just an ordinary hungry, frightened young girl.

On an impulse Suzanne put the book down, went to the clerk at the archivist's desk and asked for Mrs Stewart's memoirs. They were delivered to her, handwritten, in a binder. Good old Mrs Stewart. She had been a practical and enthusiastic early Calgarian who, in her eighties, sat down and wrote what she could remember of the town she had come to as a young married woman. She was weak on dates and details, but she gave a good feel for the place. Suzanne thought Mrs Stewart made reference to the housemaids who were chosen from among the Indian girls at the Sacred Heart Convent. There it was — just that — "We often hired the best of the Indian girls, and very good housemaids they made, too." No names, nothing more. Suzanne put her face in her hands. It was so frustrating, this search; there was nothing to give a comprehensive picture, only the oblique and random viewpoints given by diaries, newspapers, photographs.

Idly, she began flipping to the end of Mrs Stewart. A name jumped off the page. Lovingheart. Curious name. What had she said about him? "Lovingheart was tried and convicted. Many of the best women in town had to look the other way." Strange.

But it had nothing to do with Rosalie. Suzanne was very tired. She thought she was wasting her time, championing another lost cause, catching that disease of women here. The men allied themselves with progress and winning, and the women, carried along with their husbands' success, looked over their shoulders, behind, in the dust, to the losers. There was such a great gap between the winners and the losers, and no one else to bridge it. Maybe the women

felt they had no right to be in the forward group; maybe
they were absorbing the guilt of their kind.

But they were mocked for it. Time-waster! Soft-hearted!
These people deserved what they got, didn't they? Even if
they didn't, no progress was ever going to be made without
hurting a few people. All those good women Suzanne had
known in her life, dedicated to the unfortunates, and
damned by those they helped, as well as by their menfolk.
Those women seemed to be, by virtue of their good fortune
and kind hearts, forever exposed to a type of public
vandalism. It was a role Suzanne declined to play.

Suddenly in a great rush, Suzanne dropped Mrs Stewart's
memoir back to the archivist's counter, picked up her
notebook and made for the door.

At the turnstile an adolescent boy was checking out half a
dozen books on fungi; Suzanne pushed around behind him
and out. In daylight again she walked westward, watching
the city get younger. The dust was washed away. There
were no more broken window panes. The store windows
were brilliant with jewels and dresses; the shoppers carried
rustling plastic bags. She passed the brick walls of the
convention centre and entered the mall on Eighth Avenue.
It was staked out with benches and potted trees and had
become home to vendors of tacos and straw hats.

In front of the sandstone pillars of the Bay, Suzanne went
up to a kiosk. The coffee she bought was hot and slurped
into the sensitive web between her thumb and forefinger; it
made her eyes fill with water. She put the sore place in her
mouth and sucked it. She read the lettering on the side of a
pirogi stand. *Home-made. $1.85 a plate. With salad $2.25.*
Across the street, Italian boots were on sale for fifty percent
off. The air was growing whiter as the sun rose; the leaves of
the potted trees were absolutely still.

She walked over to look down First Street West towards
the train station. She couldn't help it; down there the Turf
Club had stood. Near the corner an Indian sat on a bench,
sullenly kicking a bottle that lay under his feet. His chum
stood beside him, a hand on his shoulder. The standing one

pulled his friend to his feet, and the two began to walk away from Suzanne towards Ninth. As they passed a tall, dark girl coming in the other direction, one of the men threw his hand out and caught her waist. She stopped.

The gesture, its urgency in a street filled with shoppers walking in straight lines past one another, was from another language. The three formed a circle, something was exchanged from one pocket to another, money, probably. After a few more words the men turned south and the woman continued north, directly towards Suzanne. She was wearing high heels and a shrunken T-shirt over skin-tight jeans. Her eyes shifted past the doors of the hotel she was passing. She walked slowly, strange in high heels but not ungraceful, with the air of a rare water bird making an appearance on land.

Rosalie had walked on this street, had stopped in this place, as Fisk walked up from the station. There, by what was now the hotel entrance, she had stepped forward, alone, volunteering to follow him across the street. She'd never met the man before. And she wasn't a regular. When she didn't come out, a crowd of her people had gathered, this crowd increasing until after one and a half days they saw the body carried out of the Turf Club, down the lane, behind the stables, to the undertaker's back shed, where the coffin had been delivered. There, over what was now a jewellery boutique, Rosalie's ghost had risen from the bed, passed by the men and out the door.

"It's just a story," Simon had said.

"A *true* story."

"A true story of a hooker done in by a john." And repeated what he'd said before, "You wanted me to read it. You left it by the bed."

She had left her stack of pages by the bed. But she knew why she left them by the bed. Because Miss Amy's call had woken her up, and when she had got back, Simon had surprised her before she could put the papers away. She hadn't wanted him to see.

"Are you saying it's my fault you're so curious? That I

have to put private things away, just in case you might come over?" She sounded more polite than she felt.

Simon sat calmly smiling. "Anyone would do the same."

She had gone home after their camping trip and opened the door to her room. The papers were on the desk. There was no sign of the violation. She picked up the pages and held them against her chest, aware of being melodramatic. It seemed to her she had a right to be, that he had taken advantage of her.

"I don't know why you're so excited. Some old murder. It's not exactly a state secret," he said.

But a state secret was exactly what it was. Her eyes filled with tears.

"What's *wrong*, Suzanne?"

"I don't like the way you *do* things," was all she could say.

"And I don't like the way you do things," he said with equanimity. He walked towards her. She gestured him out of the room. Backing to the door, he smiled in a kindly way. "What harm can it possibly do for me to see your research papers? You're acting as if I have some reason to be suspicious. And you've promised I have no reason, not any more."

"Oh, unfair! You're talking about Ace," she said, miserably. "But I told you, I'll never see him again." (Not after the last time, she said to herself.) "Anyway, that's a person. This is my work!" But perhaps her work was like a person to him, no more, no less than another lover.

"Who have you got hidden there?" he'd said more than once.

"No," she said. "It's simple. You're a snoop."

He came and pulled the papers out of her arms.

"Suzanne, Suzanne, calm down. You're projecting; it's so obvious. *You're* the snoop, don't you see? You and your gang of historians. That's why you're so secretive. You'll tread anywhere, over *graves*, to gain your ends. You have some secret agenda with that paper for *Studies in Western Canadian History* or whatever it is. We're all curious. We all want to know and understand. But you hide out in the past, maundering around in the dark for your answers."

It had been their first real fight. And the worst thing was Suzanne wasn't even sure they were fighting. Simon's manner was confusing. He had on his civilized face. Smiles lit on it at odd moments, smiles which were kindly, pleased, smiles at his own words. He took on the aspect of an audience to his own argument. All she knew was that she didn't want to be *known* by him, that being "known" in the total way he meant was only appropriate to the dead. Of her body he knew enough. She'd let him get in there; she didn't want to let him into her mind, to let it become a conquered territory, out of which he could coax responses she had no control over. She'd never let her psychiatrist, if she had one (she didn't, although she was beginning to think she should have), examine her tonsils.

Of course, after he'd gone she sat down to read what she'd written, herself. She had pulled up the old green leather chair, drawn the pages out of the yellow box, spread them in front of her.

She noticed the change immediately. The words had taken on a further dimension. The words were the same but they had more depth. Eyes had been on them. Not imagined eyes, the Head's, the short-sighted eyes of the evaluation committee for *Studies in Western Canadian History*, but his eyes. She hadn't wanted that invasion, but once it was made, she could not pretend it didn't matter. He had entered the work. He had become party to it. She had to ask him what he thought.

"I think you're obsessed with this Indian martyr, or whatever you want to call her. And I don't think you're writing a historical article."

It was the next evening. They were sitting side by side on the loveseat in her living room. She was twisting her hands in her lap.

"Look," said Suzanne, "I just have a feeling. I have a feeling there's more to Rosalie's story. People say it's just some aberrant sexual thing between an isolated man and a woman. That if you banned prostitution it wouldn't happen. But it's not that simple. It stands for something. That's why I want to find out about Rosalie. I don't want to leave her cast in this role forever, when there's so many things that don't fit."

"You want to redeem her," he said.

"OK, so I do."

"Fine then, as long as you've admitted it. As long as you're not pretending to be objective."

She didn't want to give up her hopes for acceptance by *Studies in Western Canadian History*. "It's an academic paper," she said. "I have to be careful."

"It's not an academic paper, don't be ridiculous. It's a *fabrication*; it's part true and part you."

Suzanne sulked.

Simon wasn't under attack now; he could be helpful.

"All right, let's talk about it," he said.

"You said it was worthless," she said.

"I didn't. It's just not an academic paper. It's something better."

Suzanne prepared to give up. What was the paper to her, anyway? A hope for promotion, for status among her colleagues? She didn't care.

"It doesn't have to have a name," he prodded. "If you're afraid to give it one."

She always denied it when someone said she was afraid. "I'm not afraid," she said.

"Then talk about it." He remembered the names, made the connections. He asked for more details. "Who was Lowry?" "What about Fisk's family?" They were things she didn't know, but could find out.

"I just have a feeling," she said. "A feeling." And as he kept asking questions, she weakened. "Oh, but it's probably nothing. I can't find anything to back it up. I'm probably wrong anyway."

"Don't do that to yourself!" He struck the arm of the loveseat as she recoiled. "You're always selling yourself short. You've got the instinct, then follow up! Follow up!"

His harlequin face was charged and generous in the light of the table lamp. He took off his glasses. His eyes were moist and slightly unfocussed. He was showing how to walk in the dark again, listening to the sounds, feeling the textures. If there were no signposts, it didn't matter. She was going somewhere no one else had been.

"Do you think I've gone a little too far with Murphy?"

"No, no," he said. "You can't go too far." He took her face in his two hands. "Just follow your instincts."

Suzanne stared. She loved Simon more than ever. "I will remember this moment," she thought, "long after my story is finished, and maybe even after *our* story is finished. Whatever else Simon does to me, he did this. He gave me this one precious thing."

Suzanne turned on her heel, threw her styrofoam cup into the mall garbage bin and strode back to the library. She spun through the turnstile and marched up to the desk at the local-history section.

"We close at one," said the archivist. He was packing up.

"Lovingheart," said Suzanne.

"Ah yes," he said. "Our backstreet abortionist."

"Aha. Didn't know we had one. Amazing name, isn't it?" The archivist looked at her strangely.

"Well, that's about all I know. There's that bit about him in Mrs Stewart's memoirs. He practised here in the eighties and he was tried, I think, in the nineties. Wait a minute."

There was very little. People don't write about abortionists; abortionists fall out of history like stones. Here and there his name was mentioned, in passing, as if everyone knew who he was and no one had to say more. Maybe she'd find something in the police records. Or maybe in the weekly *Herald* on microfilm. Still Suzanne didn't mind. She had his name. She established that he had been there in 1889. That was enough.

Freed from the requirements of *Studies in Western Cana-*

dian History, she could do anything. A fabrication was it? Then she could feel her way. She could make it up.

And now the library began to irritate her. The hissing of dry papers was in her ears. She moved her chair closer to the table; it squawked. The air felt dusty and dry; she wanted a coffee. She put the files back together and left them on the desk. She used to love the authority of archives, but something had changed. The archives were the same, so it must be her. She wanted her spare room, to lay her notes out on the bare pine floor, to bend the goose-necked lamp over a fresh piece of paper, and to go forward.

Chapter 12

Townspeople packed the immigration shed to the door. Pressed deep in their midst, noticeable only for their uncovered heads of dark hair were New Grass and his wife. Beside them was the tall and rigid young man, Rosalie's brother.

Fisk's fancy eastern lawyer stood before the judge, lightly, on puppet's feet, which lifted as he spoke.

"My first move, my lord, is to ask you to have the parents of the deceased removed from the court." Mr Justice Rouleau was a little man with eyes that pouted into his cheeks and rosebud lips under a waxed moustache. His voice made up for it; he picked his words and delivered them with a great, commanding flourish.

"What ever for?"

"Their presence prejudices my client's case, my lord. It's a known effect. They create sympathy for the deceased." The lawyer raised his eyebrows in the direction of the Indians, stopping just short of accusing them of unfair tactics.

"Indeed?" issued Rouleau. "Anyone else you'd like to see put out? Any other detractors from your case?"

"Well," said the lawyer, edging sideways to look at his

papers, his elbows up, waving before his chest. He hadn't anticipated such luck.

"I suppose the other Indian people — "

"Exactly!" boomed Rouleau. His rosebud lips broke into a merry smile. "Do you think we're that stupid, out here? If they have no right, who does? No sir, I'm afraid you're going to have to argue your case before those most affected by the crime."

Outside the wind blew. A March wind, though they called it April here, erratic and rough, a mixture of the dead cold of winter and the heathen, obscene smells of a coming spring. The shed which served as courtroom was on the south side of the railway tracks; it amused me each morning to see the upstanding Calgary citizenry pick its way across to this glorified lean-to. Its thin walls seemed to creak and rattle with the pressure of public feeling. I suppose I felt superior, not part of the gawkers, because I had my pen, my notebook.

"...that the said William Fisk feloniously, wilfully and of his malice aforethought did kill and murder one Rosalie, a Cree squaw...against the Peace of our Lady the Queen, Her Grace and Dignity..."

The handcuffed giant looked composed, too composed. He didn't open his mouth except to yawn. If he had friends around him, he did not look at them. If he trusted the lawyer his family had sent here, or if he mistrusted him, he showed none of it.

"The accused has nothing to say in his defence."

The crowd wasn't getting much in the way of entertainment. Already I'd sat through two days while they tried to empanel a jury. If Fisk's side found a man acceptable, the Crown rejected him. No one wanted the job of serving on the jury, that was it. They soon learned how to disqualify themselves. "The girl only got what she was asking for," one said straight away. "There ought to be no trial, the affair should be hushed up," said another. One fellow came out and admitted he didn't like Catholics. That was funny, because Rouleau, being French, was a Catholic just like

Rosalie. You see, no-one wanted to stick his neck out. Fisk was everyone's friend. For a while it looked like Rouleau was going to give up and move the trial, the way the eastern lawyer wanted him to. But finally, he did find six men who, when duty called, did not turn away. And the trial began.

Inside the rough wool of my suit, I felt clammy. Although the shed was poorly heated and the air outside still full of ice crystals, there was steam on the windows. I looked at Constable Dillabough, down the row. On his feet were enormous heavy boots, a thick sole of leather and uppers with laces; by the tongue of the boot I could see the grey wool of his regulation sock. I imagined his foot, white and thin and quite perishable, damageable flesh, inside, and felt distaste.

Whitbeck came on the witness stand. His face was white and he moved his lips as if they were frozen.

"Had you seen the dead woman before February 28th?" said the lawyer.

"She hung around outside the club, sir, you know how the squaws do. Yes, I'm sure I'd seen her before."

He was lying. I knew it; almost everyone else knew it too. I could feel my stomach, straining against the waist of my pants, and my underarms were beginning to itch. I let my mind go off on its own. It went off on its own all too easily now, because I was alone so much. No one to talk to. My wife gone, my son silent and seemingly hostile. We lived in the same house, passed and greeted and spoke, but the boy was a cypher to me.

They all came on the stand, one after the other, as the fancy eastern lawyer tried to set down the lay of the land, from his client's point of view. Dillabough, Murdoch. Dr Lafferty got up, finally, and described the body as it was when he found it. He was very clinical, he had to be. The injuries were to parts of the female anatomy the lay individual didn't even have names for. What a mess it all was. The ripped flesh, the blood, the bruising.

I had to say my pen paused on my paper; then it lifted

right up so I couldn't even write. I'm as interested as anyone else, in this case. And I know it'll make good copy. I could feel the spectators all around me drinking it in, the gory details of the murder, or accidental death, whatever it was. Never before had the arts of description failed me. It wasn't that I couldn't find the words. It was that I didn't *want* to find the words. I began to think, this was no ordinary death. This was death that made other deaths look easy. It didn't seem right to be scribbling notes about it. It was better to sit back and wonder.

The most amazing thing, to me, was that there seemed to be no reason for it. They said Fisk wasn't drunk, and I don't think he was. No quarrel took place, there was no theft, as far as anyone could tell. It looked like a simple exchange — sex, for money. Mind you the girl was not experienced. But there must have been some wick lit, if Fisk indeed killed her, some symbolic revenge taken.

There was no simple explanation for behaviour in sexual matters, I concluded. Take the sudden lust displayed by my previously obedient and intelligent wife! That's all the evidence one might ever need for such an argument. Still it was strange, the Indian girl meeting such a fate. If she had been a whore I could have said she had taught whoring to Evangeline. No, more likely it was a kind of madness, possibly contagious, that had touched my wife and then her maid. I honestly wished to hear no more about it.

But I was a reporter; I had to stay. And I did, I suppose, retain a sort of curiosity about horrors of this nature. It was simply from the hope, I said to myself, the *hope* that someday a cure might be discovered, a means of retrieving those lost to mental disturbances brought on by an excess of sexual feelings. Perhaps something could be done in a civic way.

By now the miserable Kelsey was speaking.

"Jumbo came out and made the remark to me that there was a little blood on the bed as this woman had her flowers. He then asked me to go into the room as he believed the woman was dead. This was before we went to supper. Yes, we went to supper."

"Where did you go?" said the defence lawyer. "Where did you sit?"

"The Windsor Hotel. We sat at the table nearest the window."

"What did you eat?"

Titters went through the shed. The lawyer was stupid. He wasn't doing his client any good having a description of the roast beef dinner he ate while Rosalie died. Or maybe he had another reason in mind. It was Kelsey he got to say it, after all. It made Kelsey look worse than Fisk.

" — and yorkshire puddin'. About half an hour it was. I looked at the clock a lot." Kelsey was almost snivelling. He got thinner and paler in the lock-up while Fisk looked just the same as the day he went in.

Oh, the trial went on some more that first day. The lawyer had men describing staircases, doorways and who passed whom at what time, but these discussions did not erase, from my mind at least, the impression that had been given. Half a dozen men in a two-storey timber building heard a woman groaning while she was torn open from the inside, and said they didn't know what it was. And the men who did know went to dinner, leaving her to bleed to death. There could be no mistaking these facts, now, seen from a distance. It seemed to me when I *was* there — I had to remind myself I *was* there — that a spell had been on us all.

The men of the jury watched the witnesses or stared at their knees. I watched New Grass and his wife. They were not old, they might be forty, they were certainly younger than me. This was not their law, nor their Queen. They stood static, indeed even ironic. They did not look a part of the proceedings. The mother caught my eye. I nodded in recognition of her grief. She looked away. What was I to her? Just another prurient gawker. If I were strictly honest, and I want to be strictly honest, in writing here, since I can not be in daily life, it gave me a bizarre sort of thrill. She absolutely did not know my connection with her daughter.

That night at home, alone, I sat, my letterbox on my knee. I wrote many letters in those days. I kept copies of everything, too, in a specially made book with carbon sheets after every page. It pleased me to see my words building up like this, final and set and dignified.

Dearest Jessie,
    The trial of the unfortunate Fisk continues apace and I only wish it over so the townspeople can go back to other topics of conversation. It is a strange and bewildering case, my dear sister; I fear its consequences will be felt for some time. It looks to my mind as if there were two murders: the physical one, caused by brutality of hand, and the mental one, by brutality of mind. These men can be like animals. Certainly, they left an Indian woman to suffer the way you would not an animal. And sadly, it comes at a time when Calgary has begun to grow, to reach some sense of itself. We are closer now to electric lighting for the streets and after that will come sewers, no doubt. I still have no buyer for my land. Thus far I have taken every opportunity to support the growth that will elevate it to the value projected when I came here. But without you, dear sister, and my wife, the whore —

There came a knock at my door. I rose, straightening my waistcoat, shaking down my pants over my long knees. I was always careful not to seem an untidy old man. I peered through the window by my door. There on the street, light falling on her form but not her face, stood a woman.

"Murphy, are you alone?"

Incredulous, I looked more closely. She wouldn't dare! But yes. It appeared to be the very devil of whom I had been writing, materialized at my doorstep.

"I don't wish to disturb you Murphy but I must talk to you."

I opened the door abruptly and drew her in, whether in urgent tenderness or in anger I was not sure. Not knowing what I intended to do, I shut the door behind her. All I could think was that the neighbours must not see.

She stood on my bit of carpet, snow on her boots and a blanket of some sort draped over her bonnet. I touched my hair, knowing, all of a sudden, that I had aged.

"Evangeline! What are you doing out? The streets are not safe!"

"Nonsense," she said, removing the shawl. I was reminded of her unfeminine lack of tact, and became irritated. But reprimand, with which I had once been so free, was no longer permitted. I turned away.

"Are you alone?"

"My son is out," I said, reclaiming the boy I had once begged her to mother. I did not offer to take my wife's outer clothes, but pulled my watch from my pocket. "You must be quick, he could come home any minute." I had decided that Evangeline must be in trouble and wanted money. I was stirred up inside, but imagined this had to do with the day, and my thoughts, to which, thank the good Lord, she was not privy.

"You are writing the newspaper reports."

"A letter," I said, gesturing.

"But you *are* writing the reports."

My nose twitched, my lips moved to the left. I have said it was one of my abilities, to smell news. I had a talent to be where news came from. One best achieved this position by seeming to be nowhere at all, by seeming to be no one at all. My instincts did not betray me that night, even before my wicked wife. I realized that she must know something. I barely nodded; best not to move too much. I absorbed the defiant set of my visitor's face, and saw that she was not frightened of me. It was not she herself, then, who was involved.

"I heard what Whitbeck was saying about Rosalie," Evangeline said. "You know it's absolute slander."

I lost my composure instantly. I could never have been

husband to this woman! I rattled my cheeks; my voice cracked out louder than I expected. "You were *there*? Your whoremaster ought not to let you go there. It's not to do with you. It's something between men — "

"He's not my whoremaster, he's my lover. And he doesn't tell me what to do. It's my business, too. She was my friend!"

"You mean that for a year she worked in your kitchen!"

"No I don't mean that. She was my friend. Yours too, a little."

"No," I said.

"You know those men are lying. Swearing on the Bible and telling lies."

I held my head still. I knew they were lying. I just could not bear to hear her say it. Women ought to believe men. It put my loyalty in conflict with my sense of truth. Evangeline had so many irritating traits. This cleverness was the worst.

"It simply isn't true she'd been in and out of that terrible place. I ran into her on the street only a week before she died, and she was the same sweet girl she'd been when she left us."

I made a vague sideways gesture with my hand. The reporter in me won out. She did know something. The other hand went inadvertently to my pocket for pen and notebook. Not there — on the desk. To reach for it would be too obvious. In the absence of a writing tool, my mind moved up from mere listening to another level, recording. Now I would forget nothing.

"You spoke to her when you saw her on the street?"

"I did." Evangeline's chin wobbled but she did not cry; for this I was grateful. I began to stroke my beard; I gazed into my wife's face. What did she know? She looked back at me clearly. I was Murphy, investigator, I saw her as if from a point two feet above and behind my head. I humoured her. She might know something but she did not know it all.

"You're right. She was a good girl."

"Make them say so, Murphy."

"You imagine I have such powers. I am flattered." Yet I was unable to leave it at that. "I suppose, if we agree on her goodness, we may yet inquire what she was doing upstairs in the Turf Club?" It was much like arguments we'd had when Rosalie was in the house. The fact that my wife was close to the girl had made me find fault. "Was it the first time?"

Evangeline just looked at me, trying to shame me.

"You're going to say she was desperate. But if she needed something why didn't she go to you for help? Or me?"

"Does it matter?" said Evangeline, surprising me.

"Does what matter?"

"Her reason for being there."

"Well," I spluttered, "to the man on trial for his life — "

"Is his crime less if she went there to earn money?"

"Not exactly, but — "

"She had fourteen dollars on her person and Fisk never paid her," said Evangeline.

"She did," I commented. It was neither a question nor a statement, the way I put it. "What do you think that was for?"

"I think I know what it was for, but not where she got it."

"You think you know." I lay my finger by my nose. "I think she intended to pay for something. She was looking for someone."

"Come, come." My hand went to my beard again and moved faster up and down. "What could she possibly...? She told you this?"

"No."

I assured myself that Evangeline positively did not know. But with her infuriating instincts, which I had to admit would have made her a wonderful reporter had she been a man, she was getting close.

"I think she needed help, a certain kind of help. There was something about her eyes. Maybe because I wanted it so long, I can always see it in a woman. I just realized today *what* I had seen in her. She was pregnant."

I spluttered. A pulse, a jagged lightning stroke, went through my eye, through my face down the right side of my mouth. Evangeline went on.

"And if that was true, she went to the Turf Club looking for Lovingheart."

For a moment I ignored her preposterous suggestion, which was only a guess. "What do you know about Lovingheart?" I demanded.

"All women know."

"Not good women."

"You don't know what women know, you never listen to them. You refuse to believe women even exist when you're not there."

The unfairness of this comment was so horrible that I struck my forehead and sprang away from Evangeline so that I might not strike her. She stepped forward. I swear her quickness was the devil's own.

"Perhaps you visited him yourself," I said terribly. Much as I hated this woman, I could remember my hopes for a child from her womb. I had blamed her for our barrenness, but never enough, it seemed.

Evangeline's little pointed lip curled. "I most certainly have not. I've had no need." Her voice became coarse when she was taunted; mine rose when I taunted her, in a kind of glee. Astonishing that these months could pass and the shattering memories recede, that she could return, and within a matter of minutes it could all be restaged, the grand opera of our mistaken, miserable marriage.

"In any case," I said, trying to get my footing back, trying to draw back my powers of reason from the cliffs where they teetered. "If," I said, "if, by any stretch of the imagination it so happened Rosalie were pregnant, it hardly argues for her virtue."

Evangeline drew back as well, and pulled her shawl up to go. "You and I never did agree on what constituted virtue."

"Just what do you mean to imply?"

"She may have been pregnant by a man she loved, one who could not or would not support her and her child."

At that my poise collapsed. My throat filled up with anger, my eyes with tears. It was too pointed, too close to the heart. I followed her to the door, bent and shambling, like a prisoner in my own house.

"Why do you come here to say this? What are you asking me to do?"

But she did not answer my question. Instead she said something odd.

"You used to believe in things, or was that a pose as well?"

She was leaving. Already I missed her. I was humbled. I was at her feet, as always. Yet I could not accept it. "Why do you accuse me? I'm a good man, I am. What is it that you think you know?"

She had that erect posture of all proper women; how misleading it was, I thought. She wasn't proper at all. The door opened and shut. I rushed out after her, and grasped her hands. I didn't care about the neighbours, once I held her hands.

"Vangie, even if you were right. What good would the truth do Rosalie now? She's dead."

"There are those she left behind."

My mind went to New Grass, his wife, and the brother. Their strangely passive hating eyes. For them, yes, but they were lost already. Their story was done. History had consumed them. They knew it; the knowledge was obvious in their eyes. The end. Amen. But that was not what Evangeline meant. She meant something larger; she had in mind for me some even more frightening task than to save these Indian parents from their doubts. She had always wanted me to sacrifice my ambitions for some generally improved moral stance. It had never made sense.

I dropped her hands. "You never did understand how the world works."

"Perhaps not. Perhaps I understand something more important." Her eyes were silken on me.

I was helpless. This was what it was about, this was what it had always been about. She was too strong, too good for me. She had to set herself against the whole world. I couldn't go with her. I couldn't let her go.

"But there *is* nothing more important," I said. I didn't want to lose her again. I could have stood arguing all night.

She withdrew gently. "My sad old man."

And then she was gone.

Chapter 13

Suzanne was making muffins. She did it every year. Raspberry, it used to be when they were kids and went picking along the river bank. Gooseberry, if they went out in the country to the north. Blueberry, when they were in season, late July and August. She had bought two little square open-topped boxes of Ontario blueberries covered with green net at the Greek greengrocer on Tenth Street. She got out her muffin tins, lined up the baking soda, baking powder, vanilla and salt on the counter, and pulled out her canister of flour. As she combined the wet and dry ingredients she looked over her shoulder at the papers on the tiny table where she had coffee in the morning. Her divorce papers had come in the mail.

"Decree Nisi," it said in ornate black lettering. There was a round raised stamp and a thick red seal. A decree was a pronouncement of high seriousness, a message from the imperial powers. Suzanne was impressed.

As the muffins browned, she picked up the papers again. She had only glanced at them when she first opened the envelope. She examined the declaration. She rarely saw her full name, or Ace's. Ashley Cummings. In the American style, his mother had given him her surname as his first

name. She had been Miss Amy Ashley. And Suzanne had
been, and still was, Miss Suzanne Margo Vail. She wondered
what had possessed her mother to give her the name of
Margo. If she had been Margo only, or even Margo
Suzanne, she would have been someone else entirely.
Perhaps a Stampede Queen, or at least a candidate. She
would have gushed when claiming her ribbons at the horse
show, "I think my whole life has been sports." She would
have had Harry the Horse at her bridal shower. She would
still be married.

Not that she regretted anything. Although Ace had
started it all with his affair with Titian, it was Suzanne who
finished off the marriage. When the court date came at
last, only a month ago, he hadn't even turned up. His
absence had caused a moment's semantic confusion.

Jennifer's friend, examining in gown, held up a black and
white photograph and said, "Do you know this man?"

Suzanne knew the man. She also knew the picture. It
was a good one, head and shoulders. Behind him and to
the right, not showing, was a chair lift. She had taken the
photo herself, in the mountains, on a ski holiday at least
ten years ago. She even remembered the jacket he was
wearing. It had been burgundy with grey trim. She had
smiled involuntarily. Yes, she knew that man. The problem
was how to indicate that knowledge, how to describe what
she knew.

"Yes," she said.

The woman lawyer put the picture down and gave
Suzanne a strange look, as if to say "you aren't helping
much." Her type was obviously not prey to these dilemmas
of category which overtook Suzanne. She would not have
understood what it was that was making Suzanne smile.
"Who is it then?" she said.

Suzanne pondered. She might have said "It's Ashley
Cummings," but that sounded forced, even pretentious,
too distant and formal. The alternative was to say "it's my
ex-husband," but that was premature, and could be taken
as presumption. They were asking the judge for this

divorce, after all, and they might not be given it. The judge might, like a schoolteacher, say they hadn't tried hard enough, they had to go back and start again. Caught between these choices, Suzanne said nothing.

"Could you tell the court who he is?" the lawyer said more loudly. Somehow the whole business of getting the divorce had come down to this: was Suzanne able to say in one simple sentence who Ace was? Who he was to *her*.

"He's my husband." She smiled brightly, too brightly. Suzanne was such a good girl, and conscious of taking up the court's time, of making things awkward for the friend of her friend the lawyer. Trying too hard, she put more enthusiasm than was appropriate in the words "my" and "husband." She sounded more like a newlywed than an applicant for a divorce. She had blushed, and had been surprised when the judge ruled that there were irreconcilable differences, and hence the divorce could go ahead. She had been sure she had not made a convincing case, and had failed the test.

But no, she had passed. Here was her diploma. Proof of citizenship in the country of free women, women with lives of their own and self-sufficient definitions, definitions which did not rely on or include someone else. Women who had lovers and did what they wanted, and survived. Perhaps, she thought, she should fold it and carry it in her wallet, like a driver's licence. But first she would display it. Gemma was coming over for tea.

The muffins rose up out of the white frill of baking cups, round hillocks touched with brown and studded with blue-purple blood of the berries. Gemma took one off the plate and began to peel back the paper. She was eating again. SWARM had convinced her that she needed some curves. She eyed the divorce papers on the coffee table a little distance away. "Don't want to get grease on them," Suzanne had said.

"You know I really liked Ace's father," said Gemma.

"Block?"

"Does he have another one?"

For a minute Suzanne couldn't think where Gemma had met Block. Then she knew. The barbecue, scene of the tennis racquet attack by her ex- (now she could say it) husband.

"He's so youthful," mused Gemma.

Suzanne poured the tea. "He's one thing I won't miss," she said.

"He asked me if I'd like to ride on the go-carts with him one day."

Gemma was putting Suzanne through a test. She was asking Suzanne to prove that she had no further interest in the Cummings family, to renounce them totally.

"You'd better watch out," Suzanne said. "That man is trouble. He's too big a fish for you."

Gemma was tearing the muffin into small pieces, and putting the pieces down in rows on her plate. "Oh, I won't go," she said. "Do you think I'm a fool? He's married."

Suzanne laughed. "It's never stopped you before."

"His wife doesn't look well though, does she? How horrid it must be for him, stuck with that *husk* when he's so vital — "

"Gemma! You're talking about my mother-in-law!"

"Former."

"For ten years."

Gemma wiped her hands daintily on a paper napkin. She tossed her hair. It was done in a new way, in shiny curls across the front of her head, like a row of pin curls invisibly stuck to her scalp. "Former," she said. "You don't have the right to be possessive about her any more, Suzanne."

She gave in. "I know. I just like Miss Amy, OK?"

Gemma shook her head as if that were a statement too insane to contemplate. "Anyway," she said, "we've got him on our list." There was no doubt who "we" were.

Suzanne and Simon sat in the three-cornered living room. They had eaten salmon steak. She had made a ceremony of presenting the decree. They were now on to the wine-soaked strawberries. She sat opposite him, on the loveseat; he was in the armchair. She felt romantic, more than romantic, electric. She felt as if her body were being drawn towards him, as if its cells were clear fluid sliding down an incline.

"I missed you all day," he said, at the same time as she said, "Don't you think it's exciting? I'm free."

"I missed you," he continued as if he hadn't heard, "in a very precise way. I needed to talk to you. I always want to speak to you when something new comes up. I really enjoy bouncing my ideas off you."

"Pardon me?"

"You're a very special woman, you know. I've tried to figure out what it is, exactly. And I think I've got it. You're independent." He said independent the way some men say "snake"; he said it as though it fascinated him and repelled him at the same time. "You don't just pretend to be, to attract a man, and then crumble, like a — like a — macaroon. You really are. So it's very good for me."

Suzanne's head was longing to be laid down on something. It was almost rolling off her shoulders.

"Strong," he marvelled. "You really are strong. Maybe you're even stronger than me ..."

The marrow had virtually vacated her bones, leaving her no hope of remaining erect. She stretched herself across the loveseat, let her head fall back, and dropped her forearm over her eyes. Simon showed no sign of moving; peeking around her elbow she saw that he was pondering her characteristics in an upright position, his elbows on the arm rests.

Music, she thought, sets a mood. She walked to the stereo. His eyes were on her back, her calves, her hips. She bent slowly to the row of record folders, touched their plasticized spines and began to push them one by one so that they flopped at the other angle. Mussorgsky, Romanian Rhapsody, Liszt, too wild. Here, Bach organ concertos. She drew the record out carefully, light fingers on its edges, before she laid it on the turntable. She knew he was following every movement. She pressed the start button and the arm lifted, finding the first groove with robotic accuracy.

"Come here!" said Simon.

She let herself be pulled to his lap, tilted back. She felt him tighten his arms around her. Sonorous chords filled the room. She put her arms around his neck and kissed his ear. She ran her hand down his shirt front. She found his belt buckle and pulled on it. Suddenly his hold relaxed.

"I can't tonight."

The organ music was a mistake. She turned it off, and retreated to her position on the loveseat. After what seemed like ages he came up to her and they lay down side by side, cramped.

"Men are very extended, very vulnerable, when they make love," he said.

She put her hand on his heart. It was thumping very slowly. He looked old.

"This was once compensated for by social factors," he continued. "Previously, if I were to make myself vulnerable to you, I would have your hand in marriage, I would have had assurance that no other man other than myself had been with you, or ever would be, for that matter..."

"You mean like several hundred years ago?"

"No, even a decade ago. You feminists have forgotten something. You don't respect the intricacies of the power balance. Everything has been disturbed now, everything. You go into love like a lioness, all confidence, no modesty."

Suzanne got up and went to the window. It was still not midnight. The sky was dark, glimmering with hints of cloud. Their first night, walking by the dull shine of the river, Simon had been quick and sure, jumping off the curb, that lightness in his feet. She thought he was like a kid. Now she knew more about that lightness. It was the agility of a mountain animal, which chose the dangerous ledges, the impassable routes, appearing on some rocky outcrop and crying danger, then running back, defying aid.

"I'm a terrible lover," he said, "you must hate me."

"I don't hate you!"

"I think I'm inhibited because I am wondering if you are comparing me to Ace."

"Ace! How could you be thinking about Ace, today of all days? All this time you've been waiting for my divorce. Now it's here." Suzanne let petulance into her tone. "What else can I do for you to show that it's over?"

"There," he said, seizing on her little indulgence with satisfaction. "I knew it. You're blaming it on me. You're sorry you got divorced, aren't you?"

"I am not." A dark suspicion came to her mind. "But maybe you are."

He gave her a long glance, and pulled himself up off the loveseat.

"You never stopped asking when it would come!"

Now he would be kind. "I know, I know. But now that it's here, I think you've changed. You're different."

"How am I different?" she whispered, looking at the streetlight across the street.

"You're available."

You're different. You're not the same. The eternal cry of lovers: you are altering yourself, altering something that is mine. How speedily the change had come. And once it came, it was relentless. At first they pretended it was nothing. They tried to outrun it, to make plans, to pin themselves into the positions of before.

Simon had news. A week after the divorce came through he dropped over to talk.

"I got a phone call," he said. A pleased and private smile was on his face. "I'm going to Washington."

"Washington?" A forlorn echo attached to her voice, despite its buoyancy. "How wonderful. But why?"

"They want a lobbyist. It's a great idea. It's high time they thought of it. I've been telling them for ages — "

"Who's they?"

"Ottawa."

He'd been telling her for months it was all over with those people in Ottawa. But tonight they were so familiar they didn't even need names.

"Aren't you excited for me?" he said. "Washington?"

"For how long?"

"Oh, just a few weeks. Now, and then again next month. I'll keep my base in Calgary."

His base. Until this minute Calgary had been where he lived. He saw her face.

"We'll buy a house, I'll put you in it," he said.

She said nothing.

"Washington is real power," he said.

"I remember when you told me the only real power was standing away." She was stiff; she was not behaving as she should. She reminded him of before; she pointed out an inconsistency.

He said he didn't want to have another fight. He had work to do later on.

"I remember when you talked about absolutes. Poetry."

He turned his back to her as if she'd said something really unkind. "That was last spring!"

"Yes. Last spring."

"I was rebounding then, from a bad experience. I said a lot of things."

"You said it was all a crock, as I recall." She pushed. She was going too far. She couldn't help it.

"Times move on, Suzanne. Last year was a whole different thing. I think I'm like a lot of people, too, I was carrying around a whole lot of baggage from the sixties. I guess I've finally got beyond that. I have you to thank."

That's right, Simon, Suzanne thought. Turn your cynicism into a necessary development, turn it into a trend. Make a slogan out of it. And then she was ashamed of having thought that unkind thing, and she pushed the thought away.

Suzanne pulled her car up in front of the door to Simon's

hotel. He materialized behind the doorman and dragged out three suitcases. When the suitcases were in the trunk, he jumped into the front seat beside her and leaned over for a kiss.

"Can you believe I've spent four months in that slum? Riding the elevator, eating those watery scrambled eggs?"

Four months. That's how long they'd been together. It was only an hour. It was nine years. They were older now than when they had met. They had been happy for four months.

"At least it was a business expense," she said, "you could write it off."

"I'd rather live in a house."

Simon was moving his things to Suzanne's house while he was away in Washington. It seemed to him silly to spend the money for the room and not be in it. Suzanne wasn't entirely pleased.

"Why don't you buy one then?"

He put his hand on her thigh and stroked it down to the knee, pinching the muscle that was tight from pushing the gas pedal.

"Buying now would be silly, unless we looked together. We'll be living together soon."

"I don't want to look for a new house. I like the one I've got."

"It's a very nice little place," he conceded. "It's just a bit small. I could probably manage, though, if I moved my work into your spare room."

A silence followed, while she spun around a traffic circle. His voice became a little testy. "Obviously the longer you wait on this, the greater the inconvenience to me," he said, with a growing tone of grievance.

"Wait on what?"

"Selling your house."

She pressed her foot harder on the accelerator. They were the push-me, pull-you beast from her Dr Doolittle books. One half going one direction, the other the opposite.

Before they could get anywhere, one of them had to give up. It wasn't going to be her. "With this slump, the market's no good for selling."

"You'll get a better price now than in a year. It's not going to get any better." They were in his territory now, prediction.

"Oh really?" He might be right and that made her angry. "Why will it get worse? Buttons and knobs again?" His clever act of legislation had been blamed for an exodus of business from the city. And now the feds were sending him to Washington, to bring the business back again.

"Anyway," Simon sighed. "It'll just have to wait. I have all I can handle with this trip east."

"Right," said Suzanne. And wondered where she would store his cases.

Suzanne and Simon slumbered in bed. As the slumber lengthened, their consciousnesses crossed. His passed downward into deep sleep, and hers rose up to wake. She had a dull ache in her stomach. She got it now every time they made love. She had been ignoring it. Tonight, however, she could not. Instead, awake at night, she examined it. What was it? It was longing. Despite the frenzy, fruitlessness. That Friday lunch feeling again. Sunday pre-dawn in your own bed with a man who wanted to move in was just as bad.

And what was she longing for? Some release that did not come from orgasm. Something further. Suzanne was confused. She had made her choice; she had (she thought) severed herself from her old life. She had moved into the unfettered future. But the future was moving on and looking like it would be different than she had imagined. It was moving on, and anyway, it was not going to be enough.

Bolder than on earlier sleepless nights, she slid out of the sheets and crept over the carpet and down the stairs to the corner of the kitchen where she kept the brandy. There she poured herself a draught and climbed back upstairs to bed. She was lonely. She wanted company. But Simon was here.

How could she be lonely? It came to her suddenly what kind of company she wanted. She wanted another life inside her, a child.

Suzanne had already had one baby: Marlyss Vail Cummings. And she had lost her. The grief, the doctors told Suzanne and Ace, was cyclical. It would ease, and then return. Suzanne said, after it happened, that she would never try again. The very thought of purposefully bringing on herself all that pain had been horrible. But now she thought: I cannot be childless. It is a false proposition. I don't have a baby but I *am* a mother; the baby I want is here, a large emptiness in my belly, a palpable ache.

Suzanne's baby was gone, the baby Suzanne had made. But the woman, the mother this baby had made of Suzanne was not gone. It was an old warning. Once a mother, always a mother. She had known this once. She had known that the baby was part of her that could not be discarded, but that her husband was an option. She had forgotten, in the interim. She, Suzanne, was a childless mother. She must have a child to be complete. She sat in the dark, and looked inside herself. She thought she knew herself before, but now the eyepiece of the kaleidoscope had been turned. All the little pieces were the same, but they made a different design.

She was ambushed by the emptiness. At first she tried to analyze it. Where had it come from? A buildup of unfertilized eggs in her system? Or from the chemistry of loving Simon? Why did it happen then, there, in that bed, at that hour, beside Simon? It was as if the old child, the phantom child, had crawled in from the night to ask for existence.

Then she embraced it, this long-resisted, now welcome thing. She wanted a child. "I want a child," she said in the still room.

Now it was true, and everything had changed. She wallowed in the new feeling. She wanted to be heavy, restful, stopped in her tracks. She wanted to be pregnant, full to bursting. She wanted her recreational self to be tuned into the necessities of life, food, warmth, shelter.

She wanted to serve in this way, and to go on from there, to fuss with tiny items of wearing apparel, the names of which she didn't even know. To tuck the edges of downy quilts into cribs while creatures with heads soft as corn silk lay helpless in sleep. And then to go on from there, to read rhymes, and make Pablum, and to take a walk for no reason at all, to go nowhere at all, with someone who stood the height of her knee. She could see the child, already, when she closed her eyes.

Simon slept on.

In the morning Suzanne put grapefruit and coffee on the dining-room table while Simon showered. She found her antique peach silk dressing gown with the lace collar. She went outside and cut a last rose from the garden, overblown and tacky, and put it in a glass bowl on the table. Simon came out of the bathroom frowning. He didn't like her shower.

"The pressure's lousy," he said, going down on the chair with a thud. She poured him coffee.

"I know you're right about us," she said, "we'll be together for a long time," she said, kissing his neck.

"It's what I've been saying since the night we met." He bent over his grapefruit.

"And that means there's something we should talk about."

"The house?" he said, hopefully.

"No. Children."

She hadn't meant to put it in the plural.

Simon looked up at her with juice running from his lips. Perhaps he thought she had said something truly fantastic, perhaps he hadn't heard.

"A child anyway." She had to be mindful of his age.

"What child?"

"Ours."

He threw his napkin in the air. "Talk about timing!" The paper napkin drifted gently to the rug without making a sound. "We never talked about a child," he said with the tone of a man whose luck has run out.

"I would like to have a child."

"Today?" He looked at his watch. "I've got a plane to catch. Are you nuts?" He picked up the napkin, and stood. "You sure pick your times."

"But Simon, if we've made this commitment..."

When a quarrel is trivial, it is possible to shout. Some are too important to be carried on noisily. Their voices were forcibly low-key; it was as if they hardly spoke. The walls absorbed it all. Movement slowed to the ceremonial, as Suzanne continued to serve breakfast.

"We *have* made a commitment but I've got to go to Washington."

"We don't have to start today."

He threw up his hands.

"Some men would be pleased." She poured herself a cup of coffee. It wasn't hot enough.

"Is that right?" he said. He turned his sharp, beady profile, his uncivilized side. "Well, why don't you ask 'some men' then?"

Tears formed in her eyes. She had no control over her behaviour. She was on this gangplank, and she was walking. He came to put his hands on her shoulders.

"I am flattered, OK Suzanne? We'll do it some day, for sure. But you just got divorced. What's the rush?"

Suzanne didn't know what the rush was. She just knew it was there. She wound her arms around his neck, and stretched her leg out of the front closing of her gown. Her foot curled like a little hand and went up inside of his leg. She drew him up on the stairs behind her to the unmade bed, loosened his tie and shirt and seduced him. It was so easy.

And then he was late. He had a plane to catch. He got up to wash. Suzanne lay on the bed, her satin dressing gown open around her, crying. The fact that he wanted her and did not want her baby offended her. She also noticed that although he had no time to talk, he had time to make love. The other night it had been the opposite; all he would do was talk. It always had to be his way. She looked at his bare feet going down the hall to the bathroom for his second shower this morning. Skinny ankles, flat feet with toes like slashes; he was not quite human.

But Suzanne excused him, and blamed herself. How could he understand? She hadn't told him about Marlyss. She began to wonder if this desire to have a child had been behind everything that had happened since the spring: a yet-to-be-conceived being had pushed her to fall in love with Simon and to get free of her latent marriage. But love, now she had it, seemed sinfully indulgent. Love was just play. Something more lasting had to be made.

Simon came back in his towel. She watched him dress to go, unencumbered. It came to her that the contraption she relied upon to be a playtime lover was a trick that men played on women. Never mind that it was her own insistence, and not his, or any man's, that kept her childless until then. She was playing by his rules. The rules left him free to leave her. For Simon she had chosen: she had put away other possibilities. He asked her to be faithful, to be with him and no one else. Now she asked him to take the next step, have a child. Fidelity was for men, for procreation, wasn't it? It was to protect his paternity. The farmer takes a wife, the wife takes a child.

Simon pulled a fresh shirt out of her closet. Suzanne had learned how to develop theories, from a master. Now she enlarged on this one. Fidelity was an invention of men to ensure an otherwise unprovable paternity, embraced by women because they needed a man's protection. Until she had agreed to that fidelity (symbolized by her divorce, from Ace in this case, not a marriage to Simon), she had had the power. But now she had given up her power. Without Ace, she could not make Simon jealous. Instead she made him fearful.

He had (in her) a womb of his own, but he did not want to fill it. He had a womb of his own, but she might as well have none, since he didn't want her to use it. He had rights over her womb, and cancelled her own right to fill it. *Unfair*, as Miss Amy would say.

Simon was tying up his tie. His garment bag was by the

door. It occurred to Suzanne that it would be no large
matter to have the metal coil — the 'mortal coil,' she said to
herself with chilly humour — inside her removed, in his
absence. He would never know until it was too late. Oh,
frail power of men. She could go right down to her local
doctor and have it done that day. Alas, she did not have the
arrogance. She could not be the only real parent of a real
child. There must be a willing father.

"Let's think of a time," she said, "when we can talk
about it."

Simon ripped the knot out of his tie and began again. He
looked as if he were preparing a noose. "I don't know
what's the matter with you," he said. "You used to be
independent. You're turning out to be just as clingy as all
the other women I've known."

Chapter 14

Miss Amy called Ace to her bedside.

"What I fail to understand," Miss Amy croaked from her stark white pillow, her flowered canopy. She was a wretched fallen thing. "What I fail to understand is that your father, who easily drinks as much as I have always done, and is no more holy, is not dying as well. You see after this many years we begin to compare fates with our spouses, and feel they should be equal. It's so unfair."

"You feel that," said Ace. He sat on a cushioned velvet stool beside her bed. His elbows were on his knees.

"Don't give me that, Ashley." She called him Ashley, sometimes Ash. "If I feel it, it's so."

"Yes Ma'am. I only meant."

"You meant." She hacked; the tendons in her throat drew up convulsively, the skin slid down.

"It's not necessary for you to suffer all the time."

"Oh but it is," she said. "That's what I do. Why do you think your father keeps me on? 'Mother of my children,' that's what he'd say. But that's too simple. I'm the reminder of old times, when he was a human being."

"Mother!" The stool was too small, but he was glad he was bent over. He'd been hit in the gut.

"He lets me bore him, and berate him, and stumble away from my own dinner table. He carries me in his arms from cocktail parties. I am the part of him which is destroyed."

"You are not destroyed. You are very alive and very wily," said Ace.

"The cunning does seem to live on," she said, not without pride. There was a pause. "However, at last I am calling in my debts."

He had been summoned; it was in the nature of a last request. Looking at her face, the cheeks collapsed inward around fine horse's teeth, lines converging in the lips, as if purse strings had been threaded and drawn there, the skin purplish, the blonde hair bleached so often it was like the dried hair on a mummy, he realized for the first time that this illness was not just one of her black jokes.

He walked to the window and lifted the flowered curtain to see the unrelenting brightness of outside. The glazed concrete of the patio, the arbour in the garden, the curved perennial beds heaped with compost. What was she going to ask him? To take his wife back? Not that he had a chance. To find a new one, and procreate? He doubted it. That was something his father was more likely to ask. Funny, he thought, turning back to the bed, if it were his father dying now he would have none of this wild outrage. *Unfair*. Her word. He hated to think anything was unfair. If you are blessed, fairness is not a welcome idea. It could only mean less for him.

"Don't leave me," he said. "Mother." And stopped himself from throwing his body down on her breakable form.

"But my dear," she said, "it's you who have been leaving me ever since you were born. I had my joy with you. I remember those grand edible toes." She looked away. "Anyway, I'm glad to see you haven't lost your looks."

"Why try to be so clever?" he asked, miserably.

"Why indeed?" She took up the cigarette lighter, black lacquer, with rhinestones down the side. Ace wondered as he had wondered before — where did she get these stage props? Some store that sold Hallowe'en costumes? "Certainly it never did me any good," she said.

"What do you want, Mother? What can I do?"

"Nothing," she said. "I want to give you something, something of mine, something to make you different from other men."

"Oh no," he said, suspecting a trick.

"I want you to have a conscience."

"You want me to feel guilty," he said bitterly. "That's not so different. Isn't that what all mothers want for their sons?"

"No, no, no!" She grew animated. It made him nervous. "Aren't you just like a man? You see anything remotely restricting your powers as subversive. No, a conscience is something very modern. It is a sense of right and wrong. It operates on its own, without external control. If you listen to it, normally you avoid guilt."

It was as if she were describing the latest bit of software for his computer. She had her power still, and no sooner had she said it than it was done. Ace stood there dazed.

"I'm sure you'll find it improves the quality of your life immensely. You see conscience in males was not invented when your father was growing up, so he never got one. That was half the problem."

Suzanne went out the back door and unlocked her bicycle where it leaned against the porch. She hopped down the sidewalk beside it, adjusting the polka-dot scarf over her nose. Car fumes had got so thick in the city that she never went for a ride without it.

"Hey, bandida, going to rob a bank?"

Ace's arm hung out through his open car window; he patted the side of the car the way people pat a dog, pretending to calm the animal when they are nervous.

"What are you doing here?" Her voice got caught in the moist cotton mask.

"You don't sound very glad to see me."

"Maybe because I don't know who you are. Ace or the

bad actor." It had been two months since the tennis racquet incident and she had not forgotten.

"Which one did you divorce?"

"Both," she said firmly. But she got down from her bicycle seat. She supposed he had got his decree *nisi*, too, with its embossed stamp and red seal. All by itself her thumb struck the bell on her right handlebar, again and again. He was grinning engagingly.

"Believe me, I'm a good guy."

Suzanne snorted, "I'd need proof of that."

"The proof is I came around here a couple of other times and saw that your friend was here, so I stayed away. I understand he's jealous."

She pulled the bandanna tighter on her nose.

"Invite me in," he said. "We haven't talked."

"No." She pushed her bike along the sidewalk towards Riley Park. She intended to go to sit by the playground and watch the mothers and children; it had become one of her favourite diversions. He followed.

"Holding a grudge, are you?" He looked so cute, leaning from the window in his old satin frat jacket, blue and white with gold lettering, that she almost stopped.

"I'm not holding a grudge. I'm just not talking to you. I don't have to. We're divorced." Now she got on her bike and started pedalling, the expensive purr of his car following. She turned the corner. So did it. Gravel popped under its tires. He had to raise his voice.

"That's what I wanted to talk about," he said.

She stopped, and pulled the bandanna off her nose. With one foot on the ground she faced him. His car drew up beside her. He worked to keep his face sombre.

"You got one of those things too, with the red seal? Impressive, no?" she said.

"Amazing. Compared to it the marriage licence was just a wee little thing."

"Mind you, this one cost more." Ace had split Jennifer's fee with her, still she was paying five hundred dollars.

"Not when you count the party." They smiled together,

remembering the wedding. After the late start, it had been a bash. There had been quantities of champagne, and game hens, tiny little things with legs like ring fingers. For fifty people, it had been a mass slaughter. Ace had made a speech. "This is the happiest day of my life," he had said. Suzanne got off her bicycle and put her other foot on the ground.

"It's quite a milestone," he said pleasantly. "I thought I should congratulate you. You were the driving force."

He had to be nasty, did he? Suzanne began to push her bike ahead. The park entrance was just around the next corner. "It takes two," she said, "to get divorced."

"A joke, OK?"

"OK." But there was a painful swelling in Suzanne's throat. She looked down at the curb. If she let him go, it might be for the last time. She might cry; she was affected by a bizarre form of nostalgia. The comfortable past collided in her memory with the chaos of the present, and the unknowable future. "I'm going to the park to look at the babies," she said.

"I'll come with you. I want to talk about Miss Amy," he said.

She dumped her bike beside the pathway and walked over to a wooden bench, where she sat down beside a young mother with a stroller pulled up between her knees. The baby had a head like a globe with a faint gloss of white hair, and he was fussing. The mother ignored him, smoking a cigarette. Ace strolled in the gate a moment later. He came and stood over her.

"My mother called me to her bedside," he said.

Suzanne took one more look at the woman — girl, really — with her baby and stood up. "Let's walk," she said. They began a slow circuit of the bed of marigolds.

"She gave me a present," said Ace. "I thought you'd like it." And he told her about the conscience.

"Amazing," said Suzanne. "I thought she was up to something."

Ace gave a sudden, humble smile. They had made a

complete circuit of the flower beds and were now standing
near the big slide. It must have been the end of nap time.
The strollers were lined up beside the sandbox; half a dozen
young mothers watched as two toddlers filled a shoe with
sand. The white-haired baby had gone to sleep. He lifted
one of her hands and kissed it.

"So I want to say this. You have every right to your new
life. We're finished. I'm sorry I acted like a jerk. What you
need is a friend. We can talk about your new man. We can
even talk about what happened with us."

Suzanne had been thinking about that. "It would have
been different if we had the baby," she said. There was a
silence.

He looked her steadily in the face. "I never think about
it."

Was he telling the truth? Suzanne dropped her eyes. The
subject would lie untouched between them a little longer.

"You shouldn't dwell on that, Suzanne."

She nodded, looking at the ground.

"Say!" he said "I know what. Do you want to have lunch?"

"Lunch!" They were standing amongst a litter of toddlers.
Lunch in the empty townhouse! Her head began to pound.
"Friday lunch! You honking for me in the parking lot...
The electric wires sticking out of the holes in the walls...
The bed made up with fresh sheets by some domestic you
write off as a business expense. Are you kidding?"

Now Ace hung his head.

One little girl teetered on the top step of the slide.
Suzanne watched her. "Mama!" said the child, "Mama!"

"How could you have done that to me?" Suzanne
whispered. "How could I have done it to myself?" she
corrected.

"I didn't mean that. I mean a real lunch."

"What do you mean, real?"

"In a restaurant."

The mother of the stranded toddler began climbing the
steps behind her child, murmuring. "Don't move darling,
don't move, Mummy's coming." It did occur to Suzanne

that with Simon out of town she could meet Ace for lunch
in a restaurant and have nothing to worry about.

"Caesar's?"

"No bad acting?"

"You're safe. We'll be in public."

"We were in public before." But he was sincere. Tears
stood in his eyes. Suzanne pulled her bandanna from around
her neck and gave it to him to use as a handkerchief.

Caesar's could have been the tomb of same. It was one of
those dark, overdecorated restaurants where oilmen eat at
noon. Walking in from the blue and yellow glare of day,
Suzanne couldn't see a thing. She asked for Mr Cummings'
table; the waiter's smile was oblique. It was a very private
kind of lunch place. They had never been here when they
were married. She could have been a blackmailer or a
mistress.

Ace was already seated, his face lit by a candle in a little
red gourd-shaped glass covered with white netting. He rose
to take her hand. He was elegant, as always; he was smooth,
and his accessories were smooth, suede jacket, silk tie, the
aftershave that left his face like cream. He took her fingers,
and squeezed them.

They sat. Faces began to poke out of the darkness, all
clustered around these little candles, leaning together,
chewing or talking. Ace still had Suzanne's fingers.

"Hey," she said lightly.

He drew the hand closer to his chest, making it awkward
for her to draw it back. Then he pulled it to his mouth and
pressed his lips on the back of it.

"Hey," she said, louder this time.

He let go. "You're perspiring. Maybe you're nervous. I
hope so." He sighed. "When you came into the room I
thought, who is that beautiful woman, I must know her, if I
don't know her now I'm going to get to know her. Imagine
how I felt when I realized it was the woman I'm divorcing."

"The woman you've divorced!"

"If she says so."

"Imagine how I feel being referred to in the third person all the time. My friends do it. My parents did it. Now you're doing it."

"When in doubt, correct his grammar. That's my Suzanne."

The wine came. Ace toasted the end of their first marriage. "Now we're freed up for the second!"

"But what about your promise?" she said. "About the friendship?" She needed to talk. To tell him that it was not going well with Simon. That all the same she was desperate that Simon and she move ahead to an understanding, a child. The new mature Ace was her hope of counsel.

"I haven't forgotten," he said.

"I want to tell you about him," she said.

"Suzanne," he said, "I don't doubt you're deeply involved with Simon. But you're involved with me too." He drank with his face muscles, drawing the liquid into his cheeks, then forcing it down his throat. "We're stronger than ever," he whispered.

"You're crazy," she said. The conversation was not going at all the way she'd imagined. But he was very serious; he made his square, innocent face clear of cant.

"I may be crazy, but I am absolutely right. I'm asking you a favour. I've been through a lot for you and I want you to do just this one thing. I have a little speech planned. Don't say anything until I'm through."

She sat back in her chair and looked into the cold white wine. He had never made a speech before, not to her.

"You probably haven't realized that the brothers are all laughing at me," he began. "My friends. They're killing themselves laughing. Celebrating because I lost my wife to a four-eyed eastern bean-counter who can't even remember what side he's on."

She dropped her eyes. This was not the kind of friendship she had in mind.

"You two make a good pair, I suppose. He's as mixed up as you are. Don't think I haven't noticed that you said you wanted out of the marriage for yourself. That you just wanted to tidy your life up with this divorce. Turned out what you wanted was to marry him, am I right? I agreed, and there I go from *nisi* to absolute in another ninety days."

He pushed back his chair and sat straight, a few feet behind the table. He put his hand flat on the table. "I must say I gave it my best shot. And I lost you. You know, I can't remember when I ever lost anything before? Except the juniors, that first year I entered."

Suzanne remembered the juniors. The juniors had been a humiliation, but the next year he won them and after that the seniors too. He won every year, every time, all the way, as far as he could go, until he quit, and he quit because he knew he couldn't go on winning. For a moment she succumbed to the memory. They had lived through his first defeat together; later he retired full of glory. He saw her smile.

"Remember the Ace-R machine that tested the shuttlecocks? It's in my mother's garden now. It always hit a perfect shot."

She hadn't thought of the Ace-R for years. She had hated it; it stood for everything that was wrong with him. "That Thing!" she said.

"So anyway now, I've lost. Can you blame the brothers for having a bit of fun? I am a big fat loser. You licked me. You threw me over. The one person I never suspected was out to get me."

"I wasn't!"

He leaned on his elbows, across the table, his hands clenched as if in prayer. "You were so soft when we met. Your yellow red hair and your pale skin. Your collar bones almost visible among the freckles on your thin chest. Your touch as thrilling and colourful as a butterfly."

"Ace! Cut it out!" She didn't know he could talk like that. He was a better poet than Simon, she thought.

"No really," he said, enjoying this. "The thing about you was that you were always there. You were so young and loyal, like a puppy. I felt no fear with you, ever. I felt kindly and fond and proud of your stubbornness, when you showed it, even when you showed it against me." An attractive look of dejection spread over his features.

"Do you know something? I'm sad," he said.

She nodded.

"I can't remember ever having been sad before, do you believe that? It is absolutely true. I cannot remember being sad. What makes people sad, after all? Being ugly, I suppose, or being poor. Being sick. But I am healthy and wealthy and handsome and I have always been happy. Or so I thought."

He leaned back and took another drink of his scotch. Swish, swish, it went into his mouth, out into the cheeks, and then down.

"Or so I thought. But you know the really curious thing about this sadness? I remember it. It's familiar. It feels like a thing I've had with me a long time and have not bothered to look at. Some large stone I've been carrying. And now I've put it down to look at. Imagine that, Suze! I've had sadness and not even known it!"

Suzanne was listening very carefully. She nodded slowly. She thought he was probably right. There was no one who didn't have some sadness, was there?

"And then I had this idea. I began to wonder if all this was why you used to say I lacked emotional depth."

He sat there, his scotch and soda in his hand, challenging her. He remembered what she said longer than she remembered having said it.

"And then I realized that I had never even considered the possibility that you were right in what you said about me. I thought you complained out of some perverse need to find the hole in the doughnut. You see, Suzanne, you were right. I am shallow."

He held up his hand as she began to speak. "I'm not finished yet. You were right. And now I am right. I'm right when I say that this is not an end for us but a beginning. Because you are the grand love of my life, as I am of yours."

Suzanne thought there must be some mistake. Another

man had said the exact same words. But Ace said them
better. She looked into his eyes. Foolish woman. She was
trapped.

"Don't expect me to make a speech in response. I'm not
prepared," she said. "Anyway, here's the food."

Her vichyssoise was a pale puddle suspended in a tiny
cup in the middle of a huge pewter ice-bucket. "I can see
this is your kind of place, Ace," she snapped. "One of those
eateries where the apparatus overpowers the food."

He watched her. His face was open to whatever she was
going to give him. Pain. Comfort. Passion. Her thoughts
flapped in panic around in her mind. She had to be clever,
she had to be.

"My kind of place?" he said, confused.

"It's all coming back. How I dislike your taste in movies
and your friends and the way you spend your money."

"Anything else?" he said. He could play along; they had
their dialogue if nothing else. "Was it all that bad?"

"All right, there were things I liked," she said. We
stumbled along for a while, but overall, we're too different.
You're just confused because lately we've been having an
affair. That was a mistake. I'm sorry if it gave you
expectations. This is what I want, the divorce."

"It was a lovely affair," he said.

"An affair is different," she said. "Easier. Ours couldn't
survive out of the rarefied air of your townhouse on the hill.
It was a hothouse flower."

Ace put his tiny fork into a shrimp and lifted it off the
edge of his cocktail glass. "You'll settle for less?"

"You don't understand my metaphors."

"I never was much for literary devices," he said, grinning again and putting the shrimp into his mouth. Suzanne
watched him.

She remembered when she first saw a shrimp cocktail,
she thought that each shrimp was a leg of an octopus-
shrimp hanging over the edge of the glass. Where was the
body of the shrimp? Then she found out that each leg *was*
the body. That was synecdoche. Taking the part for the

whole. Or maybe it was the other, taking the whole for the part. "You're taking part of our relationship that was good and saying it was all good. What about — " she floundered momentarily. "What about — "

"Don't say it, Suzanne. It's over and done with."

"The wine," she said. "It makes me want to cry. If I'm not careful, I'll let go and bawl. I do, sometimes."

"It might be the best thing."

"No," she said, "no. You don't understand. I could lose everything if I get involved with you again." She meant Simon, the baby.

He said nothing.

"Do you even know what a hothouse flower is?" Suzanne said, aggressively.

"Sure, it's beautiful and exotic and everyone should have one."

"But not to base his life on," she cried. "What I mean is that the hothouse flower doesn't belong where it is, and therefore can't support itself. It's impractical." She thought that would get him, son of an engineer and all.

"Well, what do you want, a dandelion?"

"I want," she said, "I want..." and paused to think about flowers. The metaphor was used up. She didn't know what she wanted.

The ice-bucket went away and her salad plate arrived. Ace had ordered steak. She began to think about the fact that all her life she'd been sitting in restaurants watching men eat steak while she took the baked potato with sour cream. She bit into a piece of egg and considered the possibility that men and women were actually two different species. "The amount of dead flesh men consume is staggering. Greenpeace ought to get onto it," she said.

He picked up his knife.

"This conversation is pointless. We can't possibly get back together now. We're divorced."

He chewed a bite, and then raised his fork to speak. "Suzanne, the trouble with you is that you want rules. You can't get used to the idea that we can do whatever we like.

We're lucky. We should do grand and foolish things. We owe it to the world. If we don't, who's going to get the chance?"

She pondered this logic. "Are we so special? So privileged? Maybe you are, but I'm not so sure about me."

"You've always been too guilty to admit it. Let other people make decisions by what "works," what's practical. Life leaves such a small space for gestures. We ought to be together as a gesture. I'm arguing an ecology of human happiness, OK? We ought to do it just so that it — this unusually perfect thing, this hothouse flower — can exist."

"But even then," she said, plodding along with her thoughts, "let's say that we are privileged — and I'm not even sure of that, maybe Bushmen have better lives — doesn't that mean we should serve, rather than indulge?" She sat for a minute. Her face was sad. "Sometimes I wish I was shallow. People criticize you for it, but maybe most of them are just jealous. How nice it must be to believe oneself enfranchised for extraordinary pleasures," she said.

"I look after myself. At least by looking after myself I provide the world with a good example."

She laughed out loud. "You said that before. You don't even remember. You said the very same thing the day you told me about Titian. You said..."

"I'm consistent," he said.

"You are. But I want to tell you about Simon." It was, after all, what he had said they could talk about.

"I have a plan," said Ace, "a plan for us. Let me tell you that first."

"It's no use," she said. "There is no us."

Lunch hour was over, and the men were beginning to leave. In the hollowing room, his words began to travel from the table. He had on a silver tie-pin; it pulled his collar tight around his throat. He yanked at the collar, twisting his neck. Then he leaned towards her across the table, his jaw set forward.

"Be *reasonable* Suzanne. There is an us, or we wouldn't be here. We are a quantity, a past, present or future. I know you're seeing another man, but I'm still in your life. And I can wait. At least for a while."

"Now you're going to start talking about time horizons," she said, edgily. "And broad-brush treatments and bottom lines. It's no use. We don't even talk the same language."

"Do you and Simon?"

She looked blank.

"Listen," he said, reaching for her hand again. He looked gently on her face, matching its lines to some memory. "I've thought about this so much. It was right between us. If it didn't work in the ordinary world, so what? It worked somewhere else, in another realm. In the stars. We're made to be together. I know it. So let's not be a couple, let's be a constellation."

She hadn't known he could talk like that, until today.

"I know I'm raw, unsophisticated. I know I've got a bad actor inside of me. But I'm full of energy, devotion, will. I'm like a bride with a vast dowry. Let me bring my undeveloped greatness to you. I only want to see you. You don't have to promise me anything."

He had even moved himself; his eyes were full again. That was twice since they'd met in the park. In all the years she'd known him till now she'd never seen him shed a tear.

There was almost no one left in the restaurant. The waiter moved back and forth in front of the mirrors on the other side of the room, his reflection following him like a faithful dog. Ace gave him the high sign.

She dropped her face into her hands. The organ music was soft at first, then louder. The words had never made sense. And it sounded like a dirge.

"*...As the Miller told his tale ... That her face at first just ghostly turned a whiter shade of pale.*"©

Still, she loved it. She shook her head. "That too," she said. "You're really laying it on."

"Pulling out all the stops," he said, cheerfully.

"All right," she said. "All right." She looked round. "How did you get them to play it.?"

"You gotta get some perks for eating here three times a

week." She looked up and saw his profile, the line down his cheek deeper than it had been even two months ago. In the wave over his forehead was a glimmer of grey.

"I can't stop seeing Simon," she said.

"You don't have to," he said.

The room was very still. The darkness in the restaurant had gone with the hour they'd spent there; now they could see everything. It was as if the roof were glass and the sky visible all around, the planets too, as if, when Ace gave the word, she and he might join their number. People were just small things, scattered here, open to the elements, thought Suzanne. They were here to love one another, to protect one another, to comfort. Why be singular, possessive about love? Why choose one human above others? She felt very powerful, very sad, very generous. She touched the end of his finger.

"You're wonderful, Ace. If I had another life..."

"It's not too late."

He put his arm around her. They put their heads together over the table. Tenderly she reached over and touched his cheek. A voice screamed *Simon*! How can I betray Simon? And another part answered that although she loved Simon she loved Ace too; she had loved him first. Then she leaned to him and kissed his lips.

He kissed her back, and his lips were frank and shocking, like the lips of a stranger. He put his arm tightly around her shoulders, and they walked out of the restaurant. To her astonishment the afternoon was still young.

Chapter 15

It was the third day of the trial and by now I was no impartial reporter; I was gripped like the rest. I could not shake the fascination of the case — bare hands for a weapon, the silent participation of the victim, the uncertain moment of her death. But I tried — successfully, I thought — to maintain my air of distaste for it all.

Kelsey was on the stand, asserting Jumbo had come downstairs at one point in the afternoon to ask if he could borrow a dollar. Since Fisk had chosen not to speak, the fancy eastern lawyer had only one option to clear him, and that was to destroy the prosecution's witnesses. Kelsey, whose nerves made him stammer, became the man's particular victim.

"A dollar, Mr Kelsey? He wanted to borrow a dollar? A man fresh from winnings at cards, a man who entered the Turf Club at four o'clock that afternoon and ordered drinks all around the bar? A man who had over five hundred dollars in his pocket? Why would this man have need of a dollar?"

He paused while the jury thought about it. Kelsey looked like a liar already.

"But I daresay he did come down to speak to you. Did he

perhaps have some other favour to ask? I suggest he asked you to come upstairs and have a look at the injured squaw." The lawyer toe-heeled his feet back and forth, moving from one side of the room to the other. Before Kelsey could answer, the lawyer began again.

"And I have another problem with what you've told me. You say that at around six o'clock you opened the door of the room and saw Mr Fisk at the washstand with blood stains on the floor, and the squaw lying on the bed. And this was *before* you lit the lamps. Now I just happen to have found some scientific data" — here he ruffled a few papers — "and according to the government station, the sun set over Calgary at 4:47 P.M. on February 28."

This little guy was better than I'd thought. He went on.

"Picture it, gentlemen of the jury. The one little room, with one window, a window looking north. The dark interior hallway with no lamps lit...It's six o'clock, that's night around here in winter. How could this man have seen a hand in front of his face, let alone all that he says he's seen?"

Kelsey turned this way and that. He looked away from his questioner trying to find something, courage, perhaps. He was completely mixed up.

"Maybe I didn't see the blood then. Maybe it was later, after I lit up."

The lawyer danced back to the other side of the room. Kelsey watched him like he was a swinging noose.

"You normally light up at five o'clock. Why were you late that day?"

"I suppose I was busy, I don't know."

"You don't know? May I suggest a reason? Perhaps you *did* see blood the first time you went up, when you say you only listened at the door. You see, then it was only half past four. And Rosalie was alive and maybe hurt, and Fisk said what should we do and you said 'nothing,' which means that you are as responsible for what happened to her as anyone is."

"Objection!" said the prosecutor, a little late.

But the lawyer grinned. He was content; he'd made

things look bad for Kelsey. Then he turned around and produced a surprise witness: Lowry. Lowry said he had been in the upstairs hall with a potential buyer. And he said that while Fisk and Kelsey were out for dinner he saw a halfbreed hanging around by the alley door. "By this time," concluded the lawyer, "we've established that the room Rosalie was in was unlocked. This halfbreed, or anyone else, for that matter, could have walked in and done the deed."

Well! It seemed to me all of a sudden that we were simple folk out here. We'd been trying to tell the straight tale. But Fisk's high-paid actor had succeeded better by making what had been clear, murky. Now it looked as if Rosalie's death took place in the midst of so many other inexplicable events on that dark afternoon that you couldn't say how one was related to any other. I thought I understood the case, and had previously been content that Fisk had done it, whether deliberately or not. But now even I found it unclear. I wrote on my lap and crossed out my words, wrote again, and stared at the wall. But then — lucky for Kelsey — the defence lawyer overdid it. He produced Dr Brett from Banff. Brett went dead against everything Lafferty said about Rosalie's wounds.

"Is it possible she could have made the tear with her own hands?" said the lawyer.

"Yes."

"That it happened with her assent?"

"At the very least she must have co-operated with the man who did it."

"Now you've gone too far, fella," I said under my breath. Some say that the law has no fixed rules; it's just the sounding of the public's reflexes. If that's so, old Dr Brett hit the nerve. You might get the people of Calgary to accept that some minor, shared negligence had led to Rosalie's death. They, or we, might be inclined to blame no one in particular for a murder they, or we, wished to forget. But we stopped short of blaming Rosalie. There were hisses and boos in the courtroom.

Perhaps he realized his gaffe. Lightly, on the balls of his

feet, he ducked his head, danced sideways and sat down.

And now our own prosecutor, a dim fellow who barely cast a shadow in the crowded room, had his chance. In a voice only slightly raised above the conversational, he began to try to redeem Rosalie's reputation. I hoped Evangeline was there to hear him. It was what she wanted, but I couldn't take credit. He called the Indian agent to testify to Rosalie's blameless life; he described her as "the flower of her race." Then he called Father André. Pacing to the front of the shed in his black robes, it was the priest, advantaged by his costume and his reputation which went before him (he had been confessor to Louis Riel and had sat with him all through the long night, returning him to God before his execution), who saved Rosalie's reputation.

"Especially devout," he said, "a little shy. A great love of drama."

At that I seemed to hear the high voices from the little garden. "*How now my love, prithee why so pale?*" I shut my ears to them.

"What was her future likely to be?" said the prosecutor.

"With her education, she could have hoped, perhaps, for a position of service in town until marriage to one of her race gave her a life of her own." At this point his eyes sought and caught my own. As I held my breath, he cleared his throat, and added that he had last seen Rosalie only one week before her death when she had come to the mission to make confession. He had heard the confession himself, but of course the contents were confidential. My scalp prickled as sweat broke out. I looked at my notebook and began to write furiously. He must know.

Outside the shed the unsatisfied wind circled. The crowd shifted, pushing each other; there was no room to move. The jury looked rattled by now. There had been too much information. Who or what was Rosalie? She had been a dissolute squaw; now she showed signs of becoming a holy martyr.

At this point the prosecutor played his trump card. He asked to admit one more witness, the mounted policeman who had inspected Kelsey's room in the Turf Club after Dillabough had fainted. At first he seemed to be going over old ground. He asked the man what he had seen in the room.

"A great deal of blood. On the floor, the bed, the washstand. And the walls — "

"Could you tell the jury about the blood on the walls?" The prosecutor's pale, ineffectual hands described circles in the air — go on, go on.

"I found, near the head of the bed, a handprint made in blood, quite clearly the impression of a man's right hand."

"I want the jury to listen very carefully now — was there anything special about that handprint?"

"There was a finger missing. The fourth digit."

There was a rustling from those who knew. "My lord, I request that the accused raise up his right hand."

Rouleau nodded. Eyes turned to Fisk, who had been impassive for the three days of the trial and did not move.

"Mr Fisk?"

He was handcuffed. A move was made to unlock his hands. Then a guard raised Fisk's right hand and there was the deformity, the fourth finger cut off at the first joint, a blind stump, an obscene pygmy.

"Do you see that?" cried the little prosecutor, his voice becoming piercing in his moment, his victory. "The same deformity found in the bloody imprint on the wall appears in the hand of Jumbo Fisk!"

Even I was affected. The crowd made a sound between a gasp and a cheer, and lurched forward. Pushing made for more pushing; the wall of people behind the chairs of the principals began to buckle. The mass of spectators wanted to move but was prevented by its own size and passion. Fisk went down on his knees in the centre and put his hands over his head. The guards had him. Rouleau jumped to his feet with the gavel, pounding and shouting "Order!" Only the jury obeyed.

Finally, the guards lifted Fisk out over the heads of the crowd, which was no easy task, as he was a big man. They began to push the people out through the open doors at the back. The prosecutor dusted his sleeves in a corner.

"I conclude," he said. No one but me heard.

Lucky I'm nimble. I scrambled over and through the people to the door; agitated and out of breath I ran across the tracks and around to my office. The jury was going out. It was noon, and I had a five P.M. deadline. I couldn't guess which way it would decide, but I devised a strategy: I would pen two versions, one to use in the event that the jury returned a guilty verdict, the other in case Fisk was found innocent.

I sat down to the task, suppressing my own fear of being found out. I had not forgotten Father André's look. Oh God that the church should get me yet, I thought. I've always hated the church. In the first version, the guilty version, I used phrases like "deformed fiend" and "more animal than man." In the second I called Fisk "that unfortunate citizen who got himself caught in a sordid affair." Similarly Rosalie was "a young girl of blameless reputation" in one draft, and "the type of lost woman who frequents these spots" in the other.

I found the exercise entertaining, and was diverted until well after four o'clock. At that time I looked up from my desk, consulted my watch and hurried for my coat. I crossed the tracks again to the immigration shed, expecting that the jury might have already returned. The mounted police guards were outside the door. Several dozens of the regular spectators also waited. Peering through the window, I saw that the judge was at his desk. Something caused me to draw attention to myself. Presuming on my position as a member of the Press, I knocked at the door.

"Do you expect a verdict in the next hour?" I said. "I've got to get my copy to the printer." I eyed Rouleau closely, wondering if he had any notion of my involvement.

"We're not making decisions for the convenience of the newspaper," growled Rouleau. "A man's life is at stake."

"The community is upset. People need to know," I said, more aggressively than I might have. An oily agreeability worked best, when you wanted something. I could see I'd get nowhere with Rouleau. The little man looked on fire; he had picked his side already. Fisk should be worried. It looked as if I would be using Version One of the story.

I was about to climb back across the tracks and send it in when I saw, emerging from the building where they had been closeted, the six men of the jury. They marched across under police guard, looking dour and self-proud. The onlookers pressed close to the door. When all, including the prisoner, were assembled once again and the judge was in his seat, the foreman stepped forward.

"My lord I am here to tell you that we cannot agree."

"Are you confused as to your instructions?"

"No my lord. We cannot agree." The man seemed rather pleased with his message. Rouleau read his face, blew into his closed lips and leaned back, contemptuous.

"Very well then, go back into your chamber until you can agree."

"Sir, it is almost the supper hour."

Judge Rouleau gazed down on his foreman. "Supper seems to have undue importance in our town. You would go to supper while the scales of justice teeter? Get out of my sight, and don't return until you have a verdict."

I had not bargained for this. I pulled out my two pages of copy and realized I was going to have to modify Version Two, the "not guilty" story, and use it until something further resulted. I reread it and changed the "unfortunate" to "the unhappy," "remorseful" to "sullen." I didn't want to whitewash Fisk, but my bets were that if the men were not yet agreed, they were unlikely to get unanimity. NO VERDICT! I wrote at the head of my copy. I read it again. Like the jury, I could not decide. At the last minute I removed all adjectives applying to the victim and the accused, and filed it.

Then I returned to the shed. After several more hours the foreman sent a message: still no verdict. Rouleau declared that the men should be locked in their room overnight, and told us all to leave.

Then I walked home, my crabbed legs weak under me. The boy would not be in, as he took his meals with the widow down the street. Indeed I could have done the same were I not suspicious of the lady's attentions. If Vangie had found me attractive (and me already white-haired with a gimpy leg when we met), who knew what others of her kind would set upon me? I had had enough trouble from women.

Stirred up inside, I took a sherry in my parlour. It was a war of nerves to get this trial and this young Indian girl put away. Still it was not without its pleasures. I giggled, thinking about the men locked up overnight. I wished I had ears on the argument in the hotelroom where they were kept. It was a little punishment for them, not as bad as Rosalie's own, but something of what the men of this town deserved. I hoped Evangeline was satisfied. But the more I sipped, the more the thrill of the trial deserted me; in my chest now there was a feeling like bleeding. Then I heard the voice in the kitchen, whispering, rhythmic, a voice in prayer.

"Sometime — it could be very soon, it could be a long long time — He will draw me into a place between the mountains. It is dark there but I will not draw back; I will not be afraid for —"

"Rosalie, quiet in there!" I said it before I knew I was saying it. Then I felt myself a fool. Rosalie was dead and gone. I put the glass down. I could hear laughter. They were making mockery of me, Vangie and Rosalie, in my own home. I paced to the kitchen door. Vangie was not there, but Rosalie stood before the window. She wore some light garment, it was the only way I could see her in the coal-coloured room. She held out her hand, giggling.

"Not now. You're teasing me."

She came two steps towards me, shyly inclining her head, as if she did not see me or hear my words but only felt my presence.

"Rosalie! Get away from me!"

How often had I chastized her, scolded her; I had scolded

Vangie as well, they were like two children, delighted to be
in each other's company, and me angry that their pleasure
left me out. Of course, she had meant nothing by her
gesture, only to soothe me. It had been me who first
interpreted her warmth as flirtation. But it was over and
now only Father André knew — if he knew, if I wasn't
imagining. As it turned out, my wrong to her had been only
a sub-plot; the poor girl's terrible fate had already been
approaching her in the thick, stubby-fingered form of the
blacksmith.

"You're gone now. Gone, Rosalie. Go!"

She pressed her palm to her lips and then held it out to
me, a flying kiss: Vangie had taught her that too. Then she
went to the stool by the fire and picked up her shawl — the
red shawl — and put it over her shoulders. As it went
around her the white of her gown disappeared, and with it
her face. She was gone. She obeyed me at last. I shook my
head to clear it and went to undress for bed.

The next morning the crowd was larger than before.
Rouleau looked straight down his nose at the foreman, who
was speaking. He and all the jury members had a night's
growth of beard.

"We've nothing to say,'" he told the judge. "We're
nowhere closer to a decision."

"Then why have you returned?" Rouleau was passionless
this morning; he looked out the window. "Go back to your
room and don't come out until you've got something to
say."

"We've been locked up all night. We had no supper. We
had no light, or rest," he said.

And nor does she, I thought.

"We're finished," said the foreman.

Now Rouleau snapped to life before us. His quiet voice
became a shout. "You're finished when I tell you. This is no
ordinary day's work. You must decide a man's fate."

The jurymen began to groan and rumble to each other.

"We want to go home," said the foreman.

"So do we all. Maybe your discomfort will help you come to a decision."

"Can he do that?" whispered someone beside me.

Slowly I nodded, keeping my eye on the foreman's face. "He can do whatever he can get away with."

"I'm going to have a mutiny on my hands," whined the foreman. But Rouleau was no longer listening. His energetic hair vibrating with held-back anger, he slid his papers into a pile. The jury was led away again. Rouleau was testing his luck. Only threads of decorum kept the men in his control, kept the law on top of them.

I went home for lunch, noting as I came in that the boy was there. And perhaps Rosalie, if it was like last night. It was as if her soul, as well, were waiting on the outcome of this trial. If her homeless spirit came here until its destination was decided it would not be to harm me, of that I felt sure. In fact the previous night, when I saw her, I slept better than I had all week. I made myself tea in the kitchen and carried it, together with some biscuits, on a tray into the chilly parlour.

"Is he going to hang, Father?"

The boy was standing by the window in his school clothes, but he hadn't gone to school.

"I don't know, son, I don't suppose so."

"Why should he, anyway? I don't think he deserves to."

"Is that your considered opinion?" I always did this to him. I couldn't help myself. "Does any seventeen-year-old have a right to an opinion in this matter?"

The boy flinched a little but did not look away. "Why can't they decide?"

"Because Fisk is one of them, I suppose. And they're not sure that he did wrong, even if she died by his actions."

"But what did he do, Father?"

I looked right at him and said I didn't know.

"The savages say that if a soul is murdered and the

murderer not punished, the soul will roam the earth seeking justice," said the boy.

"I expect they'll punish him a little. Perhaps they'll call it manslaughter."

The boy laughed hoarsely. He'd liked Rosalie, but then she'd left. Just as he'd liked his stepmother, but she'd left too. "I think they should call it squaw slaughter."

At that I rose up to rage. "Where do you come by this impertinence? You cannot speak like that in this house. Apologize this instant!" I could feel the pulse in my forehead: I advanced on the boy as if I would hit him, but I didn't. I never could.

The boy smiled easily. He'd won, discovered his father's feelings. "I apologize, Father."

At one o'clock in the afternoon it was twenty-six hours after the jury had gone out. The men had worked without rest and without food. The foreman's eyes were pouchy and his mouth, when he began to speak, turned down in a bitter way. He seemed to consider himself and his group to be the real victims of the affair. He glared at Rouleau.

"We have reached a verdict, sir."

"And that is?"

"We find the prisoner *Not Guilty* of the murder of —"

But the rest of his words were tossed up in the air. Our citizens, who had attended on all the bloody details with the patience of morticians, now exploded. They cheered and shouted. Men slapped other men's backs and shook hands as if they themselves had been brought back from the brink. In the centre of the uproar stood New Grass and his wife, jostled, paralyzed.

"Silence! Enough!" Rouleau banged his gavel. He was flushed from his ears upward; his rounded forehead glowed. "Silence or I'll clear the court!" On pain of missing what was to come, the spectators fell silent.

"Gentlemen," said Rouleau. His little hands, clenched to pistons for pounding, relaxed in jerks. He found a handkerchief to wipe his forehead. "That will do." He searched out the foreman's eyes and the puckers around his lips released into a small unhappy smile.

"I will not accept that verdict. You may return to your deliberations."

I could hardly believe it. I think I must have whistled. There was a confused rustle of feet around me.

"I don't understand," said the foreman.

"Go, dismissed!" Rouleau waved his short arm. "I don't like it. Get me another verdict!"

"Can he do that?" whispered a man beside me.

I shook my head. In these parts, he could do what he could get away with. There was no check on it, none but public comment, the Press. Me. Already I was making phrases... "History was made but not in the way we imagined it would be... the great tradition of English common law has broken down... the people of Calgary are being subjected to a 'tyranny of the law'..." I liked that one, tyranny of law. This case had become the most extraordinary contest between Rouleau and the people. And I was in the centre again, as I so often chanced to be; an arbitrator.

The jury marched out without a word. That was how it happened that it was later still, thirty hours after it had first withdrawn, when the jury returned to the judge, lawyers and the accused assembled for the last time. Rouleau took the manner of an exasperated schoolmaster.

"I hope you have something to tell me this time."

The foreman shook his head. "We're at the point of tossing a copper."

Rouleau's eye was full of disgust. He looked over the men and concluded that they were useless. "You can't agree?"

"We can't convict, my lord. You rejected acquittal."

"Then get out of here! I've no more patience with you!"

At this the lawyer from the east stood. Poor Fisk was half standing, half sitting. He had been alive, now he was dead again.

"You cannot continue this, with all due respect, my lord," he said. "It's simply not done —"

But Rouleau ignored him.

"I'm going to write '*no verdict*' here," continued Rouleau calmly, "and remand the prisoner for two months. And then we'll start all over. If it takes another trial to get some justice in this town, I'll do it."

There was no use arguing. The fierce little man snatched up his papers and strode through the crowd, pausing only to nod at New Grass and his wife.

Chapter 16

Gemma called Jennifer on the telephone.

"When was the last time you saw Suzanne?"

Jennifer was in her office. She was almost always in her office.

"Ages ago," she said. "She's busy all the time with Simon. The grand love and all."

"She can say what she likes about love," said Gemma, "but it's not exactly enhancing. I dropped over on the weekend. She looks awful. Her nails are worse than mine."

"What shall we do?" said Jennifer. She had never liked long telephone conversations.

"Call her up and get together. We owe it to her. We've got to do something. You phone. She'll take it better from you."

Jennifer called Suzanne at the college.

"Long time no see," she said pleasantly.

Suzanne's voice was lively, almost manic. "Jennifer! Where have you been? You know what I was thinking about? Pharaoh's Retreat. Tell me, what happened?"

"Nobody wants to know," said Jennifer. "It's not clean-hands law, remember?"

"I never said that. It was Gemma."

"Why are you asking? Is it something for your research?"

"Don't, hey?" said Suzanne. Now her voice faded a little; it sounded to Jennifer as if she had turned her face away from the telephone and was thinking of something else.

"The cops went in. Laid charges on the two guys," said Jennifer. "But this is ancient history now."

"And what happened to the women, have they been charged?"

"Yeah, but they'll plead the evidence act and help us convict the guys. At least we want them to. Otherwise their charges will stand."

"So where are they now?"

"Most of them — all I guess — out on bail. This won't come up for a few months."

"How did they get bail? Where did it come from?"

Jennifer sighed. "Suzanne, why are you asking all this? Are you just trying to prove you're interested after two months of neglect?"

"They're just pawns," said Suzanne angrily, "and you treat them like pawns."

Jennifer was beginning to be alarmed. Suzanne did not sound like herself. She didn't sound like anyone, as a matter of fact, she sounded unbalanced. She sounded like someone who had just poked her nose out of a solitary tank, responding to an imagined alarm. "Look," she said, "I didn't call up to have a political argument. I called up because we thought we'd all get together."

A long, considering breath was let out from the other end of the telephone. "Well, all right," said Suzanne. "I guess we should. We're out of touch."

"You don't sound all that keen." Jennifer laughed a little gingerly.

"No, no, it'll be good." Again her voice faded, then came back strong. "Can you make it tomorrow? I was going to go out to the cabin."

After Jennifer's call, Suzanne put down the telephone in her office, and pressed her palms into her eye sockets. They felt sore, sunken. She had not been getting enough sleep. Night after night, she woke up in the dark and lay there staring. Last night it had been four in the morning when she was suddenly awake, frightened, breathless. She'd had a bad dream which went away so fast she knew nothing about it, only that it had been there.

She tried to turn over, but was stopped by a weight on her chest. For one terrible moment she did not recognize the arm that lay across her. It was not her own, she knew, because she could not move it. It must belong to Ace, she thought. But when she peered down at it she saw dark coarse hairs. She looked at the pillow beside her: a mass of curly stuff there too, and a jutting shoulder under the sheet, hunched defensively even in sleep. Simon. She breathed in and out, temporarily reassured. She was sleeping with Simon beside her, that was all. She gazed into the dark bedroom. But now something was wrong out there; the strip of pearl from the streetlight fell on her left, not her right; the window was on the wrong side of the door. It was all backwards, like a photographic negative.

She sat up abruptly. The room tilted.

What was wrong? Everything was out of place. She tried to steady herself with her hand on the side of the bed. Then she realized that it was she who was out of place. This was the side she slept on with Ace. And she was with Simon; she should be on the other side of the bed.

It was a simple distinction. Married to Ace she had taken the right side of the bed, which in their apartment had been farthest from the door, nearest the window. When she had been with him in the empty townhouse, she had automatically done the same. The relationship of his body to hers, to the light, the door, the edge of the table, those things by which one navigates in and out of sleep, had been identical. With Simon, she always took the left side of her bed, so that her head, her feet, and her eyes struck other points of the compass. Thus she had divided one life from another, one love from another. Last night in the tangle of sex she had fallen asleep on the wrong side of the bed. The misalignment, like a change of magnetism in the poles, woke her.

Thankful that Simon slept so deeply, she pushed at his shoulder to move him and then climbed over his body so that she was on his left. Now she was by the door; the mound of his body and the slant of weak dawning light from the window were where they ought to be. She lay back relieved.

But it had been a narrow escape. In slumber she could have reached for Simon thinking he was Ace. She might have called out "Ace!" or murmured that she loved him, or even mentioned something silly from their past. Ace was on her mind, and she was no good at secrets. Simon, wakened to endearments made under mistaken identity, would be furious. He had been suspicious enough when he came back from Washington, suspicious that she had seen another man. If she slipped in sleep and made an amorous advance in the language that belonged to her and Ace, it would be all over.

Suzanne stretched out stiffly on the left-hand side of the bed. She had to be on guard; she had to keep her subconscious under lock and key as she did her writing, in the other room, since he had threatened to take that over too. She lay there and did not fall asleep. "I am a prisoner," she said to herself. "A prisoner of my own deceit, and of my submission to Simon. I thought I was choosing freedom. Why can I not stop putting myself in jail?" And it came to her how very unhappy she was.

But I can't be unhappy! she reasoned. I have found my man! She remembered all that Simon had seemed to her, at first blush, the old, wiser, man, bringing her the world on a tray. And all he had become to her since, the wildman who walked in the dark, the teacher who made her be herself. Half man, half beast; he was the satyr she had always been waiting for, not at all handsome, not always charming, ill-mannered and difficult around the house, but still the magical whiskered, hooved, sinewed man of her dreams. She thought of how it would be when they began to live together, the sharing and settling and comforting she missed in her single life. And the child. I will be happy. I will have everything I want. What were these small inconveniences, like having to guard her tongue, and control her spontaneous expressions, compared to all that? She tucked herself into his left side and tried to go back to sleep.

But she had woken up this morning tired. Getting to work had exhausted the only bit of energy she had. And now she had to meet Asp. She'd agreed to let her do some directed history studies over the summer to bring up her grade. Suzanne reached into her file drawer for her notes, pulled out a folder, and set off down the hall for the cafeteria in the yellow section. She kept her head down as she passed Nola, but she saw, out of the corner of her eye, the receptionist look up at her, and shake her head with a little *tsk, tsk, tsk*.

"My goodness dear, you are having trouble, aren't you?" Nola had said.

Suzanne was beginning to feel as if she had some wasting disease. Everyone seemed to feel sorry for her, even as, defiantly, she told them her news. "It's just the changes, Nola, such a lot to adjust to selling the house and all."

Nola did not look convinced.

"Jealous," said Suzanne to herself. "Perhaps she's jealous of my good fortune." She took the wrong hallway and ended up in the green section by mistake. By the time she had made her way back to the cafeteria, Asp was leaning on her elbow over an empty cup of coffee, looking as if she'd lost hope.

As she put her folder on the table Suzanne was hit by the full brunt of her sleepless night. Her head ached. Her eyes wouldn't stay open. Her mind, when she tried to put it in motion, flopped over ineffectually and lay down. Asp fingered some ghastly metal spike which hung from a ribbon around her neck. Her eyelids had half moons on them.

"New makeup class?" said Suzanne, absently.

"Naw. I just felt like it."

"Tell you what, let's change roles today. You've done

enough work now. Give me a lecture. You've got two minutes to think it up while I get a coffee."

When she put her plastic cup down on the table Asp was ready to go. Her back was straight, her chin thrust forward.

"You've heard the expression 'the rest is history,' " Asp said. "Well I wouldn't be so sure. History is the headline. The rest is forgotten. It's what's forgotten that interests me. History gives us the result of yesterday's race. But I want to know how it was run, and how it was judged, and why.

"History simplifies. It likes neat categories. History serves up winners and losers. Cowboys and Indians. It gives people what they ask for. People like contests, resolutions, elections. They like to feel that scores are settled."

"Bravo," said Suzanne. She basked in a rarely allowed pride. Someone had actually learned something. Asp held up a hand for silence.

"Today," she said, "I'm going to tell you about a race. Or rather three races. They were all betweeen a man called Deerfoot and a man called Stokes. Deerfoot was a Blackfoot with a narrow chest bearing the wide purple scars of cuts showing his participation in the Sun Dance ritual. He had narrow braids on either side of his face, and something that looked like a game of x's and o's drawn on his cheeks. He wore a braided band across his forehead: above it, a topknot of hair made him look taller. He wore a choker of teeth and beads, and a heavy, low-slung beaded breech-cloth. He ran in his bare feet."

"I know Deerfoot," said Suzanne.

"In the fall of 1886 Deerfoot agreed to engage in a ten-mile race at the Star Rink against an Englishman named Stokes. A thousand or more spectators leaned on the rail fence or watched from the democrats pulled up alongside. Deerfoot started ahead, and kept a good lead to the finish.

"But strangely, when the counting was done, it had Stokes winning by a lap. The judges threw up their hands: it was not what they had seen, but perhaps there was some misunderstanding, perhaps they were wrong. They declared the race off, and all bets with it."

Suzanne sipped at her coffee. She was enjoying this.

"A rematch was set for November. This time the prize was to be a medal, and each man was to take half the gate. Even more people turned out; people had talked, no doubt of the speedy Indian, whether he had indeed beat Mr Stokes. It was due to begin at eight. First, there was a delay of one hour and a half. Deerfoot was refusing to run. Then he agreed to run, but on certain conditions. His first condition was that his share of the money be collected in advance and placed in the hand of some person whom he could trust."

"Where did you get this story?" said Suzanne.

"From a book. Twelve and a half dollars were put aside. Then he said he wanted twenty-five. The hat was passed and he got the extra amount. Then, Deerfoot squatted down in a far corner of the track, refusing to move unless he got fifty dollars, two lots of land and a free pass on the CPR for life."

"You made that up!" said Suzanne.

Asp shook her head. "Anyway, it was now after nine o'clock. Deerfoot, who ran without shoes, said there was glass on the track. The track was cleared. Then he wasn't sure if it was a good night for running. Finally at ten o'clock Stokes convinced the judges to start the race. Stokes began to run. Deerfoot stayed sitting with his legs crossed in his blanket coat. Stokes did three, four, five laps...

"At five laps, Deerfoot jumped up, sped from his sitting place, and began to fly around the track. After two he'd gained one lap and was only four behind: in the next four miles he made up the difference. When the race was half run, they were equal. At one more mile Deerfoot was a lap ahead. He crossed the finish line three laps ahead."

"Wonderful," said Suzanne. Maybe she could get to like students after all. Asp was eloquent.

Asp continued. "But when Stokes flung himself over the line in the moonlight he claimed *he* was the winner. The judges began to fight. If it was only a question of who covered the ground faster, Deerfoot had won? But some said he had not been in the race at all, and that his faster running did not count. Stokes maintained that he, the Englishman, as the only competitor, had taken the race. He had been covering the ground without reference to the other man."

Asp raised her voice. "When he couldn't convince them on that point Stokes backtracked and said that for his own part, he had not been in the race either. Ten miles was not his preferred distance, and he really ought to be matched up against Deerfoot for a twenty-five mile, or sixteen-hour go-as-you-please race."

"Oh no. They're not going to go for another?"

"The twenty-five mile race was run two weeks later, before a good crowd. Deerfoot clearly came in first and was awarded the prize. Now," said Asp, raising her finger and stopping her run-on declaiming, "that was fair. Or was it?"

Suzanne said nothing.

"This is your question, Dr Miss S. Vail. Who won the race and why? Was Deerfoot right or was Mr Stokes? Who was the cheater?"

The sprouting pale green hair that had been black and orange was silver now. Asp wore what would have been a beatnik's outfit thirty years before: tight black leggings and a baggy long sweater. Suzanne looked at the girl's/woman's face and thought, with relief, that something would come of her. It was amazing to her how it did matter, now.

"So who do you think won?" repeated Asp.

"I don't know. Who do you think won?"

"Stokes got to define the race didn't he? He got Deerfoot to do what he wanted, time and again, until he finally had to let him have the money. So maybe he won, because he was the boss."

"Yes..." said Suzanne. "If being the boss and setting the terms is winning. I guess most people think it is."

"But on the other hand, Deerfoot made Stokes look like an idiot. He made them *all* look pretty foolish, really. So in a way he won."

"Maybe he had that satisfaction," said Suzanne. "I think you'd call that a pyrrhic victory."

"But he got the money too."

"It wasn't much considering where he stood in society compared to the others. Two years later Deerfoot was accused of the theft of money and a rifle. He got sick and died young. Like any other Indian."

"Maybe nobody won," said Asp.

"Is that what you think?" The clatter of trays in their metal rolling carts reminded Suzanne of her headache. She felt that Asp, suddenly, was more clear than she was on key matters.

"I think the whole point of it is that they kept on running the same damn race over and over. Over the same ground, against the same opponent. And neither one was willing to be beaten because he believed himself to be the best. The race was only an excuse, you see. They just had to keep trying. They didn't have any meaning without each other." Asp sat back and folded her hands. She smiled. It took Suzanne a minute to realize Asp wanted her to be the teacher now.

"I think that's very good," said Suzanne. "I hope you've written that all down, and that you'll hand it in to me."

They were both silent. Then, "I've got something to show you," said Asp shyly. "We've already got two hundred names." She opened her binder and pulled out a white sheet of paper. Suzanne just caught sight of a few words at the top: "reinstate," "local history," "Western Canadian subjects." She peered into the open folder. There were pages and pages of the lined paper, with black and blue and red writing on it, the names of students, she supposed. She saw a colleague's name, too.

"What's it for?" she said dimly. Usually petitions of this size went around the campus for causes like the opening of a pub, or longer hours for the library.

"It's so you can teach your course again next year," said Asp.

Inadvertently, Suzanne looked over her shoulder. Her first thought was, the Head will think I put you up to it. Her second thought was, I didn't, so what does it matter? "You've done all that yourself?"

Asp folded her binder together again. "I'm going over to the Council of Native Students this afternoon too. I know I'll get a lot more there. Don't worry, you won't be blamed."

Suzanne stared at her across the table. "I'm not actually worried," she said. "I guess I should say thank you."

"Not at all," said Asp. "It's great fun for me."

Yes, thought Suzanne, and it might actually work.

She walked back past Nola's desk with a breezy smile on her face. She didn't feel so tired after all. "Would you like me to bring you a sandwich?" she said. "I'm getting one myself."

The sky was blue china, the car a spinning top on the unfurling glaze of highway. Jennifer, Gemma and Suzanne were going out to the cabin. They had the top down; the scarf Jennifer tied over her hair pursued them flapping a sharp tattoo. The road flew up before them and then was consumed under the car.

Suzanne and Simon had had a bad fight before she left home. He wanted her to spend the day with him, since he was leaving soon for Washington again. But she had promised her friends, she said. She was looking forward to the break from her little prison. She put white cover stick over the bags under her eyes and rubbed lipstick into her cheeks.

The speedometer was up to one hundred; with the wheel tight in her hands Suzanne willed them westward. There is a point where the valley opens up, before the foothills, a collapse in the land from which the mountains rise up important and unavoidable. Just there, she pulled off the road and got out her thermos of coffee. Jennifer and Gemma had theirs in cups; Suzanne drank out of the lid.

They stood beside the car on the highway, kicking at the dirt. Suzanne had the feeling she was being called on the carpet. Gemma scanned her face.

"You look exhausted. And skinny," she said finally.

"I lost weight on purpose! I want to be really thin before Simon and I..." her voice trailed off.

"Why do women do that?" said Jennifer. "They all start to look so wasted before they take on these domestic roles. And later they get so fat. As if they wanted to make a living symbol of their sacrifice — the young virgin becomes the fatted sow."

No one answered. Gemma put her foot on the hood of Suzanne's car and began to stretch her leg. The hood was burning; it was the tag end of summer, hot sun and cool breezes. Suzanne hummed as she looked west.

"So what have we got here?" Jennifer went on. "Is this one of those fairy tales where you get your wish and it turns out to be the worst thing that ever happened to you?"

"Very funny," said Suzanne. "I told you, I'm just fine."

"What I'd like to know," said Gemma "is what, if anything, Ace and his bad actor have to do with this. Have you seen them?"

"Gone, for the moment."

"How nice for him. Just there when he needed it. Do you suppose the rest of us could get one?"

"I think they only give them out to men."

Suzanne had planned to tell her friends about the fight with Simon, but now loyalty stopped her. They already didn't like him much. They had advised her against him. If she told them all the problems it would look as if she was wrong, wouldn't it?

"Well, what's wrong then? You're not yourself," said Gemma.

"I've been really busy. What with Simon, and my work and all. I just haven't had a chance to call you. Wait till you're in love, Gemma, then you'll know."

"I don't think you're in love with him at all, frankly. I think you're in love with an idea of him."

"Is there a difference?" said Suzanne.

Gemma threw up her hands. "You intellectuals!"

"Where is this place called love?" said Jennifer, laughing. "And remind me not to go there."

"Oh, but you should!" Suzanne put her thermos lid down on the hood of the car and stretched her arms over her head. "It's not a place. It's a kind of restlessness. Hunger and anticipation. Like a bush full of birds, all about to fly off."

Gemma gaped. "I hope you don't talk like that to him!"

"We do it together," said Suzanne. It was better whipped up with words. She felt better herself. She forgave her friends their disbelief. The city was gone and the air was clean. She opened her arms wide and turned around and around. In the fullness of the notion that she loved, everything seemed beautiful; all the people in the world could be brought to her breast.

"Birds or not, your nails look as bad as mine." Gemma sighed. Suzanne kept on turning. Gemma tried again. "So what's with your research? I want you to finish that thing. I've known about it for so long. I feel as if I've been working on it myself."

Suzanne stopped. "Coming. Although I don't actually know if it's still research."

"Well, what is it then?"

"Fabrication, Simon says."

"So is this," said Jennifer. "Come on, tell us what's going on."

Gemma made a fist and banged three times. "One two three —"

"I'm scissors."

"I'm rock."

"I'm paper," said Suzanne, sighing. "All right, all right. I admit, it's not so easy. I only have one question. Don't men ever need to be alone?"

"Maybe they are alone," said Jennifer. "Even when they're with you."

This possibility had occurred to Suzanne too. That

Simon was himself with her, not oppressed by intimacy. And that she was not herself with him, not fully. She saw this as her failing, as the possibility that her privacy was too close to her skin, too easily wrecked by the touch, sound, smell of another person. It took hours from Simon's removal for her recoil to stop.

"So it's not all wonderful," said Jennifer softly.

"No, it's not." Suddenly it was a relief to talk about the awfulness. About being afraid it was over. About his two faces. About being seized by love, the force of it. "Can you understand that? It's alchemical. We might as well be two objects undergoing a transformation of substance."

"Sounds to me like a form of self-immolation," said Jennifer.

"You're turning into a masochist in your old age," said Gemma.

"No. I'm sure it's just love," said Suzanne. "Wretchedness has to be part of it." She collected their cups and put the thermos neatly back together.

They got back into the car and reached the second turnoff without speaking. The dirt road up to the cabin was narrow and full of potholes. Near to the top there was a hundred-foot pitch down to a muddy bottom and a matching climb to the house. Today the road was dry and easy; the motor churned but it made the grade. Suzanne turned into the cleared space.

Since her parents had sold their house and moved to Arizona, this cabin stood for all that had been home, to Suzanne. Her father bought it for a retirement retreat. Small, square, and built of logs, it had once belonged to a trapper, and sat on a little rise in full sun. It was the real Poverty Flats, a paean to his childhood as the only son of settlers who'd come through the depression. But when he withdrew from the gas company, Suzanne's mother scotched the plans to live at the cabin. "I don't want to be old and cold at the same time," she said. Now they lived in Sun City and drove everywhere in golf carts.

Suzanne unlocked the door and led her friends into the

main room. It was hot; the windows were closed. The chairs were dusty. She put the picnic basket on the table. Houses in the country made Suzanne fretful until she had been out; then their purpose, shelter, became clear and she was content to shut a door.

"Walk?" she said.

"I can't walk in these heels. Besides, it's dirty." Gemma sat in the kitchen rocker and pulled a copy of *Vogue* out of her bag. Jennifer and Suzanne set out.

At the top of the path, Suzanne stretched her arms into a V upward, to make herself a funnel for air. She turned her eyes down to the rutted mud then, and entered the copse of thin pines that stood over the hill. She had been this way hundreds of times, often like now, with Jennifer's firm steps pressing her from behind. Brash sun and a great burst of air met her when she came out of the trees.

"So do you have the perfect answer with your hermit?" she said as Jennifer came out of the woods behind her. For years, Jennifer had carried on a sedate relationship with a botanist who lived in the mountains where he was working on a book on high alpine meadow flowers. They saw each other about once a month and never spoke of it.

"Nothing's perfect."

"But you don't want to try for better? You know, for the whole thing, marriage, kids?"

"I don't think it's possible," said Jennifer, scrabbling ahead down the pebbly slope to the edge of the creek. "Not for me." Here the heartless sound of water running over stones took the place of words. Suzanne threw a stone and heard it crack against a larger stone.

They used to fish here, casting the lures into the deeper pools along the creek, letting the current tug their lines out, waiting for the Dolly Varden to strike. They hardly ever caught anything. They didn't really want to catch anything; they couldn't have stood to extricate the hook from the dainty open jawbone, or bang the slippery silver bodies against the rock until thick blood drooled out of the side of the mouth, like their fathers and brothers did. Instead they fussed about equipment and climbed down to the water to retrieve hooks caught under rocks. And talked. Fishing, Suzanne had told Jennifer the first time she let a boy touch her breasts; fishing, Jennifer had announced that she would be a lawyer; fishing, they had pretended not to see each other cry when Suzanne said she was leaving Ace and going away to the east. That was before they thought anything was impossible for them.

"How come?" said Suzanne.

"We didn't really have fathers, did we?"

"Simon says that too. He thinks it's why I love him. Some kind of substitute."

"Well they weren't there, were they? Not really. They just lived for work. I think that's the problem. We don't want to be like men. We don't want to be like our mothers either. That's the worst fear: you'll lose everything, your independence, your job, your sanity. The only way to be safe is to stay out of it all," said Jennifer.

"I used to want to be safe too," said Suzanne. "I used to sit around and be afraid my life would be damaged. Now I just think about how I can get what I want in a short time. I've let someone in, someone who can hurt me. In a curious way it's a relief."

"Sounds dangerous," said Jennifer.

Suzanne felt for the first time in her life that she had gone beyond her friend's understanding. Jennifer doesn't know what real love is, she said to herself. "When someone wants you so much," she said, "you lose the right to yourself. You become a kind of property of the love affair. I was tired of having myself to myself."

Jennifer jerked her neck impatiently and jumped off the log.

"It's not a matter of how much he wants you. It's just you giving up on being you."

Suzanne followed, splashing through the creek this time. Her pant legs were getting wet. She could tell by Jennifer's walk that she was really angry. "But you don't know Simon," she said. "If you did — "

"It's got nothing to do with Simon, you nitwit!"

She was very angry then.

Slipping on the rocky creek base, Suzanne began to get angry back. Did Jennifer not understand what it was to be moved beyond control, did she not have soul, spirit, passion, faith? No, she did not. She was just like everyone else in this flat part of the earth, grounded, suspicious, puritanical.

But so were you, said a voice in Suzanne. This is where you come from too. If you give up on being yourself, then who do you become? In the height of passion he once said to her, "You are so perfect. You remind me of someone I made up." What if he had made her up? Often he used both names to address her, Suzanne Vail, as if he were a uniformed messenger on the doorstep, with news of momentous import. His telegram contained plans for her life; because of his coming, everything for her would be changed, had already been changed.

"Everything between us sounds like poetry," he said. But at other times he argued: "Poetry is a game with words." Poetry is strategy, politics. And they were? Where poetry and politics met. A phrase was incomplete.

Then she thought, as she quite often thought, "Who is this man?" What if — a worse possibility, somehow — *she* had made *him* up? What if they had made each other up?

They were in draft form; two writers exchanging images. Suzanne began to feel deflated. She was back to this morning's confusion. She splashed along behind Jennifer, who, without warning, stopped and sat down on a rock at the edge of the water. She put her hand down among the rocks and drew up an imaginary rod, held it above her, then laid it slowly out.

"We did it like this," Jennifer said. Miming, she opened a tackle box and chose a lure, held it up in the sunlight and then tied it on, clipping it with tiny scissors. Squatting on the bank, she cast her phantom line, gave it a couple of seconds and then began to reel in.

"You didn't really fish. You didn't want the real prey, did

you? Imagining was better. You wouldn't really fish but you would put yourself in the position of fishing. You got cold and wet like a fisherman."

Suzanne froze, looking at her friend.

"You've always been afraid," said Jennifer. "Afraid to do anything. Now that you're actually in danger you think you've finally got what you wanted. You're out too deep, Suzanne, come back."

Suzanne closed her eyes. She was inclined to pity Jennifer, who obviously had never really been loved. She was not like Jennifer. She and Simon were having trouble, but she would not give up. Giving up would mean coming down to earth again. Giving up had somehow come to mean abandoning that other adventure too, putting Rosalie's story back between the pale covers of *Studies in Western Canadian History*. She didn't want to be narrow, safe, well-grounded. She wanted to be at risk. She had decided now, and it was too late to turn around.

"I am going to move in with him," she said. "And we are going to have a baby."

Jennifer's invisible lure made a perfect arc overhead and plopped into the water. Jennifer reeled it back in, rapidly, as if she hadn't heard. Then she stood up and gazed into the water where it ran clear.

Chapter 17

Simon and Suzanne stood side by side on the walk in front of 73 Rosebush Rise. It was brown with a roof slanting off to one side, squat, blank.

"Not this one," said Suzanne.

They were looking for a house to buy. Suzanne had wanted to stay in her part of town, Kensington. They'd seen one or two places with For Sale signs, but Simon said they looked too small. He wanted to be across the river in Mount Royal. "I can walk to work," he said. But the houses there were too grand and they couldn't afford one.

Suzanne wanted to be near a little village with a few stores, maybe a library, a couple of restaurants, a dry cleaner, a bookstore. She liked to be able to shop on foot. But Simon liked a lot of grass and wide sidewalks where he could jog. Near the river, west of 14th Street, would have suited both of them. But the houses there were flimsy old wooden structures which wouldn't be good investments, he said.

"What if we want to sell in a year or two?" he said. "We wouldn't be able to get our money out. It's got to be in a coming area."

But the coming areas were far flung and suburban and

you had to drive three miles to buy a carton of milk. "We're not buying it to sell," she said. "We're buying it to live in."

"Say if we went to Ottawa," he continued. "Or Washington."

Ignoring the warning of doom that hit her when he said this, Suzanne allowed herself to be talked into looking at this duplex in Rosedale Heights, an area which neither of them liked. It was not a coming area; it was not Kensington; it was not Mount Royal. It was a compromise, limbo, nowhere. And the house itself was distinguished by nothing. In the kitchen there was a black flecked linoleum floor, pale green wooden cupboards. The mirror in the bathroom opened on narrow shelves holding an empty bottle of aspirin. It had a rumpus room.

"You change the decorations, of course," the agent had said in an irritable voice.

You could change the decor but would it do any good? You would still be trapped in this house. Reduced to a housewife. Wasn't it the life that she had spent the last decade and a half *trying* to avoid? Wasn't this the life Suzanne's friends feared she would live?

"Not this one," Suzanne repeated.

"I don't see what's wrong with it," said Simon.

The real-estate agent had made a great show of getting her car away from the curb behind them. Now she gunned the motor, reminding them she was waiting. Simon's face was bunched in tight knots and his arms swung out from his sides while he spoke. Suzanne moved back from him a pace.

"It's only for a little while. Then we'll go back east."

"But I have a job," she said mildly. His assumptions were amusing, at the moment, because she was not in a position where she had to go along with them. Thank heaven for my job, thought Suzanne. She did not want to leave Calgary. That in itself was a revelation.

"Maybe you'll quit it," said Simon. "Maybe you'll become a poet."

His idea that she was a poet; he had to make her better than she really was. Suzanne laughed.

"Maybe you'll go into business. Maybe you'll become a real-estate agent, who knows?" said Simon.

Now the laughter turned to a cold feeling. Suzanne looked along the slightly rising crescent to the rows of houses with their trim of neat white gables, their plate-glass windows, their large white garage doors. They weren't so bad. But the house she really wanted was her own house.

The window of the agent's car moved silently downward. Her bright chestnut head of hair and red-rimmed glasses poked out at them. "I'm afraid we've got to be in Coach Hill in fifteen minutes," she said. "The owner was going to be there especially to let us in."

Suzanne hadn't known they were looking at a place in Coach Hill. "Cancel it," she said, "there's no point. I'm not going to live in Coach Hill."

"You shouldn't miss this one. It's a split-up," the agent said. "The husband has moved out; a mother and two children are living there, and they're desperate to sell because they need the money."

"No, no, no," said Suzanne.

Simon looked at the ground.

"Well then, where can I drop you?" said the agent. She knew when she was wasting her time.

"Back in Kensington."

The window moved slightly up again, and as Suzanne turned to get into the back seat of the car Simon took her arm painfully. "I don't think you want to buy a house at all."

"I want to live with you," she said. "I love you."

He did not look mollified by her protestation. "Well we've got to live somewhere. Where?" he said. "You can't live with me in your mind, in your dreams. It's got to be somewhere."

It was true; Suzanne could not imagine where this wonderful life with her wild man and his child was going to unfold. Perhaps in a large hotel room, where she would be sometimes, with him, and have her own house to escape to?

"I don't know why you care so much about the house," she said. "You're not even going to be there." Gloom descended over Suzanne. She could see it all now. He would have his own private world, Washington or Ottawa. She would have a duplex in Rosedale Heights.

Released by the real-estate agent, Suzanne and Simon went for lunch at the La Rivière on Tenth Street. He was still coming down from his trip to Washington. Suzanne looked out the window as she listened to him talk. Leaves from the poplar trees that lined the river bank were being blown along the road in clusters, little gangs that gathered and flew up in the air together, turned over and were flung onward and then separated.

"I'd forgotten about capitals, about all these attractive young women who hang around politicians. It was amazing. In every bar on Capital Hill. And all through the State Department. It's the power they're drawn to. Moths to the flame," he said, complacently tucking his napkin onto his lap.

"I don't see it. The grandeur of politics leaves me quite numb, I'm afraid."

"I know it does," he said wanly.

"I thought you liked that about me. Not playing the game and all," she said.

"I did. But that was before I knew what it was about," he said. "It's only because you don't think you're part of it. Because you don't think you measure up, because you can't imagine yourself as one of the great figures of history. It's just insecurity."

What had been her charm was now a flaw, Suzanne observed. It was strange because she was also conscious that Simon's analytical bent, which she so admired, had become oppressive.

"Don't I get to have any ideas of my own? Does

everything I think have to do with my psychological makeup?" She put this as a teasing question, and not a statement. She found it necessary, when disagreeing, to do it pleasantly, so subtly in fact, as to not do it at all. "Neither worshipper nor worshipped be," she said more firmly. "That's me."

"It's more than psychological," Simon went on, "if I dare say. It's biological. Female. A turned-in perspective. The end result of your opting out of the larger forms of social organization is this fever you now have to procreate. You realize that power in the larger sense is blocked to you and then you start having children to achieve immortality."

Suzanne considered how to take this remark. Sitting down or not? Walking out or staying, giving it the benefit of examination? Trying not to be hasty, she examined it. On the face of it, his analysis was tempting. She never had liked politics. She liked history. She wanted a child, yes. But she had not lost her lust for history. On the contrary it consumed her more than ever. She could reach the past, but the future eluded her.

"You seem to see having children as half a bid for glory, and half a useless detour," she said. "I don't think it's either. If anything it's a duty." She did not actually mean that, but she was desperate.

Now Simon twisted with amazement in his chair to examine the out of doors. "That's very elitist," he said. "Duty! Do you think your kind has a duty because you think you're better than other people?"

"My *kind*? Isn't it the same as your kind?" But perhaps not. Not to Simon. "I don't want a child which just comes from me, you know. I want to have you in the mix."

"And now you're going to tell me it's because you love me."

Suzanne turned her eyes back to the autumn whirlwind.

"It sounds pretty," Simon said, "but I don't think it will wash. It's not fair to ask someone to have a child just because you love them."

"I don't want this sandwich," said Suzanne. She got up and left the restaurant. She put her hands in the pockets of her coat and began to walk. He caught up with her at the corner in front of the bookstore. The wind was fierce; he'd had to shout for her to hear.

"Where do you think you're going?"

"I don't just want a baby. If I did that I'd have it by myself. I want you to want a baby too," she said. "Otherwise it's no fun."

"Good old Suzanne. Always upping the ante, aren't you?" he said, but he took her arm and they walked back to the house together.

Simon took Suzanne out dancing. Swing was in again, and the Western Hotel had opened up a large crescent-shaped dining room with a dance floor. They had a table near the front, and a bottle of champagne on it. Suzanne wore a strapless dress. She'd always wanted to wear a strapless dress, and this had seemed like the occasion. She'd bought it from Jezebel's Antique clothes shop around the corner from home; it was turquoise taffeta, from the fifties. The walls of the dining room were pink, and so were the carnations on the table. Simon was still talking about Washington.

"You should have seen these guys," said Simon. "I really snowed them. I had them bamboozled. The muscle is there, but the will, I don't know. They're weak. I can talk circles around them."

Suzanne was just a little bored. She had hoped that this table would be different from the restaurant tables they sat at; that this bottle of wine would be more sparkling; that they would talk about real things.

"What happens to your circles when you've gone out the door?" she said.

"That's what I don't know. That's why it's so important that I get back in a week or so — "

"That soon?"

He touched her hand. "Didn't I explain? That's why I

want to get you settled on a house, then I'll go back to Washington and prime them up again."

Suzanne pretended not to hear him, which was easy, because the music was loud. She leaned back on his elbow and they both stared at the band. The members all wore tuxedos and the trombonist leaned like a treble clef into the sky-blue shell behind.

"So you think that love's a barrel of dynamite, goody-goody!"

The waiter passed with a tray. "Drink up," he said, winking at Suzanne. She laughed. Her dress had turned her into someone who was winked at. But when she opened her mouth she didn't talk like that kind of someone.

"That's all you want. To lock me up in a little house somewhere safe and then fly off on your half-baked political mission — "

Simon had been expecting this. A smile came onto the lips which could be thin and cruel, or rounded and passionate by turns.

"You've never respected my work," he said. "I guess you'd be happier if I were some right-wing entrepreneur, making a fortune out of tennis balls or whatever it was."

"Shuttlecocks."

"Gift to mankind," said Simon, snorting down at his menu. "I would have thought someone like you, so high-minded and all, would have been above marriage to a jock."

"At least I knew what game he was talking about," she said.

"Hooray and hallelujah! You had it comin' to ya," sang the band.

Simon's eyes were red around the rim, and they fixed on one object after another around the room. They fixed on his drink, the waiter, and then Suzanne.

"You don't love me enough. You never did."

Suzanne made an attempt. "Please," she said, leaning over to kiss him on the lips. "Ace and I are just friends, remember. I wasn't happy married to him. It's you I want."

Simon rallied. He smiled his open, sweet smile, the one that rearranged the downward lines beside his nose, and brought out the impish dimple on the side of one cheek. Only his eyes did not move. "I never did have a proper talk with the guy," he said. "But maybe he'll come around when we're living together."

She put her glass carefully on the table in front of the champagne bottle.

He poured another glass. Suzanne's eyes drifted back to the dance floor. It was a crush of bodies; all these couples who wanted to do the old steps, the foxtrot, the two-step. Suzanne knew how to count them out aloud. "Solves the conversation problem," her mother used to say, when she and her father went to their dance classes. *Slow, slow, quick-quick* being what you said to your partner in the foxtrot.

She could see the couples out there that looked like one animal, like the beast with two backs. Heads pressed alongside heads, ears to cheeks, forward and backward promenading. Vacillation was the natural progress of the beast with two backs.

The clarinetist stood, raising his instrument to the pasteboard stars. In front of him the ladies moved in restricted squares, colliding with one another, for which accident their partners apologized, man to man. Suzanne would have preferred a huge ballroom floor, with Viennese waltzes. A hopeless romantic, she was. Why is the word hopeless always attached to romantic? She thought she could be a hopeful romantic.

"Let's dance," she said.

"I don't. I told you that."

"Not even at weddings?" she said. A slip. She should have said celebrations.

"So that's the next thing you're after, is it?" he said darkly.

But the evening must not go down to another of their quarrels. "You mean I'm never going to dance again?" she said, falsely gay.

"You could lose out on a lot, tying yourself down to me."

She turned back to the dance floor. She looked at the

couples and thought, yes, I would be willing to lose it too, but only knowing I could have a child. It made no sense, but there it was. Simon had taken a back seat to the phantom baby, as he called it. He never liked to take a back seat to anyone, and certainly not to what he called "one of her ideas."

"All women want children," he was inclined to say.

The phantom baby had come to live. They had this name for it, the phantom, and this habit of discussing it in the conditional, but by now it was not even a phantom, it was real. Simon was conditional. Suzanne did not know why it had come, what made it come. Simon said it was all political. Jennifer said it was to do with her parents. But Suzanne's mother did not believe in maternity as a fulfilling activity. When Suzanne had once mentioned in a passing way that she would like to have a child some day her mother had said, "Oh, you wouldn't want to do that!" Suzanne's mother had not, in fact, left her many choices. Working was not a worthwhile way to live, and neither was having children, and neither was love, "living for a man."

Her parents used to go out dancing. Her mother's clever thin feet wrapped in silver slippers, her father's staunch neck done up in a dark tie. They left Suzanne at home in flannelette pyjamas, hot and tangle-haired from the bath, with a babysitter. At the Kinsmen Club or the Palliser Hotel, they sat around a big table, the men drinking from a brown bag they passed from lap to lap, and they got up and swirled across the big open floor.

"Come on, Simon, you can learn," Suzanne said, meaning to dance.

"I can't," he said. "And I won't. So don't try to make me."

He wouldn't swim either. He claimed to be more dense than water, that his bones were heavy. The truth was he hated to swim because he hated taking off his glasses. He wouldn't swim because he couldn't see, and he only liked being in the dark when he could hold on to something, like Suzanne. When he could put his fingers on the buttons and knobs.

The music drew up to an end and the conductor tied a

knot in it, sharply, with a circular tug of his baton. Applause scattered over the retreating musicians in their black suits. Suzanne placed her glass very carefully down on the heart-shaped paper coaster. She realized that she had dressed like someone else, like an older sister, or an aunt. She looked down on herself from a distance, and saw that this sister, dressed for romance, was patronizing a lost cause.

"I suppose it's good, that you can be so clear about things like that. A good sign," she said, carefully, "I suppose." It came so easily to her, this language of compromise. He would call it constructive engagement.

He said something, but the clapping took away his words. The band was returning for an encore. People got up from their seats to dance. They pushed in their chairs and grabbed their partners' hands and ran to get a place. It was as if awful things had been said at each table, as if they were running away from the tête-à-tête instead of running towards that small, gleaming diamond of a floor. The song began again.

"And I hope you're satisfied, you rascal you."

Suzanne fixed her eye on one couple. The woman wore a red, tight-fitting dress; her thick brown hair was rolled at the back in the style of thirty years ago. She and her partner were wedged so tightly, and she wore such a dreamy smile, the smile of a person who has come to rest permanently, that it was a few moments before Suzanne realized how off balance she was, how very uncomfortable she must be, hanging off this man's shoulder at such a ridiculous angle.

They were a handsome couple, well-matched, sleek and graceful, their bodies pressed together, one firm and the other bending, supple. They were so like their era, the men in those days, thicker, harder, like one another, cut into the designated shape. And the woman too, a sharper waist, a greater curve in the hip, a dreamier eye.

Their sequence of steps became familiar to Suzanne, the same twenty-four counts, a dip and a twirl, a box step, turn into the chase, and then another step and start again. The music changed, the dance did not. The dance was set, the steps and postures so firmly learned that neither one nor the other could unlearn them. Their feet wrote the letters on the floor, a series of hieroglyphics. Suzanne could have lifted tiles off the floor and hung them on the wall. Read the message. The message was about submission and dominance, tyranny and slavery. And yet this couple was nothing extraordinary. Their dance was a commonplace enough dance, their bargains and inhibitions and restrictions were not so different from anyone else's.

The woman in the red dress, now almost weightless, was touching one spot on the floor with her toe, moving neither forward nor back. Suzanne felt sad. The effect was lovely, and it was only an effect. The image had no more power to hurt or damage her.

She turned to Simon. She put her hand on his hand. She felt they were teetering. Their debates had got away from them. They were caught up high on their word scaffolds and were about to lose sight of ground. "Come on down from there," she said.

His face was hard. His cheeks had fallen into his chin. His eyes had gone to gunpowder grey and his body had taken on a certain fixity.

Simon felt betrayed. Betrayed because Suzanne had not seemed to be like other women and now this baby thing was happening. Betrayed because he had come to her when he needed a job, and now he had one, and she wasn't properly enthusiastic. Betrayed because he thought she knew what kind of man he was and that meant she would not ask him for things which he could not give.

He had understood Suzanne, had he not? Despite the fact that she was younger. That in itself is hard, when you are the old one, when you know your skin is getting loose and she is still firm and smooth as a new bar of soap. He had given her what she needed, a little loosening up. Some belief in herself. Advice about her work, to help her out of the prissy confining little schoolmarm's jacket she put on herself. Hell, he might even have made her into a great scholar, or writer, anything. He was good at seeing what was inside people and helping to bring it out. Just like he was good at seeing what was in the country, and putting a name on it. Finding the right guy to capture the imagination of the public. That was what Simon was good for.

Simon thought Suzanne did not appreciate him. He had an important role to play, and he must not be held back. He made a fist: nature itself was against him. He wanted to say something like, "I'm a special man. It takes a special woman to keep me. You were it. You were going to show me what a woman could be. Now you turn out to be like every other dumb, dependent, cloying..."

He found he had said it.

They looked at each other. There was not going to be any going back now. He barged on.

"I can't have people depending on me, leaning on me. I have so much important work to do. I need to be free. I can't be forced into looking after a family. Anyone can do that. I have to do something else..."

Suzanne had goose pimples on her shoulders. She looked down and thought, my collarbones are too big and ugly to be wearing this. The costume, the whole evening was a mistake. "No one is going to force you to do anything, Simon."

The horns were wailing. The dancers were circling; heads back, laughter gurgled like blood out of their throats. Simon and Suzanne sat at their small table, rigid with discussion. The music was very loud. He was saying something. Suzanne put her face right up against his to hear. He shouted it in her face.

"I have to tell you something."

She nodded. She watched the dance floor. The woman with the red dress had disappeared. Her eyes sought out the chestnut hair roll. When she found her, she nodded to Simon. Yes, yes, go on.

"I can't have children," he shouted.

She turned to look at him. "Pardon me?"

She thought he'd said he couldn't have children.

"I can't have children. I tried before. With Marlene. We tried for three years. But it didn't work. There's something wrong with me. I have self-destructive sperm."

Suzanne leaned back and looked carefully to see which face he wore. It was the wild one. It was the crafty face, the face of passion. The face that looked after itself first. Not the teaching face, the giving face. At the same moment, it came to her, as in a footnote, how much they had talked and played word games in bed, but whenever they had a really important conversation, it was in public. She had a nervous desire to laugh.

"You've got what?"

"It's a rare condition. There's something in my fluids that reacts against the sperm, as soon as they're ejaculated. It kills them off before they're out of my body."

The song ended. The band leader began to tell them what wonderful people they were, what really great people, and how it was a pleasure to play for them. The dancers clapped and clapped but they could not squeeze any more music out of the band. The musicians bent over and began to pack up their instruments. The men on the dance floor put their hands on the bare backs of the women and prompted them off the floor.

Suzanne watched Simon sort through the bills in the wallet and leave some of them on the table. She watched him take out his silk pouf and lightly touch the sweat that had formed under his nose. And she thought, whether this fantastic tale is true or not, he means to get rid of me by it.

Just because it had not happened yet she was able to imagine how it would hurt. He would leave, she would cry, there would be rage, and recriminations and then worse, nothing, just the vacancy he left, beside her in the night, in every part of her body, in her work, where he had tangled so dangerously, everywhere in her house. In her mind. How much of her now was reacting against him, defining herself as not being him. And she remembered his words at the beginning.

"There's an endless stream of girls, I'm afraid, because there's an endless stream who never had a father."

How absurd that had seemed to her at the time, theoretical and arbitrary like so many of the things he said. If he was a father to her he had been judging, tyrannical and possessive (like her father) and now he was pulling away (like her father) only this time she felt it. She had not felt it before, she had not allowed herself to feel it before, and now she was going to die of pain.

Very privately, Suzanne said goodbye to Simon.

They went back to her house and made love. But it was only pretend. Suzanne knew there wasn't any more hope for her and her animal-man, her satyr on his high ledge. Suzanne lay under him wishing she had studied mythology; was it her imagination or was it true that satyrs can't reproduce? Satyrs are an end in themselves.

"I'm grateful you told me," Suzanne said, after.

"And now I suppose you'll leave me," he sulked. But he didn't believe she would.

Chapter 18

In the end with Miss Amy it wasn't the drink, exactly. She went out on a windy day. Her arthritis was so bad she couldn't properly do up her clothes. She arrived at her destination, the hairdresser's at Seventeenth Avenue and Fourth Street, in a taxicab, and when she got out, she shut the door on her coat. The taxi pulled away from the curb, upending her and dragging her a few feet.

Her foot was smashed, and her ankle. The doctors gave her a general anaesthetic to repair the tiny fractures. Block was there before she went under. He was angry.

"Where were you going," he said, holding her hand, "on such a rotten day? The rain was terrible." The doctor was asking her to count down from a hundred.

"Ninety-nine," she said. "To get my hair done. Ninety-eight. What's it to you? I was bored. Ninety-seven. And then I was going to meet Gracie for lunch, ninety-six — " she said, and then said no more.

She never woke up from the anaesthetic. The doctors were not liable; her medical history was so complicated. They left her for a week but Block couldn't stand the strain. It was too indefinite: was she dead or alive? What with the drinking and the pills, they agreed there wasn't much hope, and unplugged her, like a radio. A great silence followed.

Even though she was an invalid, her death was a shock.
She had been ill so long it had seemed that she could stay
that way forever, that it was her natural state, and not a
decline. Amy's three men stood together in a hospital
corridor. Block was trembling. He kept complaining about
the buzz from the overhead lights; he couldn't hear.

"I'm overwhelmed with feeling,'" he kept saying, shaking
his head. What he meant was that feeling was so rare to him
that any amount was overwhelming. Brault had his hands in
his vest pockets, miserably trying to stretch the fabric
around his middle.

"Perhaps it's just as well," he said thickly, "if she'd
woken up, who knows what she'd have been like?"

Ace made a disgusted noise and jammed his fists together.
He shrank from his brother's paltriness of spirit. To think
that life should end because of mere pain! His mother's
pain had been more lively than the absence of pain (of
pleasure too, for that matter) in others he could name. And
if the truth were known, Ace heard in his brother's words
an echo of what he had once said to Suzanne about the
child: "Perhaps it's just as well."

Even Block looked irritated. "Just as well, to die?" he
grunted. "Have you no respect?" Block had respect for
death: it was the only thing he feared.

"But *you* had them turn her off..." Brault had taken to
wringing his hands, an odd gesture for such a big man. The
more his father scowled and shook his large head, the more
Brault wrung his hands.

Block seemed to hear Amy's voice overhead. "Don't
blame me. You took over. I had no influence." Or perhaps it
came from down the hall where she had been wheeled. "I
can't in any way be held responsible."

"Come on, Amy give the boy a break," said Block.

"I'll give you all a break," she said. "I'll go on up now."

The three men looked at each other to see if they'd all
heard. They stood chastened, awaiting the sting of her
withdrawal, which had come for the last time. Now she

would not be there. Her wit would no longer touch them; in her destruction she would no longer put them nearer to their souls.

"Quite a woman, your mother," said Block, reminiscent.

Ace thought very probably they were all doomed.

Gemma leaned over the cards in the gift shop. A pity: bereavement did not lend itself to much zip in the way of messages. She had considered flowers or a wreath but knew that those would simply fall into the huge pile of consolation, chiefly corporate, which would have arrived. She wanted to be noticed. A personal card was the ticket.

In Your Time of Loss. No. Words Cannot Express. No. What she wanted was something along the lines of Smile, it could have been You. Or, Don't let Death carry you Away. Something that stood out. In the end she settled for a card with a picture of two young lovers under an apple tree, beside a speckled brook. One with "Message, Blank" inscribed on the back. The good thing about this card, she thought, was its utter inappropriateness. She transported it to the cashier with delicate fingers. It would seem spontaneous, ingenuous.

Later in the day at her coffee break she took out a fine-point flow pen, black. She wrote. "Dear Ace, I am so sorry about your mother." She hesitated, thinking she might make reference to the fact that he had lost his wife too, and then decided against it. "I hear your dad is having people over to the house Wednesday — do you mind if I come to pay my respects?"

She signed it — Gemma, with a little heart above the final *a* — and dropped it into the box on Tuesday, not sure if they would get it on time. Still, if they looked surprised to see her, she could say she wrote. The thing about death was that it made the mourners public property. They could hardly turn away well-wishers, could they?

The maid was counting out the sandwiches on silver trays.

The bartender was pouring generous ones. Miss Amy's hostessing had never been this successful, the crowd had never been so congenial, in her lifetime. The boys — "boys" — were in their schoolboy best and Block, his durable face gleaming faintly, had never been so loving.

Nor so youthful. His hardy gloss could not help but remind those who gathered among the azaleas of her sunroom that she had not been so impervious to time. It was unseemly for him to appear so well. But unseemly had been his way in all matters, and a most successful way. In any case, to the more thoughtful mourner, Block's persistent youth suggested more long-term punishment than victory.

And Amy was not there. Not regaling the ladies in the powder room, or splashing vodka behind the palms. And now her amazing thinness had reached its natural culmination, she was crumbling in her coffin. Here it ends, the women seemed to whisper. On the face of it, a tragedy. And yet. She did go before he left her. It might have been otherwise, had she hung around. She died in office, as it were.

Well, if you want it.

Here came one who did. Gemma, dressed in the peasant style: a blouse with white ruffles on an elastic around bony shoulders, a full skirt clinched with a soft leather belt with long fringes, a belt which cost her a month of lunches. Up to the bereaved husband she drew on humble flat feet, smiled to that shovel-shaped face, weathered but not beaten and already bored of sorrow.

"Mr Cummings, remember me, I'm Ace's friend, we met at the McBean barbecue?" How easily she had taught herself the lines; she'd been getting ready for this for years. "Gemma Starchuk?" she said, as if to ring a bell. "Friend of Suzanne's. Gemma," she repeated.

His look of dazzlement was not from being unaccustomed to having pretty young(ish) women present themselves to him for whatever purpose. She was neither the prettiest nor the boldest, nor the most imaginative. She was merely the first to get there after the death of his wife. She reached him just as he had begun to resent Miss Amy for the partiality she left behind. And she was Ace's friend. There was something in that; as his wife retired from competition, he might slide down to the juniors, again. Nothing was impossible.

"Of course, I remember." He gave her the deep sparkle, as opposed to the opaque grey glint. He gave her the knowing glimmer, which seemed such a privilege, being so rare. The barbecue? He remembered Suzanne, his son's red-headed wife. He did not recall this one. But never mind.

"I was there with my wife," he said. His chin dropped slightly on the last words, a genuine recollection of precise loss: she had hung on his arm that day, together they had watched the hot-air balloon ascend and move east. Death subtracted something from the memory. He leaned on the bar with his elbow; he was smoking a cigar, and the tip of it crumbled, falling into his coffee.

"You must have loved her very much," said Gemma, looking at his cup where ashes floated. She gestured to the expanse of the living room, which was to her like a meadow, long and flat and broken up by clusters of trees and flowers. Perhaps she felt its size was an indication of his love for Miss Amy.

"Always," he repeated and a tear wedged its way out of the triangle of his eye. "And failed her very much," he added. "Perhaps I let my work come between us. We never spoke of it." He smiled. He always smiled when he lied. She used to travel with him until the time he caught her in the hotel room reading the minutes of a meeting he'd left in his briefcase. She had dropped the sheaf of papers in the garbage, announcing that she found this plan immoral, these directors a herd of pigs, and that she did not wish to join the wives of pigs in their tour of the local art gallery.

"We had separate realms," he said. "If she didn't like what I became at least she didn't interfere." It was a release for him to speak of this. He had maintained silence to friends and relatives; there had been times, however, when the occupant of an adjacent seat on a flight from Toronto had heard his confession.

But Gemma knew nothing of travelling saleswomen. She felt only the immeasurable thrill of receiving intimacies from the flinty Block Cummings.

"Are there women who don't want their men to succeed?" said Gemma, rounding her eyes, poking out a thin elbow and bringing it to rest on the bar, so that she let her weight settle back slightly without his noticing it, to a place of rest.

Block ran his eyes along the course of her thin body from the part in her brown hair (white scalp visible) to the seamless tip of stocking in the open-toed shoe. "Nothing is that simple," he said. "When you hitch up like we did, at the start...It was more than hitching, actually, it was sort of, welding..." He was at a loss. "We shared each other's failings. We shared rather less in triumph," he added in an unguarded fashion, because the idea had just come to him.

"I wouldn't know about that," said Gemma, "I've never been in love."

By now hearts were beating fast. Gemma looked down at her hands to find she had no glass to hold. She swung back to face the bartender, leaving Block gap-mouthed, a fish lifted on a line, who did not yet feel the hook but wished to know for what reason the sea had tilted, the speed of events had increased, why something he had sensed, some glittering curiosity was missing, not knowing he had swallowed it.

"Some wine, madam?" said the waiter.

"A little, please." She looked over her shoulder at Block. Someone else had come up and was kissing his cheek. His eye caught hers. They would meet again.

Ace sought out the Weepstick. Of course he would come, he was the sort who would come. There he was, a standing scythe, his head tilted down, half patronizing, half humble, as he listened to a short woman.

"Hey fella," said Ace softly, punching his arm.

"Fella!" said the Weep. He took Ace's biceps in his two hands; he squeezed them.

"How're ya doing?"

"Super! Hey, sorry," said the Weep lightly, casting his eye over the gathering. "About your mum. Geez. Bad. Know what I mean?"

"Oh sure," said Ace, lightly. There was a funny sore tension around the corners of his eyes. Maybe he was getting a cold. Maybe he was going to cry. The Weep's consolation made it worse. "It's tough," he said.

They both shifted their feet.

"What'cha been up to?"

"The same."

"Oh yeah?" said Ace, wondering if it was possible. Were the brothers all out there, up to the same things? "Haven't seen you around."

The Weep looked proud. "Working. Yeah, I spend a lot of time in Denver. There's a guy there, he likes the same stuff I do. You know, competition, fast cars, women?" Weep laughed, a falsetto.

"Women?" said Ace, mildly curious. The Weep had never cared too much for women.

The Weep moved one fist forward and back rapidly in front of his belt. "You know, I like to keep in practice."

Ace smiled, nodded, weary. It was too long ago. He couldn't play. There was only one thing he wanted. "Say," he said. "You know what I was thinking about? I was thinking about the Ace-R." He lifted his right arm upward and back, made as if to serve a badminton bird. A woman behind him had to adjust her hat. He dropped it, quickly. The occasion. Still he had to know if the thing was still in Weep's memory, as it was in his.

"The *Ace*-R!" cried Weep, his voice dropping in pitch and rising in volume. "To test the shuttlecocks!" The Weep lifted his hands to the side, extravagantly. "Ten shots those little birds had to survive, from the Ace machine. If it fell on the circle, it went in the tin. The shot that never missed. The perfect shot!" It was as if it were his own, not his friend's; more than that, as if he had created the shot, husbanded it. "Those were the days, eh?" Then he dropped his voice. "Hey," he said. "Suzanne's over there."

Ace didn't look.

The Weep waited a minute and then went on.

"So what were you thinking about the Ace-R?" The Weep had invented it, but Ace had been the mould.

"I don't know. I was just thinking about it," he said. "It's in the garden, behind the berry patch. Maybe I'll go out, pay my respects."

The Weep's laugh shot up high. Heads turned. He curled down again, the guy had a spine like a cat's, Ace could swear. "So give me a call," he said. Ace said he would do that.

Ace saw Suzanne across the room. She was alone. Tall in her flat shoes, rangy, shoulders hunched, her hair loose. He wanted to go to her, make her stand up straight. Amy used to take her to shoot traps. She should have been good at it, with her broad shoulders and long arms, her far-sightedness. But she wasn't. She couldn't take aim. She made a better target than she did a hunter.

He saw her not as he had seen her before — a woman he loved, with a nervous face, liquid and sensitive. He saw her as a stranger, dry, locked in her solitude, which was not really solitude but singlemindedness. She had always walked with her arms wrapping her waist, clutching small things to her, tassels, purses, notebooks. Now she stood loosely, as if she had nothing left to protect. The gentle hollow of her long cheek was visible, the sharp knob of her chin lifted, the long wide-apart eyes under straight brows fixed in thought.

His eyes caught the gaze. She nodded gravely, and turned away, as if it would have been indecent to intersect longer. She turned, walked forward, but found no clear path through the crowd and stopped in confusion. He followed her and caught her arm.

"I thought we were friends," he said. "I thought we were a constellation. Up in the sky."

"That was before," she said. She shook her hair off her face.

"Before what?"

She said nothing. He put his arm out but she did not move into it. Holding off, as if she were saying, we can't let this bring us together.

"What have you been up to?" he said, understanding that she could not talk about Amy.

"Working," she said quickly. She looked off over his shoulder. "I'm almost finished this *thing* I've been writing." She looked back at him. "Simon and I..."

She used his name like a shield. But it felt weak, a shield halfheartedly raised. He pressed his advantage.

"Bad times?"

Finally she looked him in the face. "Instructive." Then again she gave up. She waved her hand and drew in a big breath. "It's just..." Her hands went up. "Everything's gone. Amy. And..."

"Your big romance?"

She didn't deny it.

"Has it then?" He was pressing her, he was aware of it, pushing her forward, aware that people, his brother, her friend, the relatives were watching. "I'm sorry," he said.

She bit her lip, and began to back away. "No, I'm sorry. About Amy."

"Are you all right?"

Tears started down her cheeks. Before he could see any more of what was happening to her face, she turned it sideways. "I've got to go," she said, and fled.

At home, she waited for Simon to call. She knew he would. When he did it was late at night, which meant it was even later in the east.

"Just checking to see if you're in," he said. He sounded different, a smoother, more threatening version of himself.

"But it's none of your business," she replied. To her the baby incident, as she referred to it, had been final.

"So I guess you miss me?" he said.

"Not really." She didn't miss him, she missed the affair.

"I don't miss you either." Then they both laughed. He said he was coming back to town and would she meet him at the airport? She would. When she hung up she cried until her eyes shut by themselves. He was nothing. He was an invention that had failed. Her lover was gone. Even his voice had lost its low marvellous electricity.

The night he arrived, a batten of cloud pressed over the saddleback roof on 11A Street. Suzanne wore a baggy cotton jacket over her jeans and T-shirt. She stood in the airport terminal, watching the businessmen come out of the gate. He had called the men steers. They did look like domesticated animals stunned for the kill, coming down their chute. He was smaller than the others, jerking as he walked, from the weight of his huge briefcase.

"Darling," he said, setting down the case carefully and opening his arms.

She stepped forward automatically. His smell came over her, a memory blow that weakened her legs.

In the house he dropped his bag by the door with a thud. He loosened his tie and made for her, his chest straining inside the cotton of his shirt. She dodged, and offered him a drink.

"Seen any houses?" he said.

Suzanne was shocked. She hadn't imagined even *he* could pretend none of it had happened.

"We won't be looking at houses," she said. "I'm staying here."

As he sat, thin fingers tense around the sweating glass, she told him.

"I mean it, Simon. I don't want you any more. I am over you." She was lying, a little bit. She would be over him, but she wasn't yet. "Over you," she repeated, her features immobile. Suzanne had got this plan right; Suzanne knew what she was doing. She saw the hard cast of her image in his eyes. Strong, independent. All the things he'd said. And getting away. No great catastrophe was going to mark this betrayal. Nothing large or odious took place.

The difference was so small, it was nothing anybody would ever know. But she felt it, a small, painless irrevocable separation in her chest, as when the yolk of an egg slides away from the white. Finished! she used to say at school and sign off with a dot, bounding her pen on the paper. *Fini. Terminé.*

Simon drained his glass. His eyes were red around the rim but he was used to sacrifices; you have to make sacrifices all the time to bargain. He managed to make a graceful exit, and for that she was glad.

But he was a habit. She still woke up wanting him, and paced the small rooms of her house trying to sweat him out of her pores. Once she broke down, and made for the telephone. He was there. She burst into a tearful tirade about what he'd done to her. After she was finished, she hung up.

She saw him once, on the sidewalk in front of the fountain at the Husky Building. He stood talking, fast, to two men, old men with white hair and paunches, and he almost looked young in comparison. She realized that his face had become familiar now in the way it was at first. The way the faces of movie stars are familiar, so that sometimes you think they are old friends, when really you've only seen them on the screen.

And then she didn't see him again. The grand love was over. The habit was broken.

She woke up in the night sometimes, crying with jealousy after dreaming that Simon was making love to one of those beautiful political groupies he talked about, who had brunch in bars and knew all about buttons and knobs. Then she would go back to sleep and he was in her arms again but she did not want him; she would twist away. He was false, a trick with words, a trick with mirrors.

Now Suzanne began to believe that there never was a Simon. He was not a person, he was an action, a reaction. He was what-happened-to-Suzanne-when-she-was-with-Simon. Whatever exaltation of molecules in her had lent an ordinary pale man this god-in-heaven glow was gone. It had passed painfully through her, a mammoth thing, leaving its mark, a hollow place inside that would harden in his print, like a fossil.

Chapter 19

I was getting my coat to leave at five o'clock, for what miserable entertainments the Alberta Hotel bar had to offer, when my editor turned up behind me, rattling a handful of sheets of paper in my face.

"Something's the matter with you, Murphy," he said. "I didn't think it was possible but you have become more objectionable than ever!"

I knew what was troubling him. It was my latest editorial, which hadn't been calculated to please. Normally the man hardly glances at them. But we'd been getting a lot of letters in about the Jumbo Fisk trial, most of them referring to it as an "abhorrent miscarriage of justice." And they didn't mean because he'd got away with it. They meant because there hadn't been a verdict. "Fisk is still on trial," the letters said. "He must be given the fullest measure of fair play in defending himself." McAra, the editor, was especially sensitive.

All I had done was write something that went against the mood of the city. And why not? I was a citizen too. If every half-cocked, law-and-order-minded resident of our fair town could have his say in the letters column, then why couldn't I have mine? Such was my thinking. Apparently

I'd been wrong. My editor had taken unaccustomed trouble in reading the copy before it went down.

"What is this horseshit?" he demanded, thrusting the pages I'd so happily written out even closer to my face.

" 'Crime weakens us all, clings to us all,' " I said, reading over his shoulder. " 'And the trouble with punishment is it isn't much better. It is least fitting where there has been the greatest wrong. To think of putting Fisk in prison for a few years only trivializes his crime.' "

McAra looked blank.

"It's a theory," I said. "for murder there can be no sentence."

"What the hell are you recommending then?"

"The Greeks had an interesting notion," I said, laying my coat on the back of my chair and settling in for a little discussion. I looked forward to it: he seldom wanted to talk about anything. "They had this concept of banishment." I pointed a little farther down my copy. I don't think he'd actually read to the end. "You see what I say here? 'The Greeks sent a criminal far away from his own land for a period of years. They believed that the continued presence of a murderer in the land would cause it to wither and sicken, and that crops would fail and waters would run dark.' " I looked at him, challenging.

His jaw fell open as he read on. "Are you mad, Murphy?"

"Not in the least. You see what I think is fitting is banishment. And then I go on a bit."

"You're damn tooting." McAra was reading now, his mouth drooping, my description of what might happen if Fisk (and his like, I meant, but didn't say) were banished. Perhaps the buffalo might come back. Perhaps the Blackfoot, starving to the south, would be suddenly free of tuberculosis. I had let myself go. I knew McAra's look. He was imagining what would have happened if he'd done his usual careless job of editing and the thing had gone to press.

He put down the papers. "I repeat, Murphy. You've let this thing turn your head around. What is *wrong* with you?"

I was prepared to talk about it. I admitted there was

something. I didn't quite understand what. I only knew that I was filled with disgust, a deep and thorough disgust, of which my former cynicism had only been a thin imitation. Fisk remained in jail with his mounted police guard. Rosalie was dead, but not buried, a ghost. The whole town stank of it. The unsolved murder seemed to have stopped time. We couldn't get past it, had been divided by it. The group who didn't want Fisk convicted included most of the big cheese, the merchants. The other group wanted the Indians appeased, and most of all wanted the ghost to go away. She was said to have made appearances in the Turf Club bar, out at the convent, even in the general store on a Saturday morning.

I wouldn't say this to anyone but I personally was not bothered, if Rosalie lingered somewhere between death and life. She died for me when she refused to come to me again. Oh yes, I dreamed of lifting her body, heaving the soft, wild-smelling skin up and over my face like a sheaf. But that shameful dream was sweetened and made pure by the fact that she was dead. As far as I was concerned she could wander the town scaring people while she waited for her place in the Happy Hunting Ground or whatever it was for as long as she liked. I just cared about justice, and cleansing ourselves of this.

McAra felt differently. Our editor wasn't exactly a man of the pen, nor did I esteem him. Daily he gave me reason not to. For example: this is how the newspaper works. McAra, who hails from that great capital of Regina several hundred miles east, gets his free board with a woman who lives a few blocks away. His landlady in turn gets her free groceries from the Hudson's Bay Company store. And for that, the Bay gets to advertise in our paper. I ask you, does this make for an independent editorial stance?

Needless to say, McAra proceeded to blow his top. He said I was crazed and berserk and that I had no business writing editorials. I couldn't be trusted to advise a dog on how to get rid of fleas. He said we were going to have to rewrite the editorial and if I didn't do it he would. I said I would. I'd had my fun writing it, as a matter of fact. I didn't know if there was anyone out there listening to me anyway. I suppose there was one pair of eyes I'd hoped to please. But more of that later. I grabbed the copy from his hand and sat down and gave him what he wanted.

"The North West cannot afford to lose its reputation for sound application of justice nor can Calgary as a town afford to stand as the only place where murderers go unpunished..." I wrote, and finished up, "The *Herald* best serves by withholding opinion."

Then I scampered on out of the office. I had an errand to do this evening. A remarkable document had come into my hands, as a result of my meddling. I'd put myself in touch with the Williams family out east early on, just because I'd met the Reverend once, and I thought, it can't hurt. You never know. I'm seldom wrong about these things, because earlier that day a letter was delivered to the *Herald* office, for Mr Justice Rouleau, in my care.

I turned over the white vellum envelope with its round, upright script in royal blue ink. I was alone at the time. I pushed my hair back from my forehead with the back of one wrist; inky fingers. My nose was itching like mad; my eyes had even begun to run. I knew it had to be a great lead, this envelope with its fragile seal. And the fact that it had come to me seemed like an invitation. They meant me to open it, I thought, seeing that the return address was Williams, in Montreal.

I turned it over again. I don't normally open other people's mail. But I felt almost as if I were obliged to interfere, since I'd been poking my nose in all along. I tore the seal. Then, my hands suddenly shy, I slowly turned over the two pages inside. The writing was so large that only three words fit on each line. The letter read:

Mr Justice Rouleau:
    Have you children?
    I have, and William Fisk is one of them. The date of his new trial, ordered by you after he had been found not

guilty by a jury, is near. People tell me he has no hope of escaping the death penalty this time. But he does have hope. I hope for him. I must. He is my son and I am charged as deeply as any lawyer, only more irrevocably, to defend his innocence. If that proves ineffective (and I must believe it will, for you have let us know you will not accept a verdict of not guilty) then I may plead, I think, for his life.

To his mother, he is no murderer. For me to believe that he had done this evil thing, would be, I think, a worse evil. Is it not essential that mothers hold faith in their sons and daughters, just as man must hold faith in the race descending from him, regardless of the terrible times in which we are living?

When he was a babe in my arms he was innocent. His fault, if he has one, he learned here on earth and not above. I blame myself for letting him go to that horrid frontier — why did I not stop him from going west, and so young — ? where men come unstuck from civilization, with the help of savage women.

But such a woman is still a living soul. Atonement must be made for her death, and your task is to choose it. It is in your power to end my son's life. Dare I say I pity you? To face the desire to take a life is to face up to a little of one's own savagery. Dare I say I also understand? For is not law another kind of motherhood; you must teach with kindness and by example of your superiority. When you resort to force you are diminished in your task. If killing is wrong, how may you order death to punish it? Must the law not demonstrate its own wisdom?

Still, you may argue, how to repay the Indian people for the wrong done to them and Rosalie? I have no answer. I only ask for mercy for my child, as they would have done for theirs. Her death is a terrible thing, but the dead, I understand, are not reclaimable, most certainly not by execution of the living.

Yours respectfully,
Martha W. Fisk

I have seldom been so elated as I was on reading it. Fancy me finding an ally in this woman, perhaps my only ally in the position I held, between the fires of vengeance and the coals of denial. Laughing to myself, I dropped the letter through the door at Rouleau's house. But I had lost the desire to drink among men, and so turned my steps back to my empty house.

And I sat down to write, at my letter-writing desk. I sometimes stay here through all the dark hours now, writing in the leather-bound books with the carbon sheets behind. I put down what I think, what I can't put in the newspaper or in letters to my acquaintances. My letters have no address, no salutation. When I finish them, I tear off the top copy and throw it away. I keep the carbon, but never look at it again. I am not unaware that it is a habit tending towards madness, the habit of making pen and paper a friend. But I need to do this writing. I need to confess, yet I am not even sure as to why. I imagine that if I just keep writing I will arrive at what I want to say.

The best news now in our stalled town, and news which is not unrelated, is Peter Prince's plan to install electric lighting for the streets. He has a generator on the Bow and wants to use his extra power to put lightposts up in the hotels and on the corners, and along in front of the station and the shops. Detractors feel that lighting the streets will damage people's health. Who knows when the electricity will jump out of the wires and get into someone, killing them? they say. I do not have such fears, none the less, I find a certain ironic pleasure in knowing that it is the same electric current which has replaced the gallows in the United States.

The debate has other amusing aspects. Will lighting the streets at night encourage or discourage immorality? What reason do folks have to be out after daytime hours, if not bad reasons? say some. But supporters claim that lighting the streets will press back these unknown forces that now go about in shadow. As one wag I listened to said, "It's sure we've got the nightlife already," meaning the ghost of

Rosalie New Grass, "we might as well give it something to see by."

But the most pressing reason for light is to enliven commerce. The shopkeepers have visions of Calgary being like New York, with windows all sparkling, and people strolling in furs to the Opera House. I must say I belong to the group that's in favour. Light, I think, is as irritating and inevitable as summer, with flies and cloudbursts. I like the night best, always have. But you've got to go with progress. Calgary will be the first Western town to have streetlights. The power project will put us on the map.

When morning came I was not in the least refreshed. The sun was high when I stepped out; there was no shade. Out of habit I eyed both ends of the street. Commerce was good, wagons were pulled up at all the shops. At noonday when the shadows were squat things close to the foot of the buildings, you couldn't tell the town was scared.

Without thinking I turned to go down to the Bow at Tenth Street: there was talk of building a dam there, so that more power could be got. The river was fast, but unpredictable, it went from deep to shallow in hours, sometimes. Now it was low, a greyish green. A channel had been made diverting some of the stream. I came to the generator and watched the heartless surge of the great wheel, and the great wheel bite into a smaller wheel, heard the machinery chunk into place. Prince had showed me how it worked at the station: the wheels turned, the steam rose, the wires were connected. Prince could press a switch, and a little filament in the test bulb turned an anaemic red.

I walked westward up the river past the last houses, past the little log huts Indians had built. Since I came to Calgary I'd stuck to streets and buildings: there was just too much of the outdoors to go out into it. I never went out of town. But I found it unexpectedly pleasant walking on the high, dried banks which rippled down to the low gravel river bed.

I took off my suit jacket and slung it over my arm. The sun and the water and the dry, clear air roused me. I'd been in a kind of stupor for months, brought on by my coal-oil lamps and my dry, stuffy parlour.

I came to a sharp rise of the land on the south of the river. It forced me down to walk on a level with the water's edge. There, pushed forward by a sense of urgency of which I had no understanding, I walked on. I had no view over the bank at all, couldn't see back to the bridge or the town behind me. The sun was beating against my face. Ahead of me there was a little low island in the water, near to the edge where I walked. The water hummed past its sides in brilliant sun. The air itself hummed. It was a spot which seemed to bestow well-being.

I looked at the island and was seized by a childish impulse to get to it. It was almost close enough for me to jump; I walked out on the tops of two rocks and then leapt. Not far enough: my right foot hit the slimy clay at the water's edge and I fell, driving the arm that held my jacket into the earth. Instantly my tenuous feeling of harmony broke. Cursing, I stood, and shook out my jacket.

I felt shaky, old and chilled. I decided to go home. As I turned back to where I had come from, I noticed a shield of dried mud and sticks pushed into the mouth of a hole. In front was a carved wooden stake, the kind the Indians made. I'd seen Indian graves before. But this one was different, apart. Only then did I realize I'd been tricked. Something had led me out to the grave of Rosalie.

"Rosalie," I said. "Was it you who brought me here?" I squatted, calling her, as one would to a small child.

"Rosalie, listen to me."

I heard nothing, but I sensed that she was there. "I want you to know something. I'm sorry for what happened to you." I broke off. I thought I sounded like a guilty man. I wasn't that. "I'm not saying anything was my fault. I'm just sorry." I could not continue.

Slowly I got to my feet. My eyes misted over; I couldn't have seen her even if she'd been there. "I was hurt, too," I said. My voice had a whining tone, even to my own ears.

My feet and ankles ached. How weak I had become! How ancient! Finally, youth gets the better of age, I thought. Without turning my back on her, I backed away towards town.

Chapter 20

Suzanne drove through the newly painted townhouses of Coach Hill and down to the old road that went west. The city reached a few streets farther than it had last fall. Near its edge, she stopped at a low, ugly shopping mall and bought a bottle of wine at the government liquor store. She found some bread and cheese in the Mac's Milk.

Within minutes the gravel road took her out of the city. The Bow River was beside her. When even the television tower was gone from her rear-view mirror, she pulled over and parked. Carrying the wine in her woven shoulder bag, she got out and clambered over stony ground to the embankment. The bank was ten feet high and grassy, and low water exposed a narrow sand and gravel beach.

She began to walk along the ridge above the water. At spring run-off these banks would be filled; now, at the end of summer, they showed rills and crevices, pockets where the water had sucked out the clay. As a child Suzanne had feared this was quicksand, that if she stepped in the wrong place the sucking would begin and she would be lost.

Opposite a small island, a little bit of land thrown like a lump of mud into the water, she sat down on the edge of the bank. The sun warmed her back. It bounced off the water in all directions. She shut her eyes and laid her head back; there was a chorus of deep and shallow sounds as the water pushed past the stones. When she looked to her right she noticed that the towers of Calgary were invisible. She thought this must be the place where they buried Rosalie.

On the north side of the river this was the only place high enough to dig a cave. But it would not be secure. Perhaps it was never meant to be. The first spring the ice would have melted under her body. The water would soak through; her imprint would go into the clay-like soil. Then — Suzanne was feeling fanciful — it would run down into the river and with the river into the town, turning the wooden wheel to make electricity, travelling along the wires to the light posts, from there floating through the air. Come night-fall, the spores of the mutilated maiden would hang over the entire town.

She put her head back and stared at the sky. Strands of windblown white cloud drifted together over her head. It looked like braid. Rosalie's braid. She wondered what happened to that four-foot rope of hair, which was sliced from her head at the Indian funeral and stuck in front of the grave on a stake.

Staring at the cloud, Suzanne remembered standing before a mirror, behind her mother, braiding her mother's hair. Her mother's head was bent, her face not visible. Suzanne held three long strands of heavy brown hair. She pulled one over, and drew the underneath one tight, then pulled another over from the other side. She kept her fingers between the strands so they did not mingle. Over and under, over and under, she pulled and wrapped the hair, making one continuous ribbon down the back of her mother's head, one stream with three tributaries, thick and lustrous and strong.

She had to be very careful to keep these strands separate, not to weave them together, otherwise she would not have this beautiful thing she was creating. She pulled and wove and admired what she had done and all of a sudden she tugged too hard and the hair came off the bowed head in

front of her and the face lifted into the mirror, and it was
not Suzanne's mother sitting there, it was an old woman,
with dark eye sockets and collapsed cheeks, bald.

Suzanne screamed. She shook the awful sight from her
head and sat up. Then, seeing she was alone, she let herself
sob out loud. Suzanne was suffering. She had never felt so
terrible. She was beset by nightmares, and grief, and she
was alone.

The progress of life had stopped for Suzanne. Her life
was like the braid that she was making. One strand was
herself, the familiar. Another was Simon, the stranger. The
last was Rosalie. Now that Simon was gone, the others
could not hold their shape. There was nothing to define one
strand against another. Her affairs were left hanging,
disordered; nothing could go forward.

There was just Suzanne, and Rosalie. Rosalie was frightening, but she had come to feel like a friend. She remembered
Simon's scornful voice. "Why make this fatal identification
with an Indian martyr?" he said. "I don't see what good it
can do you. Don't take it on."

"You are nothing to me now," Suzanne retorted. "And I
still have Rosalie. You, Simon, are over. They story is not."

But for the story to continue, Suzanne had to find out the
truth about Rosalie. Suzanne knew it was crazy but she
thought she would come here and wait for her. She tried to
invoke her. She imagined Rosalie walking into the Turf
Club behind the big dark man who had beckoned her. As
she so often had done, Suzanne tried to puzzle it out. Did
she recognize him as her death? Had she gone there to find
him, or did she think it was Lovingheart? All the women
knew Lovingheart. But perhaps not by sight, not Rosalie.
Rosalie was religious; she would be ashamed. To be there
was a sin. She must have been tormented, climbing those
stairs, stairs she would not come down alive. She would
have needed fourteen dollars for Lovingheart, and she had
it on her person. Who had given it to her?

Murphy, of course. It would have to be Murphy. Causing
it all, then writing about it; Murphy always in the middle.

And if Murphy had given her the fourteen dollars, then Murphy must have been the father.

She felt the presence rather than saw it. The red shawl made a loop over Rosalie's head; the oval inside it was too bright for eyes to penetrate. The ghost rose up the steep clay bank, her body outlined in a greyish lustre. Her hands, where they clutched the edges of the red shawl, were thin, almost translucent. The ghost moved towards her, and without reaching seemed to touch her. The feel of her was dry, rich and uneven, like pressed velvet. She did not look at Suzanne, or did not seem to. In a low even voice, she was chanting.

"Sometimes my heart is very weak and falls down, but He lifts it up again and draws me on to a good road. His name is Wonderful."

Suzanne sat absolutely still while the presence prayed.

"Sometime — it could be very soon, it could be very long, it could be a long, long time — He will draw me into a place between the mountains. It is dark there but I will not draw back; I will not be afraid; for it is there between the mountains that the shepherd will meet me..."

"Rosalie?" Suzanne whispered.

"Sometimes He makes the love rope into a whip but afterwards He gives me a staff that I may lean on..."

"Rosalie, do you know me?" But the Indian woman was hypnotized by her prayer.

"He spreads a table before me...All tired is gone and my cup —"

Suzanne spoke harshly. "Tell me why you went there!" But Rosalie finished her prayer first.

"I will lie down with the Shepherd Chief forever."

"Yes," said Suzanne, "But why?"

The ghost voice was without bitterness, her speech perfect, but slow. She hardly broke her chanting rhythm when she began to speak.

"I went to find a man, the man with the beautiful name."

Lovingheart. Suzanne had been right. "Tell me what happened."

Rosalie walked a little way along the bank and stood looking across the river. Her voice floated back across Suzanne's shoulder, a thick scarf of words. Suzanne sat very still.

"Upstairs I lay on the bed and waited. He did some things to me which were what I expected and then some which were not. He forced his hand inside me; it hurt a great deal, but he told me to be quiet. I had learned obedience from the nuns at school; I did what he said.

"I had been very bad, and I knew it. I thought this was my punishment. I could taste blood in my mouth. I sunk my teeth deeper into the flesh of my lip. I remembered God's mercy and thought there must be a mistake. This was the wrong man. I would have run away then, but he was too heavy. Then I forgot everything.

"I heard feet in the hall. Perhaps Murphy had come to help me. I tried to find my tongue. My mouth was floating in blood. I did not cry out, as I heard the key in the lock. Here they come, I thought, to save me. But the door did not open. The key turned. They were locking me in! The feet went away. I lay there and prayed.

"Sometimes He makes the love rope into a whip..."

Suzanne could feel the fear, as if she were in the locked room herself.

"It was dark and the lamp in the room had not been lit. I heard the big man stir at the top of the bed, and then the sound of water. He was washing again. He cursed the cold. I was surprised. I had forgotten cold. If this was what they called purgatory it was not what I imagined. I was lying in something very warm. All trouble was draining away from me. Sounds were escaping my lips then, groans which astonished me with their depth. The big man pounded on the floor then, a signal to those below."

"You didn't cry out! You didn't crawl away!"

"Footsteps came again and the door was opened. The men spoke, they spoke of me, and then decided to go for dinner. I thought perhaps I wasn't there, that I was dead already. But as they left, the big man said he hoped that I would get up and leave. They left the door unlocked. But I had no heart to go. I had lost the man I wanted, and now I had destroyed the child. Surely by now, I thought, the deed is done. And I was destroyed as well.

"I slept. When I opened my eyes again the room was all white, and beautiful. There were many men. The first one leaned over me, called me Rosalie, and asked me to get up. He was the one who killed me. His friend remarked upon my blood, which was painting the bedclothes and the wall and the floor. At length these men fell back in favour of another, a doctor, whose hand was gentle. At last I was covered with a fresh blanket against the onlookers in the doorway. When my spirit rose to go they all fell away, watching. I went to the door of the room, and looked back at my life, and thought it was not so much to leave behind. Goodbye life, I said. But the parting was not to be. I had a message from our gods. 'It is winter,' they said, 'and very cold, and besides you have forgotten us for some time, worshipping the white god. You are not in good standing with us. There is no room in the spirit world and you will have to wait.'

"I thought of appealing to the white man's god but I knew I should not have come here in the first place. He must be very angry. All this made me sad again. I did not want to stay in the world, but I had nowhere else to go.

"After much talk two men were taken away in handcuffs. My body was left covered, and the door locked. My spirit laughed a little at this; I was beyond harm and certainly beyond running away. I floated above the corpse, cooling now, in an ecstasy of lightness. I was happy, although alone. It would only be a little time, surely, until I could get into the spirit world."

"But you have waited a long time," Suzanne said. Her voice was loud and surprised her. She had forgotten she was alone. It was her own voice speaking, not the ghost. "Is it because there's still no answer? Why did you not defend yourself? Why did you lie there and go on bleeding, silently? Why did you obey him? Why did you become his creature?"

But the ghost began to pray again.

"Our father, who art in —"

Oh, our father, our father! Fathers in heaven teach meekness. Obedience. They teach their daughters to be good. Rosalie was "good" but Rosalie was dead. Rosalie was not in heaven. She was in limbo, like Suzanne. For the *sake* of love. For the sake of our father.

The sun was going down and it was getting cold. Suzanne lay on the bank, her eyes closed, her body curled up like a fern.

She heard that sound again. *Beep, beep, beep.* She was in the hospital and hearing the electronic warning signal.

Perhaps she was not going to make it; perhaps she would die on the table. The doctor had told her it was too late, it was dangerous. But she could not have this child. She was not ready. No one would understand that, especially not Ace. Ace didn't know. But now there was an emergency and she wouldn't stop bleeding and he was there, standing beside the bed.

"It was a girl," she said. "She looked like you."

Suzanne was raving. There'd been nothing to see. There was no child, only blood taking fabulous shapes on the sheets — now a Valentine, now a rose. And the warning signal going on and on and the nurses running in circles around her bed, and Suzanne hoping she would never wake up now.

After a long time Suzanne sat up on the river bank. The sun had declined past the rim of the mountains; it was moving farther away now, farther south. The months of deprivation would begin soon. Suzanne was cold; her eyes were swollen and sore. She was not ready to drive home yet. Feeling as if she had been beaten and robbed, surprised to find herself all right, she jumped down the bank to walk along the river's edge. She saw the cave where Rosalie was buried, and it seemed to her that Rosalie slept now, that her rest had come.

As she walked eastward the city came back into view. Shadows of the tall buildings crossed the startling yellow light of late afternoon. Not far away legions of cars drummed their hollow entrance to the bridge. A phrase worthy of Simon, she thought, and smiled.

And just for a moment Suzanne had a hint, a glimmer that the mourning would lessen; that it would, finally, many months from now, cease. A lightness spread on her, as if from a kindly, restful spirit. And then Suzanne thought, with a sudden energetic bound, she wished she could be Rosalie again. Only this time she would walk away from the hotel door! She would throw Murphy's money back in his face! No Lovingheart for me, she'd say. She would bear her child. She would go on living and the child would go on living, and there would be more life after that.

Chapter 21

Ace wandered in the convention centre. He was early for a meeting; he did not want to have lunch. Lately he'd been eating very little and drinking more than usual. He had no friends to talk to. Oh, he had a hundred friends. But his friends weren't much good to him now. For instance, he and the Weep used to have a lot in common. It was odd that Ace had never noticed before that the Weep had nothing to say. Ace chose to be alone and when he was alone he talked to himself, chidingly, tenderly. Trying to make contact again, trying to build up the old ties.

Ace wanted Suzanne to call him, longed to speak to her, not even so much about his mother's death, which was sitting in his throat, an enormous undigested painful mouthful but about his father. The old man had lost his noodles over Gemma. And everyone knew. Brault blamed Ace for introducing them. He hadn't, that hadn't been necessary. Gemma had managed it all herself.

In the first week after the funeral, Block had called Gemma and asked her to meet him in the first-class lounge at the airport. He was on his way to Texas; they sat by the window; the glass table was orange with the sunset.

"I'm in mourning," he said, seizing her hands and

pressing them to his lips. She understood how he meant it; it was the way she would have mourned, also. They played games with their fingers, on the table. They played games with their knees, under it.

"You poor man, it was all so sudden," she murmured.

"You help me, you help me to talk about it," he said. She was so surprised she forgot she'd been manipulating him. She hadn't imagined she could be helpful. That was what other people did.

"An irretrievable loss," she murmured. "Something like that changes you forever. Forty years married. There's no justice..."

"Perhaps something good will come of it," he said, rubbing one of her cold hands between his two.

"Don't you have to hurry?" she said, even as she held him back. "What time does your flight go?"

"It goes when I'm ready," he said, smiling kindly. "We have our own jet."

Block was in love with her; he was only putting in time before marrying her in order not to show disrespect to Amy. For once in her life, Gemma had been lucky. This time, the only time when it really mattered, her timing had been perfect. She was swept along, as on those wild chinook winds. Everything was so smooth, there was nothing to slow her down. Long white tablecloths, rooms paved in pale carpets, brocade sofas, marble tiles, beds with ironed sheets.

Perhaps Block thought Miss Amy would get a kick out of his loving this poor excuse for a glamorous young woman. Making amends, was he in some way making amends? But no. Block said his sons didn't understand him. Gemma needed his protection, he said. Miss Amy had never needed that. And he was impressed with how his little Gemma handled it all: the difficulties only showed up her generosity of spirit. She never said a cross word, she just kept smiling.

Her assurance of success, of being admired, brought out an unaccustomed modesty. She covered her shoulders with a shawl, cupped her hand over her laugh, and extended the back of it over the top of her wine glass, demurely. She had changed. And somehow she did seem right for the part.

Gemma could handle the cuts, the slights from the wives. She could handle Block's fooling around on the side, and she could handle the ambitious secretaries; all Block's foibles were old friends to her. It was as if all her training and experience had been for this. Gemma Starchuk. His wife's best friend. Ex-wife. Ex-friend, perhaps. Ace realized he had always hated Gemma.

Outside the entrance to the museum, Ace stopped for a moment under a stuffed head of a buffalo. It was oddly comforting. Perhaps because there had been stuffed heads of large mammals around the house as he was growing up. His father's hunting trophies, God knew where he got them, he couldn't remember Block hunting, although he did fish. The buffalo looked sympathetic, if unintelligent. Small, smooth and yellow eyes in their hiding places in the dark, dry mat of hair.

"Hello, old thing," said Ace to the animal dumb enough to run in herds off cliffs, chased by Indians on horseback, to die in heaps at the bottom. The buffalo stared steadily back.

A noble animal, said the caption, free to roam, ruler of one thousand miles of prairie until nearly made extinct in the 1880s. Sure, said Ace to himself, and now you could eat their meat in trendy restaurants run by Indian bands. Ribs, usually tough. Probably no one had ever asked a buffalo whether he would rather die out as a species or appear on plates alongside Duchess potatoes and broccoli au gratin. Perhaps the buffalo had not been so stupid as its small eyes implied, perhaps it had had a glimpse of the future and had opted for mass suicide; extinction being a grander thing than mere domestication.

Ace smiled at the buffalo. The large head with its thick brow listed slightly to the left. Its eyes needed to be dusted. The lined nose was caked like the nose of a sick dog, and the jaw parted.

"Eh, fella," he said. "King of the prairies, it says here.

They got you in the end." Would they get Ace too? As a single man he was out of the stream of life. It did not look good, for him. No mate. No chance of children. Mother gone, father entering senile phase with young floozie.

He wondered where the buffalo had gone wrong. Probably it hadn't gone wrong at all, it had just kept on being a buffalo while events got away from it. Perhaps Ace was like the buffalo, an idea whose time had gone. Suzanne had hinted as much when she had fallen for that other guy, the fast talking, jogging, silly servant from Ottawa. A softie who'd probably been in psychoanalysis or at least ought to be, judging from what Ace heard, and carried a purse. Ace liked to build things, he liked to have space to manoeuvre in, he liked to open up territory. He was not the kind of guy to move to a new town, figure out what divided people and then try to carve out his living explaining one side to the other, changing position so often that he looked like an illustration from *The Joy of Sex*. Try to steal someone's wife along the way. Served Suzanne right that he dropped her. Ace would never do that. It was unstraightforward, that's what it was. But maybe Ace was too straightforward. Like the buffalo, just too clumsy to evolve.

What he wanted, in fact, was to devolve. Simplify. His business connections were getting him down these days. He'd been thinking, all his working life, he'd really been happiest making the competition shuttlecocks. Simple, useful, healthy products. Beautiful too, in their way. That hard, resilient, heavy centre that nosed down towards earth, the feathers so clean and soft, light, heaven-bound. You knew people were going to have fun with them. You knew they were what they appeared to be, and nothing more.

He didn't like this deal he was in now. Didn't like the people he had to associate with. There was something funny going on with the hotel chain, the cops shutting down that massage club or whatever it was at just the right moment. He'd heard just a little too much to be innocent. He didn't like it, not at all. He'd been thinking about getting out even

before he got the conscience from his mother. What had
stopped him was the idea of letting the boys down, was all.
Going back on his word. But maybe there were times when
you had to.

He looked around; while he'd been standing, office
workers had swarmed in through both doors. They were
eating their lunches next door in the tropical garden,
around the fountain, eating out of paper bags and styrofoam
cups from delicatessens. There were so many of them, little
people; he had never wanted to be one of them.

Ace thought about being small, and doing the same thing
that all the others did. It made him afraid. He had seen the
future and it was crowded. It didn't seem fair (Amy's word).
As long as he could remember, he'd had special treatment; a
private sports coach, a custom-made car, chalets and clubs
and cashmere coats. There would be no more of the likes of
him, no more birthrights. He had had everything, but he
had been punished for it. He would be wiped out by further
catastrophes to his kind.

Ace walked into the garden and stood in front of the pool.
The bottom was littered with pennies. He made a wish to
the god of fountain wishes. He thought he deserved a
second chance.

Then he had his secretary call and beg off for the
meeting; he had a feeling he was going to get out of that
deal, but he wasn't prepared to do it just yet.

Free for the afternoon, he got into his car and drove up to
the townhouse on Coach Hill. There was a newer development now over the top of the hill, on the western slope.
Some of his friends were building there. The starts were in
the shape of horseshoes, some of them built into the side of
the hill, their view to the south-west, the best anywhere. He
parked his car outside one of the crescents, and walked by
the side of the road. The dry summer grasses whistled on
his jeans.

Life could be very good. Swimming pool, horses for the

kids, van to take the gang in and out of town when necessary. Big barbecues in late summer, skating parties on the pond he could build. Space. A few neighbours, just enough, but not too close.

Suzanne had been part of it. Now he could see even if he and Suzanne made up, she wouldn't want this. Not this way. It wasn't like her. They'd have to get an old house somewhere, fix it over, have a lot of books in it. Not swimming pools and barbecues but a summer camp somewhere, small and quiet, like her cabin. That wouldn't have been so bad; he could have handled that. Why had he made such a big deal all this time of going to the condo at Canmore? She'd hated it there. He was sorry about that.

He felt like giving in, but he had no Suzanne to give in to now. Someone like her wouldn't do; there was no one like her. Someone unlike her wouldn't do either. He turned back to look at the houses. He bent and picked a stem of grass, put it between his teeth and whistled. He whistled off the future he had expected. Not for him. He wouldn't have it. He wouldn't even want it now, he wouldn't have much fun with the old crowd, most of them had never had a broken heart and so none of them could understand him. He was a stranger in his own land, walking away from life as he knew it.

He would live in that townhouse instead. He would buy a black enamel bed. He'd furnish the whole thing Japanese; he'd go all Japanese, maybe disembowel himself.

Before he died, or maybe even instead of dying, he might pick up a racquet again, if he could find someone to give him a game. When he thought of love, he thought of Friday lunches, and missed them. If he couldn't have that then he'd have nothing, he'd go hungry. He couldn't remember feeling hungry before, now that he thought of it, not the kind of hungry you couldn't solve in fifteen minutes. As he became conscious of it his hunger grew; it was like the need on a hot day to dive into a pool, like the need in a blizzard to come up close to a fire. And the longer he was out in the elements, the deeper they gnawed him, and the sweeter were his memories of shelter.

The wedding was in an hour. Jennifer was at Gemma's apartment, waiting to drive her over to the Cummings' house.

"I blew my last savings on this dress," Gemma called from the kitchen, "but I figure it's the last time I'm going to have to buy anything out of my own money."

Jennifer was Gemma's bridesmaid; Suzanne had begged off, saying it would be embarrassing, with Ace standing up for his father.

Now the bride appeared. "Never thought you'd see the day, did you?" On the last day she'd ever live in a one-bedroom apartment, Gemma's hair was done in ringlets at the side of her face. Her grin was so wide it showed dimples that had never been seen before.

"Never say never," said Jennifer. "I guess you can thank SWARM."

"Huh," she said, holding up her fingernails, huge and polished white, for inspection. "They should thank me. Of course I had to resign when I got engaged. But they asked me to speak at the next meeting. "Actually," she continued, in a tone of confidentiality, "one of my club friends is going along with us on our honeymoon. So there'll be someone my own age to do things with." She said this gently, to protect Block's feelings.

Jennifer looked around the kitchen. Would the porcelain pigs come to the Cummings' house? The pad of notepaper in the shape of a balloon inscribed "Up yours"? Gemma made a fetish of her bad taste. Her gold digging — jubilant, frank — was almost a relief after all the phonies who pretended not to care about money. She didn't mind Gemma's flagrant superficiality, now she hoped it wouldn't all be lost.

Gemma was wearing a one-piece undergarment made of lustrous, heavy satin. It bore an obscure resemblance to a robe of punishment, straight-cut and plain, perhaps something worn in a convent. No, in a Ziegfeld musical set in a convent. She wanted her zipper done up. It pulled easily up her flat back. The long gown hung straight, a vestment. It was cut as low as possible, revealing her thin chest almost to the nipples. There was to be a chamber group playing on the lawn, and a tame minister had been persuaded to perform the nuptials in Miss Amy's garden. SWARM was to provide the ladies-in-waiting.

"I love old men, I've discovered. I'm so glad I waited this long!" said Gemma.

"Waited!" Jennifer couldn't help herself. "You've been desperate for years."

Gemma only smiled. "I'll do my make-up and then we'll go."

Jennifer stood by the door. The sky had gone orange, clouds which had not been visible minutes before now crowded out the blue. Something strange was happening to the weather. The clouds were low and blocklike. A wind whipped the short trim of the grass in front of the apartment, tilted the tops of the trees.

Gemma came up behind her. "That's the kind of sky farmers take out insurance against."

The hail began all at once, like the drumming of sticks on a snare drum. The stones bounced back up from where they landed. Leaves were ripped down with them. Bushes bent, geraniums disintegrated. The ice drops glazed the sidewalk, all in a couple of minutes.

Now the stones were bigger, the size of marbles. Jennifer opened the stairway door to hear the sound. Tinny, deep, hollow, the noise depended on where the hailstones landed. Gemma's face began to collapse.

"My flowers," she wailed. Over at the house the garden

had been made up for the ceremony, thousands of roses and lilies in barrels and baskets and hanging from the arbour. Jennifer put her arm around her friend.

"You heard that expression?" she said. Of course she would have, she'd lived here all her life. But she said it anyway. "You don't like the weather, wait five minutes."

A little late, but perfectly composed, the couple stood under the ruined arch, in a barren garden. Piles of hail-stones glittered in the fence corners, like mothballs hastily thrown off the scene. One basket of long-stemmed pink roses which had been indoors stood on the table, making the emptiness eloquent, as one survivor sharpens the realization of all who died.

A SWARM-ette stood beside Gemma. She had a Kleenex in her hand, and periodically reached over to dab Gemma's cheeks. The bride and groom kissed, and stepped apart, to clapping and handshakes, embraces and false clamour. Gemma's cheek was offered for kissing.

Sun was fractured in the tall crystal glasses lined up on the tablecloth. It seemed a defiance of death, of guilt; a pagan ceremony, the young virgin, or facsimile, offered to appease the gods. Ought one to worry about Gemma? Not really. She would have Block helpless as a babe before the wedding cake had crumbled under the pillows of the members of SWARM.

Amy spoke to Ace from her ironic distance in the clouds. "Your father got everything, he even got a second chance. Mind you, he was the only one who could have stood it. I'd had enough." Standing a little behind his father, Ace smiled.

"If you can't laugh," said Miss Amy, "why carry on?" Why indeed? Except perhaps to extend a kind of charity to the newlyweds.

Ace saw Jennifer, sensibly suited, usher some woman who was feeling faint through the patio doors to the kitchen. He peered around a bush: Jennifer was running water on a cloth, pressing it to the woman's temples. It was Suzanne. Ace moved through the bushes to the door.

"Come," said Ace. He took Suzanne by the hand, gently. She was white; her pink lipstick looked like the work of vandals on her mouth. Jennifer was there holding the other hand.

"Ace, is it you or your bad actor?" she said. But she was smiling.

"It's all right," said Suzanne. "You can stop looking after me now." She shook them both off. "Come where?"

"I want to show you something."

The Ace-R stood in the back of a curved flowerbed, beside the pool and behind the shed. Difficult to spot, it was half climbed by some trailing thing; its gear-jointed arms had been pressed forward to hold out a fluted tray, now a bird-bath: one of Amy's jokes. As a garden gnome the Ace-R lacked grace; he was neither Grecian nor Florentine, but a tyro, relic of the modern age.

The swimming pool was still, solid, like blue jelly in its square concrete dish, the white cots alongside the circular tables empty. There were no birds in the shrubbery, only this new-world Mowgli. The Ace-R was Ace's height, five foot ten, but appeared taller, being without width, save for the rack with halved juice cans over it which served for shoulders. Felt was glued down on the tins. The arms were simply rubber-coated wires twined around a metal bar with a hinge at the elbow. Hands had been fashioned once from a pair of Amy's old leather driving gloves. But these were gone. Now all that remained was the clamp, on the right arm, to hold the racquet.

Thighs were more juice cans, and suspended in a hoop around the iron spine was a pair of satin basketball shorts. The old blue ones had been replaced; these were red with white piping and drew neatly over the thigh bulge. The face was a shield-shaped piece of metal. Almond eye-holes were cut through; blue Christmas lights flashed when the machine was plugged in. There was a carved piece of bleached wood for hair which looked as if it had been lifted from a Christmas angel.

"Here we have it," he said. "The bad actor."

"My God. I'd forgotten this thing ever existed." Suzanne pushed her way into the leaves and walked around it.

"All unplugged," said Ace, going around the back to look, just in case. The black box where the power had come from had been behind the face. How it had been computed Ace did not know; Weep was the electrical genius. Weep had made him serve again and again there on the courts in the old Quonset hut they rented. He measured arc and angle and force, and somehow duplicated it for the Ace-R. The lower arm swung back, then made a little jerk forward; the racquet connected with the hard underside of the bird at just the right angle with just the force to make the ideal serve, high, deep, landing on the line. In the end the machine served better than Ace did. It was steadier. It did not make mistakes; as long as it was well-oiled and plugged in, it was perfect.

"The Ace-R. My best shot."

"Your inspiration, endlessly repeated."

"Yeah," said Ace. "The Weep used to joke that all he needed was to work out the other strokes and find a way to move those size ten concrete sneakers, and it would be all over me." He spoke ruefully. The act of building the thing was first adoration and then revenge: the Ace-R would get Ace, put him out of the game. "He used to say all you need is oil and electricity."

"I don't believe you liked him very much," said Suzanne.

"He scared me." Sometime during its tireless stroking the cherub-masked machine had ceased to flatter Ace and had begun to insult him. Ace was not playing with the Ace-R, he was playing against it. "He's my rival."

"The child is father to the man," said Suzanne.

"Tell me about it," said Ace grimly, thinking of Block

and Gemma behind them, obscene in their revelry. Here
was the opposite case: the Ace-R was his child, but he had
let it be his maker. Now, he could see clearly that the Ace-R
was a simple thing; it had only one trick.

"It's not much to look at," said Suzanne. No softness, no
curves, none of your poetry."

"It's perfect though. At what it does."

"Grace," she said. "The poor Ace-R has no grace. You
see you enshrined the worst of yourself, not the best."

They laughed. Ace hugged Suzanne. She was relaxed in
his arms, like she used to be, long ago.

"I mean to reclaim this," he said, digging with his toe
around its concrete feet. "I mean to take it home and put it
somewhere, in the townhouse."

"I think this is where it belongs." said Suzanne.

They stood hand in hand behind the garden shed. "I'm
gonna start playing again," he said. "Down at the club I
found a young guy who can give me a game." He laughed, a
little self-conscious. "So what if my sides have gone soft
and my arm isn't what it was? I'm human aren't I?"

"You're allowed to get old," said Suzanne. "Encouraged,
even."

He sneaked a look at her. "Perhaps I could convince you
to get married again. Stranger things have happened."

"No," said Suzanne, "not that."

"At least live together."

She said nothing.

"Find a house that suits us both."

She shook her head.

He took a deep breath. "Have a baby."

"Again?" she said. "How can we do that when we wasted
one already?"

"At ten weeks it's only a blob. That's what you said."

She looked into the still, rubbery leaves. "It was more
like sixteen weeks. And they didn't want to do it. They
warned me it was risky."

"I nearly got killed driving over. I still remember standing outside the operating-room door and seeing the stand and all the tubes," said Ace. "I couldn't do anything."

"I thought I was dying, when I woke up. I thought I deserved to."

"And I said the wrong thing."

"You always did."

"That's right, I did."

They were almost smiling now, into each other's eyes. It was as if they had not met for years, as if they had not really met since the day in the hospital, when she decided they weren't related any more.

"Anyway it's done and gone and in the past," said Ace. "Let's go forward."

Suzanne stared through the grass at her feet to the porous, bloody earth. Way down there were sparkles left over from the hailstorm. Behind her was laughter and cheers, someone making a speech, Gemma and Block being toasted. The sun was out again; it caught the hollow of Ace's cheek. She reached out to touch the place. "You're good at that," she said.

Chapter 22

Evangeline never closed her curtains. I had seen this before, when I looked towards the house from the far corner, where I sometimes passed by on my way home from the office. This night was no different. I stood out on the bare brown slope beside her house. It was at the end of the last row, unprotected, and like as not she was alone, for that man she lived with was never in town. She needn't have run off with him, she might just as well have run off on her own. But perhaps that was what she wanted all the time.

I stood outside and watched the house as the sun dropped, finally, about eight o'clock, and its light was exchanged for that of a high, nearly full moon. There were no clouds, but before all her bare windows, I saw the streaks of dazzle which meant a light rain. I could see Evangeline in there, glamorized in the explosive brilliance of her lit room. That woman always wanted a life she never had; she wanted to live in ball gowns, and waltz the night away.

I had come to see her. I had a desire to tell her of my efforts to do well by Rosalie after her death. That I had tried to have Fisk convicted but not put to death. That I wrote editorials pressing council to ban guns for children, and I'd applauded the police for arresting the man who hit a

prostitute down in the red-light district. I had some crazy
notion that Evangeline might be proud of me, that she
might even say so.

But I stopped outside her house. It now seemed obvious
that Evangeline knew I sent Rosalie to Lovingheart, had
known all the time. Perhaps she even guessed I made her
pregnant: women are uncanny. What she didn't know was
that I saw her go up with Fisk and did nothing. I can hardly
believe that myself. Often in my wakeful nights the scene
leaps up before me once again: I am sitting at the bar elbow
to elbow with my poor class of companions; Fisk pushes
through the door with Rosalie in tow; I watch her go to the
stairs. She gazes at me, a look meant to bring me shame, I
suppose, for she believes herself to be with the abortionist.
But I am furious, losing all faith in her momentarily and
believing she has come to flaunt her turn to prostitution
before my eyes. We are locked in mutual incomprehension,
and then she goes up. And through the long hour to follow I
sit, as if paralyzed, on my stool. I did nothing. We all did
nothing, while she died. Why, why, why? It was as if a spell
of helplessness fell over us, and we let evil have its way.

But I would not say this to Evangeline. I was afraid of
what she might say. She had such a power in her tongue.
This was humbling for me: I was afraid of this woman.

As I stood, hesitating, I came to another realization. I
was not alone. There was another sentry. Closer to the
house than me, he stood like a tree but he was not a tree.
Then he moved, swiftly, in the semi-dark, and stood again.

Inside the house Evangeline could be seen walking along
the hall and into the front parlour; she came close to the
window to look out. He — the Indian — looked back at her.
As the light fell on his face I knew him at once as Rosalie's
brother, Rosalie's avenger. The man who had terrified the
town by his standing, waiting, staring, as if his revenge
were out there on the horizon somewhere. Now he had his
victim in sight and it was Evangeline.

And well it might be, I thought. My need for blessing
turned to a sudden vicious desire for her punishment. It

was Evangeline's fault, if it was anyone's. She took up Rosalie's life and set it down again, pointing the wrong way. Yes, I said to myself, if he's going to get anyone it might as well be her, do the job I couldn't bring myself to do, and kill her.

My heart hard and my hands clenched in my pockets I stood in my shadow, unseen. It seemed to me right that I should have to have come here tonight, to become witness to this terrible drama; events were about to enact themselves solely for my benefit.

Moonlight flooded the house and the street as the night grew deeper. The corner where I stood grew narrower, and I hugged it. Inside her house Evangeline was exposed. I wondered, as I had before, why she chose to leave her house so open and visible this way. Only by lying on the floor could she hide from her pursuer. And she was far too proud to do that.

And she? Did she know she was stalked, trapped, by an enemy outside the house? She went to the staircase and climbed up. For a moment she disappeared but then she walked to the window of what must be a bedroom, and stood looking down. My God, Vangie, I thought, you might just as well invite him!

The lustre of the night, the open sky beyond her window set her dark form in relief. She began to move. It looked as if she were dancing, leaning back, whirling around, her face lifted to the ceiling. Really she was a most extraordinary woman. We watched this little performance for a while, I and the Indian, this little dance of death. Others have said it but love is very intimate with hate: I believe the two were joined in me then.

Suddenly Evangeline stopped and stepped up to the pane of glass and looked directly down on the Indian's head. It was a curious, triangular scene: she looking down on him, he looking up at her, and me, in hiding, looking from the flat whiteness of her face and then to him, to the part in his hair which ran sharp as a knife down the back of his head.

And as I looked I had the preposterous thought that she

was intending to seduce him. Even as this thought came to me, my whore-wife raised her knuckles and knocked on the glass. The Indian jumped back, and raised his arm, but then, seeing her, lowered it. She smiled. And then she disappeared. I hardly knew what to think for a few seconds but all hopes it was not what it seemed were quashed when in a moment she opened her door.

"Please come in," she said, loudly and distinctly. "I welcome you, and I am alone." She bowed a little, forward, and pressed her skirt back with her hands.

Imagine my feeling at that moment! I had almost — I thought I had — been prepared to see her hatchet-murdered. But could I stand by and watch this? Oh vengeance, if that was what she sought on me, for my part in the death of her little friend, oh vengeance was hers at that moment! I leaned in my corner and sobbed aloud, pounded the post in front of me, cursed her up to the heavens and back down again. I saw them climb the stairs. I saw the curtain close. I even imagined that he had come here before, that this was some rehearsed procedure, a ritual they agreed upon for their assignations.

When I left he was there still. The moon so high my shadow had disappeared. Evangeline's house was all in darkness, and the field where I walked was silvered with the joyless borrowed light of the moon.

What more is there to tell?

Fisk's new trial was efficient and without incident. The docile jury, wary of losing their night's sleep, returned a verdict of guilty of the reduced charge of manslaughter. On July 22, 1889, Mr Justice Charles Rouleau sentenced Fisk to fourteen years in the Manitoba penitentiary. I took some pleasure in the fact that he said he had intended to give Fisk life but had been moved by the letter from his mother. For his part, Fisk had not said one word in his own defence since the very first night when he approached Dillabough on the corner and blurted out, "She died on my hands."

I took the liberty of corresponding with Mrs Fisk after the verdict.

"He has been living a terrible life for some time now," I wrote, "I do think imprisonment is his greatest hope of reform."

This "reform" was to be effected at Stony Mountain, about which I knew more than she, thank God. It was an ugly compound housing, when Fisk arrived with his escort of two Mounted Police, a total of seventy-three convicts and thirty-nine insane persons. They were male and female, and some as young as fifteen years. Every year a few died, a few went insane or became violent and were transferred to Kingston, Ontario. Mostly the Indians died.

I troubled myself to discover that Fisk became convict number fifty. His companions there in the pen were a hodge-podge, victims or victimizers in the drive to close the frontier. He missed by only two years sharing space with the Indian hero Big Bear, whose son, Little Bad Man, had led the fight at Duck Lake where Fisk had lost the telltale piece of his finger.

He missed, too, Poundmaker, who at six feet in height was remembered by the warden's wife as one of the most handsome men she had ever met. His braid was three inches across and hung down to the back of his knees. It was cut, on entry to Stony Mountain, as was the hair of all prisoners. It occurs to me there must be a huge dust-heap of braids somewhere out here on the prairie, and that Rosalie's too must be upon it.

Fisk did not meet Poundmaker because Poundmaker was released, like most of the Indians serving time for their part in the Rebellion. The compound doctor was expert in divining when ailments of the heart or the body tended towards the fatal. At such times he gave passage to the sufferer and bundled him onto a train home: more than one native brave died in his coach seat.

Instead, Fisk took his place among several other mur-derers, some thieves and numerous swindlers, cattle rustlers and other small-time criminals. The compound included a small farm worked by the inmates, a blacksmith shop where Fisk was soon to find employment, a library, an infirmary, a Roman Catholic priest and an Anglican minister. This much I know from the annual reports from the prisons, which are available to the public. The priest and the minister deny annually that they compete for the souls of the convicts.

On his arrival at this Innisfree, Fisk's hair and beard were neatly trimmed and he was clothed in grey knickerbockers with red leggings. I took a certain glee in reading of this new system brought in by the warden to inspire the convicts to good behaviour. The coloured stockings comprised a "star system"; first on arrival a man must wear red, but if after several months his behaviour had been exemplary he would be given a more subtle pair of grey and white stockings. Then, six months later, if he continued to behave well, he would have grey stockings which blended with his leggings and made him even less conspicuous. At this point he would be seen to have truly joined the world to which he had come.

But as to Fisk's adjustment I had no news. I imagine that his size and strength kept him from attack, and he was still young, and with luck would escape the typhoid, syphilis and scrofulous consumption that raged. He was never cited for bad behaviour, nor for good either. I shall make a point of reading the pardons every year for the next fourteen; but I doubt that he will receive one. With any luck, in 1903 he will walk out of Stony Mountain to begin again. Where he will go subsequently I have no desire to discover. Nor I think, shall I ever know the state of his soul, his heart, or his understanding. Perhaps there is no great truth underlying why he did it; he was only a witless agent in the grand scheme where such horror is swathed in banality.

As am I, I suppose. And as such an agent I have one more part to play. As I never heard anyone speak of the true cause of Rosalie's dire injuries, I will set it down here for once and for all, and then I will be free of it.

It became a contest among certain men of ill habits to force their forearm up inside an Indian woman, just to see how far it would go. Only Fisk's drinking companions would have guessed he was playing this game and his arm became caught, and maddened by it, he tore at her to get himself free. With his bull-like strength and pent-up rage, he ripped her open. That is the fact and many knew it to be true.

And now having written it I can at last be relieved of my burden and will close the book and take my old bones to bed.

Chapter 23

This time it was Suzanne who crooked her finger at Nola as she passed the tired palms en route to her office. Fall term was about to begin. Suzanne was actually looking forward to getting back in the classroom. She felt brisk and bright; she wore a bow under her chin; her hair was curled down her back. She also carried a box under her arm. It was small and white, the kind of box boys brought to their sweethearts for high-school dances. She grinned.

Nola saw Suzanne and thought, Poor dear. I know how she set her heart on that man. But perhaps it was for the best. Nola enjoyed feeling sorry for Suzanne. Then she looked more closely. What did Suzanne have in that box? What, indeed, did she have on her mind?

Suzanne laid her hand on Nola's arm. "Be quiet," she mouthed. "Don't warn him." She turned smartly and made for the half-open door of the Head's office.

"James," said Suzanne, poking her head around the door frame. She never called the Head by his name. She never even thought of him by his name. She had her hand behind her back. "I'd like to have a word with you."

James looked up from his desk. He seemed to be writing something in his calendar. A lunch date, probably. His brows came down together. His hands, stretched out on the blotter, came together in a gesture of piety. He opened his mouth.

"I've prepared that course you've got me down to do this fall," she said. "I really don't think it's for me, but I'll do what I can."

He closed his mouth, not very firmly.

"I can manage 'Reinventing the West' again as well," she said.

He waved his hand, regretfully. "Unfortunately that's not a priority — "

"I know you feel that," she said, "but that was before the petition."

"The petition," he said, heavily. He had hoped not to have this conversation. "Yes, that was an indication, wasn't it? You're certainly popular with students." When he said "popular" his nostrils flared.

"An indication that the department should take note of," she said promptly. Asp had managed to get three hundred and twenty-seven names — more names than there were history students to begin with. "Before we get hit with guidelines."

Guidelines came down from government on topics to which the public were sensitive. Guidelines were to be avoided.

"Uh, no, I don't think there's much chance — " he began.

"Haven't you noticed in the student papers the push for more courses about Alberta? It's in the wind," she said. Suzanne spoke clearly and confidently. She knew what she had to do, and that she could do it. It had been far easier to get the upper hand than she had expected. "I'm not only thinking of me, of my interests. It is important to me not just as a scholar but as part of an organisation." She went on, speaking about contributing to the forward momentum of the university and forging identities. She was, somewhere in the back of her head, amazed at her smoothness. Simon had taught her something.

The Head, whose palms, pressed against one another, had begun to rotate, only nodded and nodded. "So glad you stepped in," he managed, at one point. But he had no chance. Suzanne was close to her goal now.

"If it is reinstated there will be no trouble to sign up the students again," she said. "I've got all their names."

"Of course," he said. "I won't commit myself. I'll have to look at the printout. But..." He waited for her to leave. Suzanne knew she had won. She drew closer to his desk.

"I feel very badly," she said, in a tone more conciliating, "that our relationship has been... less than perfect."

"Yes?" he said.

"We haven't communicated, as we might have. I really hear more about your doings from *Nola* than I do from you."

His brows bulged over the twin arrowheads where they came together. She said she hoped things would improve between them. She said that in the meantime, she had brought a little token. She reached forward and put the box on the edge of his desk.

"I hope you won't take it amiss. I know how much you like orchids."

When she swung past Nola's desk she reached for her telephone messages (Ace called. Ace called again.), and raised her eyebrows. "Bad news, Nola," she said. "You're going to have to redo that printout."

One Saturday morning at ten fifteen Suzanne walked to her doctor's office on Tenth Street. Linda was a friend; she followed Suzanne into the little room, watching with a half smile as Suzanne climbed up onto the narrow bed and firmly stuck her feet in the stirrups.

"I want it out," said Suzanne. "Can you do it?"

"Not today, not if it's a vital organ," said Linda cheerfully. Linda was one of the sensitive doctors, with a sense of humour; she kept oven mitts over the stirrups, so her patients wouldn't feel the cold metal on their feet.

"You know what I mean. The IUD."

"Just like that? No discussion?"

"I'm a big girl," said Suzanne, lying back, and draping her forearm over her eyes. It hurt, but only for a minute. When it was gone she felt naked; she walked back home with her knees together.

Before noon she called Ace at his apartment. He answered.

"Lucky you caught me," he said.

"Oh yeah?" She teetered on her kitchen chair. She could hear noises at his place. For a second she faltered; could he have a new girlfriend? She put her foot up on the edge of the table.

"I'd like to see you," she said.

He said nothing.

In the silence she heard voices around him.

"Who's that?"

"Movers. It's moving day. I'm taking over the townhouse."

"You didn't tell me that." She had mixed memories. "So what are they doing now? Packing or loading?"

"Packing. Taking out the table hockey."

"So what time will they get it over there?"

"They're talking noon," he said. "The way they're going they might just make it."

"I'll bring you lunch," she said.

She went out to the deli on Tenth Street and bought a loaf of bread, some cheeses, and pâté. Then she drove up to the liquor store and came out with a bottle of Moët Chandon. Before she got back into her car she went down to the florist and got a potted gloxinia, deep purple and white. Then she went home, had a shower, and put her hair up in a loose, feathery ponytail. She put the food and the wine in a basket and got in her car. When she turned down to Memorial Drive, she opened all the windows so her ponytail blew straight behind her. Her car shot alongside the river towards Crowschild Trail; she was humming. Then she started to hum — "*her face at first just ghostly, turned a* — " The words to that song had never made sense.

The townhouse looked smaller but also bigger, like a real place to live, stuffed with couches on end and boxes of records. Ace was walking around the kitchen, looking distressed. "Which cupboards should I put the glasses in?" he said.

"The ones by the sink. Then give up."

He gave the movers a twelve-pack and they left. It took only a few minutes to set up a table and chairs and the ghetto blaster, on the balcony looking down the hill. The *pop* of the champagne cork echoed off the bare walls.

Suzanne put sheets on the bed herself. She told him what she was doing, her aim; it would have been dishonest not to. Ace smiled. He said it was fine, it was wonderful. She said she wanted him to participate, when it happened, but that she wouldn't marry him. He said he accepted that only as a point from which to begin negotiations. She said the decree absolute was on the way, and it was final. Then he said he loved her. She said she loved him. Or maybe the words came from the green bottle, or maybe the purple throat of the gloxinia trembling slightly in the open window.

Suzanne slept, deeply, exhaustedly in the uncurtained brilliance of a perfect afternoon in the about-to-be-occupied house. In her sleep she heard children's voices, perhaps from next door, and she thought she was someone's mother already. But no, they woke up together silently, at the long end of the afternoon, and as silently Suzanne prepared to leave.

"You don't have to go." he said.

"I do, though."

He lay on his elbow in bed, watching her, and didn't argue.

At last, the short, eloquent autumn was passing. Children, wondering if they would be warm enough in paper costumes on Hallowe'en, had been counting the days. It was October 31, a Friday, it had snowed and was still snowing. Not just a light dusting to grey the streets and the hedges, allowing them the grace of age in a city with none other, but a heavy, two-inch thick muffler.

There was no wind and the flakes were falling fast, straight down. Ace and Suzanne put bags in the car. From the passenger's seat, she peered through a small hole in the frost on a side window at a trio of bandits who approached her porch.

"Hallowe'en apples! Trick or Treat!" they shouted, sweet-voiced, nowhere near devilish. She opened the door and ran back through the little group of children into her house and returned with her hands full of candies. The children opened their plastic goody bags silently, as silently gave them careful inspection and comparison, closed the bags and trudged back through the snow.

Suzanne skidded back down the walk to the car. She and Ace were going to the mountains. It was no season for golf or skiing or even hiking; they would go to a comfortable hotel, check in with two names, drink brandy before a fire and go to bed early. They'd been seeing a lot of each other.

Ace kept both hands on the wheel and passed through the parting flakes of snow which combed the sides of the car. Although the sidestreets were slippery the highway was not. It was a beautiful silent drive up into invisible mountains. It was dark when they arrived. They dropped their bags in the room, washed and went quickly down for a drink. In the bar, a boy with a guitar and a repertoire of songs made them nostalgic, singing "Bird on a Wire" and "Those Were the Days." Holding hands, they walked slowly into the dining room, exchanging the last bits of information about the week they left behind.

The dining room looked over the hot pool. They sat by the window with only a fringe of ferns between them and the glass. They remarked how they were lucky people, to be able to enjoy such things. Steam rose from the cauldron of the pool. Suzanne drank deeply from her glass of red wine. She held the glass in front of one eye: the liquid was opaque and the candle light did not shine through.

After dinner they went down to the hotsprings themselves. She had never been there at this hour of night, with the sky and the jagged rocks an absorbent black curtain and the steam making the water look like a prehistoric swamp. The hot water prickled her neck; the murky sulphurous substance absorbed her nerves. With her feet under the water she made running motions. The weight of water, pungent, stinging, was pulling the flesh back from her thighbones. She was held in the water's jelly suspense, her ability, her conviction to move absorbed.

Ace came towards her through the fog. His hands made arcs, first on one side of his body and then on the other, scooping the water out of his path. He was taller than she was; his thighs rose one after the other out of the water. In the stream he looked smooth, pearlized, the perfect inno-cent, a first man. She pretended to run, she tried, really, but the resistance was too great. She stumbled and fell forward in that sustained painless way one falls in water. Ace came towards her still, laughing as her chin hit the foam. She pulled her head quickly out of the sour water and laughed too. He was going to catch her.

As she went down, it came to her, the final scene.

Sarcee Indians in full regalia sat cross-legged on the packed earth of Stephen Avenue. At nightfall the townfolk were gathered. The Mayor — it was Murdoch this year, the honour would pass amongst all the men, it would even be Murphy's several years later — asked Peter Prince to speak. Prince said that Calgary had power now. The first town in Western Canada to light its streets with electricity! Calgary was on the map.

Men in black stood hatbrim to hatbrim; women clasping their hands before their waists withdrew under the awnings of King's store. They were all there, Kelsey, still thin from his long stay in jail; Rouleau with his proud little moustache and chubby children. The reluctant jurymen leaned by the pillars of the Hudson's Bay Company. Whitbeck and Lowry and Lee had chosen the Alberta Hotel as their new drinking spot; it wasn't to be on the lights. They lined its front, on the other side of the street. Between the two groups children in cloth caps ran, cautioned by Constable Dillabough to keep well back from the new thirty-foot cedar poles strung together with wire. The poles held up two hundred lamps each with the power of sixteen candles.

Now was the moment of illumination. Prince threw the switch.

"Aaaaaah," said everyone, and tipped back their heads.

Small pinkish lights away up there had halos like sheepish captive moons.

"'Tain't much," a voice put out. "Can't you turn it up full?"

Prince held up his hand. "Patience, please! it's the first day. And we've got to leave room for growth!"

Now they looked around their town. It wasn't the light itself so much made the difference. It was what the light showed. There was the false front sitting like a tiara on top of the General Store. The light showed up the turret on top of the Bank of Montreal, then it slid down the pale sandstone front of the Windsor, the Hull block. The light ran along the ridges of the whole row of flat-roofed buildings. It lit the white-painted wooden front of the traveller's boarding house to a ghostly glow.

It made things alive. The stuffed mountain goat on top of the toy store looked ready to leap down. And behind the black glass of the dress store, dim mannequins leaned forward to see. The light poured down the throats of the people looking up, and took away their words.

It gave relief: the drays standing idle beside the station threw shadows down on the mud; the cart wheels moved against their fallen copies. The horses, the hitching posts, the stable doors, all were thrown into a second existence. There was two of everything, the substance, and the shadow. The town had become in this instant brand new, and began to fade, already.

At length the people began to murmur. The lighted street was a triumph. A sign of how much they had conquered, how they had changed this place they had come to. Most of all it was a sign that they would stay. Darkness was pressed back.

But Murphy was not so sure. Murphy thought the strange thing about the light was the way it made night blacker than ever. He looked beyond the lighted grid of streets to the fringes where darkness had been chased. There he thought he could see the banished and the dead: the giant blacksmith in his unbuttoned overcoat, his bare scoured hands with seven fingers hanging loose, and beside him the Indian girl in her deep red shawl. Now because they could not be seen they would be there always.

The drumming began and the Indians leapt to soft flat feet. Their leather soles made no sound on the earth, but trailing beads and fringed sleeves described hieroglyphs none but they could read. The white man had taken the night and they joined in the celebration, participating, as human beings will do, in their own downfall.

When the silence became long, one man began to clap. Others followed until the whole town joined in the applause and the sound of it rang out over the flatlands.